KISSING DAISY

"Max—"

"The truth is . . ." He stepped toward her. "The truth is . . . I feel bad about giving you such a hard time at breakfast."

"Ohhhh. This is an apology."

"No, absolutely not." Max retracted the step he'd just taken. "This is absolutely NOT an apology."

Daisy huffed. Normally, she'd take great satisfaction in Max's guilt and take equal pleasure in the banter that would surely follow. However, she was a woman on a mission, and she didn't have the time, not with Otter Bite hanging by a manila envelope. "Fine. Thank you for coming here *not* to apologize and for that apple strudel thing. And"—she momentarily softened—"the money. But I just don't have the time for whatever this is."

Once again he stepped toward her. "You're making this extremely difficult."

"*This*? This *what*? What am I making—"

"*This*," he interrupted, the word melting into her mouth.

The two hundreds floated from her hand to the floor. Then her arms wrapped Max's neck, his body pressed hers, and Daisy was lost in a kiss she never expected to own . . .

Spooning Daisy

Maggie McConnell

LYRICAL SHINE
Kensington Publishing Corp.
www.kensingtonbooks.com

LYRICAL SHINE BOOKS are published by

Kensington Publishing Corp.
119 West 40th Street
New York, NY 10018

All Kensington titles, imprints, and distributed lines are available at special quantity discounts for bulk purchases for sales promotion, premiums, fund-raising, educational, or institutional use.

Special book excerpts or customized printings can also be created to fit specific needs. For details, write or phone the office of the Kensington Sales Manager: Kensington Publishing Corp., 119 West 40th Street, New York, NY 10018. Attn. Sales Department. Phone: 1-800-221-2647.

Lyrical Shine and Lyrical Shine logo are trademarks of Kensington Publishing Corp.

First Electronic Edition: June 2016
eISBN-13: 978-1-60183-686-1
eISBN-10: 1-60183-686-4

First Print Edition: June 2016
ISBN-13: 978-1-60183-687-8
ISBN-10: 1-60183-687-2

Printed in the United States of America

For my mom
Helen Vivian Shelton
1922–2000

Acknowledgments

A lifetime ago, my mother handed me a memoir. She didn't know the author, nor was she familiar with either title or story other than what she'd read in the local newspaper. I was visiting my mom in Illinois from Anchorage, where my own writing dream was withering unattended while I concentrated on my business career.

Mom explained that she went to the book signing and bought the book because one day I would be like this author and my mom wanted everyone, whether they knew me or not, to come to my signing and buy *my* book.

After that, what choice did I have? When I received my first Golden Heart nomination several years later, it was as much Mom's as mine.

My mother would not give up on my dream and she made it impossible for me to.

Thanks, Mom. This is for you.

Many have provided a helping hand to *Spooning Daisy*. Here, in the order I drew their names out of my red plaid hat with the ear flaps, are those who have left indelible fingerprints:

Lt Col Brooks E. Shelton, USAF (Ret), my big brother and an all-around good guy, gave me the idea for a pivotal plot twist, which he will surely disavow. *This page will self-destruct in 30 seconds.* Read fast.

Gretchen Brinck and Lena Hubin are *first*, talented, insightful writers who influence every chapter and, *second*, intrepid guinea pigs for my vegan recipes. Strangers to me when our critique group banded, they are now cherished friends. God-willing, we shall still be sharing tea and conversation long after the Thesaurus has been shelved.

Elizabeth (Liz) Shelton, my big sister, and "Dixie," to whom Liz has thus far devoted thirty-plus years, are the inspiration behind *Daisy* and *Elizabeth*.

John Scognamiglio, Editor-in-Chief of Kensington Books, gently tells me the bad, enthusiastically tells me the good. If not for John, *Spooning Daisy* would be just another file on my hard drive. And did I mention, *Editor-in-Chief*?

Smiling Hill, and those living here, especially dog Molly, horses Quinn and Teena, and cat Sara, everyday demonstrate that in life, as in books, animals make the story.

David Cottrell is an Alaskan's Alaskan—homesteader, business-man, entrepreneur, pilot, sailor, sportsman. By his side, I learned a lot, then shared it with Daisy and Max.

Marlene Stringer is smart, funny, loves animals, and knows talent. What else could I want? Sure, Lindt white-chocolate truffles, but I'm talking about agents. Because of Marlene, *Spooning Daisy* is CONTEMPORARY ROMANCE #1, *Embracing Felicity* is CONTEMPORARY ROMANCE #2, and *Tempting Eveline* is CONTEMPORARY ROMANCE #3.

Ken Taylor and Jerry Grover, my best buddies—gone too soon—invited me into their man caves so I might understand and write honestly, but with kindness.

Rebecca Cremonese, Production Editor for Kensington Books, guided me through the editing labyrinth much like Bartemius Crouch, Jr. helped Harry Potter survive the deadly Triwizard Maze . . . which is confusing since *four* wizards were competing. Thanks to Rebecca, revisions weren't confusing. And no one died. That I know of.

Mari Klassert and Jeanne Dolan are my yin and my yang, oldest and dearest friends, influencing every "best friend" that starts in my head and ends on the page.

Linda Rupp, trail buddy & partner-in-crime, was there for the garage sale that started it all.

Victoria (Tory) Groshong, Copy Editor, has the unenviable task of suggesting revisions to writers who like to think their every word is gold. Tory has prevented blunders such as *He screwed his face* from going to print. More like *fool's* gold.

Seldovia and Kachemak Bay, Alaska—where I scattered my mom's ashes—are the inspiration behind Otter Bite. Forever in my heart, and now in the hearts of Daisy, Felicity, and Eveline, as well. Exactly as it *otter* be.

Chapter One

"What'll ya take for this?"

Daisy Moon lifted her glazed eyes from a makeshift plywood table where she had been tidying pieces of her past. She focused on the midlife, mostly brunette whose brassy streaks fit her gravel voice. Backlit by the golden afternoon pushing into the garage, the woman appeared heaven-sent. After a closer look, Daisy knew better.

In her right hand, a cigarette was wedged between two fingers while her left hand strangled a porcelain figurine, its milky pastels and melted contours in unhappy contrast to the black polish on the woman's talons.

"I'd appreciate it if you wouldn't smoke," Daisy said politely. "There's a bucket outside—"

Too late. The cigarette was crushed between the sole of one strappy stiletto sandal and the pristine concrete of Daisy's double garage.

"So how much?"

A cloud dulled the sun and the saintly aura faded.

Stepping back to allow yet another stranger to judge the resale value of her life, Daisy answered the brunette. "Doesn't the tag say fifty dollars?" as if she couldn't remember how, in the wee hours of the morning while Lady Antebellum pleaded "Need You Now," she'd painstakingly tied the price tag around the necks of the porcelain lovers.

"Ye-ahh," the woman answered as if Daisy were dense. "But how much will you *take*?"

"Excuse me," a voice from behind interrupted. "What size is this?"

Daisy turned to a stout woman who held a Kelly-green midcalf skirt and matching short jacket. Daisy loved that suit—it perfectly complemented her Irish genes—but love wasn't a good enough reason to keep something that squeezed the breath from her. "Size six."

"Is there some place I could try it on?"

"Try it on . . . ?" Daisy imagined popped buttons and exploding seams.

"I'll handle this," Charity Wagstaff whispered, coming through the milling browsers. "You take care of Cruella."

Daisy shot her eyes toward the heavens.

"But remember," her best friend softly chided, "you're turning the page, moving on, taking risks. You're *letting go*—"

"I know, I know." Forcing a smile, Daisy attended to the brunette. "Make me an offer."

"Ten bucks."

"Ten bucks? That's a *Lladró!*"

The brunette stared impatiently, as if she were tapping a foot.

"It's a limited edition and it cost $275 *last year*. They've probably broken the mold."

"Well, if it's so valuable, why're y' selling it?"

Because it was meant to crown the top layer of a fabulous, five-tier Amaretto wedding cake . . . "Because I'm moving," Daisy said instead. "And I don't have the room."

The brunette yawned.

"It's like this—" Daisy tried to look pitiful. But it took memories of her long-departed mutt, Sophie, to produce the tears needed for effect. "My husband died and I have to downsize."

"Twenty bucks," countered the dry-eyed shopper.

"She'll take it," Charity said, sneaking up from behind.

Her auburn frizz quivering with indignation, Daisy spun toward the sunny blonde. "Have you lost your mind? It's worth more than twenty dollars. It's worth more than *fifty* dollars!"

"Let it go."

"It's so beautiful."

"It's only clay. *Let it go.*"

"I don't have all day." The woman held out a rumpled bill. "Y' want the twenty or not?"

Reaching across the plywood, Charity snatched the money.

"I've changed my mind, it's not for sale!" Daisy screamed. Charity blocked her attempt to chase the woman, who fled down the drive like a hyena with carrion.

Daisy wilted, then quickly tensed. The browsing had stopped and all eyes were upon her. A Miss Marple–type linked elbows with her equally tweedy companion and the two scurried out of the garage, pausing briefly at the garden tools displayed along the drive before glancing back and continuing their escape.

Sympathetically, Charity said, "Why don't you take a break? You've been at this for hours."

Daisy took a shuddering breath, the embarrassment and humiliation of the last year dumping on her like a sudden downpour. She didn't even know these people who were picking over the remnants of her life. Why should she care what they thought? It was *her* garage—for another two weeks. If she wanted, she could be as contrary and unpredictable as the Seattle weather.

"Maybe a *short* break," Daisy conceded, before wending her way between bookshelves and lamps and a widescreen television marked with a SOLD sign. Who could've predicted that only weeks after Jason had replaced his reliable television with a sleeker state-of-the-art model, he'd do the same with his fiancée?

Certainly not Daisy, who, nonetheless, had taken the high road, thanks to the example set by her mother, a corporate wife who always kept her smile in the face of adversity. With more at stake than just her personal relationship, Daisy had been civil, allowing Jason to move out at his leisure; she had never intended to keep either the television or the telltale Callaway golf clubs *until* she received the certified letter from Dritz Klak & Smite.

She'd fantasized about bashing the $2,500 television with the $600 driver, but the ever-pragmatic Charity convinced her to sell them instead.

"You'll get the best price on eBay," Charity had told her.

But money was less the objective than expediency; Daisy didn't have time to photograph, upload, monitor, and mail. And fear of another "Craigslist Killer" kept her away from that website. So, the old-fashioned method it was; anything remaining at day's end would be donated to the SPCA thrift shop.

Of course, Jason didn't know his precious belongings were the main course at a garage sale.

Although short-lived, the thought cheered Daisy as she passed from the netherworld of her garage into the haven of her kitchen. But not before fluffing the potpourri of carnation petals strategically placed between a crystal mantel clock and a silver-plated chafing dish.

Chapter Two

"That poor woman," Maeve Kendall said to her grown son. "Widowed at such a tender age."

"Uh-huh," Max Kendall agreed, but his attention was on a page from a surprisingly blemish-free 1952 *Superman* comic book he'd lifted from a stack of twenty. The sign in front read: $2 EACH OR $30 FOR ALL

After flipping through a few more pages, he laid the comic back on the pile, then scrutinized a set of Callaway golf clubs. Removing the driver from its bootie, he gripped Bertha and spread his feet as if he were about to swing.

"She couldn't be much more than thirty...*five*? Wouldn't you say, Max? Thirty-five?"

"I'd say she's crazy, whatever her age," proving that he was *sort of* listening. Raised with four effervescent sisters, Max tuned out most of the chatter that accompanied women. He had learned this skill from his father, who would occasionally smile and agree, then go back to his own thoughts while Maeve kept talking.

"I'm sure you would be emotional, too, if you were selling off your belongings." Maeve scanned the garage. "And she has some lovely items. She's obviously a girl of culture and breeding. Not to mention being tidy and organized. With a nice figure and a sweet face. Don't y' think, Max?"

"These clubs are custom-made graphite. With great balance. They don't look like they've been used. Way too short for me, but they might fit Dad."

"The grrrips are blue," Maeve pointed out, her brogue adding melody to her words.

"A lighter shaft might improve his game," Max joked.

"I bet her people are Irish. Don't you think she has a sweet face? A sweet *Irish* face?"

"Who?"

"The redhead."

He stopped the imaginary swing that had him teeing off at St. Andrews. "What about the redhead?"

"Don't you think she has a sweet face?"

"How should I know? You can barely see it for all that hair." He exchanged the driver for the putter; his fingers curled around the grip. Waggle-waggle. *If Max Kendall sinks this putt, he'll be the new grrrrand champion . . .*

"You should ask her to dinner."

Max lifted his eyes from his winning putt. "I'm getting these for Dad. He can rewrap the grips or sell them in the shop if he doesn't want them."

"Maybe you should go home and shave. I'll wait here."

"Okay." He returned the putter to the butter-soft leather golf bag, then shot his eyes to Maeve. "*What?*"

"I'll wait here while you go shave."

Max rubbed the stubble on his chin. "Why do I need to shave?"

"So you don't look like a bum when you ask her to dinner."

"Ask *who* to dinner?"

"The widow."

"*What* widow?"

"The widow selling these golf clubs."

"You mean . . . *the crazy redhead?*"

"Well, why not?"

Max stared at his mother as if *she* were crazy. "We're total strangers for one—"

"That's why y' have dinner. To get to know one another."

"—And she's crazy."

"All redheads have a fiery temperament." Maeve smiled, remembering her own eruptions.

"I prefer docile blondes." He fidgeted with the clubs. "Where the hell is the price tag?"

"Seriously, Max, it can't be very excitin' sitting around with Da and me each night."

"Visiting your parents isn't supposed to be exciting. Besides, I'm only here until Monday. What would be the point?"

"Not everything has to have a point. Sometimes the best things happen without having a point."

"Uh-huh. No."

"You'll probably have a great time."

"*No.*"

"I just want you to be happy and settled."

"I *am* happy and settled."

"A man without a wife is *not* happy and settled."

Max laughed and shook his head. "You have a short memory, Mom."

"That was a long time ago and it was the navy's fault."

"Whatever."

Softening, Maeve cupped his face and went eye to eye. "Max, darling, y' can't be dragging around that cross for the rest of your life."

He gently pulled away. "I love you, Mom, but give it a rest."

Maeve shook a finger at his face. "Maxim Avery Kendall, you're more stubborn than your father and you're going to end up alone in a houseful of pigeons just like your Uncle Arvis."

He took a heavy breath, having heard it all before. *Although,* this was the first time he and the never-wed Arvis had shared the same pigeon fate.

"Oh, never mind. She'd probably turn y' down."

Max frowned. *Rejection?* From a woman whose flaming hair tugged at her head as if trying to escape? *Not likely.* And when you factored in her volatility—honestly now, how many offers did a woman like that get?

Max didn't know her, but he knew all about her. This detour in her life was not her idea. She would just about kill to have someone help her steer through it. *Rejection?* No way.

"Well, just *look* at you," Maeve said, misinterpreting his frown.

He looked down on his Señorita Largatija Mexican T-shirt with its red-lipped, smiling lizard, frayed hem, and solitary sangria stain, and then to his faded jeans with a small rip in the right knee. "You thought I looked okay when you dragged me out of the house at some ungodly hour to visit every garage sale in the city."

"I was not wantin' to be critical."

"But now . . . ?"

"You're lookin' a bit too much like Seamus McGrew."

Max turned from his mother, searching again for the price tag. "I don't know Seamus McGrew, Mom."

"Of course y' do. He managed the rendering plant outside Ballyteansa. He was courting your cousin, Kyla. A nice boy underneath those entrails stains. You'll remember if you think about it."

Stopping his search, Max looked at his mother, still formidable in her midsixties, although age had mellowed both her fiery temperament and her fiery hair, now paled to a new-penny copper that layered her head in waves. The same waves that Max had inherited, although his were a perfect match to the once dark brown of his father's.

"I was fourteen, Mom." He did the math—twenty-seven years ago. "And I don't remember Smelly McGrew."

"Seamus—"

"You two have been over here a while," Charity interrupted. "Is there something I can convince you to buy?"

"My son is interested in the golf clubs."

"Your son has a keen eye. Those clubs are a steal. They're Callaways. The best."

"Some consider TaylorMade the best," Max said.

"A man who knows his golf. Then I'm sure you can appreciate what a bargain these are. They've never been used."

Maeve laid a palm on Charity's forearm. "Tell me, dear, how did the poor man die?"

Charity cocked her head. "What man?"

"Your friend's husband." Lowering her voice, Maeve sounded apologetic. "I overheard her tell that unpleasant woman about her husband's passing."

"Oh, *that* man. Well, it was quite nasty. Jason—that's his name—he, uhhh, fell into a tree chipper."

Maeve gasped. "A tree chipper? Blessed Mary Mother of Jesus!"

Max cocked one dark brow.

"Shredded him from the waist down. He lingered for days, in the most intense agony you can imagine, until he finally succumbed."

"Oh my! That poor man. Has it been long?"

"Mmmm, about a year," Charity said, trying to remember exactly when her best friend's world turned upside down and inside out. "But please, don't mention it to Daisy."

"What a cheerful name," Maeve said.

"Most of the time it fits her to a T, but she's having a tough time cleaning out the closets."

Charity sighed and slowly shook her head. "When they laid Jason in the coffin, they had to stuff his pants with packing peanuts to fill him out."

"Oh my."

Max mentally rolled his eyes. "So how much for the Callaways?"

"I'm sure the price is somewhere." Charity dug into the bag. "Daisy is quite meticulous."

Max could think of another term, less flattering, for the woman who kept her garage swept and dusted. And what was that scent? It reminded him of his mother's living room, all flowery and powdery. Garages were supposed to smell manly! Like gasoline and hot engines and car wax. Even the tables had been draped with burgundy-striped sheets, and every item he'd scanned—save for the golf clubs—had little descriptive stickers accompanying the price. Who, in their right mind, went to this much trouble to sell cast-offs?

Charity came up for air. "Let me get Daisy."

Maeve leaned into Max. "Whatever she's asking, give it to her."

"Why?"

"The poor woman is obviously havin' to sell off her belongings to make ends meet. Didn't y' see the Realtor's SOLD sign in the yard?"

"These are $4,000-dollar clubs! She'd be a fool to ask less than a thousand, and I'm not paying that. You're the one who taught me to haggle."

"Not with widows. It'll come back on y'."

"I guarantee you, Mom, she is *not*—"

"You were asking about the clubs?" Mother and son separated. "They're Callaways," Daisy said, exhausting her knowledge about Jason's passion.

"We're the Kendalls," Maeve interjected.

"Kendalls?" Daisy looked first at the petite, stylish woman and then at the rumpled, stubbled, stained hunk towering beside her.

"I'm Maeve and this is my son, Max."

"Ohhh. *Kendalls*. I thought you were talking about golf clubs. Duh." Daisy smiled. "I haven't slept much and I'm a bit . . . I'm Daisy."

Nice lips, Max thought without meaning to. The gentle lift of her mouth lit her pale complexion like the soft glow of firelight.

"You're obviously not a golfer," Max said. Her green eyes sparked. *Like kryptonite.*

"No. That's Jason's hobby. He's always chasing that hole in one."

"You poor dear," Maeve said. "Your darlin' man is still in the present with y'. My aunt Rose talked to her dear departed Henry for twenty-five years before she joined him."

Daisy narrowed her eyes on Maeve as if that would help explain what the hell she was talking about.

"How much for the clubs?" Max asked.

Daisy's smile vanished and the glow died. "I don't care. Make me an offer."

"A thousand," Maeve blurted as if this were a bidding war.

Daisy jerked back. "A thousand . . . *dollars*?"

"Mom!"

"They're worth four," Maeve said.

Daisy stared. "I . . . guess . . ."

"I don't have a thousand dollars on me, *Mother*."

"How much do y' have, Son?"

"Maybe a few hundred, *tops*."

Maeve turned to Daisy. "Would you accept a check for the rest, dear?"

"Uh . . . sure."

"I didn't bring my checkbook," Max said.

"Well, then," she began as if explaining to a child, "give Daisy what you have and you can bring the rest tonight when you pick her up for dinner."

"Dinner?" Daisy and Max said in unison.

Daisy looked at Max; he shrugged. "Mothers say the darnedest things."

"Oh, Max, you know very well we were just discussing that." Maeve turned to Daisy. "He's a bit shy."

A pained smile crossed Max's lips.

Having been embarrassed by her own mother, Daisy felt genuine sympathy for the man. However, dinner was out of the question.

"I know Max doesn't look like much now," Maeve began, lighting a motherly hand upon Daisy's forearm. "But he cleans up nicely.

And he comes from a God-loving family, y' have my word on that. An absolute gentleman. And he's quite successful, but with a kind heart. When he was seven, he raised a nest of sparrows after the mother had been killed by the neighbor's cat."

"Oh Lord . . ." Max rolled his head toward the driveway and his only escape.

Daisy didn't want to smile, but how could she not? How endearing was this to use his mother as a go-between to ask for a date? And to be honest, in baggy sweatpants and with her hair taking flight, Daisy didn't look all that appealing herself. If someone could see beyond that, she could certainly see beyond that stained T-shirt and morning stubble.

Besides, she was the *new* Daisy Moon! Moving on. Taking risks. Embracing change. The Universe had obviously delivered this man to test her resolve. And on a day when she was ridding herself of the past. Was Max Kendall her reward for sacrificing the Lladró cake topper?

Until that moment, she hadn't comprehended what *moving on* meant—*men* and *dating*. But here was her future, staring her in the face—

"I apologize for my mother. I'm sure she doesn't mean to embarrass *either* of us," Max said with a pointed glance at Maeve. "And I'm sure you have other plans."

"Actually . . ." Who was she kidding? She was still the *old* Daisy— who wasn't ready to be on the market. She didn't care what she was getting in return. She wanted her Lladró back!

"Actually . . . ," Daisy began again, trying to manufacture other plans.

"She doesn't!" Charity shouted from behind.

Daisy swung around. "Will you *please* stop doing that!"

"Excuse us, just for a minute." Charity pulled Daisy away.

"What do you think you're doing? I'm not going to dinner with a complete stranger"—Daisy surreptitiously eyed Max—"no matter how good-looking he *probably* is."

"Probably? The man *sizzles*."

"He looks a little scruffy."

"Said the pot about the kettle—"

Daisy tightened her eyes into viperous slits.

"—And don't act like you don't know it." Charity put on her sunny face and called back to mother and son, "We'll be right there. Don't go away."

She turned to Daisy and lowered her voice. "Trust me. This is how I make my living. That man knows golf, which means he's got money—"

"He could be a caddy—"

Charity hushed her with a raised index finger. "And he's kindly chauffeuring his mother around on a Saturday."

"He probably still lives at home."

"Hello—have you met his mother? If he lived at home, she would've mended his jeans and thrown out that T-shirt. Now stop being so pigheaded and do what the doctor orders."

"What if this guy is a serial killer?"

"Then you can tell me *I told you so*."

Daisy glared.

"He doesn't fit the profile."

"Even so . . . it's not like this date can lead anywhere." Daisy glanced back at Max, who had impatiently crossed his arms like Mr. Clean.

"Which is why this is so perfect! No pressure. No thoughts of the future. You can screw up and it won't matter, but you'll have gotten over the *first date* hump. And—heaven forbid—you might actually have fun and maybe even get lucky."

"*Lucky?* You want me to get lucky . . . with a stranger?" Daisy peeked at Max, who cocked his head at her, looking less pleased by the second. Obviously, Max Kendall was not accustomed to being the object of indecision.

"Sometimes, Daisy, the best way to get lucky is with a stranger from a garage sale."

"You're making this up."

"I'll bet you dollars to donuts this man knows what to do between the sheets. It would do you good to let go a little. Just remember to be safe. And *don't* fall in love."

"Love?" Daisy radiated panic. "I'm not ready for *lucky*. Why bring up love?"

"You're right. You're much too pragmatic."

"Yeah, that would explain my very pragmatic attachment to a cake topper."

"Two entirely different things."

"Uh-huh."

"This is the same advice I give clients before I hand them a bill for $150," Charity said.

"You set people up to get lucky and then you take money? Doesn't that make you a pimp?"

"A pimp with a PhD." Charity spun Daisy around and pushed her back to mom and son.

"Daisy would be delighted to have dinner with you," she said as Daisy mutely smiled. "There's a quaint Italian place not too far from here—"

"Mama Mia's?" Max asked.

Daisy's green eyes popped. How could Charity do that? She knew Mama Mia's had been her and Jason's favorite restaurant—after her own, of course.

Dark brows slid together as Max looked curiously at Daisy. "If you don't like Mama's, there's another restaurant, Fireflies—"

"No! I mean, I *love* Mama's," she insisted through clenched teeth and a forced smile.

"Mama's it is," Charity quickly concluded. "Why don't you two meet there about . . . six thirty?"

Max had tickets to the Mariners' game. "How about six?"

"I guess."

"Now you can finish your business with the clubs while I show Maeve your fabulous Royal Doulton." Charity ushered away Maeve, leaving the two strangers staring at each other.

"You've got quite the mother."

"Irish."

"Ahhh."

"You've got quite the friend."

"Psychologist."

"Ahhh."

"The truth is, she's been trying for months to get me on a date and I'm afraid you're the unlucky guinea pig. I'm . . . kind of going through a . . . splitting of the sheets."

"Yeah, I didn't think your husband really fell into a tree chipper."

"A tree chipper?"

"Your friend said—"

"Got it."

Max reached into his back pocket. "Your ex-husband doesn't know you're selling his clubs, does he?"

"Actually, he's my ex but wasn't my husband. Long story. *Longer* engagement." Daisy might have smirked. "And they're not *his* clubs."

Max lifted his eyes from his opened wallet. "That explains the blue grips."

"It does?"

"Women's clubs are usually lighter in weight with different head angles for greater loft, but you can't *see* that. The color of the grips gives them away; men's are usually black or grey." He gauged her height. "But these fit someone about five-nine. They're a little long for you."

"They're not mine."

"If these aren't his and aren't yours . . ."

"The pro shop called," Daisy confessed. "Said my clubs were in. Except I don't play golf, *obviously*. Yadda, yadda. It was a terrible thing to do."

Max grinned and his blue eyes twinkled.

Yes, *twinkled*, Daisy thought. "So if . . . So if buying *stolen* clubs offends your morality, you don't have to."

"I'm sure I'll hate myself in the morning, but what the heck." He counted the bills in his wallet. "Here's $647." He held out the cash. "And while I'm going into debt, I'll take the *Superman* comics, too."

Sheepishly, as if this were an illicit transaction, Daisy took the money.

"I owe you $380."

"Why don't we call it square?" she said, her discomfort rising like dough. She didn't want to dine with this man. And she certainly didn't want to like him, let alone find him attractive. But she might be doing all three. Worse, she had just confided her relationship woes—something every courtship guru warns against.

"Are you sure?"

"Absolutely."

"You might have some valuable issues in that stack of comics."

"I doubt it. I found them at a garage sale myself a few years back."

"Think about it. We'll talk at dinner."

"About dinner . . ."

Max jerked back. "You can't possibly feel guilty about dinner."

Guilt? Is that what she felt? Guilt, for selling clubs that her fiancé of *ten years* had bought for his girlfriend?

"Look, if you'd rather not," Max said.

"It's just that, well, you were kind of roped into it."

"So were you."

Not the reassurance she was hoping for. "So . . . if *you'd* rather not . . ."

"Hey, I'm fine with it"—the edge to his voice hinted otherwise— "but I certainly don't want to force *you*."

"I hardly think you could *force* me into dinner."

"Okay then," Max said, sounding a little too breezy.

"Okay then," Daisy said, going for the same nonchalance.

In one fluid motion, Max hefted the clubs to his substantial shoulders. Then he nested the stack of comics in the crook of one elbow. "I'm sure my mom has a few more garage sales to hit. If I don't move her along, I'll never make Mama's by six.."

"If you'd rather make it later . . ."

Max huffed. Yes, *huffed*. "Six is fine."

"Okay then. I'll see you at Mama's." An awkward moment later, Daisy asked, "You're not a serial killer, are you?"

His brows jumped, then he smiled. "Not yet."

Max collected his mother, who was paying for three Royal Doulton figurines. Along with the cash, she handed Charity a business card.

Daisy busied herself rearranging items into the bare spots while surreptitiously watching Max and his mother head toward a very new, very shiny, very expensive, very red Chevy truck with temporary cardboard plates. After putting the comics inside the cab and the clubs in the bed, he helped Maeve into the passenger seat, then went to the driver's side. Daisy watched until the truck was gone from sight.

Chapter Three

"You've done good," Charity said to Daisy three hours later when only a sprinkling of items remained. "I'm proud of you."

"If I've done so good, why do I feel so lousy?"

Charity squeezed Daisy's shoulders. "This too shall pass."

"And people give you money for this? Boy, am I in the wrong profession."

Charity ignored the sarcasm. "It's almost four-thirty. I'll take down the signs. Why don't you get cleaned up for your date?"

"Oh boy, my date."

"Stop! You're acting like this is the worst thing that could happen to you."

"No. This is the second worst thing."

"A breakup is hardly the worst thing—"

"I was talking about Fireflies."

"You'll see—this is a blessing in disguise. Now make a 'bad things' list. Bunions. Allergies to chocolate. Getting eaten by a bear—"

"Mangled by a tree chipper?"

"Just imagine how nasty *that* would be. See how lucky you are? Now go get pretty."

An hour later, Daisy came down the stairs and into the kitchen, where Charity sat at the island with a calculator beside stacks of currency spread on the granite. Clustered on her other side were a plate of crackers, a half-eaten bowl of salmon pâté, and an opened bottle of Chardonnay next to a full goblet.

Charity stopped counting bills. "You clean up real nice, Daisy Mae. What I wouldn't give to have your hair when it looks like that"—she scooped salmon pâté onto a cracker and popped it into her mouth—"an' your talen' with foo'. Mmmmmmm."

"You don't think it's too frou-frou?"

"Your hair is perfect."

"The pâté. I'm trying some new recipes. I was going for sophisticated, but maybe I should stick to basics. It's not called Wild Man Lodge for nothing." Daisy thought about the rustic cabins shown on the website and imagined what the photos didn't reveal—spiders, dust, musty sheets, screeching faucets, rusty water, mice—

"I'm sure you'll find a bunch of business types *pretending* to be wild men. They'll love your food and they'll love you."

Daisy hadn't mentioned the website to Charity. It was bad enough she was going to the ends of the earth; the third-world living conditions only made it worse. "I don't know what I was thinking when I took this job." *I was thinking I had no choice*, Daisy reminded herself as she bulldozed a cracker into the salmon.

"You were thinking you need to start over. You were thinking you need an adventure. You were thinking you need a change. And you're right. You can always come home. Lots of restaurants in Seattle would jump at the chance to have you as their chef. Fireflies is not the only game in town," she said. "And Jason's going to rue the day he lost you as chef . . . *and* his wife. I've seen his girlfriend—"

"Fiancée," Daisy corrected.

"Soon to be ex-wife," Charity quipped. "She's working her way up the food chain. Not that I'll be sorry when she dumps his cheating ass."

Daisy wasn't sure which was worse—losing her place in Jason's heart or losing her place in the restaurant she had nurtured into Seattle's most popular and prosperous.

Even the name Fireflies had been her brainchild, along with the twinkling lights scattered around the romantic restaurant and the Mason jars glowing with fake fireflies on the linen-covered tables. Like an old-fashioned summer evening—

"In a couple of months it will all be forgotten," Charity added. "People understand."

Daisy thought about her job search and all her phone calls that were never returned—something else she hadn't mentioned to Charity. "People might understand, but *men* don't. And *men* own the four-star restaurants. And *men* are the executive chefs at those restaurants. And *men* do the hiring for their kitchens. And *men* don't hire volatile, violent women. If I were a *man*, I'd have my own television show by now."

"You're *not* volatile *or* violent. The judge had just rejected your claim in the restaurant you'd given your heart and soul to for ten years! That same restaurant in which Jason had always promised you a partnership—"

Next time, get it in writing, her attorney had said. *Or get married. Never trust love to be fair.*

"—and Jason—the gutless prick—was gloating up a storm. He had no reason to fire you in the first place, let alone have his attorney do it in a letter. You showed considerable restraint. I would've torched the place and taken a meat cleaver to the man's dick."

"You're just saying that."

Charity shrugged. "You broke a few dishes. Big deal."

"A *few*?"

"What's done is done. And people *will* forget."

"Not the Royal Academy of Chefs."

"I know that gold spatula means a lot—"

"Golden Spoon," Daisy corrected peevishly. "It took me years to get it and those bastards took it away."

"For un-chef-like conduct, yes, I know. But you don't need those stuffy ol' cooks. You're no more talented with that spoon than you are without it. *Nothing* has changed."

"*Everything* has changed."

"Only circumstances. *You* are still fabulous."

"I had four stars. Four shining stars."

"You'll get it all back, Daisy. Your stars, your spoon. The great reviews. You'll see."

Daisy sighed, unconvinced, but for tonight she'd let it go—as if she had a choice. She dug another cracker into the salmon. "So you don't think it's too frou-frou?"

"The pâté is sublime."

"No, my hair." The frenzied mass had been tamed into sensual spirals that gently caressed her shoulders.

"Your hair is a traffic-stopper."

"Like an accident?"

"Stop it! You're gorgeous. I love that sweater." The teal cashmere highlighted Daisy's eyes. "Have some wine."

"If I drink that, I'll fall asleep in my marinara. I was up most of last night."

"Listening to Lady Antebellum. But you've got too much adrenaline to fall asleep. You need to take the edge off."

Daisy's hand quivered as she reached for the goblet. All she had to do was get through this evening and then she'd never ever date again. One, two, three swallows.

"Slow down! I said take the *edge* off. You're whacking the whole plank."

Four, five, six swallows . . . and the glass was empty. "How much did we make?"

"Including the big-ticket items . . . $4,722."

"Wow! And to think it originally cost about thirty thousand."

"Everything was used and unwanted."

"Not *everything*."

"Moving on."

"Speaking of which, I better go."

"You've still got time. You don't want to arrive early and appear eager."

Daisy dug out keys from her evening purse and discovered two foil-wrapped Trojans. She held them up. "What're these?"

Charity smiled. "Safety in numbers."

"I don't need safety and certainly not in numbers." But she dropped them back into her clutch. Then she cocked her head at Charity. "What're *you* doing with condoms?"

"They're for Bob's *Pretty Woman* fantasy. The billionaire and the prosti—"

"Too much info." Daisy grabbed her keys and then set them back down. "I forgot to feed Elizabeth."

"I'll feed Elizabeth. You go."

"Don't you have to be on a street corner?"

"Bob's going to the game with his buddies."

"Oh no, lawyers unleashed."

"You're stalling."

"Elizabeth can be finicky."

"I've watched you feed her a million times."

"I know, but—"

"You're going to be late."

Daisy glanced at her watch, then picked up her keys a second time. "There's an open jar of baby food in the fridge. Microwave it for *ten* seconds and put it in her dish. Give her a teaspoon of Mighty Dog on the side—"

"Yeah, yeah, go."

"—AND shred some lettuce and chop up a cherry tomato."

"I'll feed Lizzie, put her in jammies, and tell her a bedtime story. She won't even know you're gone."

"She doesn't like being called Lizzie."

"How about *The Tortoise and the Hare*?"

"Her favorite is *Beauty and the Beast*."

"Go!"

She dragged herself out of the kitchen.

"Daisy—"

Looking back, Daisy saw hope in her best friend's eyes.

"—*Try* to get lucky."

Chapter Four

Max Kendall sat at the bar and ordered an Alaskan Amber. About five-forty and Mama Mia's was emptying of Mariners' fans on their way to Safeco Field after an early dinner.

Violins crooned softly from the sound system. The subtle aroma of basil and garlic wafted through the restaurant. Candle flames flickered on the tables in the cozy dining room. But all Max could think about was his ruined Saturday night. The Kansas City Royals were in town and he and his dad had tickets. What Max wouldn't give to be driving there instead of sitting here.

Mothers!

He might still make the fourth inning if he and Daisy beat the date crowd and didn't get bogged down with drinks, appetizers, and small talk. If they were seated right now, they could be finished by seven-thirty. But that would require his date to actually be—

"Max?"

He swiveled toward the sultry voice . . . and smiled.

"I thought that was you." The blonde hugged him. "The lighting's so dim I wasn't sure. You look great."

"Ditto." Her sassy perfume enveloped him, triggering memories. "How long has it been?"

"A year."

Max frowned. "Are you sure?"

"Time flies."

"Still with Alaska Airlines?"

"Of course. How's the lodge?"

"Booked through fall."

"I've got happy memories of that place."

"We can always make more."

"I *should* come back," she teased. "Just to get a proper good-bye."

He quirked his head at her.

"You kissed me, got out of bed, and said *I'll miss you.* Meat Loaf was playing in the background. 'Two Out of Three.' That's the last I saw of you."

"I had a fishing charter and you were going back to Seattle." Not that he precisely remembered—was she kidding about Meat Loaf?—but that was his typical no-frills good-bye.

"One of these days, Max—" Tina smiled. "What are you doing in Seattle—alone on a Saturday night?"

"Visiting my parents and buying a new truck. I'm meeting someone for dinner, but they're late. Sit down, I'll buy you a drink."

"I'd love to, believe me, but I'm here with my fiancé. We're going to the Mariners' game—"

"*Fiancé?*"

Tina turned toward the dining room and fluttered fingers at an expensively dressed man who, even in the flattering light, looked much too reserved for the adventurous pilot Max remembered. Even his smile was cautious. Or was it hostile?

"Wow," Max said, catching the blinding glint off her left hand. "That's some rock."

"Three carats," she gushed. "But, look, if you're in town for a few days, call me. I'm not in the cockpit until Tuesday. Do you still have my cell number?"

"Yep."

She hesitated, then her voice became wistful. "I never stopped thinking about you, Max."

"You should have called."

"You live in the present. I want a future."

Max thought he should say something, but what? Surely Tina was joking; she hadn't actually considered *him* husband material, had she?

"It really is good seeing you." She leaned forward as if she might kiss him, stopping short. "Call me." Then she turned and navigated her way through the dining room, rejoining her fiancé, who—it seemed to Max—had a bull's-eye on him.

Max swiveled back toward the bar. *That was interesting.* But he didn't dwell. He hoped Tina would be happy with her three-carat man. Then he patted himself on the back for being a guy who never bore grudges or regrets, and always wished the best for an ex.

He checked his watch. Why were women always late? And it did seem to be a female thing. Just as waiting seemed to be a male thing. He drank his beer down to the foam. One more Amber, then he would reclaim his night.

"Sorry I'm late," Daisy said breathlessly. She laid her purse on the bar and slid onto the stool beside Max. "Traffic was a bear because of the game tonight. Anyway, you probably thought I was a no-show."

"Actually, the thought never entered my mind." Max discreetly gave Daisy the once-over as she ordered from the bartender, telling him exactly how to make her Midori and rum concoction.

Daisy did have a sweet Irish face, Max realized before checking out her auburn spirals, gleaming like the cherries in the pie slice his mother had set in front of him that afternoon. Her curls grazed slender shoulders draped in a green sweater, and it just got better from there. Who would've guessed that wrapped inside that garage-sale cocoon was a butterfly?

Drink in hand, Daisy turned back to Max, a glint in her kryptonite eyes matching the edge in her voice. "That sure of yourself, are you?"

Yes, Max thought, but said, "You don't seem like the type to leave a guy hanging."

"Actually, the thought entered my mind. About a dozen times."

"Still worried about that serial killer thing?"

"A girl can't be too careful. I once had a creepy experience when I tried to sell my car on Craigslist. Now I carry pepper spray."

"Thanks for the warning. So, why are you here?"

"I guess because . . . I'm not the type to leave a guy hanging."

"Your psychologist friend made you come."

Daisy smiled. "That, too. *But* . . . I would've come without the nudge."

She leaned close as if to divulge a secret and Max caught the provocative scent of her perfume. Spicy. Lusty. Sensual. Just what Max would've expected . . . had he previously thought about it.

"The truth is, I'm afraid of your mother. And since she knows where I live . . ." Daisy retreated to her space and drank from her tall glass.

"But not for long."

"Meaning?"

"The SOLD sign," he explained, resisting an inexplicable urge to kiss Daisy. *Daisy*. Daisy . . . *what*?

Max shrugged it off. It wasn't the lack of a last name that had him baffled, it was his ambivalence about a woman he didn't know, didn't *want* to know, but definitely wanted to . . .

"Right, the SOLD sign," she said, bringing Max back to the moment.

"So what do you do, Daisy, when you're not working garage sales?"

She took another drink. "I'm a chef."

"Really."

"Truth is, I used to be the *chef de cuisine* at Fireflies, which is why it wouldn't be such a hot idea to go there. It's all kind of connected to my breakup."

He had no idea what a *chef de cuisine* was, but it sounded like he should be impressed. "That's quite an accomplishment . . . for someone so young."

Daisy glowed. "I have four stars and a Golden Spoon."

He stared.

"It's a big deal for a chef."

Max picked up a hint of sadness. *A woman in transition.* Eager for something new. Something out of character. Something wild and crazy. Something to make her forget—for one night—whatever it was she was leaving behind. *His* kind of woman. He leaned closer and lowered his voice. "Are you staying in town? Moving to Timbuktu?"

Daisy let out a half grunt, half chuckle. "Some people think Timbuktu. Actually, for the first time in my life, I'm doing something really wild and crazy—"

Max kissed her. Just enough to tempt her, but not scare her. Then, of course, he apologized. "Sorry. I should've asked."

"That's okay. I mean, it was a surprise, but not a *bad* surprise, and I was kind of thinking about it, well, not *thinking* about it, I mean, it crossed my mind when I first sat down and saw how you look, y' know, without that stubble and T-shirt. Not that you looked bad, you just look better now. Really . . . *better*, but then who am I to talk . . ."

Her words barely registered as Max considered the rambling redhead he'd been paired with for the evening. Watching Daisy stumble her way through this explanation was like watching a puppy learn where his paws were. It was almost endearing—not that he was scouting for warm and fuzzy feelings. But if anyone needed a night

with Max Kendall, it was Daisy . . . what's-her-name. He signaled
the bartender for another drink and then the same two fingers pressed
her lips to shut her up. "Compliments aren't your strong suit, are
they?"

"I haven't slept for forty-eight hours."

"Then maybe we should get you to bed."

Their eyes locked; then, as if the inference was more tempting
than she wanted to admit, Daisy swiveled her stool away from him.

Surveying her surroundings, she started babbling again. "I used to
come here for lunch, but it's been a while. A few years ago they re-
decorated and added the fountain." A tastefully compact, three-tier
fountain gurgled in the middle of the dining room. "And they got rid
of the horrible orange carpet and put down tile. It gives it kind of an
outdoor terrace—" Daisy froze midsentence. Then she spun back toward the bar and Max. "The food here really isn't all that good. Let's
go someplace else. For dinner," she hastily added.

"I thought you liked this place."

She reached for her clutch. "Can we just go?"

"You've barely touched your drink. And I just ordered you another. What is that, five or six bucks each?"

Daisy could not believe Max was quibbling about $7.50, and her
expression reflected it. "I never asked for another and if it's such a
big deal, I'll pay for it."

"That's not the point. It just seems silly to waste—"

"Fine." Daisy reached for her icy Midori and rum. While she
drained her glass, the bartender arrived with another. Dumbstruck,
Max watched as she finished her second glass like the first, then grimaced, fingers pressing temples. "Ow, ow, ow. Brain freeze."

Max rolled his eyes.

"Can we go now?"

"Am I missing something?"

"I would just rather go someplace else."

"Burger King it is." Max asked for the tab. Before he could pay, a
menacing voice raised the hairs on the back of his neck and switched
on his defenses.

"I wanna talk t' you."

Max swiveled toward the source and faced the scowl of Tina's
three-carat man. Tina could make any man *possessive*, but Max saw
possessed. Taking the offensive, he introduced himself.

"I'm not here t' make friends," three-carat man slurred. "I jus' wanna know—"

"Look," Max said, experienced with dodging. "There is absolutely nothing between us."

Daisy drew back. "Why're you telling him that?"

"Please, Daisy, this doesn't concern you."

Copper brows jumped. "It doesn't?"

"I don't give a damn 'bout you and *her*," three-carat man said.

Max nodded in Daisy's direction. "I'm not talking about *her*."

Daisy frowned at what didn't sound like a compliment. "Thanks a lot."

Max turned to Daisy. "Do you think you could just sit there *without* talking?"

"Hey!" three-carat man interrupted. "I just wan' back wha's mine."

"That's what I'm trying to tell you," Max said. "Tina *is* yours—"

"Tina?" Daisy and three-carat man said in chorus.

"—We haven't seen each other in a year."

"A *year*?" The man's face flushed crimson.

Daisy laughed. "Oh, Jason, this is so rich! The cheater becomes the cheated!"

"Shu' up!"

Daisy gasped. Then her face angrily knotted. "I don't have to take this from *you*."

"There's no reason to be rude to Daisy," Max said.

"No . . ." Daisy slid from her stool. "That's *your* job."

"You're not going an'where—" Jason blocked her escape. "Not until—"

"Jason, please, you're causing a scene," Tina said, coming from behind. "Let's just go."

"Ol' pilot buddy, huh? You screwed him! While you were screwin' me!"

"And you were screwing *her*." Tina huffed. "Let's go. We can talk about this later."

"That's all right, Tina," Max said. "We're leaving."

"I'm sorry, Max. He's had one martini too many."

"Get used to it," Daisy said.

"He only started drinking when he saw you!" Tina shot back.

The women exchanged daggers.

"Do you two know each other?" Max asked.

Daisy turned her daggers on Max. "Apparently not as well as you two."

He frowned.

"*She's* the golf clubs."

Under the weight of his predicament, Max sagged, then he shot his eyes to the heavens. His plans for the night vanished. Like he wanted to.

"You three can work it out," Daisy huffed, trying to skirt the group.

"You're no' going an'where." Jason grabbed her arm. "Until I get the clubs."

"Bite me!"

Max stood. "Let the lady go."

His height advantage didn't sway Jason or loosen the grip he had on Daisy. "Butt out, flyboy."

If only I could, Max thought, surrounded on all sides. "Why don't we all just take a step back."

"Jason, *please*." Tina glanced at the waiters starting to circle. "You can settle this later." She latched on to his free arm and pulled.

Sirens wailed in the distance.

Trying to free herself, Daisy smacked Jason with her clutch.

Tina lunged for Daisy. "Leave him alone!"

"And by the way, I sold your TV for $200!"

"You mis'r'ble little b—"

A wave of beer drowned his last word as Daisy used Max's remaining beer to aid her escape. Alaskan Amber splashed off Jason's face and splattered the tile.

Within seconds, the four of them were tangled like last season's Christmas tree lights.

A sudden, searing pain shot through Max's knee. Then the lights went out for Max Kendall.

Chapter Five

"Daisy!" Charity Wagstaff rushed to her disheveled friend among the battered and bloodied Saturday night casualties in the emergency room. "Are you all right?"

"Thanks for coming."

"Of course I'd come." She sized up the two uniformed cops she had passed on the way in, recognizing one. "I called Bob. He'll be here soon."

Daisy tensed at the mention of Charity's husband. "Do I really need an attorney?" One green eye, heavy with exhaustion, looked at Charity. Daisy held an ice pack over the other.

"It never hurts to have the district attorney in your corner."

"I guess he was pretty pissed about missing the game."

"They're playing again tomorrow. Let's see the boo-boo."

Daisy lifted the pack.

Charity gasped. "Did Max do that?"

"Oh God, no!" Daisy returned the ice to the swollen, purple mess. "At least I don't think so."

"You don't think so?"

She groaned. "Everything happened at once. It could've been Max. It could've been Jason. But it was probably Tina—"

"Jason and Tina? But on the phone you said that you and Max had gotten into a fight."

"We did. With Jason and Tina. It's a long story."

"In a nutshell."

"We were at Mama Mia's. And I saw Jason. Then everything kind of snowballed."

"A larger nutshell."

She recounted the evening's events without interruption until—

"Did I hear you right? Max knows *Tina*?"

"In the biblical sense. They had a thing a year ago."

"What are the odds?"

"Apparently very good." Daisy moaned. "Hearing that was like lighting the fuse. It seems all men prefer Tina. I just lost it. And, by the way, I told you so."

A sympathetic murmur.

"I threw a beer in Jason's face."

"Good for you."

"Not good. It was like some demonic force had control of my hand."

"Hell hath no fury . . ."

Daisy lowered the ice pack, giving her arm a rest.

Charity reached for Daisy's free hand to offer a supportive squeeze.

"Ow-ow-ow," she squawked. "My wrist. I think it's sprained."

Gently pulling back the cashmere, Charity asked about the brown smudges along the sleeve. "Is that blood?"

Daisy looked at the cashmere. "Huh. I didn't even notice."

"Is it yours?"

"I don't think so."

Charity didn't dare ask whose it might be and instead focused on Daisy's swollen wrist, looking out of place against her slender, artistic hand. "Can you move your fingers?"

A slow wiggle later, Charity said, "Well, at least it's your left hand and it's not broken. Put the ice pack on it." She looked around the large room. "Where's the rest of the party? Don't tell me you're the only one who got clobbered."

"I think Tina broke a nail. She was holding up a finger and bitching. Or maybe that finger was aimed at me." She paused, trying to remember, then let it go. "Jason might have a couple of cracked ribs—that's what I heard the nurse say. Tina's with him in one of the exam rooms."

"And Max?"

Daisy groaned yet again and smothered her face in the ice pack.

"Sweetie, I can't understand you. What happened to Max?"

She lifted her face from the ice, looking both remorseful and mortified. "He tore the meniscus in his knee and he might have a concussion. That's what the paramedics said."

"A torn meniscus *and* a concussion? How in the world . . . ?"

"No idea. The waiters jumped in and then the cops arrived—I remember the sirens. There were arms and legs everywhere. I got an elbow in my face and I must've fallen on my wrist. Not sure what happened to Max." Daisy tried to shake off the memory. But she couldn't forget the dazed grimace on Max's face—*was blood trickling over his eye?*—as the paramedics loaded him into the ambulance. All of that anguish directed at her. Not that she blamed him, really, although it wasn't *completely* her fault. If they had left the restaurant when she'd wanted, none of this would've happened. If Max hadn't been so cheap about her $7.50 drinks, they would've been out the door. If he hadn't confessed about Tina—*what the hell was he thinking?* But Jason was most at fault. This disastrous night happened because Jason was an ass!

Charity consoled her best friend with an embrace. "Daisy, Daisy, Daisy."

The ice pack went back on her eye. "I'm cursed."

They sat silently for a minute then Charity looked thoughtful. "Just out of curiosity, before the fight, you didn't get lucky, did you?"

Pulling away, Daisy dropped both her jaw and the ice pack. "Are you kidding?"

"Were you at least having fun?"

Daisy stared.

"Well, were you?"

She pondered the question, remembering Max's kiss. "It wasn't the worst night . . ."

"That's the important thing."

"I don't think that's the important thing."

They sat in silent commiseration, for the first time aware of the conversation hum around them. Then Charity heard a familiar laugh and looked over her shoulder. Her handsome husband—a silver-haired poster boy for Eddie Bauer—chatted congenially with the two police officers. Catching his wife's gaze, Bob Wagstaff excused himself and joined her.

" Evening, ladies."

"What took you so long?" Charity asked.

"I had a Louixs and a snifter of Rémy Martin to finish. And I made a few phone calls."

"Phone calls?" Charity griped.

Bob held up his hand to halt the protest. "So, Daisy, the crime spree continues, eh?"

Daisy moaned from both her humiliation and her throbbing wrist. But mostly from humiliation.

"Here's the good news," he said. "The police aren't pressing charges. I talked with Pietro at the restaurant and persuaded him to handle this privately, but he expects someone to pay for the damages."

"Well *I'm* certainly not! Jason started it!"

"Calm down, Daisy," Charity said. "I'm sure Jason can be persuaded to share half—"

"Half? But it was *all* Jason's fault!"

"Why don't we discuss this after you've had a good night's sleep and are thinking more clearly?" Bob suggested.

"I'm not paying a penny."

"Uh-oh," Bob mumbled.

"What?" Charity looked around.

"*Clod* Standish." Bob smiled at a fifty-ish man with bronzed skin and teeth white enough to bring a ship into port at night. "It looks like Jason has brought in the big guns. I'd better go see what we're up against."

"He looks familiar," Daisy said, still irritated. "I think I've seen him in the restaurant. Of course, slaving over hot burners doesn't let me hobnob much. Jason always did the social stuff. So who's Claude Standish? Why is Bob so worried?"

"Actually it's *Clyde*. Bob doesn't like him." She gave Daisy a moment. "Clyde is *the* attorney when it comes to personal injury. Remember the guy who got scalded by coffee when the lid came off his cup? Clyde got him three hundred grand. And that pregnant airline passenger who was manhandled by airport security? Two million."

"Maybe I should hire *Clod*."

"By the look on Bob's face, I'd say Jason beat you to it."

Bob returned. "Well, ladies, the plot thickens."

"What's Clyde suing for?" Charity asked.

"Oh, who cares?" Daisy snapped. "Nothing will stick. There are witnesses—"

"Shush."

"Well, for starters," Bob began with his courtroom face, "assault. Battery. Fraud. Misrepresentation. Loss of business. Loss of wages. Loss of good name. Pain and suffering—"

"What?" Daisy shrilled. "This is so lame!"

"—And Clyde is threatening a restraining order, so stay away—"

"A restraining order! Against *me*? Jason is the one who needs to be restrained!"

"Let's remember, Daisy, you do have a history," Bob reminded her. "Which Clyde will happily use against you."

"One time! And it was completely justified! Charity said so."

"She did, did she?"

Charity ignored her husband's disapproval. "Calm down, Daisy. I'm sure this is all swagger." She addressed Bob. "You don't think Jason can win any of this, do you?"

"Doubtful," Bob said.

"See, Daisy, you're getting all worked up over nothing."

"Unfortunately," Bob added, a twinkle in his eye, "Clyde's client isn't Jason."

Chapter Six

The Alaskan ferry M/V *Columbia* eased out of Bellingham under gunmetal-gray skies. The cold salt wind stung Daisy's cheeks and flung her hair as she pressed the rail and waved bravely from the deck at Charity, who returned her farewell from the dock.

Daisy no longer babied her left wrist, healed from the incident at Mama Mia's three weeks earlier. All that remained as a reminder of that dreadful night was a mottled yellow-and-lilac shadow cradling her right eye. That—and Max Kendall's lawsuit. But she'd given *that* problem to her lawyer, along with a $3,000 retainer after being warned by Clyde Standish to stay away from his client or be arrested. Nonetheless, she had shown up at the hospital with a vase of carnations. But after the nurse had refused admittance to Max's room—apparently there was an unwanted-visitor list—she left the bouquet at the nurses' station, then stomped off, passing Tina on the way out. She'd never have to see Max Kendall again, her lawyer had assured her, promising to handle everything on her behalf, which suited Daisy just fine. After all, she had enough to be miserable about, losing her home, *her* restaurant—no matter what the judge had ruled—and now, her best friend.

"You're not *losing* me. I'm only a phone call and a three-hour plane ride away," Charity had insisted before Daisy drove her Lexus onto the ferry.

Actually, it was a fifteen-minute flight in a tiny plane from Otter Bite into Homer, then a thirty-minute flight in a small plane from Homer into Anchorage, and *then* a three-hour flight to Seattle on a 737. But there wasn't any percentage in dwelling on that.

Tears welled in Daisy's eyes as the waters of Puget Sound swirled below her and Charity shrank from view. She could scarcely believe this was happening, but the drone of the massive engines, the smell of diesel exhaust, the ebb and flow of the *Columbia* as it forged its way to sea, proved too real to deny.

On deck for the departure, her fellow passengers soon abandoned Daisy for warmer, brighter quarters inside, safe from the worsening late-afternoon weather. Daisy watched the mainland slowly disappear under a gray, depressing shroud.

A raindrop pinged her nose. Another splattered her cheek. Snuggling into her jacket, she frowned at the skies, which seemed to be one more force against her.

Turning into the rolling tide, the *Columbia* shimmied and lurched as it collided with whitecaps and a crosswind. A landlubber down to her floral panties, Daisy grabbed the polished teak rail with both hands.

"First time at sea?"

Turning her head, Daisy met a distinguished-looking man in a starched white uniform. Maybe ten years older than she, he had the commanding presence of an ancient mariner. She released one hand from the rail only long enough to chase hair away from her eyes.

"Shouldn't you be driving the boat?" she asked, only half kidding.

The man chuckled and joined her at the rail. "Actually, the *Columbia* qualifies as a ship and I'm not the captain, but thank you. I'm the medical officer, Dr. Adam Bricker—"

Adam Bricker? Why did that name sound familiar?

"—And it would please me immensely to be of service to you, Miss . . ."

"Daisy," she answered, attempting a smile at his officer-and-a-gentleman demeanor.

"Miss Daisy? It sounds like I should be driving *you*."

"It's not *Miss Daisy*. I mean, Daisy is my *first* name." She sighed. "Daisy Moon. Landlubber."

His smile was disarming. "So why would a landlubber be on a slow ferry to Alaska when a jet can get you there in three hours?"

"First of all, *landlubber* extends to the air as well." She paused, thinking she ought to save some of her problems for the next poor schmuck who stumbled across her path. But Dr. Bricker's expression was so warm and inviting, his concern genuine, his demeanor commanding, his shoulders broad, his uniform so very white and starched . . .

"The thing is, I'm sort of moving to Alaska and I have my SUV packed with stuff, and"—Daisy rolled her eyes as if she couldn't believe what she was spilling—"there are no roads to where I'm going. Only ferry and planes. So here I am. On a slow boat—sorry, *ship*—to Otter Bite."

"Sounds like you're in for some pretty vicious otters—"

Daisy laughed. As if she hadn't a care in the world.

"—and judging from that shiner, it looks like you've already encountered one."

Daisy's right hand flew to her cheek, then just as quickly returned to the rail. "Actually, this happened because of something I *otter* not have done."

Adam chuckled. But he had been right about the otters in Otter Bite—or at least one of them.

Upon first hearing the name, she had expected Bite to be *Bight*, but fifty-some years ago the residents of the tiny bay community chose a play on words after a sea otter bit an inebriated Vincent Ostrovski during a fight over a fish. What started as a joke, the Otter Bite website explained, ended with an official name change.

Dr. Bricker pulled back and appraised Daisy. "So what brings a charming young lady to a bend in the coast where the otters most certainly outnumber the people?"

"That, Doctor, is a long and not very interesting story."

"I doubt it's not interesting and as for being long, we have five days before we make Skagway."

There it was again, that disarming smile. "Actually, four days. I'm getting off at Haines."

"Then we *otter* not waste a minute. You can start your very fascinating tale at dinner tonight."

Daisy inched back.

"I'm an officer *and* a gentleman," Adam said.

"I'm sure, but—"

"You're married. Of course. Please forgive—"

"No," Daisy said in a rush. "I mean, I was involved, but I'm not now. It's just been a little difficult getting back into, y' know, *life*."

"It's only dinner."

"Yeah, well, the last man I went to dinner with is suing me." Did she really confess that?

"Now I'm hooked."

Still hesitant, Daisy silently sped through the worst-case scenario. It was a large ferry with space for 134 cars and 931 passengers—the largest of the Alaskan fleet, in fact. Daisy had made sure of that when she booked passage; she wanted a lot of buffer between her and the deep blue sea. Surely, if dinner was a fiasco, she could avoid Adam for the duration of the trip, even remain in her cabin if need be—it was the best cabin available, with a queen bed and a sitting area *and* an outside window. Not bad accommodations for hiding out—if it came to that.

"Tell you what, Daisy," Adam said when Daisy hadn't answered. "If you decide to grace me with your presence at dinner, I'll be waiting in the lounge at"—Adam slid back his jacket sleeve for a consult with a watch that looked like a Rolex—"eighteen hundred. In the meantime, why don't I escort you safely back to your cabin. Unless you prefer standing in the rain."

Soot-colored clouds were assembling like an invading army. On her cheeks, Daisy felt the beginning pricks of their cold, wet assault. She started to shiver. "I guess it would be stupid to stay here."

Adam offered his cocked elbow. "You have to let go of the rail."

Daisy glanced at her frigid hands, still throttling the teak. "You never know when the next wave will hit."

"I guarantee smooth sailing."

She looked skeptical.

"If not, I know where the lifeboats are. I'm a veritable cornucopia of information, and someone you *otter* know."

Daisy smiled. If only Charity could see her now—cold and shivering but moving on, taking risks, letting go . . . as soon as she could unclench her frozen fingers. Maybe Charity had been right. Maybe Max Kendall—however much she never wanted to think about him again—had actually done her a favor. No date could ever be as disastrous as that encounter.

"Go ahead, ask me anything," Adam said.

"There is something I'm curious about. The initials in front of the ship's name, *Columbia*. What does the M/V stand for?"

"And here I thought you'd be asking about the lost gold."

"The lost gold?" Her eyes opened into saucers before she realized the joke. "Okay, I'm gullible."

"Better gullible than jaded," Adam said. "And the M/V stands for maritime vessel. *Now* may I escort you inside?"

Chapter Seven

Daisy woke in the dark, disoriented; she had to think where she was. When she started to rise, the cabin swirled and she fell back into bed. Was she seasick?

The Inside Passage had been unusually rough last night; she felt every subtle vibration, every infinitesimal thrust and retreat of the ship as it fought the waves. But the bottle of wine she and Adam shared at dinner had been tranquilizing; her head barely hit the pillow before she was out like a light.

She dismissed the possibility of a hangover. Three glasses of wine spread over four hours would hardly put her under the table. No. It must be the sea; her inner ear simply wasn't accustomed to constant rocking.

She took deep breaths and the dizziness subsided. She slowly rolled her head toward the bedside clock; the illuminated numbers glowed red: *4:28.*

The last she remembered knowing the time was about ten o'clock last night. She and Adam had finished their crème brûlées. Daisy went to the ladies' room and while there, looked at her watch. She'd been surprised by how late it was. *Time flies . . .* When she returned to the table, they finished the wine. After that, her recollection was spotty.

She switched on the bedside lamp; soft light washed the soothing seafoam-green walls. Feeling steady, she eased out of the sheets and into her slippers. Without a single wobble—perhaps she had finally found her sea legs—she walked the short distance to her window and parted the damask curtains.

Towering lights illuminated the dock, banishing the night as workers moved into and out of her sight, readying the ferry for its

Alaskan journey. No wonder she was steady—they weren't moving. A slight shudder and Daisy felt the engines come alive. Barely in her view, a line of cars started to advance. This must be *Columbia*'s first port, Prince Rupert in British Columbia.

Releasing the curtains, she turned toward her cabin. The best available, it was still small. On the lower deck were passengers without a cabin. She seemed to remember them from last night, rolling out their sleeping bags in the ship's solarium—mostly the young and adventurous who didn't mind sleeping among strangers or sharing communal bathrooms. Daisy shuddered at the thought. Besides, she had Elizabeth to think about. She couldn't exactly cart her around and she wasn't about to leave her unattended in the open where anybody could snatch her. And Daisy wasn't good at roughing it. This cabin was about as rough as she cared to get. As it was, she had brought her own sheets and pillow for the bed, thanks to a television exposé about hotel sheets and body fluids that didn't come out in the laundry.

Yet, here she was on a slow boat—"Boat, ship, whatever!" Daisy grumbled—heading to Otter Bite and the Wild Man Lodge. The idea of being executive chef at Wild Man hadn't sounded so bad when it was just something she was going to do. But now that she was actually *doing* it . . .

Trying to bolster hope, Daisy retrieved the manila envelope from her suitcase, spread open on the compact couch. Inside the envelope was everything she knew about Wild Man Lodge: the PR brochure, a copy of the menu, photos off the website, and correspondence from Rita Jakolof, including the letter offering Daisy the job and the agreed-upon salary.

Rita had come to Seattle to interview Daisy, as well as three other applicants. *All men*, Rita had confided, intimating that Daisy's gender gave her the advantage—although she heard Rita mumble something about catching hell. Apparently in Otter Bite women were at a premium, and Rita was starved for female friendship. Nor did it hurt that Rita couldn't get enough of Daisy's cooking, being particularly enamored of her mango chutney on salmon. One thing could be said about Rita, she was a robust eater. Four hors d'oeuvres, two salads, one soup, three entrées, and four desserts later, she had found her chef.

An Otter Bite native who could trace her fraternal roots back to the Russian settlers of the 1800s and her maternal roots back to the Alutiiq people a thousand years before that, Rita was the lodge manager and a Jill-of-all trades handling a plethora of duties including supervision of the kitchen and housecleaning staffs. With long raven-black hair, luminous brown eyes and latte skin, she might've been plucked from the pages of a Zane Grey novel, except of course for the designer jeans and tight sweater accentuating her voluptuous figure. Rita was as easygoing as Daisy was tightly wound, seemingly unconcerned that the lodge was fully booked for the season and had no chef. Nor did she care about Daisy's impressive credentials—

"The royal what?" Rita had asked when Daisy rattled off her membership in the Royal Academy of Chefs. "And all they give you is a spoon? Doesn't seem worth belonging."

Nor did the reason behind Daisy's job search faze her; Daisy hadn't cared enough to gloss over it. In fact, her problems with Jason seemed to be a plus.

"Grandmother poisoned Grandfather once," Rita had said. "She found him messin' with Kitty Shelikov. Wasn't lookin' to kill him. Just wanted to give him something to think about."

Rita Jakolof was immensely likeable.

Perusing the brochure, Daisy wished now that she'd asked more questions; for instance, who was this M. K. Endall listed as owner/pilot, and what was he like? Wearing a baseball cap and sunglasses, the man was but a small part of the photo, which was consumed by an old float-plane looking glued together and bearing the faded words *Wil Man odge* on its fuselage. A website photo had him holding a fishing pole on the deck of a small barge that looked like it had been resurrected from the ocean bottom. But Daisy hadn't asked that question or all the others now filling her head because she hadn't actually expected to take the job. She'd sent in her résumé between Thanksgiving and Christmas, when she was at her most depressed and the prospect of getting out of Seattle seemed like a godsend. Two months passed. Two months of unreturned phone calls and no job offers. She had forgotten about Wild Man, and then Rita called. The day of her cooking interview, Daisy had received two rejections from restaurants in San Francisco. In a panic, she'd accepted the job at Wild Man, grateful for someplace to go and relieved to be wanted. The questions never materialized. At least the salary was generous—surprisingly generous, given the dilapidated look of the lodge—and it came with room and board, although she dreaded what that might entail, since that was another question she hadn't asked.

Daisy could've stayed in Seattle, *if* she didn't mind being the cook at Adam's Ribs for $11.75 an hour. Yes, she had actually gone to the interview—something she'd told no one, not even Charity. That's when she knew she was desperate. And desperation makes a person do crazy things. There was no way she could suck in her pride and work for Adam's Ribs or the Lobster Shack—she had answered that ad, too—or any other establishment that offered bibs and takeout.

But Wild Man Lodge at least *sounded* intriguing, and her friends applauded her adventurous spirit; some even commented that they wished they had the courage for such a daring move.

If only they knew, Daisy silently lamented, returning the envelope to her suitcase.

Her lawsuit against Jason had cut her savings in half. She made money on the sale of her house, but she had to pay for the china she'd broken or have her misdeed become a police record. Fortunately she hadn't destroyed all the dishes or her restitution would've been four times what it was. Then there were the damages at Mama Mia's. And now Max Kendall wanted $25,000.

If she had left her job at Fireflies without a fuss, she'd have all that money plus the $50,000 Jason had offered as severance—if she had signed a "non-comp" agreement. She might even have her own restaurant instead of working for someone else—again. But her pride wouldn't let her be dumped like dishwater. Not after *ten years*.

Maybe, *hopefully*, Charity was right. Maybe, in a few months, memories would fade and Daisy would no longer be the pariah she seemed to be now.

Besides, she had a plan. She would put Wild Man Lodge on the culinary map, just like she'd done for Fireflies. That kind of recognition would surely get her back in the good graces of the Seattle restaurant establishment, not to mention the Royal Academy of Chefs. Sure, she was being punished *now*, but when it came to filling dining rooms, people wanted talent. When it came to food, Daisy had talent. She *would* get her Golden Spoon back!

Not that it was going to be easy, adding stars to a restaurant that actually had *fish 'n' chips* on its menu, but the alternative was permanent exile in Otter Bite . . .

Daisy shook off that nightmarish thought. Even in the wilderness, she was a chef to be reckoned with!

Feeling much better, she exchanged her oversized sleep shirt for comfy sweats, intending a few laps around the deck. This early it would be quiet and the poor schmucks without a cabin would be hunkered into their sleeping bags.

"I'm going for a walk, Elizabeth," Daisy said, tying her shoelaces. "I won't be gone long." She searched the cabin for her key, but had no luck. She stopped and thought, trying to retrieve her memory like a file from a crashed hard drive.

Adam. He had used her key to unlock the cabin door, then his lips brushed hers—true to his word, Dr. Bricker was *mostly* a gentleman; afterward, he gently steered Daisy into her cabin.

Surely not. Racing the few steps to the door, she swung it open and looked down at the knob. Her key was still in the lock, its pendant with her cabin number hanging from the key chain.

"Oh my God," Daisy groaned, thankful someone hadn't come along and taken it . . . or worse. How lucky was that?

Lucky. With key in hand, she paused. She had been *lucky*. Not an experience she'd had lately. But last night with her handsome doctor she'd felt really lucky. Lucky that the evening ended with a kiss and not a lawsuit.

It seemed like forever since she'd had blessings to count, but maybe her rough seas had finally given way to smooth sailing.

It was breezier on deck than Daisy had expected and crisper, too, but it felt great to be out of her cabin and walking in the early morning salt air. Deck lights blended with the fading dark; it was hard to distinguish where one began and the other ended. Voices reached her from the dock below, mingling with the shrieks of seagulls floating on invisible winds, chasing the fleeing night. The rhythmic *slap-slap-slap* of a jogger came toward her then faded behind, a nod of greeting exchanged as he passed. Skirting the occasional puddle, along with the occasional stalwart passenger cocooned in a lounge chair, Daisy stopped at the forward observation deck, outside the solarium with its glass walls. She looked east toward the city of Prince Rupert and the pink and golden glow rising off the horizon; she watched until the sun crowned, birthing a new day. Continuing her walk, she rounded the corner to the starboard side, where a blast of wind flailed her curls about her face.

"Oh, *maaaan!*" Blinded, she pushed into the glass door of the solarium and cleared the hair from her face. In climate controlled comfort, she headed toward the heart of the ship, her eyes drifting over sleeping bodies, each claiming a small piece of the solarium like a squatter.

Something familiar snagged her gaze. She stopped and cocked her head, fighting the urge to run. Craning her neck, she focused on the snoozing bundle only a few lounge chairs from where she stood glued to the speckled teal carpet. Pushing out the side of the unzipped sleeping bag was a socked foot. The attached leg seemed to be wrapped in a hard plastic brace or splint with Velcro fasteners, but the sleeping bag prevented Daisy from seeing above the calf.

She jumped at the sudden rattle of dishes and the accompanying raft of voices from the awakening cafeteria. Daisy was tempted to go with her first urge and flee, but curiosity forced one step, then another.

Inch by painstaking inch, Daisy crept between empty loungers and sleeping passengers toward the object of her dread. As she closed the gap, her heart leapt into her throat.

She stopped short of the socked foot. Her gaze traveled the length of the bundle and rested on the face at the other end. Stubbled, just like the first time she'd seen it. And, yes, still pleasing—as if that mattered—in spite of the discontented furrow marring its brow. But near the hairline, above the temple and just tickling the forehead, was a healing wound she'd not seen before.

Or had she? She thought back to the brown stains on her cashmere sweater, the grimace on this same face, to the blood flowing over an anguished blue eye. It all belonged to the man looking most uncomfortable in the chaise before her.

Of all the places Max Kendall could be, of all the boats, what was he doing here, on *hers*? And why in the world hadn't he booked a cabin? *Probably too cheap*, she figured, remembering their disastrous date and how Max insisted she finish her drink. If only they'd left when she wanted, she lamented yet again, before deciding this was not the time or place to be lamenting anything. She'd verified her fears and now she needed to get out of there, fast. If Max woke and saw her . . . well, she didn't want to think about his reaction. The lawsuit hanging over her head said all that needed to be said about Max Kendall's spite.

As if retreating from a snoozing bear, Daisy slowly backed her way to the next lounge chair and was starting to turn for the exit when the ship bellowed its departure. She froze as those around her woke. Her eyes locked on Max's face, expecting at any second to meet his blue eyes . . .

But his eyelids stayed shut without so much as a flutter. Daisy stared, disbelieving her luck, before those moving around jolted her senses. Feeling their questioning gazes, she spun from the scene and headed quickly for the outside door.

Why did she look back?

Max scarcely believed his eyes. Was that his date from hell? He blinked and Daisy disappeared through the door, tassels of red hair streaming behind her. *Impossible*, he insisted, although he didn't doubt for a moment that he'd just seen the woman who'd put him in this splint and given him a new scar and forced him into the cattle car of the observation deck. Of all the places she could be, of all the ships, what was Daisy doing here, on *his*?

He groaned from both the uncomfortable chaise and the unwelcome sighting; he reached into his shirt pocket to calm the small alarm clock vibrating against his chest. Freeing himself from the top portion of his sleeping bag, he plucked the foam plugs from his ears. Sounds of the morning came at him from all directions. The ship bellowed again and Max knew they would soon be leaving Prince Rupert. If he hurried, he might get into the bathroom before the throngs made their morning pilgrimage.

Three more *long* nights he'd have to sleep—or rather toss and turn—in this lounge. Three more *long* days he'd have to go without a shower. And now he'd have to contend with that demented mop-top stalking him.

Why me? He raised his eyes toward heaven while his knee throbbed like hell.

It took two quivering hands for Daisy to unlock her cabin door. Breathing hard, she scrambled inside and immediately latched the door behind her as if she expected Max to be nipping at her heels. While her heart drummed, she tried to figure out what to do.

Four hours later, she was hungry and still no closer to a plan, but at least she'd forsaken her vigil by the door. Sensitive to every shimmy and surge of the ship, she lay on the bed, watching the passing sky through her window.

Her stomach yowled. She looked over to the bedside table at the jar of baby food she'd recently opened for Elizabeth. Beside it was a small can of minced dog food. Sitting up, she retrieved the spoon she'd used to mix the two and brought it to her mouth. Bits of Elizabeth's breakfast remained on the stainless. She scrunched her eyes closed and swiped the spoon with her tongue.

"Uck-uck-uck-uck!" Gagging, she thrust her tongue from her mouth as she scrambled for the bathroom faucet.

"I can't believe I did that," Daisy said to the mirror. "Why don't you people have room service?" Obviously, sharing Elizabeth's food was not an option, nor was staying in her cabin. She'd have to go out. Soon. She'd simply have to keep an eye open for Max. There were over nine hundred passengers on the *Columbia*. Surely, the odds of bumping into Max *again* had to be slim, especially if she ate only in the dining room. Max Kendall was too chintzy to eat there. He was probably in the cafeteria robbing the condiment tray and making tomato soup by mixing ketchup and hot water.

She cracked a smile at her reflection. Yep, that was Max's style, all right. If only she knew why he was here.

She pulled her brush through her hair, fluffing the curls. He wasn't here because of her . . . was he? She narrowed her eyes suspiciously. Just how spiteful was Max Kendall? Had he discovered her plans for Alaska? Had her lawyer said something to his lawyer? Too distracted by her life to deal with something so outlandish as Max Kendall's lawsuit, she'd left everything to her attorney.

"Probably just a frivolous nuisance," her attorney had assured her, accepting her $3,000 retainer. "I'll be in touch."

Now she wished she'd taken a little more time. But she never ever, ever, *ever* thought she'd see that man again. Her face scrunched as her brain scrambled. What did she really *know* about Max? Maybe he was more of a loon than anyone suspected. Maybe his mother was a loon, too. Maybe the Kendalls were a whole family of loons!

"Stop it!" She would never leave her cabin while those thoughts swam in her brain. There was undoubtedly a logical explanation for

Max Kendall's presence aboard this ship, and it had absolutely nothing to do with her!

Besides, she had an ace in the hole. Her very handsome doctor would surely come to her rescue if needed. As a matter of fact, they had a dinner date for tonight. Adam and all his officer buddies would keep Max from threatening her. It was like having her very own navy.

But just in case, she would keep her pepper spray handy.

"I'm going to breakfast, sweetie," Daisy cooed to Elizabeth as she put her in the compact shower stall for a little safe exercise. In one corner, she placed her food. "I'll bring you some lettuce. Yum-yum."

But Elizabeth seemed unimpressed with the promise as she slowly ate her pureed peas and minced beef.

Daisy went for her purse, sitting atop her sweaters in her opened suitcase. Spotting the open zipper, she pulled the bag wide and gasped. Where was her wallet? She rummaged in the side pockets. And her hidden stash of extra cash? She scrambled for her second pair of shoes—gold flats—and took out the socks she'd stuffed in the toes.

Her eyes popped, her mouth gaped. "Oh my God!" she squeaked. Then, as the situation registered, she inflated with rage. "That lying, thieving, miserable rotten bastard!"

Chapter Eight

"I've been robbed!"

The seasoned purser lifted her eyes from her computer screen and considered the frantic woman who'd just stormed the office. "Are you all right? Try to relax. Are you all right?"

"There's no time for questions! He's getting away!"

"Ma'am, we're at sea. There's no place for him to go. Are you hurt?"

"I'm fine. Mad as hell, but fine."

"I'm calling security." The purser punched in numbers. After a short conversation she hung up the phone and focused on Daisy, who paced the utilitarian office, one short fuse from exploding. "Ma'am, what's your name?"

"He broke into my cabin while I was *sleeping*! Can you believe that?"

"Maybe I should call the medical officer—"

Daisy abruptly stopped. "Yes, please." It would be nice to have Adam's arm to lean on when she confronted Max Kendall. "Call Dr. Bricker."

An understated gray brow lifted slightly. "You want me to call Dr. Bricker?"

"I know it's not really a *medical* emergency, but it is an emergency, and he does know me." Daisy spoke as if spilling a secret. "We had dinner last night."

"Oh," the purser answered, as if the request now made sense.

"I'd feel much better if he were here. If he's not, y' know, saving someone's life."

"I doubt that." The purser lifted the phone from its cradle. "And your name, ma'am?"

"Daisy Moon. Adam knows me."

"Adam?"

"Adam Bricker," Daisy said.

"*Adam Bricker?*" Now both her brows were raised.

"Yes," Daisy confirmed, fearing that this polite, grandmotherly type was losing her faculties. "*Dr.* Adam Bricker."

"Isn't Adam Bricker the doctor from *The Love Boat?*"

Daisy reflected back on the '80s television show she had occasionally caught in reruns during the wee hours of the morning after coming home and winding down from the restaurant. She had bought the series DVD for her mom, who loved the sitcom as much for the G rating as for the old movie stars who made guest appearances—Van Johnson was her favorite.

"Huh. No wonder the name sounded familiar," she said, more to herself than the purser. She shook off the coincidence. "Would you please call him? *Now?*"

"What's the extension?"

Daisy's face contorted, her hands flailed. "How the hell should I know? Don't you people have a phone list?"

The purser eased back. "What's his cabin number?"

Daisy cocked her head at the daft woman. "Just call sick bay or the infirmary or whatever you boat people call it. He's probably there."

Easing back a little farther, the purser punched in the numbers for the medical office. "Don't worry, ma'am, we'll find your Dr. Bricker."

Two uniformed men, one older and relaxed, one younger and intense, arrived at the office.

"Sorry for the delay." The older man introduced himself as Chief Security Officer Stone and his taller assistant as Deputy SO Keller. "We had something come off the wire as we were leaving. Now"— he addressed Daisy—"you were robbed?"

"Yes! And I know who did it. If we hurry, we can catch him in the cafeteria making tomato soup!"

"Tomato soup?" Stone questioned.

"Or maybe not," Daisy reconsidered aloud, oblivious to Stone. "He's probably eating in the dining room with *my money!*"

"If we could take this one step at a time, Ms.—?"

"Moon," the purser interjected.

"Daisy Moon," Daisy confirmed. "And we have to hurry or he'll spend all my money out of spite. He might even throw it overboard!"

"I know this is very upsetting, Ms. Moon, but we need more information. Start at the beginning. When did you discover the robbery? Did you see the man—"

"His name is Max Kendall," Daisy interrupted. "And I didn't need to see him to know he stole my money and credit cards!"

The two men exchanged glances. "You *know* the man who robbed you?"

"Yes! Well, not exactly. Kind of. In an odd sort of way."

Stone took a deep breath while Keller pulled out a pad and pen from his shirt pocket. "Please, sit down, Ms. Moon," Stone requested. "I'll have Purser Smith check the passenger list for a Max Kendall." The grandmotherly woman moved to her computer screen. "Now, Ms. Moon, take a deep breath and start at the beginning."

Daisy sat down on the vinyl sofa, took a deep breath, and started from the beginning. The *very* beginning, from when she first met Max and his mother at her garage sale, then detailing her date with Max and his subsequent lawsuit, before moving on to his surprise appearance on the ship and finally ending with the theft of her wallet and the cash which had been tucked inside her shoe—"a leather basket-weave in matte gold." She even mentioned Otter Bite and her new job at Wild Man Lodge so they would understand why she was on the ferry in the first place. When she was done, the two men shared an uneasy look.

"I think he's stalking me," Daisy finally suggested.

"It's certainly coincidental," Stone said ambiguously. "And you're positive the man you saw this morning is the same man from your garage sale?"

"Chief?" the purser interrupted. "I found Max Kendall on the passenger list. No cabin. But he's on a wait list. I remember him now," she added, intimating just how memorable she thought Max was. "He's in a full leg splint and those lounge chairs are pretty hard on him."

"Told you," Daisy said, ignoring the purser's sympathy for an undeserving thief.

"But there's no Adam Bricker," the purser added. "*Anywhere.*"

"Adam Bricker?" Stone asked with suspicious eyes.

"Yes. He's a friend of Ms. Moon's. They had dinner last night."

"He's not my *friend*," Daisy countered. "I mean, he *is* my friend, but *first* he's the medical officer. I can't believe you people don't know your own crew."

Stone and Keller quirked their heads in unison as if they shared the same light bulb.

"Believe me, Ms. Moon, we do know our crew," Stone informed her. "Now tell me about this Adam Bricker."

Picking up the ominous tone in the chief's voice, Daisy looked first at Stone and then at Keller. She started to speak when a figure in the doorway caught her attention. Her eyes widened and her right hand flew into a point. "Oh my God! That's him. Right there! That's *him!*"

All eyes shot to the doorway and lighted on the dark-haired man with stubbled cheeks and a mix of dread and disbelief on his face.

Stone mustered an imposing stance. "Are you Adam Bricker?"

"No!" Daisy squawked. "He's Max Kendall—the man who stole my money!"

Fifteen minutes later, Daisy stared at a fax with a fuzzy photo of Myron Porter, aka Dr. Adam Bricker, aka Captain Merrill Stubing, and aka Julie McCoy.

"Julie McCoy?" Daisy asked incredulously. Apparently, women were not Myron's only victims—whom he typically drugged with sleeping pills so he could safely rob their cabins.

Stone shrugged. "In this work, after a while you see everything. So, Ms. Moon, is that the man you had dinner with last night?"

Daisy returned the page to Stone. "I think so. Damn." An officer, a gentleman, *and* a cross-dressing felon.

"All we can do is alert the Canadian officials and hope they find him. At least he left your passport and travel documents. But I wouldn't hold out much hope for recovering your money or finding your Lexus anytime soon."

Tears welled in Daisy's eyes. "But he was wearing a uniform." Her lower lip quivered. "And he knew what the M/V stands for in front of *Columbia*," as if that made her trust in a stranger seem doubly reasonable.

"I'm afraid, Ms. Moon, it's not a maritime secret that M/V stands for motor vessel."

"Motor vessel?" she squeaked.

Max Kendall turned away from the pitiful sight. "Can I go now?"

"Not so fast," Keller said, obviously sympathetic to Daisy.

"What Deputy SO Keller means is—"

Max held up a palm to halt further explanation. From his wallet, he presented his Alaska driver's license. Stone looked at it and handed it to Keller.

"You won't be insulted if we verify this?" Keller returned the plastic to Max.

Max stuffed his ID into its slot. "Can I go?"

"Of course, Mr. Kendall," the security chief told him, shooting a warning glance at Keller. "Sorry for the mix-up. But I'm sure you can understand how Ms. Moon—"

"No," Max tersely interrupted. "I don't understand how Ms. Moon does *anything*." He struggled to rise on one leg from the seat he'd been forced into while defending himself against Daisy's accusations.

Yes, it was coincidental that he and Daisy were on the same ferry. But the ferry he originally booked—with a cabin—sailed three weeks ago, and three weeks ago he was in the hospital, he'd informed them as Daisy averted her eyes from his accusatory stare. He was on the ferry now because he'd bought a truck in Seattle and was taking that same truck to Alaska, departing the ferry in Haines. He didn't elaborate on his final destination, figuring the less Daisy knew about his life, the better, and by then Stone seemed satisfied that Max Kendall was just an innocent bystander in Daisy Moon's mixed-up world.

Why Daisy was on the *Columbia*, Max didn't know. But he'd stopped himself from asking. The last thing he wanted was to get involved in Daisy's life. He didn't care what her latest turmoil was or what tragedy had caused her to flee Seattle. The woman was an albatross.

"What am I going to do?" Daisy asked to no one in particular. "I have no money, no credit cards, no Lex-us," she lamented, her breath in little hops. "My pots and pans, my knives . . . my *recipes*," she added, just now realizing what the theft of her Lexus meant.

Max turned a deaf ear to Daisy's plight; he had troubles of his own.

"Don't worry, Ms. Moon, we'll get you back to Bellingham," Stone assured her. "Tomorrow, when we dock in Ketchikan, we can put you on a ferry going south."

"But . . . I'm not going to Bellingham."

"If you continue, what will you do when we reach Haines?" Stone asked. "You'll be stranded. We arrive Saturday and the banks will be closed. Even if money is wired to you, you won't get it until Monday morning. Where would you stay the weekend? You have no vehicle, no way to keep going—"

Daisy's gasps grew stronger and louder as she tried to keep her tears in check. She'd been so certain of Max Kendall's guilt that she'd overlooked her missing keys. If only she'd checked her purse earlier. If only Max hadn't been on this ship. If only, if only . . .

"—You must go back to Bellingham," Stone insisted. "If you choose to continue, we can't be responsible."

Daisy buried her face in her palms.

Max glanced in her direction, shook off his sympathy. Trying to skirt Daisy's disaster, he hobbled toward the door, unaccustomed to the burdensome splint immobilizing his knee.

Stone put a hand on Daisy's shoulder. "At home, it will be easier to put in your insurance claims and get new credit cards. That's hard to do at sea."

Daisy inched her eyes above her fingers. "But my job . . ."

"I'm sure your employer will understand. In the meantime, Ms. Moon, Purser Smith will accompany you to sick bay for something to help calm you."

"I . . . I would rather just go to my cabin. At least I still have that."

Cabin? Max stopped outside the door. Of course, she had a cabin. The woman was a nitpicking control freak. She'd probably booked passage a year ago. Too bad she wasn't as particular about the men she dated—present company excluded. Max peeked around the jamb, instantly regretting it. *God*, was Daisy pathetic, with her eyes puffed and her face splotchy and her nose shiny red like his new pickup. And hair falling this way and that. But she did have a cabin. Which meant she had a bathroom and a shower and—thank his lucky stars—a bed.

He didn't know how, Max decided, peg-legging like a pirate down the corridor, but by hook or by crook, he was getting into Daisy Moon's bed.

Chapter Nine

What now? Daisy wondered at the persistent knocking. She dragged herself off the bed and opened the door. "Oh, great."

Max held up two plump white paper bags and cocked his head. "Is that a black eye?" he asked of the mottled shadow beneath her right eye.

Daisy looked at the bags, then at Max. "Yes. And . . . ?" She shot a questioning glance to the bags.

His brow furrowed. "From . . . *that night*?"

"Yes, *and* . . . ?"

"I brought lunch."

Daisy's green eyes brightened, then quickly narrowed. "Why?"

"Because I'm a decent guy."

"Yeah. That explains the lawsuit."

"That's business."

"It feels personal."

"Do you want the food or not?"

Daisy hesitated. It was either swallow her pride or swallow Elizabeth's dog food. She took the bags. "Thank you," she grumbled.

"You're welcome."

"Anything else?" she asked when Max remained.

"I thought maybe I'd join you. Unless you have another date. Jack the Ripper?"

Daisy clenched her jaw and narrowed her eyes into venomous slits. "After my date with you, *anyone* would be an improvement."

"That explains Dr. Bricker."

"As a matter of fact, it does."

Max huffed. He felt like shutting her up by telling her she looked like she belonged in *Les Misérables*, but he didn't want the door slammed in his face. "Can I come in, Daisy? Please." The *please* felt like a root canal.

Daisy huffed right back at him. "Is that really necessary?"

"If I go, the food goes."

"I guess being a *decent guy* has its limits."

Max lifted his brows.

"Fine." Daisy stepped aside.

"It must be hell being you."

"And what does *that* mean?"

"All that pride, all that self-righteousness . . ." Max nudged her suitcase a few inches, then helped himself to the sofa. With a satisfied moan, he eased into the cushions and relaxed his imprisoned leg.

"I certainly am not—"

"For someone up an ocean without a Lexus you could be a little nicer."

Daisy clutched the bags of food to her chest. "I *am* nice. I'm *exceedingly* nice. I'm one of the nicest people I know—"

"—And then you've got that indignant, Victorian thing going on."

"Victorian?" Daisy screeched, before deciding better of sparring with Max. Setting the bags on the small vanity, she spread them open one at a time. "I don't see how you're in any way qualified to discuss *me*."

"I have the battle scars, remember?"

She looked squarely into his eyes. "You think *you* have battle scars? Sweetheart, you don't have a clue."

Maybe it was the intensity of her expression or the electricity in a pair of eyes that had intrigued him from the start—or maybe it was the sultry, hard-edged, Angelina Jolie way *sweetheart* had flowed across her lips—but whatever combination it was, Max thought he might've been trumped. It was a very odd sensation that inconveniently started his blood flowing in the most unexpected place. "I brought turkey sandwiches," he said, trying to ignore his misbehaving appendage.

"No mustard, I hope."

Max responded with an expression reminding her of her predicament.

"I can scrape it off."

"There's no mustard." His tone conveyed disbelief in the importance Daisy put on that condiment.

"I don't like mustard on turkey."

Not a contrite bone in Daisy Moon's body! Max turned his attention to the deluxe cabin with its queen bed and adjoining bath. The sunny day spilled through the window, brightening the green walls. The cabin was small by hotel standards, but large enough to accommodate a sofa, vanity, and a chest of drawers, as long as you didn't plan on doing the tango in between. There was even a small closet with an accordion door where he could stow his gear. *Yep*, Max decided, *this will do just fine.* And right about then he noticed the jar of baby food beside the opened tuna-size can of dog food atop the nightstand.

While Daisy pulled the napkins from the bag, his eyes darted around the room. He stretched toward the bathroom for a peek inside. Seeing nothing obvious to explain the jar or the can, he leaned forward in his seat, inching toward the bed and its skirt to check out what might be lurking beneath.

Sandwich in hand, Daisy turned and discovered Max with his chest pressed against his knees and his chin inches from the floor. "What in the world are you doing?"

"I've, uh, always been curious. Are these beds bolted down?" He quickly lifted the bed skirt and discovered a solid pedestal supporting the mattress. "I guess this bed won't be going anywhere."

Daisy held out the sandwich and a couple of napkins.

"A pedestal bed is very practical," he said, taking his lunch. "You don't have to clean under it and you can't lose things there."

Daisy stuck a straw through the plastic lid on a cup and handed the drink to Max. Then she sat on the small stool belonging to the vanity and unwrapped the paper from her sandwich. "You lose a lot of stuff under your bed, do you?"

"Just the occasional woman."

"Maybe they're hiding from you."

"Where would *you* hide some—"

"Lettuce!" Daisy squealed, lifting the top slice of bread and peeling off the green leaf. She turned to Max. "Are you going to eat your lettuce?"

Her smile was like a kid's at Christmas, and Max was totally unnerved. He could find no evidence of either a baby or a dog, and yet there was Gerber and Mighty Dog. And now this lettuce thing. Could Daisy get any weirder?

Wondering what Daisy planned for lettuce *she* wasn't going to eat, Max opened his sandwich and peeled off his leaf.

Daisy took both pieces and went into the bathroom.

Max stared at the closed door. What the hell was Daisy doing?

As she shook the water from her lettuce, Daisy caught her reflection in the small mirror. And oh, how she wished she hadn't. She and tears had never gotten along; even happy tears turned her face into a puffy, splotchy mess sure to cause nightmares among young children. She wasn't even going to start a discourse on her hair.

She set torn pieces of lettuce in the shower stall with Elizabeth, then, reluctantly facing her reflection, eased a brush through her rambunctious curls.

Sometimes she did have gorgeous hair, as Charity often said. And her green eyes could be spectacular when they weren't squeezed between pregnant eyelids. As long as nothing upset it, her complexion had a creamy radiance like Belleek Irish porcelain. She was a bonny lass, her grandfather had always told her, although she rarely agreed.

So why the hell didn't Max tell her how bad she looked? Why that question suddenly popped up and where it came from, Daisy wasn't sure, but it was there now, and it got her thinking.

Max had only a few bites left of his sandwich when Daisy exited the bathroom looking . . . not quite the same as when she entered. Her hair had been smoothed, the shine on her nose had been powdered, and her lips glossed. Even her eyes, while still suffering from the effects of Daisy's tear-fest, looked calmer and less dire. Could that be why she wanted the lettuce? He'd heard of cucumbers for the eyes, but maybe in a pinch . . .

Even so, that didn't explain either the chicken pâté or the pureed peas. Neither did it explain why Daisy suddenly cared about her appearance, when he was surely the last person she wanted to impress. To Daisy, Max must seem as ruthless and heartless as Caligula.

A half smile lifted his lips. He had a passion for history, especially ancient. He absolutely believed that *those who forget the past are condemned to repeat it.* But he'd never actually dated a woman who shared his interest, let alone one who knew about the infamous Roman emperor. Not that he liked his women dumb—although why

Tina was with Daisy's ex, Max couldn't fathom. But even more un-fathomable was Daisy and Jason. What had she seen in that guy?

"What?" Daisy growled, feeling Max's eyes on her.

"I didn't say anything."

"You're staring at me."

"This cabin is small. I have to look somewhere."

"Well, look over there." Daisy waved in the direction of the bed.

Max tried, but the dog food creeped him out. "I'm . . . gonna go."

Daisy stopped mid-chew and swallowed hard. "You are?"

He eased off the sofa. "You sound disappointed."

"Surprised. I didn't think getting rid of you would be this easy."

Yep, Daisy Moon was a whole 'nother species of woman. And he'd bet the farm she knew exactly who Caligula was. "I've got a proposition for you."

"No such thing as a free lunch, eh, decent guy?"

Max stayed his course, but he smiled. "If you can tell me who Caligula is, I'll buy you dinner."

"Are you kidding? What's the catch?"

"Just tell me who he is and dinner is yours."

Max Kendall rubbed her like a cheese grater, but she had no money, no food, and if she worked it right, she could probably stretch dinner into a doggy-bag breakfast. "First of all, he's not an *is*, he's a *was*." Her tone suspicious, Daisy continued. "His real name was Gaius. Caligula is a nickname that comes from the word for the boots worn by Roman soldiers. It means *little boot;* his mom dressed him in those when he was a kid and the name stuck. He was a real terror; some think insane. He ruled only four years before he was as-sassinated at twenty-eight. But he really loved his horse."

"And?"

"That's what I know." Thanks to the President's Scholars history course she took in college and the term paper she had written. But she never imagined it would be useful information. She almost felt lucky, but the last time she felt like this, she lost her money, car, and credit cards.

"*And*," Max prompted again, "I remind you of him."

Taken aback, she paused. "Maybe around the eyes."

Max wasn't sure whether he felt surprise . . . or relief. "I'll meet you in the dining room at six." He squeezed past Daisy at the vanity, wincing as the blood pounded into his bound leg.

"You will shave and shower, won't you?"

"Unfortunately, Ms. Moon, the chaise lounges in the solarium do not come with a private bath. And the on-board public showers are too hard to manage with my knee."

"Bummer."

"Yeah, well, I'm dining with you, so we pretty much cancel each other out."

His hand was on the doorknob when Daisy said, "You're more the Machiavelli type."

He looked over his shoulder. The gleam in her eyes harbored something he couldn't quite discern. But he should probably be cautious.

"If you can tell me who he is, I'll let you use my shower."

He turned. "Niccolò Machiavelli was a sixteenth century Italian politician who believed that all is fair in love and war, including cunning, duplicity, and bad faith."

"Not quite. Machiavelli believed that results counted, and nothing else."

"Like I said, all's fair."

"*In politics.*"

"Politics is about power. Same for love and war."

She looked at him curiously. "War, maybe. But do you really believe love is about power?"

"I believe . . . I'll take the Fifth."

Chapter Ten

"Okay, Elizabeth, you stay in here—" As if she could go anywhere. With Elizabeth safe in her carrier, Daisy set it inside the compact closet. "—And later I might have some lettuce or maybe even a tomato. Yum-yum. Now eat your dinner."

Beside the carrier was a plastic bowl filled with ice where Daisy had nestled the opened can of dog food and the jar of baby food. Not exactly a refrigerator, but it worked well enough. She closed the accordion door, leaving a gap for light, then made herself as comfortable on the bed as possible—knees up, magazine open against her thighs—but without messing up her hair, clothes, makeup, or bedspread. Which meant she wasn't comfortable at all. With any of this. But she was desperate. Comfortable, no. Desperate, yes. And desperation makes a person do . . .

She jumped at the knocking on her door, took a calming breath, and vowed to be pleasant. "Come in."

The door cracked open. "Ms. Moon?"

Daisy bounced off the bed.

"It's Purser Smith."

Daisy grabbed the knob and pulled. "Did they find my Lexus?"

"I'm sorry, no. I brought you meal vouchers," the grandmotherly purser said. "I meant to bring them earlier, but a pregnant passenger went into labor and the day got away from me."

Daisy took the slips of paper and studied the top one.

"You can use these in the cafeteria or dining room," she said. "Just present one when you're ready to pay. We'll pick up the tab."

"That's very kind," Daisy said. "Thank you."

"We can't let you starve now, can we? I bet you haven't eaten all day."

Daisy shrugged and tried to look pitiful. Being the recipient of sympathy was not a bad thing.

"Why don't you have dinner? If you need anything at all, come by the office." She started to leave, then didn't. "You haven't seen Mr. Kendall, have you?"

Daisy snorted. "That would be unlikely."

"I suppose so."

"Is there a problem?"

"I've been looking for him, that's all. The couple with the new baby are leaving the ferry tomorrow in Ketchikan and their cabin will be available. No worries. Mr. Kendall will probably come by the office sometime. Enjoy your dinner, Ms. Moon."

Daisy again thanked Purser Smith and shut the cabin door.

"This is a pickle." Should she tell Max about the available cabin? How about the vouchers?

Why was she debating this? Her meal vouchers were none of his business. And it was none of *her* business that Purser Smith was searching for Max. But Daisy feared she might have a less than laudable motive for keeping silent.

Startled by knocks on her door, she dropped her gaze to the vouchers in her hand as if they were a smoking gun and she stood over a body. Three more knocks got her moving; she stuffed the vouchers inside her purse, hopped on the bed, and assumed her former position.

"Come in."

The door eased open, tentatively at first, and there was Max, duffel bag in hand, as if he were coming for a long visit.

"You know where the shower is." Daisy sounded nonchalant, but the butterflies in her stomach took wing as Max gave her a quick once-over. She snuggled into her bulky Kelly-green fisherman's sweater, which perfectly matched her eyes, and tried to ignore her discomfort. "Don't make a mess, okay?"

"It will be hard, but I'll try to contain my barnyard inclinations."

"Your beard," Daisy explained in a huff. "Shavings get all over the sink. There's nothing more annoying than cleaning up after a grown man."

"Really? *Nothing?*" He maneuvered his bulky bag and his bulky leg through the limited space and stopped at the slender bathroom door. He gave Daisy a pointed look, his blue eyes both intense and playful. "I can think of so many things more annoying."

Daisy shot him her own look. "Obviously you've never had to clean up after anyone."

"Well, you're right, Daisy—"

Her eyes softened at Max's unexpected acquiescence.

"—That's what women are for."

"Ah, well, that explains it."

He hesitated, knowing he shouldn't ask. "Explains what?"

"That ridge across your brow."

"Clever." Max sighed. "I might be a Neanderthal, but at least I haven't romanced you out of your money and your car." He shoved his bag into the bathroom with more gusto than necessary. "You might want to keep your perspective . . . since you've lost everything else." Then he stuffed himself inside with his bag, fighting to close the door behind him.

Daisy slumped into her pillows. She'd sworn she'd be pleasant. What was it about Max Kendall that brought out her defensive guns? She always seemed to be shooting first and never asking questions.

"The man is suing me," she said aloud so that her words would register. "Damn, why didn't I throw that back at him?"

How could she possibly let her guard down with his lawsuit threatening her like Poe's pendulum? And it didn't help that Max had slept with Tina. It was ridiculous, of course, to hold that against him, but it was obvious Max liked Tina and Tina liked Max and neither liked her. As much as Daisy didn't want to care, it had really galled her that Tina was allowed to see Max in the hospital while she'd been given the bum's rush.

It wasn't fair; she was a good person—her china insanity notwithstanding—and it wasn't her fault Max clobbered his head and banged his knee. It's not like she'd walked away unscathed. Besides, she had tried to get him out of Mama Mia's, but he had been too cheap—

Enough, already. Nothing would change that night by going over and over and over it. Tina was as much to blame as Daisy, but obviously Max couldn't sue an old lover and he couldn't sue an old lover's fiancé, so Daisy had been selected as the scapegoat. Just like in her breakup.

"You're no fun anymore," she could hear Jason saying. "You're too critical, too compulsive, too controlling, too rigid, too picky, too *clean*, too tired for sex, and too scared to fly."

Of course she was all that. She had a 4-star restaurant to run. Interestingly, Jason never complained about that. While she was making him money, he was spending it on someone else. She knew about Tina's three-carat rock, had seen it *that night*. Ten years with Daisy and Jason hadn't offered her so much as a diamond chip!

Again and again and again, she had tried to enjoy flying in Jason's Cessna, but five thousand feet above the ground in a small plane that bounced with every ripple of air was not where Daisy cared to die. She'd taken flying lessons, figuring that if she were in control, she might do better. But Daisy couldn't control turbulence and she couldn't control fear. So finally, after seven years, she gave up. Did Jason at least give her credit for trying? Not one crumb.

The more their relationship faltered, the more she threw herself into the restaurant, and the less she cared about Jason's complaints. For better or for worse, she was who she was. And look where it had gotten her.

A duffel bag pushed through the partially open bathroom door. Clutching the handles was a fist attached to a very buff naked arm—with five tattooed stars, each the size of a quarter, trailing down from the muscled shoulder, ending above the elbow. Then Max's head appeared with his naked chest.

"It's a little tight in here," he explained, using the door as a shield for his lower extremities. "I'm just trying to make room."

Daisy didn't move, as if Max's nudity hadn't registered. The door closed and she stared a few seconds longer, thinking about the dark, downy whorls covering Max's chest; they merged in the center then trickled down the valley between his washboard abs and disappeared behind the door.

That was interesting, Daisy thought. His chest lingered in her mind and the stars begat a question. Why *five*? She brushed the scene aside and tried to hop back on her train at the spot where she'd jumped off.

Oh yeah. Her current situation. *Between a rock and a hard place.*

What happened with Max tonight would determine whether she went crawling back to Seattle and the Lobster Shack, or marched on to Otter Bite and the Wild Man Lodge. *No*, she couldn't go back. If she didn't go on, if she quit now, she'd be forever haunted with bad luck, consumed in the bowels of misfortune, shunned like a leper in the abyss of hell—

"Yes, you've proven your point," Daisy said to her melodrama. The less dramatic point was, she had to do something to break this seemingly endless cycle of horrible things happening to her.

It would take a grand gesture—

The bathroom door opened again. This time Max's splint came through the crack. It was abandoned outside the door by the wall while the arm and hand retreated inside the bathroom. The door shut.

Daisy waited for the next act, but instead she heard the shower spray.

Okay. Rock and hard place . . . grand gesture . . . Max Kendall . . .

She got off the train, tossed her magazine aside, and crawled to the edge of the bed, where she considered Max's duffel bag and his plastic splint. She looked up at the door; behind it Max was in her shower. *Max in her shower.*

How in the world had Max Kendall finagled his way into her shower? Yes, she knew she offered it to him, but that's not what she meant. Just thinking about all the coincidences that landed him there boggled her mind. Life was certainly good at taking the long way.

If they hadn't run into Jason that night at Mama Mia's, would this scene have played out three weeks ago? That's where Max was headed that night at the bar. She remembered his kiss, how he put his fingers to her lips, how he suggested he put her to bed, his blue eyes inviting. She was a little rusty, but she was pretty sure that was foreplay. *Pretty sure.*

It made no sense that Max was in her shower now, after everything that had happened. So why was he?

Scrambling from the bed, Daisy kneeled by the duffel bag, wishing that she'd learned a little more about Max from her attorney. But, at the time—never expecting to see Max again—she hadn't wanted to know anything about a man who could be so mean as to sue her.

She leaned near the bathroom door, listening to the water, then returned her attention to the bag; she unzipped and spread the canvas. Surprisingly, the contents were neatly stacked, with the flannel shirt he'd worn into her cabin loosely folded on top. She rummaged through the clothes, searching among the shirts, sweaters—taking a moment to feel the silky, steel-blue one—cotton-knit jockeys, socks, jeans, and T-shirts. She smiled at the Señorita Largatija T-shirt Max had been wearing at her garage sale, looking freshly laundered and ironed—in spite of the stain—and neatly folded. Maeve Kendall, Daisy assumed. She kind of liked Maeve, or maybe it was admiration for any woman, mother or not, who held sway over Max.

Back to her search, she stopped when she hit the cowboy boots at the bottom. That fit the profile of a rogue; she ended her trespass and zipped up.

Another glance at the door, another listen for the shower, and Daisy hit the end pockets. What exactly she looked for she wasn't sure; maybe just some clue to the man whom Fate had dropped in her cabin.

Stuffed in the end pockets were three paperback novels, two Louis L'Amour and one Stuart Woods. Not that she expected Deepak Chopra. She quickly thumbed through the pages for anything hidden between. Switching to the lone side pocket, she unzipped, her heart thumping as the clock ticked down on her available time. A wallet and a manila envelope. Why hadn't she looked here sooner? She'd make a lousy detective.

She grabbed the cognac–colored wallet first, appreciating the expensive leather, still gleaming but with worn corners. Credit cards and ID stacked neatly inside, their top edges peaking from the pockets. She didn't really have time for this, but she finagled one of the IDs from its sheath. *Pilot's license.* Flying—the bane of her existence. Daisy stuffed the plastic back in. She spread the currency sleeve and was taken aback by all the bills. Dozens. All with the same portrait of Ben Franklin.

She could take one or even two and Max would *probably* never know. She tugged at a single hundred. Only a loan—if she didn't need it, she could give it back. She *would* pay him back, once she got to Haines and a bank. If not there, she would send him a check when she got to Otter Bite. *Oh hell*, Daisy swore, swiping the bill and tucking it in her jeans pocket. *All is fair.*

Stuffing the wallet back into the side pocket, she then grabbed the envelope. She squeezed the brass wings together, lifted the flap, and dumped the contents.

Passport; two envelopes, one green, one orange; itinerary; and ticket carbons for the M/V *Columbia* and another set of tickets for the M/V *Tustumena* between—

Daisy did a double take.

Valdez and Otter Bite . . . ?

As valuable seconds ticked away, her brain scrambled for what this could mean. *The truck's final destination?* And then what this could mean for her.

Setting aside the tickets, she grabbed the green and the orange envelopes she suspected were get-well cards. The green envelope contained a card signed *With all our love, Mother & Da,* and had a religious theme with rhyming verse and lilies. The other card had a photo of a basset hound on the front, and inside the single word *Heal.* But the real message was in the handwritten words . . . and the heart dotting the I's.

If you need anything, just whistle.
Love, Tina

Well, doesn't that just figure? Daisy stuffed the card back into the envelope. Only a couple of business envelopes remained—cream-colored expensive stock. The return address was printed with the name and address of Max's attorney, Clyde Standish.

No stamp on the envelope; the flap was unsealed. She pulled out a set of pages in a fold.

The shower. Daisy leaned toward the door. There was no sound of water. How long had it been off? And how long before Max opened the bathroom door? If he caught her going through his things, he'd never take her to Valdez in his very new, very expensive, very red truck. Pushing her luck, she quickly unfolded the letter.

Mr. Max Kendall
c/o Royce Raymond, Esq.
1407 W. 2nd Ave.
Anchorage, AK 99503

Daisy stared at the Anchorage address. *Jiminy Christmas,* how many lawyers did Max have? What did that mean, *in care of?* Maybe Max filtered all his legal entanglements through his attorney in Anchorage. Maybe Max traveled. Maybe Max was between homes. Maybe Max didn't want anyone to know where he lived . . .

That fits, but it didn't explain his ticket to Otter Bite on the M/V *Tustumena*—as it so happened, the same date as her departure, assuming she got to Valdez in time to make that date. Daisy started reading.

Dear Mr. Kendall:
Based upon our recent discussion, I am withdrawing the com-
plaints filed with the court on 3 May against Ms. Daisy Moon
and instead

A bump against the inside of the bathroom door. Her heart drummed in her ears as Daisy quickly fumbled the letter back into its envelope, stuffing it, along with its unread mate, into the manila envelope. She scooped up the remainder of items and poured them inside with the letters.

"Are you all right?" Daisy called, zipping up the evidence. She scrambled to her feet as the bathroom door cracked open.

Max poked his towel-draped head through. "Did you say something?"

"I heard something hit the door. Are you okay?"

"My knee. I lost my balance." His eyes reflected suspicion at Daisy's concern. "I should probably put my brace on."

Daisy looked down at the brace and saw Max's passport, the words *United States of America* in gold script peeking out from beneath his duffel bag.

"I'll get it," she volunteered, stepping on the writing and grabbing Max's brace.

The door opened wider and specters of steam escaped into the cabin. Wearing jeans, but bare from the waist up and still suspicious, Max took his splint from Daisy. "Thank you."

"You're welcome."

"All right, what's up?"

"Nothing." Daisy smiled. "I'm just being helpful."

"Exactly."

Her smile waned. "Just because you and I have some . . . unfortunate history—"

"Unfortunate history?" Max rubbed his head with the towel, then slid the thick white cotton from his head and let it drape his naked shoulders. "That's an innocuous way of putting it."

Amusement sparked her eyes at the sight of Max's damp, tousled hair, poking this way and that like a punk rocker. "Look, what happened at Mama Mia's wasn't my fault. I know you think it was, which is why you're suing me . . ." Daisy paused, giving Max the perfect moment to confess that he'd withdrawn the lawsuit.

"I told you, it's business."

She huffed. Why was Max continuing this charade? "My point is," But there was no way she could argue to the contrary without making her own confession, "just because stuff happened *that wasn't my fault* doesn't mean I'm completely unsympathetic. I got hurt, too."

"That's what happens when you throw beer at an angry drunk."

"He grabbed me!"

Max leaned toward her. "He was *drunk*. You were taunting him and then gloating about it. That's not how to walk away without a black eye."

Daisy leaned forward. "He was flaunting his floozy."

"Tina isn't a floozy. If anything, she was trying to get him out of there. And did I mention he was *drunk?*"

"Well, I was a little drunk, too! I had just chugged *two* Midori-'n'-rums because *someone* was too cheap to leave the restaurant."

"I am *not* cheap. I didn't understand what was going on. Why the hell didn't you tell me your ex was there?"

"Because it seemed soooo—"

"What?"

"—pathetic."

Max flinched at the unexpected response; at Daisy's unexpected vulnerability.

"I mean, you'd already seen my meltdown at the garage sale. And there was Charity's lie about the tree chipper. And then the golf clubs. And I confessed about losing my job. You knew too much about me that wasn't very . . . flattering. Having to leave Mama's because of Jason and Tina wasn't something I wanted you to know."

His blue eyes softened. "Believe it or not, Daisy, I would've understood."

"Right, like you've ever run away from an ex."

"God, no. But I can understand how a woman like you—"

Her left brow came perilously close to shooting off her forehead.

"What I mean is, a woman like you who has committed herself to a man and . . . is no doubt faithful, and then finds out her fiancé isn't . . . well . . . Retreat is a good option . . ."

"Oh, please, stop." Daisy rolled her eyes at his pathetic backpedaling. "Dry your hair. You look like a punk rocker."

Max finger-combed his waves. "Your feelings . . . wanting to run . . . it's really not pathetic."

"But *you'd* never do it." She shooed him away. "Just drop it."

Max hesitated, then pulled the bathroom door closed.

Daisy fumed. The man was insufferable. The way he described her as being *no doubt* faithful made her sound like some Victorian throwback. Unlike Tina, who hadn't a single Victorian inclination. And just how many exes did Max Kendall have? Probably one in every port—

Daisy shot her eyes to her foot and bent to grab Max's passport.

The bathroom door opened. Daisy practically catapulted up, whipping her guilty hand behind her back.

Max looked at her, flashed on his bag, and then returned his eyes to her. "I hate to ask a favor," he began after another glance at his bag. "But my hair dryer isn't working. Can I borrow yours?"

"Sure." Daisy curled her lips into a smile so contrived even she wouldn't buy it.

"Anytime soon?"

"I'm, uh, trying to remember where I put it."

"Suitcase, maybe?"

"Noooo . . ."

"A drawer?"

She shook her head. "Doubtful."

"Closet?"

"Maybe." She scrunched her face as if wrestling with a real dilemma. "Why don't you go back into the bathroom and when I find it, I'll knock."

Max stepped forward, Daisy stepped back.

"I need my bag," he said, bending to reach it. "Which, by the way, is where I normally keep *my* dryer."

"Yeah, but your dryer is broken."

"Okay." He stepped back into the bathroom with his bag. "I'll be waiting in here."

"Okey-dokey."

The door latched.

That damn, damn, damn passport! Of all the things not to put back in his bag. What if he needed it? What if he had a trip planned? Even crossing the border into Canada required a passport.

"This is what happens when you steal," Daisy chastised herself. Well, she'd just have to figure some way to get it back in there before he discovered it missing. But that meant separating Max from his bag and he was surely taking it with him after they finished dinner. *Unless . . .*

Max straightened his knee then strapped on the splint over his jeans. He wiped the fogged mirror with a corner of his towel. But instead of checking his reflection, he turned away and lifted his duffel bag to the lidded toilet. A quick check here, a quick check there, everything seemingly intact, Max decided he was being paranoid. But it didn't stop him from licking the flap on the manila envelope and sealing it, just in case. Because Daisy definitely looked guilty of something, even if it was just intent. Maybe he caught her *before* she'd snooped, not that he worried she'd find anything useful to her.

Money. But he'd checked his wallet and, although he didn't count the bills, the wad was still pretty thick. Besides, Daisy might be a lot of things, but she was too proud and too honest to steal, no matter how dire her circumstances. Never mind that she'd sold Jason's widescreen TV and Tina's golf clubs. That was payback. But with Max, she'd been totally up-front about whose clubs they were and had even given him the chance to renege on the deal. He had found that amusing and admirable, in a weird sort of way. If all else failed, there was always guilt to keep Daisy on the straight and narrow.

A triple knock. He opened the door on a smiling Daisy with hair dryer in hand.

Speaking of guilt, Max thought about her excessive smile . . . *and recently-glossed lips?*

"Here y' go," she said as if she might break into song.

"I'll be out in a few minutes."

"Take your time. I'll be out here. Waiting."

Yep. Something smells rotten in Denmark. Max plugged in the dryer and faced himself in the mirror. A few minutes of hot air and he was done. Raking fingers through his dark waves, he let them fall naturally. Appraising his clean-shaven reflection, he caught the line of pink skin over his right temple. He fingered the healing gash.

So why hadn't Daisy visited him in the hospital?

Of course, he was *suing* her. And he had slept with her ex-fiancé's fiancée. *Ouch.* It was probably safe to say that Daisy didn't *like* him all that much. Maybe even stronger than that.

Still, Daisy hadn't even tried to see him while he was in the hospital; not a card, phone call, flowers, nothing. He couldn't decide which bugged him more—that she hadn't tried to see him or that it bugged him that she hadn't tried.

Pride. Pride had kept Daisy from his bedside. Had he really expected differently?

He regretted the lawsuit. But he had hospital bills and now he couldn't work, which meant he'd have to hire someone else to do his job. On top of that, he was out $647 when he'd given the golf clubs back to Tina . . . who, by the way, had visited him in the hospital *three times*, not to mention the visit he'd made to her condo after his release.

Besides, Daisy obviously had money. She had just sold an expensive house in an expensive neighborhood and she owned a Lexus—until it was stolen. Still, she'd been the executive chef at a posh restaurant, undoubtedly well paid. Bottom line, Daisy could well afford $25,000 to help him out of the predicament she'd put him in.

Not only that, Daisy still hadn't apologized for all the damage she'd caused—or, more recently, for accusing him of being a thief and a stalker—although she'd had plenty of opportunity this afternoon when he'd bought her lunch.

"That's right," Max said to the mirror. "I bought her lunch." It didn't matter that he'd had ulterior motives; she still got fed, which was obviously all she cared about. When it came down to it, for all the pain and suffering she'd caused him, Daisy was getting off pretty damn easy.

If only she'd told him why she wanted to leave Mama Mia's. Never mind that fleeing from Jason was a *little* pathetic—although he actually did understand. Those few minutes they'd spent quibbling over her drinks could've been spent escaping. And Max wouldn't have this brace on his leg or a scar above his eye or Daisy on his hands.

But not for long. Max patted aftershave on his neck and cheeks. Tomorrow they docked in Ketchikan and Daisy would be off the *Columbia* and on a southbound ferry to Bellingham. Max would be in Daisy's cabin, on his way to Haines. Like two ships passing, they'd never see each other again.

Chapter Eleven

"This place is busy," Daisy said while she and Max waited at the hostess station for a table. A wall of windows port, bow, and starboard showcased the reason most were on this ferry—cloud-piercing mountains, voluptuous spruce, and diamond-blue waters. All washed by a golden sun beginning to drop in a cerulean sky, but far from sunset. Nowhere in that vast wilderness was the tiniest evidence of human intrusion. Alaska wasn't called the Last Frontier for nothing, Daisy thought, entranced by the landscape.

Max looked around the dining room as if he hadn't already noticed the crowded tables or the waitstaff hustling from one place-setting to the next like hummingbirds to nectar—pouring water, delivering food, clearing dishes. Happy voices rose above the background noise of silverware on porcelain and congenial conversation as a casually dressed foursome entered the room.

"Captive audience," Max said. "Not a lot of options."

A half frown. "I think the food is pretty good."

"That's right. You had a hot date here last night."

Daisy's intended retort was thwarted by the hostess.

"Reservations?"

Daisy looked at Max, rolled her eyes, and said no.

"Table for two?" the sunny hostess asked, pulling menus and a wine list from the rack without waiting for confirmation.

With Daisy and Max following, the hostess wended her way between diners and oases of plants while cutting through spheres of translucent amber shining down from the ceiling. They arrived at a far table crowded against a wall in a partial alcove. She handed each their menu, promised a waiter, then left, still smiling.

"Well, it's not the greatest table," Daisy remarked, scooting her chair in. "We should've made reservations."

"I like it." Max pushed up the sleeves of his cobalt-blue sweater and landed his elbows on the table. "I've got my back covered and I can see all the action."

"Expectin' trouble, Hopalong?"

"I like privacy," Max explained, his voice deep and his words slow. "Besides, it's the food I care about."

"Dining out should be as much about ambience as it is about food. Subdued lighting, flickering candles, sparkling crystal, gleaming silverware, where each of the fork tines are perfectly aligned and the pieces match in pattern—"

Max glanced down at his setting, noting the slight bend in the outer tine of the dinner fork. Like he cared . . .

"—And the linen should be crisp and *creamy* white, never stark white, without a wrinkle, or a stain, not even a water mark. The napkins folded precisely, each edge and corner aligned with the next, and the china evenly glazed without the minutest dull patch—"

Speaking of dull . . . Daisy's dedication to precision and perfection reminded Max of his navy flight commander, "Knife" Newton. He'd never met anyone as obsessively compulsive as Commander Newton *until* Daisy Moon. If she didn't end her monologue soon, his brain would be as glazed as his dinner plate.

"Actually, that's kind of why I'm on this ferry . . ."

Max nodded, his thoughts on a lone thirty-something blonde spilling out of a low-cut sweater two tables behind Daisy. The blonde smiled at him. He could sit here, look in Daisy's direction and flirt with the blonde, and Daisy would be none the wiser. That would keep things interesting until she finished her discourse on napkins.

Picking up a breadstick, the mystery woman discreetly licked the sides, then slowly worked the shaft through her red lips. *Lucky breadstick.* His thoughts came to a screeching halt when a well-dressed, white-haired man—maybe twenty years older than Max—returned to the table that held only dessert dishes and coffee cups. When the man looked his way, Max diverted his eyes to Daisy. Then, sensing it was safe, Max looked at the blonde, who held him in a side-glance.

". . . Otter Bite."

Max nodded, wondering if he'd heard right, then went back to his fantasy. This woman held promise, assuming there wasn't a gold band hiding beneath that large sapphire on her marriage finger. Max Kendall didn't do wives. Fiancées, possibly; girlfriends, definitely. But he wouldn't be an accomplice to breaking vows. It might be a fine line, but it was his fine line and he'd never knowingly crossed it.

"So, Max, what do you think?"

Max blinked at Daisy, who was leaning into the table, intent on him, her eyes . . . hopeful? He had no idea what he thought, but it was probably best to be amenable or risk an even more boring verbal treatise on God only knew what. Of course, he could tell her that he'd been flirting with the well-endowed blonde and hadn't been listening . . .

"What do *you* think?" he asked instead.

Daisy frowned. "I just told you what I think. Weren't you listening?"

The bane of every man's relationship with women—the *weren't you listening?* complaint! He could confess that no, he wasn't, but judging by Daisy's expression, he figured frankness might end his chances for her cabin.

"I just want to be sure you've thought it through," Max said, having had practice with the song and dance.

"Oh." Sounding apologetic. "Well, I have. I know it's a little unorthodox—"

What? Max silently joked. *Folding a napkin on the diagonal?*

"—But this isn't the nineteen fifties and we are adults. With a little tolerance and patience, I think it would work. As I see it, commitment is the key to success."

"Commitment?" Max asked suspiciously.

"Well, sure. Every plan requires commitment. Otherwise you'll never get through the rough spots. Right?"

Max wasn't sure yet again what he was agreeing to—*rough spots?*—but if it could move Daisy to a conversation he had some participation in, he was all for it. "Sure."

Daisy scrutinized him as she'd done the silver. "Not very convincing."

"If it works for you, it'll work for me."

"Really?" Sounding grateful. "I'm . . . surprised. Honestly, I thought you'd have reservations or at least an opinion."

"Unlike you, Daisy, I don't have an opinion on *everything*."

If he had intended to shut her up, he succeeded. Daisy eased back in her chair with a look that reflected insult. She opened her menu and put her icy attention there.

His shoulders drooped. Individuality aside, when it came to being pissed, women were all the same. He debated an apology, but the silence was a welcome relief. At least he was no longer groping for a response to unknown questions. After a final glance at the blonde, he vowed that he'd now pay attention to Daisy. He opened his menu. After all, he was working up the nerve to ask for her cabin. There would be plenty of time later for blondes.

"Can I get you something from the bar?"

Max and Daisy looked up from their menus at a twenty-something waiter they hadn't seen coming.

"Bombay and tonic," Max answered first. "Sapphire if you've got it."

"And for you, miss?"

She flashed him a dazzling Irish smile that lit up her eyes like sparklers. Or so Max thought.

"A Coke would be lovely. Thank you, Andrew."

Max frowned at the pair, until he realized that a name tag was pinned to the waiter's crisp white shirt.

"Our dinner specials are listed on the insert. Everything is fresh. The halibut has been going over very well and we've had a lot of compliments on the scallops. The seafood salad is always popular. I'll give you a few minutes and be back with your drinks."

"Thank you, Andrew," Daisy said.

Why can't you be that sweet to me? Max wanted to ask, but reached for the wine list instead. "Would you like a bottle of wine?"

A half smile in his direction and her voice dripped honey, but the sparklers had become daggers. And no amount of honey could dull those blades.

"No. Thank you."

Yep, still pissed. "They have some nice wines here."

"Yes, I know."

"That's right—" Max stopped himself.

Daisy kept smiling. As if her lips were frozen into that curl.

"Not even a glass? We can toast to . . . our truce."

Daisy leaned into him, her voice as soft and seductive as the dark auburn spirals drizzling past her cheeks. "I would, Max, but I'm such a klutz that my wine might end up in your face." That smile, those daggers.

"I'll ask the waiter for a lid and a straw."

"It's going to be tough flying with just one eye."

Max couldn't help but smile. "Call me crazy, but I think I'm safe."

The daggers slowly disappeared until only a teasing glint remained.

However much Daisy annoyed him—and oh, how she annoyed him—she was equally entertaining. He couldn't remember the last time he'd experienced this kind of mental calisthenics where he was simultaneously exhausted and invigorated. And tonight, with her green sweater sparking her eyes and her hair tamed into finger-tempting waves and her mouth glossed so the light shimmered on the lush swell of her lower lip—

"I suppose I do have an opinion on pretty much everything," Daisy said.

—and the alluring tendrils of her perfume . . .

"A virtual cornucopia. *But*—" Max said, accepting her apology, "there are worse things in life than having opinions. At least you think about things."

It sounded like a compliment. "Charity says I *over*think."

Max was gratefully spared a response by the waiter, who unloaded their drinks from his small tray.

"Sir, you may want to try your Sapphire and tonic," he said with a pointed look at Max's napkin. While Max reached for his drink—peeking at the blue ink on the underside of his napkin—Andrew asked Daisy for her dinner selection.

Daisy looked up from her menu. "What do you recommend?"

"Everything is good. The seafood salad is light, but with a nice variety of salmon, crab—"

Over the top of Daisy's head, Max saw the blonde rise from her chair, her skirt—no panty lines—as short as her sweater was tight. Their eyes met, they exchanged smiles while her companion studied the dinner bill. Max discreetly tipped his glass her way, took a sip and carefully placed his drink to the side of the napkin.

"—However, my favorite is the scallops. They're baked in a rich cream sauce with Gruyère browned on top. Very nice."

"Scallops it is." Daisy then accepted the waiter's recommendation a second time for her salad dressing, which she asked for on the side.

"Halibut," Max said, his cocktail napkin now tucked inside the front pocket of his jeans. "And blue cheese."

"How is your drink, sir?"

"On the money," he replied, calculating Andrew's tip for this particular service.

Then Max and Daisy were alone again with a crowd of strangers.

"That showed remarkable flexibility," Max said.

"What?"

"The scallops. It must have been really tough to go with the waiter's suggestion." He paused. "Or were you intending to get the scallops all along?"

"Let's just say, I lucked out."

It was an awkward moment of congeniality. Each reached for their drink as if not knowing how to interact without sarcasm or criticism.

"Daisy," Max began when he'd captured her eyes with his and she seemed uncharacteristically receptive.

"Yes, Max?"

"Daisy," he began again, trying to find the words to ask for her cabin that wouldn't make him seem like an opportunist.

"Yes, Max?" she answered, this time with more curiosity.

"Daisy . . . ," he tried yet again, looking into shimmering green eyes that were distractingly trusting. "Let's get a bottle of wine."

"That's not what you really want to say."

"It's not?"

Her head tilted ever so gently and one delicate copper crescent lifted slightly. "I think I know what you're trying to say."

"You do?"

"Yes. And since you're being so incredibly magnanimous—"

"Magnanimous?"

"Well, yes."

Max narrowed his eyes on Daisy. "Do you know what the word means?"

Daisy flinched. "Of course I do."

"I don't think anyone's ever called me magnanimous."

"I must bring out the best in you." She smiled.

Max didn't. Instead, if what was going on inside his head was any indication, he pretty much looked clueless.

"Okay, maybe not," Daisy amended when her quip seemed unappreciated. "But, given the circumstances, I'm the one who should probably say something. And please"—she flashed her palm—"it won't be easy, so let me get through this without interrupting." She reached for her soda.

The way Daisy sucked down her Coke, it looked like she needed Crown Royal in it.

She put down her drink, took a deep breath, and rushed her words. "First and most important, I'm really sorry about what happened at Mama Mia's. I'm sorry about your knee. I'm sorry about your head. The whole evening was a complete disaster and if there was any way I could take it back, I would."

It's about time. Yet Max somehow managed to keep his expression neutral.

"I wanted to tell you weeks ago—and God knows I tried—"

His dark brows crept together.

"—but you had that restraining order—"

"What restraining order?"

"Okay, maybe there wasn't an *actual* restraining order, but your attorney threatened one if I didn't stay away from you."

"Are you sure?"

"I'm not making it up if that's what you're implying—"

"No, not exactly."

"Not exactly? That's a vote of confidence. Ask your lawyer—or better yet, ask Tina."

"Tina?"

"She was at the hospital when I came to see you. I even brought you carnations, the peppermint ones . . . ?"

Max stared.

"They're striped red and white, like peppermints. I thought about white, but those seemed too plain and red seemed too"—she waggled her head—"intense. But then I saw the peppermint ones and they seemed so cheerful, which is what people need when they're in the hospital."

Max stared harder. "*Tina . . . ?*" he prompted.

"So I had your carnations—in a vase, by the way, with a beautiful red bow—and a nurse stopped me. She checked my name on some paper and said I wasn't allowed to see you. And that's when Tina waltzed by like the Queen of Sheba, so I left my carnations and marched the hell out of there, and swore I'd never think about you again. But now Fate has kind of screwed that up."

Something is screwed up. "You sure?"

"Puh-lease." Daisy dipped her chin. "Call Tina. I'm sure you have her number."

Max shifted in his chair, feeling inexplicably defensive . . . and tongue-tied. He *had* gotten a vase of carnations, just as Daisy described, but Tina had brought them into his room and Daisy had never been mentioned.

Daisy rolled her head as her way of acknowledging that Tina had given him more than her phone number. "That's just perfect." She took a bull's-eye on Max and leaned forward. "What is so damn special about Tina that has men breaking engagements and crawling from hospital beds just to get next to her?"

"I don't think this will help anything."

"It will help *me*," Daisy countered. "Please . . . I really want to know."

Max felt a bit unbalanced by the sudden depth in Daisy's gaze, by the sadness and confusion reflected there, by an expression that seemed to be questioning her own worth.

"Well . . . she's pretty—"

"Duh. And she's blond." Anticipating his next descriptive, she said, "And yes, she has breasts—"

Killer breasts, Max silently amended.

"—But please, it has to be more than that. Men want more than *pretty and blond and breasts* . . . don't they?"

Not really. But Max knew better than to say so. Besides, some men wanted more. Some men wanted auburn spirals and kind eyes and a rapier wit and a brain who knew Caligula—

Not Max. He wanted pretty and blond and—"She's easy," he said, ending his long pause.

"You mean sex?"

"Sex is important. But I'm talking *easy* in the sense of not requiring a lot of effort. Not a lot of rules and expectations. A guy can be who he is. A few beard shavings around the sink won't be his Waterloo . . ."

She gave him the look.

". . . and a little cigar smoke isn't treated like an eruption of Kilauea."

"I've always wanted to see the Big Island," Daisy digressed. "Is Volcanoes National Park as awesome as they say?"

"It's pretty amazing." Max remembered the acres of black hardened lava and the stream of liquid fire trickling from the dome. However, the woman he'd seen it with wasn't quite as memorable—he couldn't recall her name and her face was fuzzy—but no doubt she was pretty and blond with killer breasts.

This trip, however, he'd remember for the rest of his life, along with the fiery redhead who'd made it so memorable.

Daisy sighed. "Is there more?"

"I think you get the gist."

"So, in a nutshell, you want a woman who will let you be a thoughtless, inconsiderate slob."

Imagining himself at his worst, Max frowned. "I think you're making this too simple."

"Isn't that what you want? Simple, easy, spineless . . . a doormat?"

"I knew this was a bad idea."

"You're right. I asked for it. Sorry, I shouldn't shoot the messenger. At least I understand why no man wants me. Looks aside, I'm definitely not easy."

Max cocked his head at her. No siree, Bob. Daisy Moon was not easy. She was like a 1500-piece puzzle, where all the pieces are really tiny and similar in shape and color, but are nonetheless different, and it would take weeks, maybe even months, just to get the edges put together.

"Don't look so surprised," she said. "I know I'm not exactly laidback. Okay, maybe that's being kind," she responded to Max's smile. "But I'm an incredible cook. And a really good speller. Not to mention having a humongous vocabulary. I came in fourth in the national spelling bee championship when I was fourteen."

Without meaning to, Max pictured Daisy at fourteen, in a prim white blouse and a demure plaid skirt with her hair tied back in a ribbon, triumphantly spelling words like . . . *concupiscence.*

"Do I know what men want, or what?" Now Daisy smiled . . . at herself.

Taking the cue, Max leaned in to her and spoke sincerely, but resisted the urge to cup her hand. "Somewhere there is a man who wants a pretty redhead who's difficult and a great cook with a really humongous vocabulary who can spell . . . and next time it won't be a cross-dressing felon."

Daisy moaned.

"I'm kidding . . . about the cross-dressing felon."

Daisy shook her head. "It's not that. Although I wouldn't mind if you never brought it up again. I'm remembering how I accused you of stealing my money. And how the security chief gave you the third degree. And in spite of everything I've put you through, you're still willing—"

"Champagne vinaigrette for the lady, on the side," the waiter announced, setting Daisy's salad in front of her. "Blue cheese for the gentleman." A couple of twists of his peppermill and Andrew was on to the next table.

"You were saying?" Max asked, wondering *what* he was willing . . .

But Daisy had moved on. She retrieved a plastic baggy from inside her purse. Very delicately she selected several pieces of lettuce and a cherry tomato and dropped them into the bag. Then she eyed Max's salad. "Are you planning to eat your tomato?"

Max lifted his plate toward her; she plucked the tomato from his mound of romaine. Thanking him, she returned the baggy to her purse. Then, as if the interlude had never occurred, she drizzled vinaigrette over her remaining greens.

Right when Max was beginning to think that Daisy was more normal than not, she had to remind him of her lettuce fetish. Now she'd added a cherry tomato to her puzzle. And he still hadn't figured out the Mighty Dog or the Gerber. Imagining it mixed together, he grimaced. Of course, he could just ask her—

"Excellent dressing," she said, swallowing her first bite.

—but how much information about Daisy did he really want? He picked up his fork. He was already accustomed to her face, her eyes, the blush of her cheek, the slope of her nose, the swell of her lips, the curve of her chin . . .

Max stabbed his lettuce. Even her fountain of hair was intriguing as he imagined what those dark curls might look like spread across a white pillow—

He stuffed a forkful of crisp lettuce into his mouth. Getting to know Daisy Moon would not serve his purpose. It was better if he never discovered the reason behind the dog food and the lettuce. It was the blonde and her killer breasts he wanted.

"How's the dressing?" she asked.

"Fine."

"On a scale of one to five."

Max scooted the plate toward her. "You tell me."

Daisy scooped dressing onto the tines of her fork. Max watched as she judged the flavor, her expression a quick series of quirks, flinches, and scrunches.

"Actually, pretty good, with just the right twang from the blue cheese. You'd be surprised how often blue cheese dressing is just ranch with cheese thrown on top. I give it a four out of five."

And what would Daisy rate him? Max drained his gin and tonic. Screw his low score. He'd been putting this off long enough. And quite honestly, he didn't think he could stay awake through another of Daisy's critiques, especially since there was no blonde for a diversion. He held up his glass and caught Andrew's attention. Then he turned to Daisy, who was finishing her salad.

"Daisy," Max began.

She dabbed her lips with her napkin, then returned it to her lap. "Yes, Max?"

"Daisy..."

"Yes?"

He chickened out. "What'd you ever see in Jason?"

She stopped cold; it had been a long time since she'd thought about Jason's good qualities. "He wasn't always the jerk he was that night. He used to be fun and spontaneous and romantic..." Daisy sighed. "But then, so did I. And he was a good chef. It just seemed that the more money he made, the less he cared about cooking—which is what we had most in common. He likes the prestige of owning the most successful restaurant in Seattle."

Max looked at her... and realized he was actually listening.

"Yeah, okay, I like the prestige, too," she said. "The four stars, the great reviews. But I *love* being a chef. Jason became all about the money. But... he's really not a bad guy."

Daisy remembered how Jason had lifted her off the floor in Fireflies, broken china all around, and held her while she sobbed. He could have called the cops; she was grateful he didn't. But she was less than grateful when he sent her the $30,000 bill. Considering all the money she had made for him, he could've picked up the tab. She was angry all over again and their brief truce had ended. Hell, he'd probably spent that and more on Tina's diamond—

"If you say so," Max said when her defense of Jason had apparently ended.

She shrugged. "Tina isn't complaining."

Max knew better, but he wasn't opening that can of worms. And he'd stalled long enough. "Daisy?"

"Yes, Max?"

"About your cabin . . ." He tensed, watching for any movement toward the glasses . . . or any other dish. After all, Daisy did have a history of destroying china.

"What about it?"

"This is kind of awkward, but I was wondering if you've thought about—"

"Under the circumstances, you should get the bed. I'll be fine on the sofa."

The waiter returned with Max's drink. He immediately took two swallows. "I've got the bed . . . and *you* have the sofa?"

Daisy smiled at him. "You didn't think we'd be sharing the bed, did you?"

"No." Then realizing, "No!"

Daisy frowned at what didn't sound like a compliment.

"I mean . . . *I* expected to sleep on the sofa."

"Oh." She paused. "So sharing the bed never crossed your mind at all, huh?"

Max teetered between the devil and the deep blue sea.

"I'm kidding. It's fun to watch you squirm."

Max tried to grin, but he was paralyzed by what he didn't understand. When had he finagled himself into Daisy's cabin?

"Are you okay? You look a little pained."

"I'm sure it's my leg."

"Not to bring up a sore subject—no pun intended—but how did that happen?"

"Don't know." He sighed, stretching and repositioning his leg. "My calf went one way, my thigh the other, and my knee was caught in the middle. I banged it up pretty good a few years back and it's been an accident waiting to happen. I should've had the operation then," he admitted, then he remembered his lawsuit. "But my knee was fine until I slipped on the spilled beer."

Daisy looked a little pained herself. "Kind of a freak accident, huh? No one's really to blame."

"If this is about the lawsuit . . ."

Daisy very nearly radiated anticipation.

". . . I don't think we should talk about it. It's not personal. I just don't have a lot of options," he added, saying more than he should. "For the sake of getting along, let's not discuss it . . . ever."

"We'll have to discuss it eventually."

"That's what attorneys are for."

"If we could just talk about it, you and me—"

A brick wall, that's what Max became.

"Fine," Daisy huffed, turning her attention to the dining room. "Is the service slow or what? I certainly hope Andrew doesn't expect a big tip."

"Why is it the waiter's fault? Maybe the cook is slow."

"That's typical, blame everything on the chef!"

Daisy looked everywhere but at Max; Max stared at nothing while imagining the easy blonde he'd be laying tomorrow—after Daisy had finally left the ship—while the hum of the dining room filled in the silence between them.

In what felt like forever, but was only minutes, Andrew arrived with their dinners. They ate their food with cordial but stilted conversation, declining dessert and coffee, although Max ordered a Grand Marnier in a snifter; he drank it while Daisy took her time in the ladies' room. As they left their table, Daisy glanced at the bill, shooting Max a disapproving look at the hefty tip.

Chapter Twelve

The dawn tickled Daisy's face; her eyelids fluttered. The sofa back greeted her. She shifted her sights to the window above; a pale gray sky blushed with pink. Last night she had spread the curtains to prevent the room from becoming pitch-black, and now she debated whether she should close them for another hour's sleep. Not that she was particularly tired, but one more hour asleep would be one less hour awake trying to pass time. As she discovered yesterday, apart from the mind-blowing scenery, there wasn't much entertainment on a ferry, unlike a cruise ship with endless diversions. But today the *Columbia* would dock in Ketchikan and she would be back on terra firma for a few hours. The next instant she realized that the waves hadn't disrupted her sleep last night, unlike Max's periodic snoring that had intermittently forced her head under the pillow.

She listened for her cabinmate. Hearing nothing to suggest Max was awake, she closed her eyes, hoping to drift back to sleep.

The sofa wasn't the softest, but considering it was Daisy's ticket to Otter Bite, she wasn't complaining. With the back cushions removed, it wasn't *too* much narrower than a single bed and long enough if she kept her knees bent. But wrapped in her own jersey knit sheets with her head cradled by her pillow, she could sleep almost anywhere . . .

"You brought your own sheets?" Max had asked last night, watching Daisy pull off her lilac sheets from the bed, revealing the white sheets that came with the cabin.

"I don't like to sleep in sheets where hundreds have been before."

"You use the towels."

"That's different." Although Daisy hadn't explained how. And

Max, with a couple of head shakes, had let it go as if it was useless trying to make sense of Daisy Moon.

Which suited Daisy fine. She didn't need Max to understand her. She only needed him to take her—and Elizabeth—to Otter Bite.

Her eyes popped open and sought the soothing dawn sky. She'd have to tell him about Elizabeth, and soon. It would, no doubt, be one more thing Max didn't understand. Last night at dinner, she thought for sure he would ask about the tomatoes—which would've been the perfect opportunity to mention Elizabeth—but, no, he just kind of scrunched his brow, offered his plate, and said nothing.

Max Kendall was not an easy man to decipher. Daisy humphed at herself. *Kind of like the pot calling the kettle black, eh?* But *she* would've been curious enough to ask about the tomatoes. Max didn't seem to care. Or maybe, Daisy speculated, remembering what he'd said about liking his privacy, maybe he was simply respecting hers. When it got down to it, prying was more of a female inclination. Still, asking about tomatoes could hardly be construed as prying. So why was Max taking her to Otter Bite and feeding her to boot?

Yes, it was a leap from tomatoes, but that was the real mystery. Except for the comment about her cornucopia of opinions, he'd accepted her proposition without a flinch. Of course, he was getting a cabin, a bed, and a shower, but if that Mexican T-shirt was any gauge, a few nights roughing it in a lounge chair probably wasn't all that big a deal. It was easy to imagine Max in a south-of-the-border cantina downing shots of tequila with a sultry, dark-eyed señorita, her arms draping his neck, before he squired her off to some cheap bungalow where they had sweaty, raunchy sex in a dozen different positions until they finally, mercifully, succumbed to seismic orgasms with the break of day—

Daisy thrashed off her sheets. Not that she really needed them. Her sleep shirt and a pair of long underwear bottoms had kept her cozy. Not as cozy as a warm body . . .

Admittedly, Daisy had thought that, maybe, in exchange for sharing his shiny new truck, Max expected to share a bed—and all that implied—but when she broached the subject, albeit facetiously, he'd practically jumped out of his skin.

She wasn't Tina or a seductive Spanish vixen, but surely she was good enough for sex. She had breasts and a vagina, and a pretty face when it wasn't splotchy from tears. What else did a man require for mindless, uncommitted sex? She had given him the perfect opportunity to demand *her* as part of the bargain. And although their ill-fated date a few weeks back was a little foggy in her mind, she was sure Max had flirted with taking her to bed. So why, last night, was he appalled at the idea?

You'd think the guy was gay . . .

She brightened, then dismissed the possibility. Unfortunately, Max Kendall was not gay. That would've been the easy, face-saving explanation. In reality, Daisy just didn't have what Max wanted.

Not that Max had what *she* wanted.

Who was she kidding? Max had what *every* woman wanted—between the sheets, at least. She could pretend otherwise, but the man was hot. Charity thought so. Tina undoubtedly *knew* so. Even the purser-slash-grandmother seemed to believe it. Not to mention the blonde with the breadstick. And judging by his chest, Max was testosterone dynamite.

Of course, Daisy would never experience that dynamite. She wasn't blond, she wasn't sultry. She wasn't pretty—enough. Moreover, she didn't have zeppelin-sized boobs nor was she, herself, a boob. Besides, Max could annoy the hell out of her without saying a word. A single arrogant brow raised here; the beginnings of a cocky smile there. And his baby-blue eyes—flashing, deepening, changing with his mood.

It was all very irritating, including her attraction to Max, and she wondered what Charity would say. Unfortunately, there wasn't cell service, so any conversation with her best friend would have to wait. But what she would give for a second opinion on why he continued this charade about the lawsuit. It was almost as if he wanted to keep an obstacle between them. And worse, she couldn't confront him without showing herself to be a snoop—

Damn! She meant to put his passport back in his duffel bag during the night.

Slowly, as if any movement might wake the sleeping giant, Daisy rolled to her other side, away from the window and toward the bed—

"Good morning."

Daisy shrieked.

"Did I scare you?"

"Of course not. I always scream when I wake up." Daisy protectively gathered her sheets and sat up. Finger-brushing her unruly morning hair away from her face, she looked at Max, who rolled to his side and propped himself up on his left elbow, his chest disappointingly hidden beneath that damn Mexican T-shirt. "How long have you been awake?"

"Long enough."

"*Long enough?* How hard would it be to give me a straight answer?"

"Not a morning person, are you?"

Daisy drew her knees to her chest. "As a matter of fact, I'm not. I'm used to late nights and late mornings."

"One more thing we don't have in common—"

Daisy heard what sounded like regret.

"—Not that it matters."

Or maybe not. "You snore."

"Like a jackhammer. Or so I've been told."

"It wasn't *that* bad."

Max smiled.

Daisy could clearly see the curve of his lips and his morning stubble shading his cheeks. Not to mention the boyish waves that adorably tickled his forehead.

"You should have thrown something at me," Max said.

Like myself?

"I saw that," he said in mocking accusation.

"Saw what?"

"Your expression. When I said you should've thrown something."

"I don't know what you're talking about."

"Yeah, yeah." He sat up. "Lucky for me, you don't have a ton of bricks."

Daisy gasped. "You must think I'm the worst person in the world if you believe I'd throw a brick at you, let alone a ton!"

About to ease his bum leg over the side of the bed, Max stopped and looked intently at Daisy. "Easy does it, I was only kidding."

"As a matter of fact, it never entered my mind to throw *anything* at you!"

Max raised his hands in surrender. "It was a joke, Daisy. Honest. Boy oh boy, you really *aren't* a morning person."

Realizing she'd overreacted to her own embarrassing thoughts, Daisy relaxed. "I guess I'm a little muddled this morning. It's hard for me to sleep in a strange . . . sofa . . . with someone else . . . in the room," she added. "I'm sure *you* can sleep with just about anyone, anywhere."

The speculation wasn't an intentional barb, it just came out that way. But whatever Max thought about it, he didn't comment.

"Do you want the bathroom first?" Max asked.

"What I meant was—"

"I know what you meant. If it makes you feel any better, you're probably right."

About what? The anywhere or the anyone?

"So . . . you first? Or me first?"

"You go ahead," Daisy said. "I might try to sleep another hour or so."

Concern bridged his brows. "You *are* getting off in Ketchikan, aren't you?"

"Oh, sure. But we don't dock until noon. It's not like I have much to do until then."

"I thought we'd have breakfast." Max stood beside the bed in his T-shirt and boxers.

Is that what he'd slept in? Daisy had been under the covers last night, her face to the sofa back, feigning sleep, when Max had returned to the cabin after a walk. Suggesting she might want privacy, he'd excused himself when she removed her sheets. But Daisy had suspected he wanted respite from the stress of their dinner. Not that she blamed him. *She* was the one with the short fuse who took every comment the wrong way. But she hated being indebted to this man; hated having to rely on him. Yet if she was getting to Otter Bite, she'd have to suck in her pride and stop being such a bitch. She would stop dwelling on her bad luck and thank her lucky stars for Max Kendall, 5-star stud.

Surely not.

"Daisy? Breakfast?"

"That's really kind of you, Max," she said sweetly. "And generous."

Max inched back. "It's only breakfast."

"It may seem like only breakfast to you, but to me it's just one more magnanimous gesture—"

"Will you *please* stop saying *magnanimous*? Breakfast is not a magnanimous gesture!"

Now it was Daisy's turn to ease back. "Maybe *magnanimous* isn't the best word. But you have been very kind and understanding and generous—"

"Oh, brother."

"You have to admit, Max," she added, annoyed at his refusal to accept her new leaf, "few would be doing what you're doing. And I just want you to know that . . . you're practically saving my life."

"I slept in a bed last night, Daisy. And now I'm taking a shower. And I have a cabin I can return to this afternoon. And the same for the next day, and the next. Believe me, Daisy, I don't do anything for free. So you can stop being thankful or feeling indebted or all of those other misplaced emotions. This."—he flashed two fingers between them—"is a simple trade. You have something I need; I have something you need. I am not saving your life. You're a resourceful, tenacious, determined woman. You would've figured something out."

Daisy stared at him, fearing she might cry but not knowing why. All Max had done was point out the obvious. After all, she'd been the one to suggest this deal in the first place. So why did it seem so cold and calculated when Max parroted it back to her?

"The truth is," Max continued, "I'm selfish and self-centered, and completely without conscience and incapable of remorse. Thank your lucky stars you'll be rid of me soon."

A few minutes ago, she *was* thanking her lucky stars—and counting his. "Fine," Daisy said, in a semi-sulk. "But just for the record, no one without a conscience confesses they don't have a conscience."

"Of course they do. It absolves them of any guilt."

"But if you have no conscience, you have no guilt."

"It absolves them of guilt the other person tries to lay on them."

"Nice try, but you're not quite the sociopath you claim to be."

"Can we just agree that I'm not magnanimous and that you're really annoying?"

"If you like."

Max huffed. "I'm taking a shower and I'm using all the hot water."

"All right by me." Daisy punched her pillow then lay back down on the sofa, pulling the sheets around her. "I take my showers at night."

"That kind of defeats my purpose." He limped toward her and Daisy went eye to knee with his six-inch incision. Far from healed, the surgery site was still swollen, pink, and tight. With every flex of his knee, Daisy feared the skin would split open. Other than that, Max Kendall had handsome legs with just the right amount of muscular definition and an appropriate mesh of dark hairs. Neither girly nor gorilla, just good strong limbs. Or at least they would be once his knee healed.

"Not too pretty, is it?"

Daisy looked up. "I'm sure your particular brand of woman will find your scar immensely sexy. Especially if you come up with a really good story to go along with it."

Daisy rolled over and faced the sofa back.

"Like what?"

Daisy lifted her head. "Like what . . . kind of story?"

"Yeah."

"Oh, I don't know. Say you got shot while working for the CIA."

"Please. My *particular brand* of woman is not an idiot."

Daisy lifted her brows at him.

"Contrary to what you want to believe."

"Like I care," she said, laying her head back down.

"So what kind of story would *you* believe?"

Daisy lifted her head again, only to discover that Max had taken a seat at the end of the bed, his injured leg stretched out in front of him. "I thought you were taking a shower."

Max shrugged. "Are we in a hurry all of a sudden?"

Daisy gathered her sheets and sat up. "Well, judging by that T-shirt of yours—"

Max looked down at his T-shirt as if he'd forgotten what he was wearing.

"—I'd probably believe you got knifed in a bar fight over a woman in some south-of-the-border cantina."

"Doesn't make me sound very heroic."

"Which is exactly why I'd believe it."

"A few minutes ago, I was magnanimous. Now I'm chopped liver?"

"It could be sort of heroic, depending on whether the woman was married or not. So, was the woman married?"

"That's debatable. But there was no knife. So what else might you believe?"

Daisy cocked her head at Max, who looked appealingly rumpled in his Señorita Largatija T-shirt with his uncombed hair and his morning stubble. "Okay, forget the bar. But keep the woman, only she wasn't a lover. She was younger . . . the daughter of an old army—no, navy—buddy . . . who had gone down to . . . Acapulco . . . for spring break, but hadn't returned. Your friend asked you to find her, because you know your way around Mexico . . ." Daisy paused. "You once ran a fishing charter there for the tourists. How am I doing so far?"

"I'm looking better and better."

"So, did you find your friend's daughter?"

"Ellen," Max interjected. "That's a good wholesome name for my friend's daughter, right?"

"It's your story. So . . . you found *Ellen*, but she had inadvertently gotten mixed up with one of the local drug lords, who had wined, dined, and romanced her into a quick marriage with a huge diamond ring, but soon after, she discovered who he was and where all the money came from and she tried to leave, and that's when he got violent. So, long story short, you found Ellen at this guy's villa, and you did save her, but not before you fought off a half dozen thugs and two really big Rottweilers, but one mauled your knee. In spite of that, you didn't hurt the dogs because you're an animal lover."

After a moment, Max asked, "And you'd believe this story?"

"It's possible."

"Meaning?"

Daisy faltered, debating how much she wanted to help Max dupe his next blonde. "You wouldn't actually use this story to get some unsuspecting woman into bed, would you?"

His laugh was immediate. Daisy realized how ridiculous her allegation was. Max Kendall's particular brand of woman didn't need lies to motivate her into his bed. His women were fun and adventurous and, unlike Daisy, didn't have impossible expectations.

"I thought we were talking about you," he said with a dying chuckle. "But if you think you're helping the enemy . . ." With his good leg bearing the brunt of his weight, he rose from the bed. Grabbing the handles on his duffel bag, he slowly stepped toward the bathroom.

"If the lights were dim and the music soft and the wine expensive."

Max turned at the door. "And?"

"And what?"

"I don't believe for one second that you, Daisy, would be under-mined by lights, music, and wine."

"*And* . . . if I thought you were . . . *special*."

"And what makes a man special?"

Daisy hesitated at the fork in her road. She could give Max an honest answer or . . . "Well, for one thing, he's *very* forgiving—"

His eyes crinkled as his grin returned.

"—And he would never use all the hot water just to prove some ridiculous point."

"I guess I'm not the only one who has trouble giving a straight an-swer. See you when the water runs cold." The bathroom door clicked shut.

"And he makes me smile," Daisy murmured, smiling.

Chapter Thirteen

"More coffee, sir?"

Max nodded and the waitress freshened his cup. The roasted aroma lingered before fading into the inviting breakfast redolence of the busy restaurant.

Max met the eyes of the young woman—probably working summers between college semesters—and acknowledged her service with a half smile. He returned to his magazine as she left his table. Finishing a page, he sipped from his coffee, then went back to his article. Ten minutes later he'd drunk half his cup and finished his third article from the magazine he'd bought on his way to the dining room. Setting the publication aside, he read the menu and set that aside, then he looked toward the entrance, *again*. A dozen people waited, but no Daisy Moon.

He'd been there forty-five minutes, alone for thirty minutes longer than he was supposed to be.

The waitress returned. "Do you expect your party soon, sir?"

"I wouldn't really describe her as a *party*."

"We have a number of people waiting," the waitress continued, either not grasping Max's joke or not thinking it funny. "Perhaps you'd like to order."

"Perhaps I would, but I think I won't."

Her dark brows tipped together.

"Why don't we give my party another fifteen minutes."

The waitress attempted a smile, although she was obviously unhappy with the wait. Not that Max felt otherwise, but it was, after all, his and Daisy's last meal together and he wanted to send her home on a full stomach.

Bored with his magazine, he checked out the other diners. Mostly middle-aged couples, a few families with children, and a few groups of twenty-somethings. He suspected that most passengers were eating in the less expensive cafeteria, where he would've been had it not been for this plastic leg of his. Not that money was the issue; Max didn't need the frills of a restaurant, especially for breakfast. Those orange twists and parsley sprigs cost money, and who eats the garnish? Then there was the added 15 percent to get your meal from the kitchen to the table and coffee from the carafe into your cup. But, in his present situation, it was a relief not to tax his leg by standing in line and getting his own coffee. Nice, but nonetheless, frivolous.

And speaking of frivolous, there she was, being led by the hostess straight toward him. Max smiled. She smiled back. Right before she finger-combed her silky blond strands from her bronzed face—a healthy glow in contrast to the white in her snug blue-and-white striped top with its sailor collar. Her white hip-hugging capris exposed tanned calves, slender ankles, and pampered feet strapped into sandals with a wedged heel.

Nautical with a hint of naughty. Exactly Max Kendall's particular brand of woman. Judging by the discreetly turning heads, he wasn't alone in his attraction.

The hostess seated the blonde at a nearby table that had a RE-SERVED sign. He scanned the restaurant for her escort from last night. When he couldn't find the gentleman, his eyes drifted back to the woman, who was now talking to a very attentive waiter. Unexpectedly, they both glanced his way.

Max took this as his cue. He rose and started toward the blonde. And that's when he saw her. Being led by the hostess straight toward him. He raised a brow at her lousy timing. She smiled, right before she brushed an errant cherry spiral from her porcelain cheek. She wore nothing to spark his fantasies—faded jeans and a light green sweater set. Just an everyday woman . . . except for that froth of curls, those kryptonite eyes, and a mind that cut him no slack.

He glanced at the blonde, then did a double take as she slowly applied cherry-red lipstick. When she looked straight at him and pursed her succulent lips, it took all his willpower to drag himself back to the table in time for Daisy's arrival.

"Sorry I'm late." Daisy took the chair to the left of Max's. "Were you leaving?"

"Just getting the kinks out." He sat down. "I've been here awhile."

Daisy quickly opened her menu. She corralled her curls to one shoulder and Max caught the glint of gold dangling from her ear. The petite chandelier twinkled and winked at him and drew his attention to her sleek jaw and the soft vulnerability of her neck. Then her auburn curls fell against her skin like a curtain closing.

Daisy glanced at him. "So what are you getting?"

"What I always get. Two eggs over easy with sausage and toast."

This time, her eyes lingered. "But there are some interesting things on the menu. The lemon soufflé pancakes, for instance. And crab cakes Benedict."

"Sometimes I order bacon instead of sausage."

"Don't you ever want something different?"

"I've been known to make waffles the morning after."

"Impressive."

"I know what I like. I know what will satisfy me. It's only food, not the Holy Grail."

"*Only* food?" Daisy looked shocked. "That's like saying it's only air. It's *food*, Max. It's what sustains us. It's life, it's—"

"Look," he interrupted, dipping his chin at her. "I'm hungry. Will you please just choose something?"

A momentary pause, then Daisy went back to the menu. Max watched as she considered the selections. A scrunch of her brow at that one, a pucker of lips at the next one . . . He could practically read her thoughts. And he didn't read a single thought that included him . . . well, in any *friendly* sort of way. Unlike the blonde, who had *very* friendly thoughts. In fact, Daisy always seemed to be donning armor. Like this morning when he'd joked about throwing bricks. What was that about? And the way she gathered her sheet around her like she needed protection. And speaking of sheets . . . Just how many bubbles off plumb was Daisy Moon?

At least she wasn't boring. Annoying, irritating, frustrating, yes. Boring, no.

Nonchalantly, Max looked in the direction of the blonde. The gentleman from last night had joined her. As Max watched the blonde dote on her *whatever*, he decided that while Daisy had idiosyncrasies—the dog food niggled at him—she was undoubtedly loyal, probably to a fault.

"Do you know her?"

Max snapped his attention to Daisy. "What?"

"I said, do you know her? Or are you just *planning* to know her?"

"Who?"

"Please, Max. Give me a little credit."

Max gave her the most sincerely perplexed expression he could muster—head cocked, brows fused, eyes radiating puppy-like innocence. "I don't know what you're talking about." And the hurt in his voice complemented the halo above his head.

"Oh, for Pete's sake—or should I say for Saint Peter's sake? I saw you watching her last night. And you're doing it again now. As you so clearly pointed out this morning, our arrangement is strictly business—I need a ride and you need a cabin. You're free to make any side deals you want with whomever you want. And apparently you want her." Keeping both her composure and her dignity, Daisy stood. "I'll leave so you can finagle her away from her . . . *whatever.*"

Max reached for her arm. "Please, Daisy, sit down." From the corner of his eye, he glimpsed the waitress come near their table, then stop and make an about-face. At this rate, he was never getting fed. "It's not what you think."

"If I want lies from a man, I have an ex who tells them in spades."

"But you've got it all wrong."

Although Max didn't have an alternative scenario—yet—this was no time to upset Daisy, not when he was so close to getting her cabin. Regardless of how open-minded Daisy claimed to be, his being distracted by another woman probably pushed the envelope. But Max was a sucker for an easy blonde, while Daisy was the most difficult red—

His thoughts came to a screeching halt, then backed up. *Did Daisy say she needs a ride?*

After hemming and hawing, Daisy finally sat down. "So tell me. What do I have wrong?"

Max gave her the same innocently perplexed expression as before, only this time it was genuine. "What did you just say? I need a cabin and you need a *what?*"

"Quit stalling," Daisy said, poised to spring from her chair.

"I'm not—"

She started to rise.

"I wasn't looking at her," Max said in a hushed tone. "I was looking at *him*."

The anger melted from her face. "OhmyGod. Are you gay?"

Max jerked back. "No!"

"Well, why in the world would you be looking at *him* and not *her*?"

"I was looking at them *both*," Max huffed, mentally congratulating himself for his quick thinking. "He's the state representative from Seward. But that is definitely *not* his wife."

Daisy narrowed her eyes. "Really?"

"No. I'm making it up."

"That I believe."

"I guess this is one of those times when a uniform would come in handy, eh?" Max might very well have dislocated a shoulder from patting himself on the back until he saw the pained expression on Daisy's face and realized the low blow he'd struck. Suddenly there it was, in the pit of his stomach, a small knot of guilt. All because he couldn't admit he was looking at the blonde. *No.* Because he couldn't *stop* looking at the blonde. *No.* Because he *wanted* the blonde. And Daisy's cabin.

This was why he never involved himself with a complicated woman!

"Daisy . . . ," Max began, not sure what to say but willing to say almost anything to get rid of this foreign feeling.

"Y' know what, Max? You're absolutely right. First, your personal life is none of my business—any more than what you eat for breakfast is. And I had no right to imply you were lying. After all, why would you lie to me—it's not like you're trying to get *me* into bed." She paused, then softly added, "I guess I'm a little sensitive about blondes." The corners of her mouth almost lifted in a smile. *Almost.* "But I shouldn't take my frustrations out on you. And from this moment on"—thumping the table with her right index finger—"I'm going to stop being defensive and critical and . . . and analytical and . . . opinionated. Instead I'm going to be—

"Bland and boring?" Max realized too late he'd spoken his thoughts.

Daisy perked, then looked at him sideways. "I thought you liked bland and boring."

"I like *easy*. And *that* you are not. You're critical and opinionated and a little odd—"

"If this is about the sheets—"

"The sheets, the lettuce, the dog food—" *Damn*, Max silently swore, regretting he'd brought up the subject.

"The dog food?"

But since he had... "I saw the can of dog food yesterday, on the bed stand . . . next to the jar of baby food."

"Ohhhh. I can explain."

"Unless you're hiding a dog somewhere, I don't want to know."

"It's not a dog, it's a—"

His hand shot up. "Sometimes it's better not to know too much about a person."

"Max, you're being ridiculous. I have a perfectly legitimate reason—"

"Look, Daisy, I'm sure you can make anything taste good, but I don't want to know about it. We're just two ships passing. And there's a lawsuit between us, remember? It's better if we keep it . . . superficial. So, please, *don't* tell me about the dog food."

Daisy stared at Max. Max stared at Daisy. Then, without a word, Daisy returned her attention to the menu.

Not only was the knot still there, it had grown, like a ball of string you kept adding to. He took a breath, feeling very nearly desperate. "I think you're . . . *interesting*."

She lifted her eyes from the menu.

"Annoying, yes, critical, opinionated, and odd, but *interesting*. You can't change who you are. Which was what I was trying to say before we got off on the dog food."

Her green eyes softened but still harbored something indiscernible, while the corners of her mouth lifted slightly. "I have a turtle. A western box turtle. Her name is Elizabeth. Which is why I have the dog food and the baby food and why I was begging your lettuce and tomatoes. So I'm not as odd as you think."

Max stared. "You have a turtle? And you named her . . ."

"Elizabeth."

"And you brought her with you?"

"I've had her since I was twelve," she answered defensively.

He slowly shook his head. "Daisy, you *are* as odd as I think."

"What's so odd about having a turtle?"

"Name one other *adult* who has a turtle." He didn't know what pets, if any, the women passing through his bed had. In fact, until he visited Tina's condo, he hadn't known she had a cat.

"Jiminy Christmas, Elizabeth's a turtle, not a platypus. So what if I don't know anyone else who has a turtle? It's not like *you* have to take care of her. Why is this a big deal?"

Because it was one more piece of the Daisy Moon puzzle he didn't want to have. Because he'd unwittingly flashed on Daisy as a twelve-year-old—with scraped knees and pigtails. *And* the notion that, for twenty-plus years, this woman next to him had been hauling around a turtle, was somehow endearing, if not inspiring. Loyalty like that didn't come around that often. All of which made Max feel like racing to the nearest exit . . . or marrying her on the spot.

"It's *not* a big deal," Max insisted. In a few more hours he'd be forever rid of Daisy and, hopefully, these unsettling feelings. "It was just unexpected. I never pictured you with a turtle named . . ."

"Elizabeth," Daisy reminded him yet again with impatient emphasis. "So what *did* you picture me with?"

"I didn't."

"Really?" She sounded a little hurt. "I pictured you with lizards and snakes and frogs and—"

"All manner of reptile?"

Daisy twitched back. "Not *only* reptiles, but that was a clever comeback." She smiled. "I pictured you—as a kid, I mean—with all sorts of animals. A real softie. Maybe because of what your mom said about that nest of baby birds you raised—"

Ah, yes, his *mis*-matchmaking mother.

"—Now I figure you have a dog."

"Can we please order breakfast before it becomes lunch?" Max craned his neck in an exaggerated search for the waitress.

Daisy frowned. "A cat?"

"No and no."

"I know you have *something* . . ."

Max pressed the table and leaned into her. "*This* is the annoying part I keep talking about. You don't know when to quit."

Daisy winced but was spared further response by the arrival of the waitress. Max ordered his usual plus a refill on his coffee while Daisy ordered strawberry crepes, orange juice, and hot water. The waitress scribbled down their choices, took their menus, and left, seemingly relieved.

It took a few moments, then Daisy looked at Max. "Y' know what I just realized?"

"The mind boggles."

"I just realized that I know practically nothing about you. And none of what I do know has come from your own disclosure."

"Maybe that should tell you something."

"It's beginning to tell me a lot. Like maybe giving you the key to my cabin isn't such a good idea."

"I don't recall confessions being part of the deal." Actually, Max didn't recall any of the deal, or even if there was one, but he was pretty sure confessions never came up. "And if you want confessions, then you can just keep your damn key."

Softening, Daisy said, "I'm not asking for *confessions*. I just don't see the harm in telling me a little bit about yourself, like"—she glanced at the *Flying* magazine beside his fork—"you're a pilot. That's not too personal, is it? As a matter of fact, it's something we kind of have in common . . ."

As Daisy talked, his memory started to rewind. She had mentioned something about him flying, and recently, but what exactly had been said? And how had she known?

"Max? Hello?"

Max refocused on Daisy's hand, waving like a metronome in front of him. "What?"

"Oh, never mind." She dug into the front pocket of her jeans and slapped a key on the table. "Here's your damn cabin key. That's why I was late for breakfast. I picked up another key. Well, that and I stopped by the purser's to see if, by some miracle, they'd found Myron Porter or my Lexus, but no such luck. Anyway, I thought you should have your own key so you can come and go as you please."

Max looked at the key, then looked at Daisy.

"What?"

"Nothing." He reached for the key.

"No, go ahead. You obviously have an opinion."

Max wanted to ask why she'd gone to the trouble for a few hours' inconvenience; why she didn't simply give him *her* key when she left, but, looking at Daisy's steeled expression—as if she was waiting for his criticism—said instead, "That was very thoughtful."

Her steel melted. "Oh."

The seconds ticked. The waitress arrived with Daisy's orange juice and hot water, then poured coffee into Max's cup. Daisy retrieved a tea bag from her purse and pushed it into the little pot of steaming water. It wasn't long before spicy tendrils spun into the air around the table.

Max wondered if Daisy always carried her own tea—like his mother did—then berated himself for his curiosity. He didn't care if Daisy always had a stash of tea. It was just another detail he didn't need. He scrunched the sleeves of his sweater up his forearms and reached for his cup.

"That's a nice sweater," Daisy finally said, remembering it from the duffel bag. "What is that? Silk?"

Max reflexively looked down on the steel-blue, knobby weave his mother had bought him.

"No idea."

"You obviously don't do your own laundry." Daisy poured tea from her pot into her cup. She looked up, then rolled her eyes at Max's stony silence. "Oh, come on. *Laundry?* Don't you think this privacy obsession of yours is bordering on the pathological?"

"I can see how you might think so, Ms. *I'm an open book.*"

"I'm not either an open book. There are lots of things you don't know about me."

"Like what?"

"Well, for starters—"

"*Really?*"

Daisy bunched her brows.

"You're about to prove my point." Then his words took on steam. "Do you realize that before I even knew your last name, I knew you were going through a messy breakup, that your fiancé cheated, you were moving, you're a clean nut and a control freak, that you're sentimental with high-end taste *and* that you're a chef without a restaurant." Max breathed and calmed his speech. "This is exactly why Myron Porter picked you. And the same reason your fiancé screwed you out of the restaurant."

Daisy looked stunned.

"My point is, Daisy, that you're too damn open and too damn honest and too damn trusting. And you expect everyone else to be like you and they're not. *I'm* not."

After a moment, Daisy shrugged as if Max's speech was water off her back. "Well, maybe I should be a little more guarded. But it wouldn't hurt if you were a little *less* guarded."

"Then who would pay for breakfast?"

"Look," she said. "I'm just going through a little bad luck. But this *blip* in my life hardly defines me. Before this nightmare, I was executive chef at a four-star restaurant. And I'll be that again. I might even fall in love again. And while I won't be quite so blind next time, I will never be so . . . so . . . *afraid* . . . that I can't talk about *laundry*."

"Nice speech. Try paying the check with it."

Daisy considered whipping out her meal vouchers, but Max needed a dose of guilt. "Fine," she said, snatching her purse where it hung from the chair back. She rooted inside and pulled out a notebook and pen. "Last night I had the scallops and a Coke"—she scribbled on her pad—"plus tip . . ."

"What are you doing?"

She glanced up. "Oh, and one cherry tomato for Elizabeth . . ."

"Daisy—"

Pen to paper. "And for breakfast I'm having the crepes and juice plus tip . . ."

"This isn't necessary. We have a deal."

"Surely they don't charge for hot water . . ." She wrote something down anyway. "But I am *not* paying for lunch yesterday. You showed up on your own without any suggestion from me."

"You still ate it," Max teased. "And you took my lettuce."

"I'll pay for the lettuce." She scribbled in the notebook. "Twenty-five cents?"

Max grinned. The lengths Daisy was willing to go to for a point! "I'm kidding. I will gladly sacrifice my lettuce for a twenty-something turtle. As for the rest of it—"

"I'll pay you back," she said, zipping up her purse.

"I don't want you to pay me back."

Daisy looked at Max with the most soul-baring eyes that had ever been cast his way.

"Do you think I *like* relying on you?" she began with honest emotion. "Do you think I'm having fun eating off your charity? I *hate* that you have to feed me and Elizabeth. I *hate* the situation that I'm in, and I hate that I let myself get in it. Although, I still think your lawsuit is a crock. But," she continued before Max could comment, "I promised myself this morning that I would stop taking my problems out on you, so excuse me if I'm just trying to make a little lemonade from my lemons. I had no idea laundry held such a hotbed of emotion for you. And from now on, we *won't* talk about anything even remotely personal and I *will* pay you back because the last person in the world I want to owe is *you*." For a few more seconds her eyes blazed for emphasis, then Daisy primly attended to her tea.

Well, he *might've* had that coming, Max allowed, politely appearing not to notice Daisy's trembling hands as she poured from her teapot. He *was* being kind of a prick this morning for reasons he didn't completely understand. Not that he would admit that. No, this situation called for something light and witty. Some clever quip to break the tension. Thanks to the arrival of their breakfast, he had a moment's reprieve to think about it. Daisy smiled her approval to the waitress, and after confirmation that nothing else was needed, the young woman happily moved on.

Max picked up his fork. "Bon appétit." He inwardly cringed as the words cleared his mouth. Light and witty? More like dumb and dumber.

Daisy cocked her head at him. "*Vraiment? Vous voulez jouter en français? Allons-y!*" She waited, superiority sparking her eyes.

Of course, Daisy spoke French, Max realized too late. And while he should've been guarded about what was surely to come, he was instead oddly intrigued.

"Ahh. *Vous ne comprenez pas,*" she said sympathetically when Max offered no response other than a curious expression. "*Vous ne parlez pas français. Vous êtes un imbécile ignorant.*" She shook her head sadly. "*Quel dommage.*"

Yes, indeed, nothing made a woman's lips more kissable than a little French, even when those same lips were calling him an ignorant fool.

"*Aussi,*" Daisy added coyly, when one dark brow inched up roguishly. "*Aussi, vous êtes beau, charmant, et spirituel, mais désagréable, ergoteur, et difficile. Pourquoi?*"

The seconds ticked as the words lingered, chipping away at his resolve. Then he shook off the spell. "You have me at a loss."

Daisy smiled sweetly. *"La plupart du temps."*

"Okay, you can stop now."

Napkin in her lap, Daisy picked up her fork with a self-satisfied air. Two bites of egg later . . . "So, where did you learn French?"

Daisy dabbed her lips with her napkin and looked at Max. "A little personal, don't you think?" Back to her crepes.

His plate was almost clean before he tried again. "I do my own laundry."

Daisy turned toward him. "Really?" As if their French interlude had never occurred.

"Well, most of it. I do send stuff to the dry cleaners."

"You own clothes that need to be dry-cleaned?"

Max indignantly raised his brows. "Well, I do have a Sunday go-to-meetin' suit."

"You have a suit?"

"I have five suits, to be exact, plus a number of sport coats, and this is exactly why I don't like talking about personal things. I tell you I do my own laundry and now you know how many suits I have. You have no limits."

"You have five suits *and* sport coats? What do you do, Max? When you're not moving trucks north."

"Enough," Max declared. "Max Kendall has left the building."

"I studied French in high school and college," Daisy began. "And then I spent two years in Paris at Le Cordon Bleu. In Seattle, I belong to a French-speaking lunch group. There're five of us. Charity and me and three others who get together twice a month to practice our French. That's where I met Charity, actually, over ten years ago."

"How old are you?" Max asked, kicking himself afterward.

"Now *that* is personal." But Daisy smiled as she said it.

"Forget I asked. Really. I mean it."

"Thirty-five. I graduated high school at seventeen. And the rest adds up."

Max mentally bowed to his mom's intuition, then braced himself for Daisy's inevitable next question, which, of course, he'd have to answer because she had answered his.

Instead, Daisy reached for her orange juice, draining the glass.

"Well"—she glanced at her watch—"I guess I ought to get going. We should be docking in Ketchikan soon and I want to spend as much time on dry land as possible." She scooted her chair away from the table. "I don't suppose you're getting off. . . ?"

"Walking around Ketchikan for three or four hours probably isn't the best thing for my knee. But you'll like the town and especially some of the shops—" Max stopped when his brain caught up with his mouth. "Sorry."

"Actually, I can shop without spending a dime. Looking is almost as much fun as buying. And it's not like I need anything." She paused. "Actually, I need everything. So, are you going back to the cabin?"

"Naaah. I think I'll sit here and finish my coffee, then maybe go up to the solarium."

Daisy stood and Max politely followed suit. "Thanks for breakfast and I guess I'll see you when I see you."

It was one of those awkward moments where the best good-bye was less than obvious. Should he shake Daisy's hand, peck her cheek, give her a hug or—

"Catch y' later, Max."

She left before Max had even gotten through his choices. He watched her maneuver through the restaurant until she was out the door and gone from view. Then he took his seat, regretting that he hadn't done something to acknowledge their parting. At the very least, he should've insisted she take some money.

The ship bellowed its impending arrival in Ketchikan.

But it wasn't too late. They hadn't docked yet. Daisy would still be in the cabin. For Daisy's sake, he should give her the kind of good-bye she would remember. The kind of good-bye that would take the edge off her lousy trip. The kind of good-bye—

"Excuse me, sir?" The waiter held out a small pink envelope; its perfumed scent sparked his imagination. "The lady asked me to give this to you."

His spirits rising, Max took the envelope, was about to lift the flap when he realized the young man still stood by the table. He'd never paid out so much in tips, Max silently groused, handing the waiter a five.

Alone at the table, Max pulled the folded stationery from the envelope and got a dose of Chanel. He read the script, his spirits flagging by the final word.

He returned the note to its envelope and stuck it between the pages of his magazine.

Another soulful call to the passengers, and diners rose in concert. Soon the restaurant looked like a scene from a disaster flick. With Max as the lone survivor.

He relaxed into his chair, stretching his legs in front of him. He had a system. And it worked. So why rock the boat, make waves, go against the current? Why look for trouble, tempt Fate, spit into the wind?

Why fix something that ain't broke?

"Are you done here?"

Completely and totally, he thought but answered the waitress with a simple yes.

"Can I get you anything else?"

"What else could I possibly need?"

The young woman curled an errant strand of hair behind her ear, then began collecting plates and silverware. "Apple strudel?"

Obviously, the waitress didn't recognize a rhetorical question. "I'll just take the check," Max said.

"Be right back," she said, her hands laden with dishes.

"And maybe," he added before she completed her turn, "a very small piece of apple strudel."

Daisy could not believe her lousy luck. In one hand, she held Max's passport. In the other, the sealed manila envelope it was supposed to be in.

"This is what happens when you steal," she chastised herself. "Remember that, Elizabeth," she warned the turtle, who was plowing a corner of the cabin. Daisy put down the passport and envelope and crawled the short distance to Elizabeth. Lifting the turtle, Daisy looked into her trusting eyes, kissed her little turtle nose, then turned her one-eighty. Soon Elizabeth was off and, not running, exactly, in another direction. If only Daisy had someone who could pluck *her* out of corners.

Obviously Max didn't trust her, she thought, more indignant than the situation warranted. But what, exactly, did this sealed envelope mean? Did Max know his passport was missing—and she was the culprit? Was he now challenging her to put it back? Or had he only *suspected* Daisy's snooping—overlooking the missing document—and thus sealed the envelope to prevent her further prying?

Whatever the scenario, Daisy couldn't win. She had to return his passport. Somehow, some way, before they disembarked at Haines. He couldn't get off the ferry—at any port—without it. And to think she'd suggested he might want to join her in Ketchikan. Of course, that was before she knew about the sealed envelope. Still, how lucky for her that he'd declined.

Luck certainly was fickle. One moment it was lousy, the next good. Back to her lousy luck and the sealed envelope.

Examining the seal, she wiggled her little finger into the tiny space between flap and envelope, but there was no way she could pry the flap free without ripping. She was pretty much stuck with no choice—confessing and begging for mercy. She shuddered at the distasteful image. Besides, knowing how Max guarded his privacy, she wasn't sure of either his compassion or his forgiveness.

As her mind dwelled on her latest corner, she moved Elizabeth from *her* latest corner into the shower stall, where she left her with the first of her two cherry tomatoes. She looked at the remaining cherry tomato . . .

Another cherry tomato! That's all she needed. Or, in this case, another envelope. It was so obvious, why hadn't she thought of it sooner?

Her heart pounding with hope, she scrambled for her own suitcase, lying open on the sofa, and burrowed beneath her clothes for the manila envelope containing the information on Wild Man Lodge. And just that quickly, her hope was gone. Why must she label every damn thing?

She returned the envelope to its designated spot, then looked out the window. On the dock, half a dozen workers tended to the ferry's arrival while a flock of seagulls watched from the pillars. A hodge-podge of tourists—from one of the cruise ships, no doubt—milled about the dock while local fishermen walked past.

Her eyes traveled from one direction to the next and saw a town that looked, well, uncomplicated and inviting. Towering spruce crowded the hills beyond and tickled the underbellies of marshmallow clouds. Spots of brilliant color hailed her from flowerbeds and hanging baskets. She could practically smell the ozone. Similar to the semi-isolated islands off the Washington coast, Ketchikan portrayed a virginal inexperience with the seamier side of life.

She turned from the window and slumped on the sofa. Maybe she could find a job in Ketchikan, she ruefully thought, since once Max discovered her trespass, he'd surely call off their deal and she'd be wherever her fanny landed.

"How stupid *am* I?" She wasn't looking for a chanterelle mushroom. How hard could it be to find another manila envelope somewhere on this ship? Possibly the purser's office. And if not there, surely in Ketchikan.

That meant, however, that she'd be stuck with Max's passport for a few more hours. But at least he wasn't going anywhere. If she hurried, she might even take care of this problem *before* she left the ship. Then she'd have a couple of carefree hours in Ketchikan without a ticking bomb.

Relief washed over her; she returned Max's manila envelope to his bag and stuffed his passport underneath her extra pairs of panties. She closed her suitcase. Then she locked it. She set it on the floor beside the bed before thinking better of that location. She looked at the closet. *Out of sight, out of mind.* Just in case Max did come back to the cabin, there was no reason to tempt *him* with *her* suitcase. Not that he would snoop. Max would probably find the whole idea beneath him. And he wasn't that curious about her. Besides, as he'd said, she was pretty much an open book. Still, better safe than sorry.

With suitcase in hand, she'd taken only the first step when she heard the key rattling the cabin door lock. She stopped. The door opened and Max Kendall dwarfed the frame, looking very Max Kendall. Boyishly appealing, yet roguishly grown-up.

His eyes caught hers, then dropped to the suitcase in her hand before returning to her face.

"I caught you."

"Caught me doing what?"

"Caught you before you left," he explained, with a head cock after.

She relaxed. "I thought you weren't coming back to the cabin."

"I, uh . . ." Then, as if realizing he was still standing in the doorway, Max stepped inside and shut the door behind him. "I, uh . . . wanted to give you some money . . . for Ketchikan." He gently tossed his magazine on the vanity and reached for his wallet.

"No way, Max. Not in a million years."

Max grabbed her free hand and stuffed two hundred-dollar bills into it. "You can pay me back," he said, forcing her fingers closed. "With interest."

Daisy hesitated, feeling like pond scum for the previous hundred she'd stolen. Still, she was in a very precarious financial position. "With interest," she insisted. "And . . . thank you."

Max stuffed his wallet into his back pocket. "What I really . . . I . . . came because I didn't like the way we left things."

"Oh?"

"I, uh, thought we should have a better good-bye."

"Oh."

"Actually, I thought, *you* deserved a better good-bye."

"Oh?"

"I don't suppose you could put your suitcase down for a minute?"

"Sure."

"Y' know"—Max inched back as if assessing Daisy—"I think this is the least talkative I've ever heard you."

"Well, it's a little hard to come up with conversation when you're speaking Greek."

"Yeah, okay, maybe this *is* a little out of character for me . . ."

Her brows flicked up.

"I had apple strudel. I never have apple strudel. It's not my usual."

"You came here to tell me you had apple strudel?"

"The thing is . . . I liked it. For a change, I mean. Once. Not every day, of course."

"Max—"

"The truth is . . ." He stepped toward her. "The truth is . . . I feel bad about giving you such a hard time at breakfast."

"Ohhhh. This is an apology."

"No, absolutely not." Max retracted the step he'd just taken. "This is absolutely *not* an apology."

Daisy huffed. Normally, she'd take great satisfaction in Max's guilt and take equal pleasure in the banter that would surely follow. However, she was a woman on a mission, and she didn't have the time, not with Otter Bite hanging by a manila envelope. "Fine. Thank you for coming here *not* to apologize and for that apple strudel thing. And"—she momentarily softened—"the money. But I just don't have the time for whatever this is."

Once again he stepped toward her. "You're making this extremely difficult."

"*This*? This *what*? What am I making—"

"*This*," he interrupted, the word melting into her mouth.

The two hundreds floated from her hand to the floor. Then her arms wrapped around Max's neck, his body pressed hers, and Daisy was lost in a kiss she never expected to own.

Chapter Fourteen

"*This* was unexpected."

On so many levels, Max thought, looking down on the meandering part in Daisy's hair as she nestled against his bare chest. In the bed. Under the sheets. Naked.

If awkward had a moment, this would be it.

"Yep," Max agreed. "*Very* unexpected."

"But you know what's really amazing . . . ?"

That we're so good together? He relived the frenzied intensity of two people who couldn't take each other fast enough.

". . . that I'm actually in these sheets."

Max frowned. *That, too.* Twirling an auburn curl around his fingers, he took the opportunity to check his watch. He was wondering how to delicately move this moment along when . . .

"I suppose I should get going." She lifted her face toward his.

Max was caught off guard by how inviting Daisy looked with her tousled curls and flushed cheeks and thinking eyes. Had it been any other woman—less complicated, less troublesome—he might've asked her to stay . . . for just a while longer. Of course, Daisy would want to vacate these sheets as soon as possible, maybe even shower. So instead, he nodded and said, "Yeah. You don't want to miss Ketchikan."

Thankfully, Daisy had a southbound ferry to catch, because an affair with Daisy Moon would not end well. And it would end. For however good they might be in bed, out of bed was a whole 'nother story. And Max was not in the market for a bad ending. It was better—*for both of them*—to let it go now.

"But I want you to know, Max," she added, "this was the best *un*apology I ever received."

"It wasn't an ap—"

Daisy gently pressed her fingers to his mouth. "I'm sure you know this, but—" She rolled her eyes. "What am I saying? Of course you know this, I mean, I'm not the first woman to say this, but, really, Max . . . *wow*."

"It takes two."

Shyly, as if doubting the compliment, she smiled. Then she reached for his lips with hers and left a soft remembrance of what he wouldn't have again. Never. Ever. Unless he said something right then and there.

Silent seconds later, Daisy slid from the bed and demurely gathered her clothes on her way to the bathroom. She stopped in the doorway. "What are the five stars for?"

Max grinned. "I'm a five-star stud, baby."

"Seriously."

"Are you saying I'm not a five-star stud?"

"I'm saying you wouldn't advertise it on your arm."

"I might."

She smiled as if she knew everything about him—for instance, he wouldn't give her a straight answer—then she disappeared into the bathroom, closing the door behind her.

Max lay there for several indecisive heartbeats. Then he scrambled from the bed like it was on fire, jumped into his jeans, and jerked on his sweater. Pulse racing, he snatched his boots and splint. Hearing the bathroom door click, he hopped from the cabin on his good leg, slamming the door behind him.

"Max?" Daisy peered out from behind the bathroom door at an abandoned bed. She opened the door wider and looked around. "I guess he didn't want to talk," she said to Elizabeth, who was in the shower eating her tomato.

A little chagrined by his hasty departure, Daisy nonetheless felt sympathy for the man. What do you say after something like this; something that probably shouldn't have happened.

Probably?

She and Max were so mismatched it was like fitting a round peg in a square hole.

Okay, bad comparison. Because the one thing that *did* fit together—

Stop it! She should be grateful Max wasn't there for that awkward after-the-lovin', see-ya-later moment.

They'd have to talk about it eventually—*wouldn't they?*—but this temporary separation at least gave them time to digest this ... this ... anomaly.

"And that's all it is," Daisy insisted, brushing through her curls. An anomaly that absolutely would not happen again.

Finished attending to herself, she attended to the bed. Grabbing one corner of the sheet, she pulled the cotton taut.

Charity was right. Max Kendall was not a man a woman risked her heart on, although her exact words were a little more succinct. *Don't fall in love.* Not that Daisy was entertaining that. No, no, *no!* She was merely stating the obvious. For emphasis.

Daisy moved to the opposite corner. Speaking of sheets, Max absolutely knew what to do between them. Charity would say she had gotten lucky. But Daisy didn't feel all that lucky. There was too much going on in her life. The last thing she needed was an impossible relationship. Even if nothing was going on in her life, the last thing she needed was an impossible relationship. Too bad she didn't think of that before she ended up naked between the sheets with Max Kendall, *5-star stud.*

She smoothed Max's pillowcase. Pausing, she lifted the pillow to her face. And breathed in.

It amazed her that all men smelled like men and yet each was unique and distinct. Not that she went around sniffing men. But there were a few ...

Her father smelled of Old Spice and crisp cotton and expensive suits. Her first love, Bobby, smelled like Ivory soap and dirt. Of course, he was twelve at the time. Mark smelled like new books and old money—he was British. Alex smelled like leather and lanolin, bourbon and cigarettes. Roberto smelled of freshly baked bread, basil, oregano, and nutmeg. He was Italian, a chef, and absolutely yummy. And Jason drowned his natural scent with pricey cologne, which should've been her first clue. As for Max ...

He smelled rugged, like the wilderness outside her cabin window. Sunny and clean, with pinches of cedar and wood smoke and musk and all of it carried by a refreshing mountain breeze with a hint of ...

Another whiff.

... vanilla and honeysuckle?

She pulled an auburn spiral across her nose, breathed it in, then sighed it out. Before she knew it, they'd be finishing each other's sentences.

You're much too pragmatic.

"That's why I'm inhaling his pillow," Daisy challenged an imaginary Charity. She plopped the pillow in its place, followed suit with the other one, and pulled the top sheet over them both. A little smoothing, a little tucking, the bedspread on top, and she was finished.

Checking her watch, she shifted into gear. Wrangling her suitcase into the closet—just to be safe—she checked on Elizabeth still in the shower. After glancing in the mirror one more time, she grabbed her purse, found the two hundred-dollar bills she'd dropped on the floor, put Max Kendall on the back burner, used all her willpower to ignore a wrinkle in the bedspread, then smoothed it, and dashed out of the cabin in search of a manila envelope.

Chapter Fifteen

"Playtime over," Inga lilted, as only a buxom, blond Swedish au pair with cherry lips and an allover tan could. She rolled toward Max and plopped her chin on his chest as the ship's call reverberated through the cabin. Golden afternoon seeped around the closed curtains into the grainy dimness of the cabin.

With the second of two long baritone blasts, the M/V *Columbia* again summoned her passengers. Although she had the ship in sight, Daisy stepped up her pace. Soon she funneled into a boarding queue along with other northbound travelers.

"You have beautiful chest, Max. Very manly." Inga stroked the hairs with her fingers. "First time I see you I think *here is very beautiful man*."

"Ditto."

Inga lifted her chin from his chest. "What is ditto?"

Max looked into crystal-blue eyes that belied an innocence sharply contrasting with Inga's expertise under the covers. "*Ditto* means you have a beautiful chest, too."

Inga giggled. "You funny, Max. Maybe tomorrow we play again? *Ja?*"

"Maybe," he answered, surprisingly ambivalent. What the hell was wrong with him? This was exactly the kind of situation that suited him. Eager blonde. Fun sex. Light conversation. No commitment. Easy, simple, uncomplicated. So why was he about to pass on a second helping?

"Depends on my orders," he added solemnly. "I'll probably be working."

Inga frowned. "CIA is tough boss, *ja*?"

"*Ja*." Max spiraled a blond strand around one finger.

"Shoot leg and make you work. Not good boss."

"Well, in fairness, the CIA didn't shoot my knee. It was a Mexican drug lord." He released the strand; the curl fizzled.

"Max beautiful *and* brave. Five stars not enough." She pecked him on the lips. "Inga must go. Boss needs me." Tossing off the covers, she bounced from the bed as only a buoyant, buxom, blond Swedish au pair could. She blew him a kiss before disappearing into the bathroom.

What man wouldn't need her? Max thought about the gentleman he'd seen with Inga. Poor guy was probably wrapped around her little Swedish pinky. Which probably explained the Chanel veil draping Inga. When it came to gifts, men were pathetically unimaginative and traditional. How many bottles of Chanel had his own mother accumulated from his dad, who figured anything with a name and a price had to be good?

It was probably the same with Inga's boss. The way she'd fawned over him, Max figured he and Inga were an item. Who would've guessed she was nanny to his kid? And where was that kid? Max wondered. Probably with its young mommy while Daddy played with the even younger nanny.

A scream jolted Max from his thoughts; he shot off the bed and collided with Inga, bolting from the bathroom.

"Big bug in shower!" She threw her arms around Max.

"Is that all?"

"No," Inga said, her eyes wide. "BIG bug. Max protect Inga!"

Max unhooked her arms from around his neck. "Yes, okay. I'll take care of it." A few steps into the bathroom and he grabbed a wad of toilet paper to nab the spider he was sure to find. He looked inside the shower, jerked at the surprise, then started laughing.

"Inga, this isn't a bug—"

"Ms. Moon!"

Nearing the stairway that led to her deck, Daisy turned.

"Ms. Moon!"

Searching the faces of the passengers who meandered past, she saw Deputy SO Keller—all spit-'n'-polish in his uniform—waving at her.

"I was just coming to your cabin when I saw you." He guided her to the side of the corridor, away from the traffic. "How did you like Ketchikan?"

"Charming," was the first word that came to Daisy's mind.

"And you did a little shopping." A nod to Daisy's paper sack.

"Only postcards. I found a few bucks in my jeans pocket," she lied, answering his unspoken question.

"Lucky."

"Real luck would be if I got my Lexus back and new credit cards."

"In that case, Ms. Moon, consider yourself *half* lucky."

Daisy listened to Keller, feeling strangely ambivalent about the $1000 and a credit card from her Seattle bank, waiting for her in the ship's safe.

This meant, of course, that she no longer needed Max or his shiny red pickup. She could fly out of Haines, since she had no vehicle to transport, and with a few more connections, get to Otter Bite. She could forgo the five-day drive and possibly spend a day or two in Anchorage replacing some of her stolen belongings. This was very good news. She should be elated. Ecstatic. Turning cartwheels.

"Well, this certainly is good news, yes indeed," Daisy said with forced enthusiasm. "And I don't know how to thank you. Really."

"The captain and Chief Stone really deserve the credit. Once they realized how determined you were, they pushed hard to get things squared away."

"Well, don't I feel special."

"After the tough time you've had, you deserve a break."

"Yes, I do," Daisy agreed, wondering why she couldn't get one.

"So . . . would you like to get your money and credit card now?"

"Actually, if you wouldn't mind, I'd just as soon get it in the morning. I'm pretty tired and I'd like to think about my travel plans . . . now that I have some options."

"Of course. To help you—"

Please, don't help me anymore.

"—we have a number of brochures with flight information. All these ports have air service. I'm assuming, of course, you will be *flying* out of Haines."

"That certainly seems the prudent thing."

"If we can be of further assistance, let us know." A tip of his hat and Keller left her.

Daisy looked up the stairs that loomed like Everest. Should she tell Max the good news or keep it to herself a wee bit longer? Or should she forget to mention it altogether? After all, it wasn't any of his business . . .

Even as she thought it, she knew that excuse was wearing thin.

Then again, maybe Max would ask her to come with him in spite of her other travel options. She could share the driving and the expenses and they might have a really good time. *Or* . . .

Not.

The speed at which Max had left the cabin after their *whatever* you wanted to call what happened in bed . . . probably indicated how uncomfortable he was. She was uncomfortable, too. But not in a bad way. More of a confused, uncertain, butterflies-in-the-stomach, wondering-what's-next kind of way.

Maybe Max was right—they were two ships passing. So why not enjoy each other for the moment and when it was over, just say goodbye and walk away. She could do that. Sure, she could. She could.

I can, Daisy insisted.

"Of course, Max doesn't know I can do that," she mumbled to herself, taking the first stair. "He probably thinks I'm all smitten and ga-ga over him."

Smitten and ga-ga? The man sizzled and she was hot for him.

The point was, Daisy could be as carefree and breezy about sex as Max. She was the new Daisy Moon—*remember?*—moving on, taking chances, letting go. She would be fun and—

How had Max described Tina? *Easy?*

That's what she would be. Fun and easy. She'd prove to Max there was nothing Victorian about her!

As Daisy climbed the carpeted stairs toward her deck, she felt the vibrations of the *Columbia*'s engines as they pushed the ferry into open waters.

At the top of the stairs, she slowed and pressed the wall, allowing space for the passengers behind her to go around. In a matter of seconds, she'd be at her cabin and be face-to-face with Max Kendall. What would happen then?

*   *   *

"Get dressed and get out!" Max shouted, flicking on the lights. In a whirlwind, he snatched Inga's clothes from various locations around the cabin, then forced them into her arms.

"But I have no shower yet."

"No time. Daisy will be back any minute. You have to get out."

Inga had an armful of clothes but seemed in no hurry to put them on. "What is Daisy?"

"The woman I'm with, sort of, but not really," he said, trying to clarify in his own mind exactly what Daisy was now that they'd crossed into that landmine of sexual intimacy.

"Ah, Daisy is CIA partner," Inga said. "Your *cover?*"

"Yes," Max agreed, remembering the lie he'd told. "And she will be very upset if she finds you here"—with a pained expression, Max looked upon Inga's perfect body—"like this."

"But you say partner is gone."

"Apparently I was wrong," he said, wondering why Daisy *wasn't* gone. And she wasn't gone, Max knew, because no way would she leave Elizabeth behind. "Now, please"—he turned her toward the bathroom—"most beautiful, sweet Inga. Get dressed!"

"I think Max lie to Inga," she said as Max eased her into the bathroom and shut the door behind her.

"Well, duh," he mumbled. In the next instant, he was fluffing the pillows on the bed. Then he pulled the sheets taut and grabbed the spread, letting it settle before he straightened the corners.

It had been years since he'd juggled women, although this time it wasn't his fault. Daisy was supposed to be on a southbound ferry . . . wasn't she? Hadn't they talked about this last night at dinner? Isn't that why she'd given him her cabin?

Max struggled to remember anything she might've said, but all that came to mind was her discourse on table settings. Unfortunately, with his focus on Inga, he'd tuned out Daisy. Surely he would've picked up something indicating her change of plans . . .

Obviously not.

Then again, maybe Daisy had decided at the last minute to keep going north. Maybe—and Max started to sweat—maybe she had read too much into their moment between the sheets. Maybe she had decided to stay because of *him!*

In spite of his Catholic upbringing, Max wasn't particularly religious, but he was making all sorts of promises to the Almighty in exchange for a little help.

Max breathed. *Just calm down.* He'd tempted death too many times to count, yet Daisy had him cowering like a new recruit. He'd sort this out later—when he wasn't neck-deep in Sweden.

The bed looked reasonable. Not like Daisy had left it, all tucked and prim, but passable. And if he could just get Inga dressed and out—

"Holy shit." *He* was still naked. Surveying the room, he found his crumpled jeans by the sofa where Inga must've tossed them after pulling them from his legs. But where were his boxers?

He was just about to forego underwear when he spotted the wad of cotton between the bed and the nightstand. And lucky he did, because in the same locale was an empty Trojan wrapper. But only one. He scrambled to the opposite side of the bed and found the second incriminating foil. The contents had already been flushed.

Grimacing at the pain in his knee, he tugged the faded denim over his boxers and carefully zipped up. He stuffed the torn wrappers into his front pocket for a later disposal where Daisy wouldn't find them. Then he scrambled for his sweater, pooled on the vanity stool.

Fingers through his hair, another calming breath. "Inga, honey, how're you doing?"

The bathroom door opened. "Inga done."

"Wonderful," Max gushed, not really registering the sexy capris and the cute sailor top that had captivated him before. "Let's see if we can get you outta here."

"Inga need shoes."

The two started looking as if on an Easter egg hunt.

"Got one!" Inga proudly held up a stacked sandal.

"Here's the other."

While Inga strapped on her sandals, Max limped to the door, his knee aching from the various contortions Inga had required. But there would be plenty of time to ice his knee as soon as Inga was safely out of the cabin.

He turned the knob. Ever so slowly, he eased the door open . . .

Snuggled against the hallway wall, Daisy rummaged through her purse. Key in hand, she froze as the cabin door slowly parted from its frame. She caught a glimpse of Max. "Max?"

He froze along with the door. "Daisy." And then louder. "Daisy!"

Daisy left the wall and faced the door, bending slightly to see Max. "What're you doing? And why are you yelling?"

"Am I yelling?" he shouted.

"Yes."

"I think my ears are plugged up. I might be getting a cold."

She pushed on the door but Max didn't budge. "Will you let me in, please?"

"I can't move. I'm, uh, having a back spasm."

"A back spasm? Are you kidding?"

"I, uh, could use some help walking it off."

"Shouldn't you lie down instead?"

"No! I mean, walking always helps."

Daisy huffed. "Okay, fine. Let me check on Elizabeth—"

"I just checked on her. She's fine. But my back is killing me." Max eased the door open just enough to fit through. Hunched and limping like an old football player, he quickly shut the door behind him, then looped his right arm around Daisy's shoulders, leaning into her. She glanced back at the cabin, torn between staying or going, then together they started slowly toward the stairway.

"Did you like Ketchikan?"

"It was absolutely beautiful. There's a park downtown—"

"Whale Park," Max interrupted, then quickly added a moan.

"Are you sure you don't want to lie down?"

"No, no, I'm fine. Tell me more."

"The flowers were amazing. Geraniums, delphiniums, petunias. Absolutely beautiful. And I saw all the totems—"

"Totem Park."

"Actually it's called the Totem Heritage Center."

"Only *turistas* call it that."

"And I walked along the boardwalk—"

"Creek Street."

"—where all the whorehouses used to be."

"Where both fish and fishermen went upstream to spawn," Max said, reciting local history.

As they took the first step down, she said, "So is that where you went spawning?"

He smiled, enjoying the congenial moment, forgetting his ulterior motives. "Actually, they closed down the brothels in the fifties."

"Too bad."

"Yep, that's what the men thought."

"Now there are some cute little shops. For the women."

"And what did you buy?"

"Nothing."

"What's in the bag?" Max asked, nodding toward the large, flat paper sack clutched in Daisy's right hand.

"Just postcards."

"So you had a good day . . . ?"

She looked at Max, feeling none of the discomfort she thought would surely be there. "I did. I really did."

"You sound surprised."

"I guess, in a way, I am. This trip hasn't exactly been a walk in the park. It's always nice to find pockets of sunshine."

"That's Alaska for you. She's too grand, too beautiful, too wild, too intense, too laid-back and too awesome. Problems pale in comparison."

Daisy glanced into the cool, glacier-blue of Max's eyes and wondered if Alaska was only part of the reason for her rising spirits. "I suppose that's possible." After the last step, they paused for traffic, then headed for the deck. "How about you? How was your afternoon?"

"The truth?"

"If you can tell it."

"I would've had more fun in Ketchikan."

"Except for your—" Daisy stopped and pulled away. "Where's your brace?"

"I thought I'd try walking without it," he said, grimacing. For real.

"That's not very smart, Max."

Tell me about it. "Let's just keep going."

She again tucked herself under his arm and they went outside and into the wind. Her hair scattered. "How long before your back relaxes?" She winced as her curls assaulted her face.

"Once around the deck should do it."

"By the way," Daisy said as they headed toward the bow, "your sweater is inside out."

Chapter Sixteen

Daisy dabbed her lips with the linen napkin and laid it neatly beside her empty dessert plate. "Are you sure you didn't leave it somewhere?" she asked for the third time.

"For the third time, I didn't buy anything so I never used it."

"Then you must've left it in the cabin."

"But I didn't take it out of my back pocket," Max insisted.

"Maybe it fell out when you took off your pants."

"What makes you think I took off my pants?"

Daisy stared at him. "You took off your pants at least once today."

It was the first time either had referred to their late-morning *whatever*. They'd managed to finish their walk, return to the scene, and get through dinner and dessert without either of them so much as alluding to what had occurred between them that morning. Daisy had even showered and changed while Max lounged on the bed, icing his aching knee. Not once was there an awkward moment, until now.

"Oh. Right," Max said, with an expression on his face Daisy couldn't quite read. "But I'm pretty sure I had it when I left the cabin."

More like when you fled *the cabin.* "But if you didn't use it . . ."

He shrugged. "Maybe you're right."

"Really?"

"I don't know where else it could be."

"When we get back to the cabin, we'll do a thorough search. I still have the money you gave me. We can pay the check with that. I'll just finish my coffee—"

"I'm heading back to the cabin. I'm not going to relax until I find my wallet."

"Do you have your key?"

Max patted his front jeans pocket. His brows lifted slightly—that damn Trojan wrapper. "I've got it. I'll see you back at the cabin."

The evening sun still shone above the horizon, tinting the port windows orange and casting a glow over the restaurant. Daisy watched Max wend his way around the tables of first-seating diners, most with gray hair, although a few families with small children were also seated. Like she and Max, most diners had finished their meals and were leaving. It had been a little early for dinner, but neither she nor Max had eaten since breakfast.

And speaking of breakfast . . . Max's exit came to an abrupt halt at the hostess station. Daisy craned her neck. Waitstaff and diners challenged her view, but even so, she was sure it was the blonde from breakfast whom Max ushered out the door.

Her red velvet cake soured in her stomach. She hated these reactions that gave away her true feelings. No matter how much she wanted to pretend otherwise, she was not easy.

"Give it back," Max growled to Inga. Clenching her upper arm, he led her to a deserted nook.

"Max hurt Inga," she whimpered.

"Cut the crap and give it back. Or you'll be spending the night in the brig."

Inga smiled as if she understood. "Max strip search Inga, *ja*?" She pressed against him. "Max think Inga spy?"

"I'm serious." He squeezed her arm.

"No hurt Inga, Max. I do what you want. We go your cabin, *ja*?"

"What're you talking about?"

Inga cocked her head at him. "What're *you* talking about?"

Her speech was suddenly American. Out of sheer surprise, he released her. "So much for being Swedish."

She stared at him harder. "Yeah. Like you're CIA."

Max shook off his disbelief at being trumped. "I want my wallet."

"I don't have your wallet."

"I don't believe you."

"I don't care."

Max struggled to connect the dots.

"Look, Max, I didn't take your wallet. I'm just a bored wife enjoying a harmless fantasy. I figured you were doing the same."

"You're married?"

"Please don't tell me you actually thought I was an au pair. How dumb are you?"

Max wasn't dumb—his summa cum laude graduation from Annapolis proved that, not to mention his many subsequent successes. But since Daisy had come into his life, he felt like he was flying in fog with only a joystick.

"Look, Max, I love my husband," Inga said. "But he's thirty years older. Howard and I have an understanding. Which obviously you and your wife do not."

"She's not my wife."

"Wife or not, you don't want her to know about me—"

That was true. But why did it matter? There were no promises, nothing to imply a future. In fact, Daisy had said straight out that he was free to make any side deals with *whomever* he wanted. But that was *before* . . .

"—so if you want to keep this secret, take her to bed and do what you do so well until she forgets every suspicion. If you feel like confessing, find a priest."

Max smirked. *Nothing says love like lying.* "Advice for advice?"

Inga shrugged.

"I've seen the way Howard looks at you. This sex-on-the-side? It's not harmless."

Inga pulled back. "You're one to talk."

"Actually, I am."

Daisy nursed her second snifter of Grand Marnier. Should she confront Max with her suspicions . . . or turn a blind eye, as she'd done with Jason?

Of course, this situation was different. She and Max had no commitment, no promises, *no future.* They barely knew each other. It was premature to start making demands on him, let alone ultimatums. Considering she would never see him again after she got to Otter Bite, why was she entertaining this dilemma?

It was ludicrous, this idea of fidelity among strangers. And she, Daisy Mae Moon, would have no part of it. Max Kendall could do whatever he wanted and *whomever* he wanted, as long as she didn't know about it.

Daisy drained the last sweet puddle of liqueur, used a meal voucher for her dinner and paid cash for Max's, meandered out of the dining room, and ran smack dab into Deputy SO Keller.

Max closed his book for the fourth time. *Where the hell is Daisy?* He checked his watch against the nightstand clock—did that belong to Daisy? He refocused. Forty minutes was plenty of time to pay the check and be back at the cabin. So where was she?

His knee throbbed—like a steel drum. Easing out of bed, he retrieved a bottle of painkillers from his shaving kit, took one capsule, then washed it down with a palm of water from the bathroom faucet. He returned to the bed and his book, although the words on the page didn't register.

This was so unlike him . . . and he didn't like it. Of course, he could've just confessed his dalliance to Daisy. But then he wouldn't be lying in this bed. After an unfaithful fiancé, Daisy wouldn't be inclined toward forgiveness. Inga was right about confessions, even though this situation was clearly not the same as with Jason. Max and Daisy had no commitment, no words of love between them. They barely knew each other.

Still . . .

Maybe it was time for a stroll around the ship.

He rushed on the same clothes he'd taken off forty minutes ago. A few steps later he turned the doorknob and—

"Mr. Kendall?"

—jerked back.

Purser Smith glanced at the numbers on the door, confirming she was at Daisy's cabin, then looked again at Max . . . and smiled. "I guess you don't need that other cabin."

Chapter Seventeen

How sweet, Daisy thought, of sleeping Max. The soft light from the bedside lamp stole gently across his face and bare chest. A Louis L'Amour western had fallen to the side, atop the sheet draping his abdomen and legs. Even the sudden rattle of a lone snore and the shadow along his cheeks didn't alter her perception—undoubtedly clouded by the two snifters of Grand Marnier followed by the two drinks she'd had with Deputy Security Officer Keller, now known to her as Steve. Their chance collision had been serendipitous right when Daisy was feeling inadequate. But Steve had buoyed her spirits, plying her with compliments about her determination, tenacity, and pluck. Which any woman in competition with a curvy blonde really wanted to hear. Oh well. If she couldn't be beautiful, blond, and buxom, at least she was determined, tenacious, and plucky. *And* a good speller with a great vocabulary. Let's not forget that. In fact, Daisy could probably out-spell Max's blonde *sinistrodextral* and *dextrosinistral*.

Yep, good spelling and big words always keep 'em coming back.

But, in fact, whatever Max may have done this afternoon, he *was* back.

Daisy stared as if seeing Max for the first time, resisting the urge to smooth the dark hairs from his forehead and touch his scarred temple. The way she was feeling, it was better not to wake him. Better if he stayed on his side of the cabin and she on hers. Better if she put her heart in its holster and backed away slowly before anyone got hurt.

Ever so delicately, she lifted the book from beside his hip, holding her breath when Max briefly stirred. Then she set the paperback on the nightstand beside his wallet—*wallet?*—before switching off the bedside lamp. Only light slivers from behind the partially closed bathroom door intruded on the darkness. She turned toward the light.

"Hey," came the groggy voice. "Where y' been?"

"I didn't mean to wake you."

"Come sit."

"I was just going to get ready for bed."

"I took a pill. For my knee," Max mumbled, as if he understood her reluctance. "I'm harmless."

Daisy doubted Max would ever be harmless—especially in the dim light with his hair appealingly mussed and his torso invitingly naked—but she sat down on the bed anyway because she wanted to.

"What time is it?" he asked, sounding more coherent.

"About ten."

"Ten? Where've you been?"

"I ran into Steve Keller."

"Who?"

"Y' know, one of the security officers."

"Oh," Max answered, as if he wasn't really sure. He sat up and stuffed a pillow behind his back.

"I had drinks with him."

"Really?" Max suddenly seemed very awake. "Why?"

Daisy eased back at what sounded like, not jealousy, but disapproval. "Why not? He's nice. He's not married. He's cute. And he asked me." *And you were escorting the breakfast blonde out the door*, Daisy thought, but decided not to play that card.

"Isn't he a little old for you?"

"That's Stone. I had drinks with Keller."

"Isn't he a little young?"

"He's thirty-one. It's hardly a May-December romance. And it was only drinks. Why are you picking on me?"

"Did it ever occur to you that I might be worried about you?"

"No, actually, it didn't."

"Well, I was. And I didn't like it."

"Really."

Daisy sounded unimpressed. Max leaned forward. "Am I missing something here?"

One Mississippi, two Mississippi. "Where'd you find your wallet?"

"Uh . . . over there," he said ambiguously. "You were right. It fell out of my pants pocket."

"Lucky you found it. It's awful to lose important things."

After a few moments of uncertain silence, Daisy started to rise.

Max grabbed her wrist. "What's wrong?"

"What could be wrong?" She pulled from his grip.

"I don't know, but I'm pretty good at sensing these things." Sarcastically said.

"I'm just tired—"

"Then come to bed."

"I can't sleep in those sheets."

"You can sleep on top of me."

"Where thousands have been before . . . ?"

"Not *thousands.*"

Even in the dim light, Daisy saw his playful, cocksure grin.

"And you were there this morning and you didn't seem to mind."

"I *did* mind," Daisy said. "But apparently not as much as you."

"What're you talking about?"

"You fled the cabin like it was on fire. Doesn't really inspire confidence for an encore."

Without apology, Max said, "That's because *we* were unexpected; *you* were unexpected. But now I know what to expect."

"Yeah, well, I'm not sure *I* know what to expect."

"Meaning?"

"I don't like being juggled."

His brows lifted. "*Juggled?*"

"You know what I mean."

They held each other's gaze for a silent moment, the light from the bathroom casting alluring shadows, then Max said, "Look, Daisy, this thing happening between us, well, it's a little nutty if you ask me, and certainly nothing I would've planned." When Daisy looked pained, he hastened to add, "but I'm up to my neck in it now and *juggling* is not my intention."

"*Up to your neck in it?* Wow. Be still my heart."

"Hey," he said, his tone edged with anger, "I'm not making a bunch of poetic promises I won't keep. I don't know what's happening tomorrow. I sure as hell never saw *this* coming. Did you?"

He had her on that one. Never in her wildest dreams had she expected this conversation, let alone the reason for it.

Max leaned closer. His voice was soft and seductively sincere.

"Moments like this don't come around all that often. Don't throw it away because you're afraid it won't come again."

Her heart pounded; Daisy was sure Max could hear it. Should she mention the blonde? She didn't want lies, yet she feared the truth. Although neither would change what she really wanted *at this moment* that didn't come around all that often. But could she actually live in the moment, without any thoughts beyond?

She leaned toward him, breathing in the great outdoors—the cedar, the wood smoke, the musk—drawing her in, crumbling her resolve.

Max lifted her chin with his fingers. "*Permettez-moi de vous aider à se déshabiller.*"

Daisy twitched back. "You . . . speak French . . . ?"

"In a dozen different ways."

His words alone caused a spasm. Daisy gave up the air in her lungs and seemed unable to find more. Her eyelids dropped, her lips parted. Her accusation was on the tip of her tongue . . .

I saw you with the blonde.

But the words never made it past her lips, which were otherwise engaged with Max's mouth.

"Midori and rum," Max noted, after a long, lusty kiss. "Remind me to thank Keller."

With ease—and as Max had promised—he relieved Daisy of her clothes, and soon he had her between the sheets, pinned beneath him, their lips rhythmically coupled, locked in a moment Daisy thought for sure she could live in forever . . .

His good knee parted her thighs.

. . . Except, of course, she couldn't . . .

His fingers milked one nipple.

. . . Because none of it was real . . .

Her pelvis reached for him.

. . . It was all an illusion . . .

He teasingly pulled away.

. . . *Max Kendall* was an illusion . . .

She struggled against his retreat, gripping his back, feverishly seeking consummation, her emptiness screaming for him.

. . . And he would disappear like a magician's rabbit . . .

He slowly rocked against her until the sensation very nearly drove her insane.

. . . But before he vanished, Daisy Moon was getting hers. In French. "*Maintenant. MAINTENANT. **MAINTENANT!**"

"*Mmmm, bébé, restez calme,*" Max murmured against her lips. "*Ce n'est pas un sport de sang. Vos ongles . . .*"

Her eyes fluttered open. Oblivious to the intensity of her grip and the bite of her fingernails, she now forced their release as Max had asked. "*Désolé.*"

He looked into her face and smiled. "This go-around we're doing it the old-fashioned way. One . . . slow . . . inch . . . at a time."

That she didn't need in French. Or English. Or words. She only needed what Max promised for this one moment. "Shut up and do it."

And he did.

And he did.

And he did.

And he did.

And he did.

And he did.

And . . . he . . . did.

Chapter Eighteen

"You lied."

"Probably," Max muttered, his eyes closed. He lightly stroked Daisy's naked back as she cuddled up against him. "Be more specific."

Daisy gently burrowed her fingers beneath the silky hairs on Max's chest, lifted and burrowed again. "You said you were harmless."

He sighed, long and heavy.

Daisy lazily breathed in the rugged scent of him layered with her own soft scent, and basked in the thousands of pheromones sprinkling the air like fairy dust.

Max affectionately pressed her to him and in a low, sexy, sleepy growl, said, "You wouldn't want me if I were *really* harmless."

Daisy stopped her burrowing and scrunched her brows. Mulling that over. She lifted her head. "That's not completely true."

Max groaned. "Can we debate this tomorrow?"

"It is tomorrow."

"No, it's today."

"But today is tomorrow."

Max opened his eyes and dipped his chin toward Daisy. Light from the bathroom metamorphosed the darkness into a dreamy ambience. "Babe—"

Her insides flip-flopped. No one had ever called her *babe*. Never mind that Max undoubtedly called every woman babe. Probably 'cause he couldn't remember names. She still liked it. A lot.

"—I'm really tired and my knee is killing me."

"I thought you took pills."

"One pill. It wore off."

"Tell me where they are." Daisy started to rise. "And you can take a couple more."

"I don't need them." Max pulled her back. "I'll be fine."

"There's no reason for you to be in pain."

"They really knock me out. Just stay here and I'll fall asleep soon enough."

Daisy tried to get comfortable beside him, but couldn't quite. After a few minutes, she said, "The thing is . . . I can't sleep in these sheets."

"You're sleeping on me."

"Yes . . . but eventually I'll be sleeping in these sheets."

"You've been in these sheets for the last two hours."

"Yes . . . but I was distracted."

"I suppose I should take that as a compliment."

They lay together a few more minutes, Daisy really wanting to move, but Max's embrace keeping her from it.

"Max . . . ?"

"Oh Lord." He took back his arm and flung away the sheets. With a groan, he dragged his leg over the side of the bed and sat up.

A momentary fear gripped Daisy. "Where're you going?" She sat on her haunches and immediately felt the ghost of his erection.

"I'm taking drugs. I need something to dull the pain of this ridiculous conversation."

"I'm sure you mean that in the kindest of ways."

Max grabbed a pillow and playfully heaved it toward her. "Just put your damn sheets on the damn bed."

Daisy clutched the pillow to her bare breasts as Max hopped toward the bathroom and his shaving kit within.

Maybe now was a good time to try—yet again—to rid herself of this aversion she had to community sheets. After all, they'd probably been washed in very, very, very, *very* hot water, and bleached on top of that.

"They're clean," Daisy quietly insisted. She placed the pillow against her cheek. "They're clean," she told herself again. She breathed. Again. Her brows collided into a knot. She breathed more deeply.

"What're you doing?"

Daisy spun her head toward Max, who stood in the bathroom doorway.

"I thought you were changing the sheets," he said.

"I am."

He shook his head. "Do you really think *now* is the time to work on your sheet phobia?"

"It's not a phobia." Daisy watched Max grab his jeans from the vanity stool. "It's an aversion. If it were an actual phobia, I wouldn't be able to be in these sheets at all. Why are you getting dressed?"

"I'm going for ice." He grabbed the plastic bag he had used earlier to ice his knee.

"I can—"

"No! *You* change the sheets."

"Are you coming back?" She instantly cringed at how needy she sounded.

His hand on the door handle, Max turned toward her. "We're on a ship, Daisy. Where the hell would I go?"

It wasn't exactly the reassurance she'd hoped for. But what bugged her more was that she needed reassurance. And yet . . .

When the door closed behind him, her nose went back to the soft cotton, sniffing like a bloodhound. Was she worrying over nothing? But the gnawing in her gut—and the perfume on the pillow—told her otherwise.

Chapter Nineteen

While the sunrise fought rain clouds, Daisy made her way through a ship beginning to awaken; she was surprised, but nonetheless relieved, to find the purser's office already open for business.

"Twenty-four seven," the young man said. "In case of emergency."

Daisy stopped rolling her suitcase and set it on end. She put Elizabeth's carrier on the cropped-pile carpet. "I'm Daisy Moon." She addressed the man she didn't know—*Dobbs*, according to his lapel pin. "I should have a thousand dollars in cash and a credit card in your safe, please."

Dobbs thumbed through his clipboard of notes and papers. "Here it is." He looked up. "Could I see some ID? Driver's license, passport?"

"My driver's license was stolen, but I do have my passport." Daisy retrieved the thin leather-look book from her purse.

Dobbs compared the photograph with the flesh-and-blood woman before him, then he closed the document and smiled, returning the passport to Daisy. "Are you leaving the *Columbia* in Wrangell, Miss Moon?"

"Yes. I have a job waiting for me in Otter Bite, but I need to get to Anchorage first."

"You can certainly get to Anchorage from Wrangell, but it will take a few planes to do it."

Daisy had figured as much, and the thought didn't thrill her, but it was better than wondering who Max Kendall would next have between her sheets. And they were *her* sheets—technically, if not morally—because it was *her* bed in *her* cabin. Bought and paid for by *her*. She still couldn't believe that Max had actually invited another woman into that bed after he and she—

"It will take me a few minutes to get this for you," Dobbs told her. "I have to locate the officer on duty."

"No problem." She took a seat as he left.

Daisy glanced around the neat and orderly office, remembering the first time she'd come here in a panic. "Some trip, huh, Elizabeth?" she said to the turtle, who was buried beneath a mound of moss in her carrier. "Well, pretty soon we'll be on our way and this will all seem like a bad dream."

Daisy yawned and stretched her neck this way and that, trying to purge a bad night's sleep. Of course she'd put her sheets on the bed—no way she was getting back into those other sheets after she knew what had happened. It creeped her out. Even now. Just thinking about it caused unhappy goose bumps.

Which was why, when Max was safely in a three-pill drug-induced slumber, she left the bed and took a shower.

She'd considered confronting him about the breakfast blonde—and surely the source of the perfume—but then she decided on another tactic. A tactic that Max himself had undoubtedly employed a time or two. That meant, of course, that she'd have to forego her righteous indignation along with the satisfaction of nailing that bastard—

Daisy breathed, trying to release her anger.

Instead, Max would always remember Daisy Moon and wonder why . . .

So early this morning, after several hours of restless dozing, Daisy got dressed and packed. She wrestled with keeping Max's passport just to make things *really* difficult for him, but then relented in her fantasy for revenge, and used the envelope she'd gotten in Ketchikan to hide her prior snooping.

With Max's documents tucked safely back into his duffel and Elizabeth in her carrier, there was only one thing left to do.

She had to sacrifice her sheets, of course, what with Max still asleep in them. But they would only remind her of Max, whom she never wanted to waste another thought on. Plus, she could buy sheets in Anchorage. A new, clean, fresh, never-used set that didn't remind her of anyone.

She'd eased first Elizabeth and then her suitcase out of the dark cabin and into the bright hallway. She had lingered in the doorway, a block of light spilling into the cabin, to look at Max one final time, almost wishing he'd wake up just so he could see her walking out, but in the next instant she felt ambivalent. Before she could talk herself out of it, she turned and shut the door on Max Kendall.

"Sorry for the delay," Dobbs said, returning. He handed Daisy a small manila envelope and asked that she verify the contents. She smiled at the valuable piece of plastic that would take her away from all her recent mistakes and to a new beginning in Otter Bite. The crisp $100 bills were just icing on her cupcake.

"I guess you've had a tough time," Dobbs commented, as if he wasn't quite sure of the details.

"Mistakes were made," Daisy said, figuring he could get his answers elsewhere.

"If you could just sign this receipt . . ."

Daisy happily scribbled her name and then asked for two envelopes, which Dobbs obligingly gave her. Digging into her purse, she found near the bottom her small notebook and pen. Pulling them free, she quickly tallied the numbers. The total came to $122. Back to her purse, to the inside pocket where she kept her lip gloss and emery board, and where she now kept her money—or rather the money from Max—since she no longer had a wallet. She pulled out all the bills and began sorting on her lap.

She would return the $200 he'd given her for Ketchikan, less what she paid for his last night's dinner, of course, although technically the money had been a gift, so she could rightly keep it. *And* Max was getting her cabin.

"Let's see," she mumbled to herself. "Two nights without me . . . two nights with me is half that . . ." She scribbled on the paper: *Less the $200.* Taking the high road, but counting the $100 she'd taken from his wallet as payment for her sheets.

And minus the $122 for meals comes to . . . Daisy perked up. Max Kendall *owed her* $53!

With her bills and receipts, Daisy placed all the cash back into its envelope and stuck it in her purse. After jotting a quick note at the bottom on the small page, Daisy ripped the paper from her notebook, neatly folded and placed the page in one envelope provided by Dobbs, sealed the flap, addressed the front, and set the envelope aside.

On a separate piece of paper, Daisy carefully penned a note to Steve Keller, folded the sheet and placed it in the second envelope, sealed and addressed it.

"Could you see that the man in my cabin gets this . . . *after* the *Columbia* has left Wrangell?"

His expression reflecting unspoken questions, Dobbs took the envelope from Daisy.

"And could you see that Security Officer Keller gets this?" She handed the remaining envelope to Dobbs.

"After we've sailed?"

"Any time is fine."

As the *Columbia* proclaimed its impending arrival in Wrangell, Daisy collected herself and Elizabeth. "Thank you very much, Mr. Dobbs."

"My pleasure," Dobbs answered with equal politeness. "And Miss Moon?"

One step from the door, Daisy turned.

"Good luck."

Max woke to a hammer inside his head. Eyelids heavy, and groggy from his drug-induced slumber, he checked the empty space beside him. He looked for the time, but the nightstand clock was gone. Rainy daylight spilled into the cabin from the window, casting the room in a gloomy, one-dimensional pallor.

"Daisy?" The hammer pounded, only this time he recognized the source. Groaning, he freed himself from the sheets and shuffled to the door. He turned the knob. "Did you forget your—"

The uniformed man on the other side of the door lifted his brows at Max's nudity.

"—key?" Max finished, realizing too late that it wasn't Daisy doing the knocking.

"Mr. Kendall?"

"Yes," Max said, oblivious to his own immodesty until an elderly couple walked by and chuckled.

"Hang on a second." Retreating to the bathroom, he grabbed a towel and flung it across his offending appendage, very much awake, and tucked the terry around his waist.

"What's the problem?" he asked, returning to the open door.

Dobbs presented the envelope. "This is for you."

"What is it?"

"Miss Moon asked me to deliver it. Have a nice day, Mr. Kendall."

Frowning at his handwritten name, Max stepped back and closed the door.

Chapter Twenty

Mud splattered the belly of the Cessna 206 as it touched down on the rudimentary airstrip. With earth solidly beneath her, Daisy Moon sighed relief.

It had been a fifteen-minute flight from Homer to Otter Bite, but crammed into that short flight was some of the most spectacular scenery of her long journey, like traveling back in time—not hundreds of years, but thousands—to a world before man.

Epic mountains, white-capped against a royal-blue sky, plummeted into lush green valleys spotted with snow, then rose into furry forests of centenarian spruce, in turn giving way to icy, meandering streams pooling into shallow, mirrored lakes reflecting their mountain sentinels. And that was just the east coast of Kachemak Bay.

To the west, frothing and foaming in rolling waves, Kachemak Bay metamorphosed into a deceptive turquoise sheet before it reached the far shore fifty miles away and disappeared into a mist. Rising from that ether, the Alaska Range stretched north and south like jagged shark teeth, enameled neon-white with snow. Taking center stage, hulking Mount Iliamna loomed at over 10,000 feet; its plume of volcanic gas lingered ominously above its cone against a pale blue sky. A little farther north, dwarfed by distance but nonetheless magnificent, Mount Redoubt hovered like an apparition.

To the north, from where Daisy had come that morning, Kachemak Bay flowed into the relaxed, silty waters of Cook Inlet and Turnagain Arm, which corralled Alaska's largest city to the west and south.

Surprisingly sophisticated, Anchorage had been exactly the respite Daisy needed. Rather than arriving early in Otter Bite, she had spent a week in Anchorage shopping for replacements of her stolen items, making frequent calls to Charity, and just plain collecting herself for her next challenge at Wild Man Lodge. She'd even shopped for locally made wine at the Alaska Denali Winery, picking up a novelty bottle of Lime Margarita. To that purchase she added a lovely imported Pinot Gris found at a small wine shop called—she smiled—Grape Expectations.

At the Moose's Tooth she'd eaten the best wild mushroom gourmet pizza ever and bought a souvenir T-shirt for Charity. Two days later, she went back for their Hungarian mushroom soup. From the display in the entry, Daisy learned that the restaurant owed its name to a rock peak in the Alaska Range that looked like—no surprise—a moose's tooth.

From her hotel room window at the Captain Cook, Daisy had a view—on clear days—of North America's tallest peak, the mountain with two names: McKinley for those in the Lower 48 and Denali, as Alaskans called it. Googling the name, she discovered the mountain actually had several names, depending on who was talking. The Anchorage-area Athabaskans called it Dghelay Ka'a, or High One. The Alaskan Aleuts, who had numbered close to thirty thousand before the Russians decimated them, called it Traleika. Even the Russians had a name for it—Bol'shaya. In 1975, the Alaska legislature scrapped "McKinley" and officially named the mountain "Denali." Forty years later, the Federal government followed suit, making the name nationally recognized. But whatever the name is, was, or had been, the Great One rose 20,000 feet; in summer, climbers from all over the world attempted to reach its summit.

Daisy had purchased a mini version of the mountain in Artique, a fine arts gallery on G Street in downtown Anchorage. Entitled *Aurora*, the Byron Birdsall print was already framed but, at 12 x 22 inches, still small enough to fit inside her luggage. Since Myron Porter had stolen her art along with her Lexus, this Denali would be hanging solo in her Otter Bite home.

Studying the maps in her travel guide, Daisy had read about Otter Bite's nearest neighbors to the south, the coastal villages of Seldovia, Nanwalek, and Port Graham. Had she for some unfathomable reason traveled farther, she would've reached the Barren Islands and then Afognak and Kodiak home to the world's largest grizzly bear, the Kodiak brown. By then she would've been into the turbulent waters of the Gulf of Alaska, but still a Dr. Jekyll in comparison to the Mr.

Hyde of the Bering Sea. Neither for the faint of heart nor faint of craft, the brutal and defiant ocean regularly claimed the lives of crabbers, making the profession the deadliest in the world and the star of a television show.

But today in Otter Bite, Poseidon required no sacrifice. With the midday sun shining and a cool breeze blowing, Alaska seemed as docile as a newborn seal pup. Whatever Daisy might've felt about her epicurean exile, she could hardly lament its breathtaking beauty.

The Cessna rumbled past a dozen small planes, parked and tied off the strip. A sign over a little lean-to welcomed visitors to OTTER BITE, WHERE YOU OTTER BE. Next to that, an Alaskan flag—eight stars of gold, configured into the big dipper and the North Star, on a field of dark blue—fluttered and relaxed with the variable wind. Parked nearby was a late model Land Rover—that should've been Daisy's first clue—with the words *Wild Man Lodge* stretching across its doors, the *n* and the *L* obscured by Rita Jakolof, who leisurely leaned against the vehicle.

The Cessna braked to a stop and the propeller abruptly quit. The pilot opened the door and Daisy struggled out of the plane with Elizabeth in her carrier, following two other passengers who had the grace of experience.

"Miracle of miracles, you made it!" Rita threw her arms around Daisy in a welcoming hug that squeezed the breath from her. Nonetheless, Daisy smiled. It felt good to be wanted . . . if only for her mango chutney.

"Amazingly," Daisy agreed when she'd found her breath. Then she found it again, luxuriating in air as Mother Nature intended, without all the byproducts of a modern world.

Her thick braid of black hair falling forward, Rita bent over and peered into the small carrier. "This must be Elizabeth . . . somewhere."

"She's hiding under the moss."

"We'll meet later." Rita returned to eye level with Daisy. "Let's grab our stuff and get outta here. We'll have lunch at the lodge."

Daisy had only her suitcase and two boxes. Eight additional boxes with household items were still in Homer, coming over on later flights. But there were a number of boxes and packages for Wild Man Lodge in the cargo hold.

"Stocking up," Rita explained. Then, with the expediency of a longshoreman, she hefted each piece into the back of the Land Rover while Daisy climbed into the front seat with Elizabeth.

"I would've helped," Daisy said, when Rita slid behind the wheel.

Rita flicked off the comment with her hand. "I do this all the time." She closed the door, but before she started the SUV, the pilot hailed her.

"Hey, Doug," Rita called back through the open window.

Obviously happy with his life, Pilot Doug had a confident and continuous smile that partnered well with his dark glasses, blond ponytail, and barrel chest. *Just one of the guys,* Daisy thought, who probably wanted no more out of life than flying passengers and freight up and down the bay with a cold beer after.

"Got time for me tonight, RJ?" Doug cupped his hand over the window frame.

"Sorry, sweetie. This is Daisy's first night and I want to get her settled. Check with me later this week."

Never relaxing his grin, Doug peered around Rita at Daisy.

Even through his dark glasses, Daisy felt Doug's unchivalrous scrutiny.

"Down, boy." Rita started the engine; the expensive import purred. "She's off-limits to pudknockers. She's our new cook."

"Is that what you're calling 'em?" Still grinning, Doug rapped the vehicle with his knuckles. "Catch y' later, pretty Rita."

"What did he mean, *what you're calling them*?" Daisy asked after they turned onto the road.

Rita shrugged. "Who knows."

Daisy suspected she did know, but didn't want *her* to know. "If you want to go out, I'll be fine. I don't need a babysitter."

"Please." Another dismissing flick. "Doug isn't going anywhere. And I should warn you," she said, glancing at Daisy, "there'll be a lot of *Dougs* sniffing you out—"

Daisy reflexively cringed at the crass description and the un-wanted image it provoked.

"—I know you're coming off a bad breakup and your hormones are kicking in. But it's better to go easy until you get your bearings. There's an old Alaskan saying about finding a man up here: The odds are good, but the goods are odd."

Had Daisy not been rendered speechless by Rita's inference that she was in heat and on the make, she might've informed her that she was no more interested in finding a man than she was a bear. But by the time she collected her thoughts to say so, Rita was pointing out the highlights of Main Street, with buildings on one side and a bay on the other.

"That's the mercantile." They slowly passed a brightly painted building sporting a colorful sign proclaiming OTTER BITE MERCAN-TILE. "Jen and Bud Owens. She came here from Idaho a few years back and married local. He's a charter fisherman. Both on marriage number three."

Also belonging to the Owenses, the Kachemak Kaffé was next door, its odd spelling forced by the Kachemak Café in Homer and the Kachemak Kafé in Seldovia. Outside, two women sat together at a table drinking what looked like lattes.

"That's the local bar—"

LIGHTHOUSE INN, the crudely painted sign announced; it hung on a building which looked like a crazy quilt of construction leftovers.

"—And the post office. And the general store. They have the staples, but not much extra. We get most of our groceries in Anchorage and Homer. But fresh fish we get right out of Kachemak Bay."

On the opposite side of the road, its back to the sheltered waters of relatively tiny Sedna Bay, home to Otter Bite's marina, the last building—a house looking like it belonged on the historical register—had a mural across its front, protected by a wraparound porch. The colorful underwater ocean scene included otters, dolphins, orcas, seals, starfish, seahorses . . . a mermaid? . . . and a sea turtle. Daisy smiled, although she doubted turtles—or mermaids—were in these cold waters. The image reminded her of a Wyland. But the name of the shop baffled her. "What's FLuke Eleven-Nine mean?"

"Don't know. Felicity won't tell."

"Felicity?"

"The proprietor. She said something about Excalibur and the shop's name being set in stone . . . But then, Felicity is kinda an odd fish."

"You mean *duck*."

"Sure. Go with that."

They passed a small fleet of independent charter boats waiting for the start of the season, only days away. Floating on outstretched wings, seagulls screeched overhead demanding a handout from the men working on their boats. The breeze carried the aroma of the docks: a salty mixture of ozone and fish.

"That's our girl there." Stopping the Rover, she pointed to a sleek 75-footer, with a flying bridge sprouting whiplike antennas and the Alaska flag. "*Molly-Anne.*"

Molly-Anne looked scrubbed and speedy . . . and nothing like the barge on life support pictured on the website. "She's big."

"And sexy," Rita added. "Comfortably accommodates twenty. Men get hard just looking at her."

For that comment, Daisy couldn't think of a single response, but she winced at the scene she imagined. Middle-aged men, bellies over their belts, crotches bulging, gazing at this boat as if she were a centerfold. Then again, maybe she was. "Who's Molly-Anne?"

"The one who got away."

"Really?"

"Well, there's no Molly-Anne now, soooo . . ."

As they drove off, Daisy quickly inventoried the other, smaller boats. *LuLu. Alaskan Star. Mystery. Heavenly Daze. Maggie C.* And the last one Daisy glimpsed—*Sea Mistress.*

On the next hill sat a closet of a church, but well cared for, painted white with robin's-egg blue shutters, a gold, onion-shaped dome on top, and the triple-bar cross Daisy recognized as Russian Orthodox. A small crop of headstones and crosses sprouted from the manicured lawn beside it.

"Pretty little church," Daisy commented, as the sun gleamed off the dome.

"We like it. It's on the National Register. Once in a blue moon, a priest comes for services. But usually it's every sinner for himself. Two widowed sisters, Sylvie Atukaluk and Millie Charkoff, take care of it, but the door is always open and there's a candle to light if you have the need. Just remember to leave a buck in the cookie jar."

Daisy wasn't Russian Orthodox or anything in the vicinity, and most of her prayers were the short, *Oh God!* variety, but maybe a lit candle now and again wouldn't hurt.

Soon they were on a wooded, winding road with enough washboards and ruts to put a tank out of commission. When her curls tried to escape out the open window, Daisy raised the glass.

"Nice road," she quipped as they bumped and skidded around a muddy corner.

"The state comes over BT and AT to grade it. They're late this year."

"BT and AT?"

"Before tourists and after tourists."

Local lingo. Daisy filed it away.

Every now and again they passed a trail and Daisy glimpsed a house nestled in the trees, each rectangular box a clone of the one before.

Rita braked and swerved to miss a black bear who'd loped out of the woods then crossed the road into the woods on the other side.

Daisy gasped and twisted in her seat to follow the fellow's getaway. "That's a *bear*."

"They come out of the woods spring and fall. They avoid people," Rita added as if she sensed Daisy's worry. "But they love our garbage."

Daisy made a mental note not to hang out with the garbage. And to wear her bear bells, as recommended by her guide book. *And* to carry her giant-sized canister of cayenne pepper spray recommended by the hotel concierge who had chuckled at the lipstick-sized vial she carried in her purse to ward off muggers. Both bells and spray were purchased in Anchorage at a sporting goods store from a clerk who thought a rifle was a better bet, but nonetheless took her money.

"So, have the cops found your SUV yet?"

"Uh . . . no," she answered, still lingering on the bear and the bells and the spray.

Reluctantly, Daisy had confided to Rita about her *Columbia* woes—not her Max Kendall woes, of course—but she hadn't seen any way around her missing SUV and her cooking implements, since she was supposed to be arriving on this morning's ferry with all of that.

"And I don't think they ever will, but I've talked with my insurance company and they're sending a check to cover the loss."

"Well, you don't really need a car since there's no place to drive, and the lodge has a couple of Jeeps you can always borrow. Besides, it's better to tear up someone else's car on these roads than your own."

They shimmied around a corner.

"So how far is the lodge?"

"It's at the end of the road. About seven miles from town."

Occasionally the trees cleared on the driver's side and Daisy sighted

Kachemak Bay, then the road curled inland and the forest took over. She hadn't thought it possible, but the road actually worsened, narrowing into what could only be described as tire tracks. Yet Rita continued to drive as if they were on the interstate. One hole separated Daisy, who held Elizabeth on her lap, from the seat. "Jiminy Christmas!"

"It's like pulling off a Band-Aid. Gotta do it fast."

Daisy wasn't convinced, but it didn't seem worth arguing about. Besides, up ahead was a carved wood sign proclaiming WILD MAN LODGE. Roped to towering, rough-hewn poles, three flags stretched and fell in the variable breeze; flying tallest, the American flag was flanked by the Alaskan flag on one side and—was that Ireland's flag on the other? As they turned into the drive, dread of the unknown made her heart race.

Thinning forest gave way to thick, spring-green willows and budding salmonberry bushes, dappled with sun. At the end was Daisy's new home.

Constructed with spruce logs gleaming like honey, the tripledecker lodge stretched on either side of a tiered grand entrance ablaze with scarlet and salmon geraniums and soothed by an understated rock waterfall. The drive circled beneath a two-story overhang supported by massive totem posts while the carved hardwood double doors of the entrance could easily dwarf any member of the LA Lakers.

Rustic elegance, Daisy thought; it reminded her of the luxurious celebrity lodges found in Aspen. After a short pause for Daisy's awe—eyes wide and mouth gaping—Rita eased the Land Rover past the entrance, to the north and around back.

Daisy turned to Rita. "When was the last time you updated your website?"

Rita smiled. "Not what you expected?"

"Not what *anyone* would expect. This isn't even the same place."

"The cook's cabin is around back," Rita said.

"*Chef*, actually."

"Sorry. I thought we'd get you settled and then we'll go to the kitchen for a little lunch and afterward a tour."

"Great," she said, barely able to contain her anticipation.

The back of the lodge was no less impressive than the front, albeit more subdued. No totems, no grand doors, but manicured and tidy with an expansive deck, solid outdoor furniture, additional flowers, hummingbird feeders, and maintained walkways. *Hummingbird feeders?*

"You get hummingbirds up here?" Daisy asked.

"Sure. The guys like to sit out here and watch them."

Mulling that over, Daisy looked past the feeders. The view of Kachemak Bay and the distant Alaskan Range was inspirational. Each of the twenty guest bedrooms—ten to a wing—shared this same vista from their private balconies.

Daisy smiled at the rustic sign pointing in the direction of the beach; even in summer the ocean never warmed above forty degrees, a temperature only polar bears and sea otters found inviting.

"That path there goes to the hot tub," Rita said, nodding to the next sign. "A word of warning. Some of our guests like to experience it au naturel."

Daisy mentally grimaced at a repeat image of big-bellied, middle-aged, wild man wannabes, now naked.

"And don't be surprised if they ask you to prepare their *catch of the day*, whatever that might be."

"Whatever that might be?"

"The Japanese guests eat anything and everything. Octopus to seaweed. One time, Scully Jones rode his old horse, Buster, to the lodge, left him grazing outside for a couple minutes and when he got back, poor Buster was surrounded by a foursome with horse-chops on their minds."

Daisy didn't believe—

"Scully almost decked one of 'em. All because these guys have no boundaries when it comes to food." Rita shook her head as if the incident still amazed her.

"Every culture has traditional food."

"*Horse* is not a traditional Japanese food."

"No . . . but you eat whale blubber. I read it in my guidebook."

"Okay, first of all, *I* don't eat *muktuk*. I'm Alutiiq. But if you lived in the Arctic where all you had was whales and snow, you'd make do, too."

Daisy turned to her surroundings, allowed a few seconds for the air to clear, and then said, "This is incredible, Rita."

"I know." The drive veered away from the lodge and headed back into the trees. "This is where we live."

The drive widened into a parking lot; a dozen log cabins in the same honey-gold appeared among the trees with walking paths leading to them. Rita parked the Rover and cut the engine.

The gravel disappeared into the woods. "Where does it go from here?"

"The equipment and maintenance sheds are back there and the trash Dumpster and the greenhouses—that's why we've got flowers in May and fresh vegetables—and farther on, the road swings back toward the cliffs and the boss's house."

"Oh?"

"But don't go snooping. I made that mistake early on, and holy Jehovah!" Rita leaned into Daisy and spoke as if the trees had ears. "We'll sneak a tour when the boss goes fishing for the day."

"Is that what you call him? *The boss*?" Bruce Springsteen came to mind.

"That's what he is." Rita unlatched her door. "Let's get you unloaded."

Rita's cabin was on the first turnout off the main footpath; Daisy's was the third. In between, Rita told her, was the cabin for the guide-slash-pilot. The year-round groundskeeper also had a cabin, as did Jasmine, the year-round masseuse. The rest of the cabins were for seasonal workers who came in late spring and left in the winter. Not that it really mattered since all the cabins were pretty much the same. Several local employees had homes in Otter Bite.

"I thought *the boss* was the guide-slash-pilot," Daisy said after a reflective moment. "Isn't that what the brochure said?" *Although . . .* the brochure wasn't exactly an accurate source of information. And now she was again wondering—

"You've got to have more than one, especially now, with the boss out of commission."

"What do you mean?"

With Daisy's large soft-side in hand, Rita walked up the steps to the small wood porch and opened the door. "He had some freak accident a few weeks ago." She stepped inside with Daisy close behind.

Any follow-up to Rita's disclosure was set on the back burner as Daisy checked out her new home. Setting down the suitcase, Rita opened the blinds on the two large windows, and the room awakened with natural light.

"Living room, kitchen, dining room," Rita said, pointing to the counter and the two stools separating the living room from the kitchen. "Bedroom and bath," she added, her finger shooting from one darkened doorway to the next. "And furnace and hot water heater," she noted, referring to the closed door on the other side of the bathroom.

The air smelled of pine, which Daisy attributed to a recent cleaning. She set Elizabeth's carrier down on the little blue squares of vinyl flooring. Without having to change directions, she considered the living room. Nubby beige sofa, Naugahyde recliner, pine coffee and side tables, sky-blue rug and ancient television. Pine paneling throughout shone as if freshly polished. Shifting her eyes, she took in the kitchen: U-shaped laminate countertops in speckled blue, pine cabinets, old microwave squeezed into one corner, beige refrigerator, beige stove, beige dishwasher, and stainless steel sink. Daisy quirked her head at an outdated beige wall phone, which hung above the far counter and sported a cord like a curled ribbon that dropped down to the floor.

Picking up Daisy's focus, Rita said, "Local calls are free, but you'll be charged for long distance."

Who the hell would I be calling around here? Daisy wanted to ask. "I can use my cell."

"Coverage might be spotty unless you stand on the beach. But we have Internet. You can always e-mail."

Daisy took a fortifying breath. "This is . . . cute."

"A little smaller than your house, eh?"

A *little* smaller? The whole cabin could fit into her living room and kitchen—with feet to spare. Heck, the kitchen alone was smaller than her master bath—without the Jacuzzi. But what had she expected? Actually, this was better than she had expected given the website and the outhouse-sized cabins it portrayed. *What's up with that website?*

"Yeah . . . but it really is cute," she assured Rita. And herself as well.

She passed Rita on her way to the bedroom. She flicked on the wall switch. The etched glass ceiling fixture shed light. Queen bed, twin pine nightstands, twin lamps with off-white linen shades, one with a slight stain—*how does a stain get on a lampshade?*—matching pine dresser, and a closet. Daylight leaked around the edges of long, beige drapes which hid the sliding glass door—she presumed—to the back deck.

Rita peeked in. "You can dress it up."

"It'll be a cinch to clean."

"You don't clean. Housekeeping does that once a week. Kind of a perk. And the lodge has washers and dryers you can use for your clothes. Or you can pay Evelyn—she's the head—to do it. Personally, I like to do my own laundry."

"Great," Daisy said, mustering enthusiasm. She took a couple of steps out of the bedroom and opened the coat closet—in the truest sense of the word. If she took the broom and dustpan out, she might have room for one coat.

"Jerry—he's head of maintenance—picks up trash on Monday and Thursday mornings. You have a bear-resistant receptacle around back. But don't leave your trash there overnight. Take it out in the morning, on your way to the lodge. And if you have to get rid of trash any other day, call Jerry or just take it to the Dumpster yourself."

Daisy wondered where she'd store Elizabeth's carrier.

"I'll bring in your boxes."

Another few steps and Daisy was in the bathroom. She flicked on the switch; four frosted vanity lights illuminated the room. She sighed. Thankfully she'd not be sharing the bathroom with anyone; it was going to be a tight fit with just her and Elizabeth. Leaning against the doorframe, she sagged, as if the events of the past month had finally caught up with her in this tiny bathroom and were heaped on her shoulders.

Rita was already setting the second box on the kitchen counter when Daisy turned around. She made a feeble play to help, which Rita ignored.

"Change is always tough," Rita said. "Especially big change, and you haven't exactly had an easy move. Give it a little time. Before you know it, this place will feel like home."

Daisy smiled, hoping to God that bathroom never felt like home. A few months. That's all she had to endure. She'd put Wild Man on the epicurean map, reclaim her golden spoon, and then she could go home and live like a person and not a packrat.

"Here's your house key." Rita set it on the counter. "But every-one knows everyone, so . . ."

Daisy wasn't sure if that meant she didn't need to lock her door, shouldn't lock her door, or that a locked door wouldn't keep anyone out.

"I'm going to my place. Come on over when you're ready and we'll walk to the lodge."

"Great," Daisy gushed.

Grinning as if she knew the score, Rita shut the door behind her.

The first thing Daisy did was to take Elizabeth out of her carrier and let her stretch her short, stocky reptilian legs on the living room rug. She found scissors in a kitchen drawer, mingling with cheap cooking utensils, and slit open her boxes. Removing wads of crumpled newspaper, she set bottles and canisters of cleaning supplies on the counter and nabbed her rolls of drawer liners. Then she stopped, checked her watch, and changed course.

Elizabeth had crossed the rug to the television stand and was now paddling at the wall as she slowly followed the molding toward the corner. Leaving Elizabeth to her adventure, Daisy grabbed her suitcase, foregoing the wheels, and carried the rotund soft-side to the bedroom; the bubble-wrapped Denali print had taken more room than expected.

Heaving the case atop the mattress, she unzipped the top and pulled the print out from under a layer of clothing, setting it aside. Folding open the closet doors, she was greeted by a hodgepodge of hangers, some wire, some plastic, a few wood. A column of narrow shelves was to the right, a set of white sheets in one cubicle. On the top shelf, which spanned the length of the closet, was an iron and a small tabletop ironing board.

"All the amenities." Daisy turned and assessed her small bedroom with just enough room to maneuver. Most of her clothes were of the folded variety, but she hung up a fleece jacket and a classic navy dress and her robe. Three pairs of identical khaki chinos went on the wood hangers, with camp shirts over the shoulders. Everything, it appeared, could use a hot iron touch-up. But that would have to wait.

She ferried her cosmetics case and shampoo into the bathroom, checked herself in the mirror, and discovered the dismayed expression Rita had undoubtedly noticed. Yes, her current situation was a bit of a plummet from her glory days, but she had only herself to blame—well, herself and Jason, that deceitful snake. Speaking of deceitful, she wondered how many more women Max had finagled into *her* sheets after her departure. She could imagine his face as he read her letter. The outrage, the incredulity. She almost wished she could've seen it, except, of course, she never wanted to see Max again. Which didn't explain why he kept popping into her head with annoying frequency. And it didn't help to know that Max was only a plane ride away in Anchorage. Not that she'd ever try to find him. It was just disconcerting that he was in the vicinity. Which reminded her to call her attorney. He'd been out of town when she'd called him from Anchorage and his paralegal had no updates. Further, he was surprised by Daisy's news that Max had dropped his lawsuit. But at least that ridiculous pendulum no longer swung overhead. Max Kendall was finally and forever out of her life.

Chapter Twenty-One

Daisy found Rita on the back deck of her cabin, relaxing in a patio chair, face to the sun with her eyes closed. It was clear from the hanging baskets of purple petunias and the beds of scarlet geraniums and the used barbecue grill and the tabby cat stretched in the sun that Rita was a permanent resident and not just summer help. Daisy already knew that, but the accoutrements drove home the point.

"Your flowers are beautiful," she said, standing in the spring shoots of grass.

Rita dropped her face from the sun. "I can't take credit. Freddie—the groundskeeper—takes care of them. All I have to do is bring them in at night until it gets a little warmer. I'm sure if you asked—"

"No, no," Daisy quickly said. "It's not like I'll have the spare time to enjoy them. Is this your cat?"

"Samantha."

The unimpressed cat lifted her head and flicked her tail tip then returned to her nap.

With lazy effort, Rita separated herself from her chair. "If you're ready for lunch . . ."

"Sure," Daisy answered, although her tumbling stomach disagreed.

Rita parked the Rover in back of the lodge and she and Daisy entered through the deck doors . . .

. . . and stepped into the testosterone zone.

Wee-ooh, wee-ooh . . .

If a man's home was his castle, the Wild Man Lodge was his kingdom. Wainscoted walls stretched twenty feet to the ceiling, where wrought iron chandeliers flickered with the illusion of candlelight.

Gilt-framed paintings of bears and moose and mountains and sea—punctuated by an occasional sconce—hung against muted plaid wallpaper. Beneath Daisy's feet, irregular slabs of gray slate defied destruction from the heaviest of footsteps.

"Wow," Daisy breathed, walking forward.

"It's something, isn't it?" Rita said with obvious pride.

It was definitely *something*. "Is the whole place like this?"

"Pretty much. It ain't called Wild Man for nothing." Rita pointed out the stairs to the lower level—"We don't call it a basement"—where the gym, swimming pool, and sauna were. Down the hall was the billiards room with a wide-screen television.

"Twenty-four-seven sports," Rita explained. A few steps later, she pointed out the bar; Daisy peeked inside the dimly lit room. More chandeliers, barrel chairs in leather, cherrywood wainscoting, and wallpaper with mountains, log cabins, and moose. A wide-screen television hung in one corner. A gleaming cherrywood bar, sparkling crystal hanging above it, spanned the width at one end with a dozen padded stools for its patrons. On the opposite wall, a massive stone fireplace anchored the floor and climbed to the ceiling. The room evoked Arthurian sensations, although Daisy was *pretty* sure none of Arthur's knights sat around in padded chairs drinking from Waterford crystal and watching ESPN.

Rita pointed out the entrance into the kitchen behind the bar, then she led Daisy across the hall and through an arched doorway into the dining room.

Airier than the bar due to the wall of windows showcasing Kachemak Bay, the generous room still managed a masculine ambience with burgundy and forest-green striped wallpaper and butcher-block tables with overstuffed leather chairs.

Fit for a king, Daisy thought, or at least for men who wished to be kings.

Rita took her the length of the room, past the massive painting of Mt. McKinley—*Denali* now that Daisy was a local—and around a quick bend into the kitchen.

"Holy-moly," Daisy muttered, scarcely believing her eyes. From every direction, stainless steel winked and teased and tempted her. Whatever medieval fantasies Wild Man inspired, its kitchen was the new millennium.

Rita took a stool at the butcher-block island as Daisy waltzed around the kitchen, caressing surfaces and exploring drawers and cabinets, looking like a kid at Christmas. Her fingers brushed gleaming pots and pans hanging like culinary wind chimes above the griddles and gas burners. Her eyes danced across the black knife handles protruding from wood scabbards. She nearly hugged the refrigerator, barely containing her ecstasy over the hulking appliance. Her expression as bright as the silver surrounding her, Daisy turned toward Rita. "It's absolutely fabulous. And so *clean.*"

"How 'bout we eat?" Rita suggested, lacking Daisy's predilection for metal.

"Let me." Simultaneously opening the refrigerator's double doors, Daisy audibly sighed at the vast interior. After a string of similar reflective pauses—at the razor sharpness of the knife blade, at the walk-in cooler, at the half-dozen bread-makers—Daisy and Rita were finally sitting together at the island enjoying turkey sandwiches with lodge-grown lettuce and freshly baked bread. And drinking diet sodas out of Waterford tumblers.

"So . . . ," Rita began after finishing the first half of her sandwich. "You like the kitchen?"

"Mmm-hmm." Daisy nodded, her mouth full. She followed up a swallow with soda, then dabbed her lips with a paper towel. "It's fabulous."

"So, it'll make up for your cabin?"

"In spades"—she stopped—"I mean—"

"I know what you mean. It's hard to lose everything and start over. But isn't there a saying about losing everything to gain everything?"

Daisy was pretty sure that Biblical reference didn't refer to breakups or getting ripped off by Myron Porter, but she merely shrugged and finished her sandwich.

"So when do the guests arrive?" Daisy asked.

"There's a party of four coming next week, but we'll have a full lodge the week after for pretty much the rest of the summer and into the fall. You have a few days to finalize your menu and make a list of what you want from Anchorage. I'll set up a meeting with the kitchen help tomorrow morning . . . about ten?"

"Sure."

"You remember that we're open to the public for dinner?"

Which accounted for the forty leather chairs in the dining room.

And she also remembered that breakfast was served to the guests, but lunches had a limited, set menu and were usually "to go" for whatever excursions the guests had selected. The middle of the day was Daisy's downtime.

"This Sunday night we have a dress rehearsal for the locals—invitation only—and we always have a full dining room. But since it's free, no one ever complains if things aren't quite perfect. It'll give you a chance to work out the kinks."

"Kinks?"

"Well, you are in Otter Bite. And the boss likes to hire residents whenever possible . . ."

"Yeah . . . ?"

"When you add in the cleaning staff and the groundskeepers and the kitchen help and the waitstaff and the deckhands, we're the largest single employer in Otter Bite."

"Yeah . . . ?"

"The boss is very proud of that," Rita said, taking the dishes to the sink.

"Okay."

"Kinks come with the territory."

A slight twitch of an auburn brow was Daisy's only response. "So when do I meet *the boss*?"

"Right now," a voice growled from behind.

Chapter Twenty-Two

Daisy ignored the pounding in her heart and on her cabin door; she snatched her blouses and khakis from their hangers and stuffed them into her suitcase.

Her life had become a free-for-all, where everything was unfair or, by Machiavellian standards, *fair*—and nothing made sense and she seemed to be continually battling bad luck. But now wasn't the time for thinking. She had a plane to catch. Or a boat. Hell, she'd hitch a ride with an otter if she had to.

"Daisy—"

She jumped at the sight of Max, every hunky inch of him, standing in the bedroom doorway. "Get out!" she demanded, shooting her arm in his direction.

"I own this cabin."

Her eyes blazed. "Well, you don't own me."

"Actually" crossing his arms and leaning against the doorframe—"I sorta do."

Daisy sputtered air. "In your dreams!"

"We have a contract—"

"Sue me."

"I will."

Daisy paused, envisioning herself in front of a judge and explaining about the perfume on the pillow. "Why would you even want me here?" she asked, disbelieving the hope she had for his answer.

"I don't—"

She swallowed her hope and set her jaw.

"—Unfortunately, I don't have time to find another cook."

"*Chef!*"

"Whatever," Max spat back. "The point is, I need a *chef* and you need a job."

"Don't tell me what I need."

"A four-star *chef* doesn't come to Otter Bite, Alaska, unless she needs a job."

"I needed a change of scenery," she countered. "But instead it's just the same old view."

Daisy's opinion of him was obvious, but the reasons behind the ice still had him guessing. He paused and softened his approach. "We'll hardly see each other."

"*Hardly* is still too much."

Max frowned and leaned into the room. "What is your problem?"

"My problem? *My* problem? *You're* my problem."

"Yeah, I gathered that from your note."

"So that's it." She stepped toward him. "You can't stand that *I* left *you*."

Max came off the doorframe and threw up his arms. "Like I care enough to care."

Daisy shook her finger at him. "You may not care, but you *care*."

"What the hell does that mean?"

But Daisy wasn't about to explain the obvious to the obtuse. "Why didn't you tell me you owned this lodge? And who is M. K. Endall? And why is he on your brochures?"

Max paused, the typo on his brochures long forgotten, but not the 50 percent discount he'd gotten for the error. Besides, the brochures, the website—they were red herrings he barely paid attention to.

Daisy cocked her head at Max's silence as the answer to the puzzle revealed itself. "M. K. Endall. M. Kendall. Max Kendall." A head cock the other direction. "Why the subterfuge?"

"You always see the worst, don't you?"

A lifted brow challenged his contention.

"It was a typo, for Chrissakes. And no big deal since my repeat guests know who I am and new guests don't care."

"And you got a discount, of course. Is that why you haven't bothered to update it?"

Max rankled at the insinuation that he was cheap. It was just another variation of the Midori-and-rum argument. "Why didn't *you* tell me you had a job here? Why'd you hide *that* information?"

Daisy jerked back. "I didn't hide it!"

"Your note doesn't count," he said, remembering Daisy's instructions on where to send the $53. "And, by the way, I owe you zip! You should pay me for putting up with you. You are so boring, the way you go on about napkins. And don't get me started on your weird sheet phobia."

"It's not a phobia!" Daisy reined herself in. "I don't know why I'm even talking to you. In fact, I'm not." She turned and made an exaggerated show of packing.

"That's what I thought. You never told me you had a job here."

Daisy spun toward him. "I did too!"

"Where the hell was I?"

She held out her arms as if beseeching heavenly help. "Sitting across the dinner table from me!"

"I don't remember that."

Daisy rolled her head from shoulder to shoulder. "Fabulous. And I suppose you also don't remember agreeing to drive me to Valdez so I could catch the ferry to Otter Bite."

Max did remember *something* about Otter Bite, but he was pretty sure that was about the time the Chanel blonde had been seducing a breadstick. *Uh-oh*, Max thought, keeping his thoughts far from his face. Could Daisy *know*? But *how*?

"Sorry," Max said, allowing her no satisfaction.

Daisy planted her hands on her hips. "Why the hell do you think I let you share my cabin?" Making her point, she stepped toward him. "I traded my cabin for a ride. You agreed. We had a deal. Why else would I give you the bed?"

"How else were you going to get me *into* your bed? And as I recall . . ."

Her eyes exploded into green fire. Something between a scream and a howl escaped her as she went for his throat.

Max took advantage of her attack, snatching her wrists and locking them behind her as he corralled her in his arms. Then he did what he did best.

Daisy was unprepared for his lips and she was torn between what she wanted and self-preservation. She shared his kiss only long enough to collect her senses before pulling free of his grasp.

Eyes locked, there was barely space between them for Daisy to breathe; when she did, his scent filled her lungs. Her heart pounded through every inch of her and she feared she might very well explode.

She wanted him and she hated that she wanted him. She had to break the spell—

The sting of her palm against his cheek jolted Max's senses. His mouth tightened and his eyes blazed as he grabbed her wrist, warding off a second strike.

But Daisy was satisfied by her single slap. *Against lyin' cheaters everywhere*, she thought. "*That*," she snarled, her eyes locked on his, "is for *her* perfume on *my* pillow."

Chapter Twenty-Three

"Find another cook," Max snarled to Rita as he stomped with his one good leg through the kitchen and into the bar.

Rita looked up from the list she was making; Max hop-sprinted by her like a whipped pup. "Hey," she called, leaving her stool and chasing after him.

Max was already pouring his favorite scotch into a rocks glass when Rita caught up with him in the dark bar. She clicked on the ceiling cams and rose light dusted the polished wood.

"Shouldn't you be using your crutches?"

"Don't start."

"It's too soon for you to be stomping around."

"I mean it."

"So what's this *find another cook* crap?" she asked, grudgingly changing the subject. "It took me three months to find Daisy, and let me tell you, we lucked out. Thank God for that cheatin' ass of a fiancé—"

Max took a hearty swallow of Glenfiddich and grimaced at the burn.

"—or we'd be stuck with some hash-slinger. Just wait 'til you taste her cooking. Her mango chutney is to die for."

Max slammed his empty glass on the gleaming cherry bar. "Mango chutney! *Mango chutney?* Men don't eat mango chutney! Men eat raw meat smothered in A-1. What the hell were you thinking? Mango chutney!"

"Just because *you* haven't changed your eating habits for twenty years—"

"Hey!" Max poured another two fingers of scotch. "Just the other day I had strudel for breakfast."

"Well, excuuuuse me. I had no idea you were capable of such derring-do."

Glass in hand, he stopped it midway to his mouth. "Derring-do?"

"It was the March sixth word on my word-a-day calendar. It's the only one I haven't used yet. Opportunity for *derring-do* doesn't come around much in Otter Bite."

"No," Max said, slugging down his last round of scotch.

Rita opened her mouth, but words failed to follow. She narrowed her eyes on Max's left cheek.

He caught her focus and offered his right profile instead.

She softened. "Did you really fire Daisy?"

Max stared vacantly into the room. "She quit."

"Wow. She's got no job, no place to live, no place to go, had her car stolen . . . and she actually *quit*?"

"Yes."

"Man, you musta really done a number on her."

"I did *not* do a number on her."

"Yeah, that would explain her gold-medal dash outta the kitchen when she saw you."

Shaking his head at an argument he couldn't win, Max grabbed the scotch bottle by its neck—leaving the glass—and moved to a table.

"You gonna tell me about it?"

"She's certifiable."

Rita leaned on the bar. "Daisy doesn't seem nuts. She's just going through a tough time. That can make anyone erratic."

"Erratic would be an improvement."

Rita earnestly asked, "Why are you being so hard on her?"

"You just don't know her like I know her."

"Duuuh."

He shot her an unappreciative glance. "She has a turtle."

"I know."

"But did you know she's been lugging around that turtle for like twenty years?"

"Hmmm."

"The turtle's name is Elizabeth. *Elizabeth*," he added incredulously.

"As compared with *Napoleon*?"

A longer, harder look.

"You wanna tell me what's really bugging you?"

Max drank from the bottle, then answered. "If you must know, Daisy is the reason I'm in this brace."

Rita searched her memory. "Daisy is the garage-sale woman?" She stifled a laugh, but couldn't stop a smile. "The one who put you in the hospital? What're the odds?"

"Apparently very good."

Rita came around the bar and joined Max at his table. "Look . . . we both know your knee was just an accident waiting to happen. You've been putting off this operation for as long as I've known you. I'm not so sure this isn't a blessing in disguise."

"Daisy Moon is not a blessing, she's an albatross."

"You know what my grandmother Lupine always said—"

Max looked up from staring at the bottle label, dreading Alutiiq wisdom.

" '—ducunt volentem fata, nolentum trahunt.' "

Max wasn't an expert in Native languages, but that wasn't one of them. "Your grandmother spoke Latin?"

"And why is that so hard to believe?"

"Sorry."

"She learned it from the Anglican missionaries who came from Kodiak a while back. Didn't care for English much, but thought Latin was a hoot."

Max could just imagine the old Alutiiq, clothed in her traditional cotton *kuspuk*, sitting in her barabara in the glow of an oil lamp . . . reading Seneca.

"Want the translation?"

"No."

"But it's so perfect for your situation."

"First of all, it has *nothing* to do with this situation. And second, your grandmother isn't the only one who can quote Seneca."

Rita bunched thick brows. "What's Seneca?"

"*Who*, not what, and he's a first-century Roman statesman from whom your grandmother *borrowed* her pearls of wisdom."

Rita mulled that over, then said, "We're really going to be up shit creek if Daisy leaves."

Exhaustion laced his sigh. "We'll find another cook."

"Chef."

Max glanced at her.

"Maybe if you talk to Daisy, ask her nicely, *apologize*—"

"Shouldn't you be trying to find another chef?" His eyes warned her against further suggestion.

"Fine," Rita said, pushing back her chair. "I'll stock up on A-1."

He shook his head at Rita's dramatics and reached for the bottle.

At the door, she turned to Max. "I was wrong. You didn't do a number on Daisy; Daisy did a number on you."

Max stared at her. Hard. "You know who pays your salary?"

"Yeah," Rita answered before her exit. "The same guy sharing his afternoon with Glenfiddich."

It wasn't a flattering portrait Rita painted, and although Max disdained her assessment, it nonetheless gave him pause. He pushed the bottle away.

Had Daisy done a number on him?

He rubbed his cheek where her palm had struck. Maybe he could add *assault* back into his lawsuit. "And while I'm at it, why don't I just throw in the kitchen sink?" he quipped to no one.

How had his life become so messy? It had been over a decade since anything, let alone a woman, had catapulted him to the nearest scotch bottle.

But Daisy Moon was no woman. Daisy Moon was his albatross. His bad penny. The siren calling him to the rocks. His bug light. *Zap, zap, zap!*

Daisy Moon was his *nemesis*. And to think it all began so innocently at a garage sale. So much for chivalry.

Amazingly, even as his mother was pushing them together, Daisy had already been hired as the new coo—*chef*—at his lodge. It was as if Fate had a backup plan. If, of course, you believed in Fate, which he didn't, in spite of what Seneca claimed.

However, Max did believe in facing down his enemy. If you ran from one bully, you'd have to deal with a bigger bully next time around. And there were all sorts of bullies just waiting to lay a guy flat.

"But not today." Fists clenched, Max rose from his chair. "Today I strike a blow against conniving women everywhere!"

Chapter Twenty-Four

Daisy was propelled backward into the refrigerator by the tornado of Max's entry, by the energy whirling around him, threatening everything in his path; then she quaked, along with the walls, at the slamming front door.

"You used me!"

Daisy gasped. Not at the accusation, which barely registered, but at the power behind it.

Max moved toward her like a menacing lion . . . with a hurt paw. "I may have gotten a little on the side with Inga—"

A little on the side with Inga? Okay, that registered.

"—but you, *you* used me for my money!"

"I nev—"

"And when you didn't need me, you dumped me like last week's salmon!"

"I most certainly did not!"

"Then how come as soon as you got money and a credit card, you left?"

"How'd you know—"

"Purser Smith stopped by your cabin while you were having drinks with Keller."

"Oh."

"Oh?"

"I mean . . . so what?"

"*So what?*" Max asked incredulously. "Well, it's an interesting coincidence."

The wheels in her brain raced as she tried to mount a defense. "For your information, I wasn't even going to tell you about the money and credit card."

Max jerked back at her confession. "Really."

Okay, that sounded bad. "What I mean is, I didn't want to tell you about the money because..." She paused, knowing that the truth would give away her feelings.

"Because?"

"Because... if you knew I had money, there'd be no reason for you... to drive me to Valdez..."

"So?"

The seconds ticked and then her brain clicked on. "If you wouldn't drive me, that means I'd have to fly... and I really hate small planes."

"But somehow you overcame that."

Finding indignation, Daisy trembled with it. "You had another woman in MY BED!"

"What a crock. You're just looking for an excuse. And if I recall," Max began, suddenly recalling, "didn't you say I was free to have *side deals*?"

Daisy *had* said that. But... "That was *before*. But once you and I... after we..."

Max smirked. "You can do it, but you can't say it. *Sex.* We had sex. You and me. And it was damn good."

The memory fogged her brain. "Yeah, maybe, but... I *never* said you could have your side deals in *my bed*."

"My mistake. I should've asked to read the fine print."

Daisy glared. "This conversation is over." She started for her bedroom, the only haven in her small cabin.

"Once you start losing an argument, the conversation stops. And it wasn't your bed. It belongs to the ship."

She spun around. "It belonged to the cabin that I paid for. That makes it mine. And it was the same damn bed you and I had shared just that morning. Which *really* makes it mine."

"Tell me this, Ms. *I'm-so-principled*. If you hadn't gotten the money, what would you have done? Kept your mouth shut? Ignored the perfume so you could hitch a ride?"

Daisy stopped at the bedroom door; she hadn't considered an alternative scenario. "Well, I certainly wouldn't have gotten into *that* bed again with *you*."

"I see. No sex, but no problem using my truck and my money."

"It was a loan!"

"Loan or not, it was still my money and you needed it. Fess up, Daisy, you used me until you didn't need me. You're not principled, you're pragmatic. So what if I took someone else to bed?"

"We had a deal!" Daisy shot back.

"I don't remember fidelity being part of the deal."

"You can't even remember the deal. How the hell do you know if fidelity was part of it?"

"Well, was it?"

"It was *implied*."

Max rolled his eyes. "Oh. The *implied* fidelity. More fine print."

"Along with decency and good taste!"

He rankled at the insinuation that he had neither. "You were supposed to be on a southbound ferry!"

"Maybe next time you should concentrate on the woman *you're having dinner with* instead of some blonde three tables over. Then you would *know*."

"Say what you will, we had no commitment and no promises."

"Ah, yes, the male mantra."

"Did you or did you not say I could make—in your words—*side deals*?"

"Interesting. You don't remember agreeing to drive me to Valdez, but you remember *that*. And just for your edification, side deals no longer apply once two people . . . *you know*."

Unfortunately, Max did know. He softened. From exhaustion or compassion, he couldn't tell. "We'd known each other, what? Five days? We'd had one horrific date three weeks earlier. I'm suing you, for Chrissakes! How could you have possibly expected—"

"It was my bed . . . *our* bed. You had no right to bring another woman into it! And just out of curiosity," Daisy said, ignoring all of his variables, "didn't you think about the evidence left behind?"

Max remembered the speed at which he'd stripped Inga of her clothes, and the speed at which he'd tried to put them back on her. With Daisy's return breathing down his neck, he barely had the wherewithal to think about the Trojan wrappers, let alone Inga's perfume on the sheets.

"Once again, Daisy, I didn't think you were coming back. And I'm not Martha Stewart."

"Or Sherlock Holmes, apparently."

"Actually, the turtle registered."

"*Oh my God*. Inga was still in the cabin when I showed up that afternoon." Her words slowed. "That's why you wouldn't let me in. That's why you pretended you'd hurt your back." Daisy groaned. "How stupid am I?"

"If I'd known you were coming back—"

"Sure, I understand, no reason to let the bed cool down."

"That's not the way it was!" Although he doubted a jury would agree. "It was a misunderstanding."

"Boy, I'll say. I really misunderstood the kind of man you are."

"Yeah, well, you're a disappointment, too. You can't see anyone's virtue but your own. I'm surprised you can see your own reflection for the glow off your nimbus."

"If you think all this sweet talk is gonna make me stay . . ."

Max leaned forward, his expression hard. "I don't give a flying fig if you stay. But I'm not about to take the blame for you welching on this job. And just for the record, it wasn't *me* who suggested I share your cabin."

"You got a bed and a shower—"

"Oh, please. I can go weeks without a bed and a shower. Offered, I take them. But I won't trade my freedom."

"—and you got *me*."

"That was mutual, so I'm not buying a ticket for that guilt trip." He took a fortifying breath. "The bottom line is, I didn't need *you*, but without me, you and Elizabeth would've starved."

"I had meal vouchers!" she blurted.

"I know," he said quietly. "And yet you let me spend my money."

"If you weren't paying, there was no reason to eat together!" The instant she confessed, she wished she hadn't. "You can wipe that smug look off your face. I only wanted to spend time with you because . . ." But her brain was in knots. "Because . . ."

"Think fast," Max said.

Her face pinched. "Because . . ." Then, as if a light switch flipped . . . "Because I was trying to get information that would help me fight your lawsuit."

"Sure you were." He took his smug look to the front door where he stopped halfway through and looked back at Daisy. "On second thought, I will take the blame. You're fired!" Then Max Kendall slammed the door on Daisy Moon.

Chapter Twenty-Five

"Daisy?"

Daisy looked up from a bottom cabinet where she was taking inventory. "Good morning, Rita."

"What are you doing?"

"Getting acquainted with my kitchen."

"But Max said you quit." Rita took a stool on the other side of the island and put her elbows on the counter.

Daisy rose from her squat. "Can I get you a cup of coffee?"

"Uh, sure."

Daisy poured from a freshly brewed pot. The robust aroma wafted through the gleaming kitchen. "Do you take anything in it?"

"Milk." Still half asleep, she wondered if Daisy was a dream.

Daisy scribbled on a generous notepad. "Half-n-half," she said, before reaching into the refrigerator for a small carton of milk. She set it in front of Rita along with a spoon. "From now on we only serve half-n-half with coffee."

Rita stirred her coffee and sipped. "Mmmm-mmm. Great coffee. What's your secret?"

"Today it's cinnamon, nutmeg, and rum extract. But just a touch. And always, *always* start with ice water. And of course, freshly ground coffee. I wasn't sure what you'd have, so I bought some in Anchorage. I couldn't find a coffee grinder. Do we have one?"

Rita looked like she was thinking hard on the question. "I thought so, but the last cook—"

"Chef."

"No, Frank was a cook. I don't think he bothered using fresh ground coffee. The grinder might be in the storage room. I'll look for it later." She sipped her coffee again. And a little more. Ecstasy washed over her face. "Really good. So . . . you didn't quit?"

Daisy shrugged. "Yes and no."

"You can't do both."

"Not simultaneously, but consecutively you can."

"What?"

Daisy warmed her own mug with more hot coffee. "It's like having your cake and eating it too."

"You can't have your cake and eat it too."

"Actually, you can. First you have it and then you eat it. But you can't *eat* it and then *have* it."

"It's only seven thirty and my brain doesn't wake up until my fourth cup of coffee."

"All that caffeine isn't good for you, Rita. You should switch to decaf. Or better yet, rooibos tea."

"Tomorrow. *Today*, I need to know if I'm looking for a new chef."

"No," Daisy said.

"Yes!" Max countered, entering the kitchen.

Rita rolled her eyes and mumbled, "Oh, for pity's sake."

"Y' know, Max, you really ought to stop spying and sneaking up on people," Daisy said.

"I own this lodge. I can damn well do whatever I want. And I *fired* you."

"You can't fire me. I have a contract."

"Sue me."

"I will. For sexual harassment."

"*What?*"

"You heard me."

"I heard you. I just don't believe you."

"Well, let me refresh your memory."

Rita, suddenly wide-awake, darted her eyes from one opponent to the other as if she were following a ball.

Until Max looked at her. "I want to talk to Daisy alone."

"Oh, c'mon," Rita groaned. "This is just getting good."

"Out!"

"Don't you think—"

"NOW."

Rita dragged herself from the kitchen, taking her coffee with her.

Staring at Daisy, Max made his way around the island toward her. "What's this crap about sexual harassment?"

"Yesterday you attacked me."

"I attacked *you*? You attacked *me*."

"You have a very selective memory, Mr. Kendall." But her bravado shrank as Max neared her.

"Remind me," he said, backing her into a corner.

His energy pressed into her. "You were doing exactly what you're doing now—"

"Walking?"

"*Stalking,* actually."

"With a bum leg?" He made her sound ridiculous.

"That bum leg doesn't seem to restrict you under *any* circumstance." She made him sound . . .

"You went for my throat. I was only defending myself."

"With your lips?"

Max gripped the counter on either side of Daisy, trapping her. "Whatever works."

He was inches from her and close enough that she smelled the fresh soap scent lingering on his skin from that morning's shower, close enough to spot a tiny razor nick on his chin, close enough to remember why Max Kendall was absolutely the worst thing that could happen to her.

"I won't be intimidated."

"*Jamais de la vie, bébé.*"

"Or seduced," she added with unexpected resolve, her heart breaking into a gallop at the memory of their last French lesson.

His smile seemed to contradict her. But Max didn't test his presumption. Grabbing a mug from the cupboard, he poured coffee. "I'm not easy to work for."

"I doubt your standards are higher than mine."

His jaw tensed. "We have rules around here."

"I can imagine."

"Rule number one: Don't ever disagree with me in front of guests or staff. Rule number two: Don't ever disagree with me *period*."

"Oh, puh-lease—"

Max stopped right before his first sip of coffee. "You think I'm kidding?"

"I think you're being a prick for my benefit."

"I do nothing for *your* benefit."

"Whatever you say."

"That's right. Whatever *I* say."

"But while we're throwing down the gauntlet, let's get one thing straight. This is strictly business. You need me as much as I need this job—for the moment anyway. So keep your *French* in your pants, *bébé*."

Max's blue eyes actually twinkled, or so Daisy imagined.

"That won't be a problem for me. I just hope it won't be a problem for you."

"I can manage. But if I start to weaken, I'll remind myself what an opportunistic cheat you are."

His jaw tensed as if he were trying to hold back words. Then he sipped his coffee . . . and frowned. "What the hell did you do to my coffee?"

Daisy jerked back. "The coffee is fabulous."

Max took another swallow. "It's not coffee, it's . . . something else."

"It's *good* coffee."

"It's not *my* coffee."

"You mean, campfire sludge?"

"I mean regular, old-fashioned coffee."

"It's just a little cinnamon, rum flavoring, and nutmeg. Rita loves this coffee, and so will everyone else who isn't stuck in a culinary time warp."

"Wild men drink coffee that tastes like coffee—"

Daisy started to roll her eyes.

"—and they don't eat mango chutney!"

Halfway through their orbit, Daisy's eyes were back on Max. "That explains the case of A-1 in the pantry."

"Yes, it does. So don't try to turn my restaurant into some wimpy West Coast bistro. *Comprenez?*" Max banged his mug on the counter, splashing the coffee over its rim and onto his hand. "I want real coffee!" He marched from the kitchen, trailing smoke.

"That went well." How would she ever reclaim her Golden Spoon if she had to serve sludge and bottled sauce? She began to rethink her decision to stay. Not that she had many options.

She could go to Anchorage, but the upscale hotels and restaurants she'd want to work at would probably show her to the door once

Jason gave them an earful about her *violent* streak. And he would. Because Jason was still pissed about the golf clubs and the wide-screen TV *and* Max Kendall. It wasn't Daisy's fault that Max and the future Mrs. Jason Whittaker had known each other in the biblical sense. But Jason had it in his mind that the evening at Mama's had been a setup so Daisy could rub his nose in his fiancée's infidelity. In a way, it was both flattering and insulting. Flattering that he gave her that much credit; insulting that he thought she cared enough to go to the trouble.

When it got right down to it, the thought of Max and Tina probably bugged Daisy as much as it did Jason. If anyone had had a nose rubbed in their shortcomings, it had been Daisy. And Max had managed to do it again with the blonde.

"Just get over it!" Daisy demanded as she turned her attention to a second coffeemaker. Because having few options wasn't the only reason Daisy was staying—

. . . without me, you and Elizabeth would've starved.

Max had remembered her turtle's name. In a flash, Daisy had seen Max in a less jaded light. She could barely admit it to herself, that's how bizarre it was, but there was more to Max than met the eye.

It had taken Jason months to even acknowledge Elizabeth, let alone call her by name. Mostly he referred to her as *the turtle,* if he referred to her at all. Even Roberto, her very sensuous Italian chef, had disregarded Elizabeth, except as a possible soup du jour. Only Bobby had afforded Elizabeth the respect she deserved.

I should've stuck with Bobby. Where had the decades between then and now taken her first boyfriend?

Now there was Max, the man who . . .

Well, the list was long and varied, but in this particular case, the man who *knew her turtle's name.* A small but immense gesture and one impossible to ignore. An oxymoron. Max Kendall.

Then again, maybe Max was one of those men who finagled his way into a woman's heart by way of her vulnerabilities.

Her brows scrunched. Except Max didn't seem to be all that interested in her heart. In fact, he seemed genuinely *dis*interested in her heart—and every other body part. "Stop it!" She shouldn't be thinking about Max Kendall; she should be thinking about the Royal Academy of Chefs. Max Kendall and his antiquated taste buds were standing between her and her Golden Spoon.

* * *

"So . . ." Rita hedged. "Am I looking for a new chef?"

Max looked up from the papers on his desk at Rita in his doorway. "Yes."

"Yes?"

"What'd you think? We'd all live happily ever after?"

Coffee mug in hand, Rita ventured a few steps into Max's office. "But Daisy said—"

"Daisy can say whatever she wants. She's only here until something better comes along. And then"—Max snapped his fingers—"that's how fast she'll be outta here."

"I can't believe Daisy would leave us in the lurch."

"Get some ads out. Use my attorney's address in Anchorage for replies. Just in case."

"Just in case?"

"Just in case Daisy should stumble onto one of the ads. And Rita?"

"Yeah?"

"Remember where your loyalties lie."

Rita sipped from her mug as if she needed a moment to see Daisy as Max did. She shrugged. "Well, she makes really great coffee."

"Why don't you get on those ads?"

Rita started to leave, then turned back. "Almost forgot. Ferris Fitzsimonds called. Heard you were looking for a pilot."

"Hmm."

"You're not hiring Fitz . . . are you?"

"It's hard to find good pilots this late in the season. All the charters had their pilots booked months ago."

"But he's a drunk."

"Not when he flies."

"That's a fine line."

"No," Max said. "That's a bush pilot."

"Sounds like an excuse."

"It's a characteristic."

"*You're* not a drunk."

"I'm not a bush pilot."

"You were."

"And I was a drunk."

A deep furrow lodged between her brows as Rita tried to reconcile Max's confession with the man she'd known for seven years.

"Did Fitz leave a number?" Max asked, to save Rita from thinking so hard.

"He's staying in Seldovia at the Boardwalk Inn."

"Anything else?"

She shook her head and turned for the open door, leaving Max alone in his office sanctuary.

He returned to the pile of e-mails confirming reservations. Flipping through papers, he smiled at the personal comments from returning guests, but stopped at the reservation for his former navy flight commander, Peter "Knife" Newton.

Pete came every year; in between visits, Max received a Christmas card from him and the missus, updating their lives. No longer in the navy, Pete owned a very successful construction company with his son-in-law, building roads and highways all over the South.

And of course, there was always a Christmas card from their daughter Ellen. She was married again—although no one considered her first marriage legitimate—and now had a three-year-old son named Max and a baby daughter named Avery. A third child, if there was one, would be named Kendall.

"Knock-knock."

Max looked up from Pete's printed e-mail.

"Wow," Daisy said, stepping into his office of wood, stone, and leather. "You got a lotta testosterone going on in here."

Max nodded to the mug in Daisy's hand. "Is that my coffee?"

"Campfire sludge." Navigating between the plump twin leather chairs on the guest side of his expansive mahogany desk, she set the mug down near the sleek computer monitor. Her eyes traveled the length of the desk. "Aren't you missing a mattress?"

Max leaned back in his buttery-soft cordovan chair and let Daisy get it out of her system. As she focused her attention on his office, Max brought the mug to his lips . . .

. . . and gagged with his first sip. Tears moistened his eyes as he stifled a cough. But he would not give Daisy the satisfaction she wanted.

"Jacques Cousteau called. He wants his fish back." Daisy stared at seven impressive feet from tip to tale of a stuffed swordfish above the stone fireplace. Then, as if the thought just struck her, she turned to Max. "That's not from around here."

"It's from Mexico."

"I bet it was something to see when it was *alive*."

He considered telling her that it wasn't *his* catch when—

"I'm surprised there aren't more dead animals on your walls."

"I bet you are."

Her brows tweaked together. "You spend a lot of time in Mexico?"

"Used to."

"Anywhere in particular?"

Max paused at the sudden congeniality lacing their conversation. "Acapulco."

"So your T-shirt is the real deal, huh?"

"The real deal?"

"Not just a week's vacation."

Suspicious of conversation that had no purpose, he asked, "Is there something you want?"

Daisy started to answer, then sighed. "How's the coffee?"

"You could blacktop a road with it."

"Then it's to your satisfaction?"

"It's horrible and you know it."

The corners of her mouth lifted. "Y' know, Max, we both want the same thing, maybe not for the same reasons, but Wild Man's success works to everyone's benefit."

"But it's at the *definition* of success where we part company. I don't care what some magazine critic thinks about my lodge. I care what my clients think. I'm not in this for the *spoons*. I do this because I like it."

"But why not have both?"

"I don't want to be blinded by my own brilliance."

Her brows arced. "Blinded by your own brilliance?"

"I have work, Daisy, and so do you." He diverted his attention back to the stack of papers.

"Y' know, Max, compromise is the cornerstone—"

He hammered the desk with his fist; Daisy winced.

"Enough! Go do your job and let me do mine." He held out his coffee cup. "Take this tar with you and do it over!"

Mug in hand, Daisy left Max's office in a sizzle.

Chapter Twenty-Six

"He's an absolute jerk!"

In a comfy pair of sweats after a long day, Daisy paced the length of her cabin, stretching the telephone cord then releasing it to curl back into itself while she filled Charity in on the events, right down to the A-1 and the campfire sludge. This was the sixth time she'd called since arriving in Otter Bite yesterday.

"He's inflexible and rigid and uncompromising and . . . and . . ." Her face puckered as she struggled for yet another unflattering descriptive. ". . . *tyrannical*. His way or the highway. He's Otter Bite's version of Attila the Hun!"

"Daisy, breathe," Charity said. "And try to remember that this isn't forever."

Her best friend sounded distant. "It just seems forever."

"I know it's a challenge, but you can handle Max Kendall. A little charm, a little cunning, a little flirting, a little flattery. You might even get lucky—"

"Charity!"

"You admitted he was great in bed. And whether you like it or not, you're hot for him. Might as well use it to your advantage. A little bit of nice goes a long way."

"I can't believe you're suggesting I use sex to get what I want. What kind of feminist psychologist are you?"

"The kind who wants you and Elizabeth back in Seattle where you belong—"

Daisy glanced toward Elizabeth, making her way slowly across the living room rug.

"—And I'm talking subtlety and suggestion, not necessarily follow-through. It's up to you how far you go."

"So now you want me to be a tease? Whatever happened to an open and honest relationship?"

"That comes with vows." Charity paused. "More or less. Up until then it's all about making the right moves on the game board. You've got to use whatever power you have. Think like a man; act like a woman."

Daisy mulled that over, glancing around her cabin as she did, and imagined how wonderful it would be to return home. With a fistful of 4-star reviews and a dozen job offers.

Then again, with the money she was making, coupled with her savings, she might be able to swing a down payment on a small café of her own. Then she wouldn't need to kowtow to another man ever again. Too bad she had spent so much money on that lawsuit with Jason. She needed this salary; that meant staying in Otter Bite until the winter closing. Months and months of A-1, campfire sludge, *and* Max Kendall. If she thought her circumstances were bleak before . . .

"Not that I would consider it, but I doubt Max would come near a bed with me in it, real or imagined."

"Yeah," Charity agreed. "You have kind of dug yourself into a moral hole. Which is not to say you can't dig yourself out. But it would be easier if you hadn't already played your ace."

"But, Charity, he was standing there looking all hunky and full of himself, denying we'd ever had a deal, and suggesting I was the one who had seduced *him*! And it absolutely galled me that he thought he'd gotten away with the blonde. I had to let him know I knew."

"Y' know, Daisy," Charity said soothingly, "it's really not the same situation as with Jason."

"Close enough."

"But there really might have been a misunderstanding."

"Are you actually defending him?"

"Of course not. But there was no commitment."

"He had her in *my* cabin, in *my* bed!"

"I'm merely saying that sometimes men are not very smart—"

"That's your argument?"

"I'm not done," Charity snapped.

Daisy rolled her eyes.

"And don't roll your eyes."

Daisy frowned at the phone. It was just plain eerie how well Charity knew her.

"Men are not very smart," Charity repeated. "But they're not necessarily malicious. They're kind of like puppies—"

"Max Kendall is no puppy, believe you me."

Daisy heard Charity's long-distance huff. "The world to a puppy is like a new relationship to a man. It's both frightening and exciting. They explore and test their limits and their boundaries, and they don't always understand what's expected of them or what dangers exist. Sometimes they pee in the house. But with firm and gentle guidance, a little patience and lots of love, they can grow into faithful, loving, and loyal companions . . . who are housebroken."

A few seconds of silence, then Daisy said, "You may be right—"

"I'm the doctor."

"—I should get a dog."

"I wash my hands of you, Daisy Mae!"

"Do I need to remind you, Char, that I'm in this mess because I followed your advice in the first place?"

"What advice?"

"Have you forgotten my garage sale? You insisted Max was just what I needed. Had I followed my own instincts and *not* met Max at Mama's that night, none of this would be happening."

"Well, some of this would be happening."

"But not like this!"

"But it might be happening different. It might be happening worse."

"How could this be happening *worse*?"

Three raps on her door. Daisy stopped dead in her pacing and stared at the solid pine panel. "If that's some old guy with a sickle—"

"What?" Charity asked.

Daisy glanced down at the mouthpiece. "Someone's knocking at my door. I'll call you tomorrow."

The knocking repeated as she hung up the phone. She stepped over Elizabeth. Her heart picked up its pace as she turned the doorknob . . .

"Howdy, neighbor. I'm Ferris Fitzsimonds. But ever'one calls me Fitz."

The surf spilled across the shore, frothy fingers sweeping and stretching, reaching for the knife-edged sea grasses, chasing the bent-winged seagulls shrieking into flight before dragging back, empty and exhausted, into the ocean, leaving the sand polished and glistening in the evening sun.

On a cliff above, caressed by a salty breeze, Max relaxed on his deck and watched the intercourse of sea and sand.

In another week, this tranquility would be a luxury. Soon Wild Man Lodge would feel like an ant farm, with guests wandering here and there, leaving footprints in the sand while their voices mingled discordantly with the chittering of eagles and the ocean waves.

There would be laughter and cigar smoke, snifters of brandy and late-night camaraderie beneath a midnight sun, then early mornings, misty and damp, giving way to crystal afternoons of diamond seas and salt air and sated evenings and sore muscles and aching backs—

Max tensed in his lounge chair. "When did I become such an old man?"

"Old man! Old man! *¡Hombre viejo! ¡Hombre viejo!*"

With a grunt, Max trained his eyes on his teal-feathered companion. "Napoleon—"

"*¿Dónde está la cocaína?*"

"Napoleon," he began again, this time smiling at the parrot.

"*¡Policía! ¡Tiren sus armas!*"

"Okay, okay," Max cooed as Napoleon bobbed up and down on his perch, flapping his wings.

"*¿Dónde está el dinero?*"

Max pulled himself off his lounge chair, his knee throbbing from the sudden weight. "Let's talk about something else, shall we?"

"Cocksucker!"

"Bad Napoleon," Max said as the parrot grasped his fingers. "How many times have I told you not to say that word? I think we should fill your beak with a cracker."

"Cracker! Cracker!"

"Good Napoleon."

"Max is hot!" the parrot squawked as Max entered his house with Napoleon perched on his fingers.

"Yes, I am."

Napoleon hopped onto the kitchen counter, then waddled across the smooth granite surface toward the cracker jar.

"Max loves Jackie!"

Max slowly shook his head. The women visiting his life couldn't resist teaching his parrot that phrase or its reverse. And once a phrase was part of Napoleon's vocabulary, it was absolutely futile trying to delete it. All he could do was encourage his next random phrase.

"Max loves Tina!"

Holding a cracker, Max looked sternly at Napoleon. "If Daisy hears you say that—"

Max frowned as Napoleon crunched the cracker. Why should he care what Daisy heard? Or saw? Or thought? Or did? Or anything else, for that matter? They were done with each other. Ended. Over. *Terminado. Fini. Finito. Kansei shimashita. Finished.* And moving on.

"If only Daisy would move on," Max grumbled. *Mango chutney. Rum and nutmeg.* What next? Napkins folded like swans? Before he knew it, Daisy would have her silver spoons into everything. *And everyone.*

"Daisy loves Tina."

"Oh man," he said, realizing the mistake he'd made mentioning Daisy. He gave Napoleon another cracker and said, "Max loves Napoleon."

"Max loves Daisy," Napoleon said instead.

"Now that would be real trouble," he mumbled. "Max loves Napoleon."

"Max loves Napoleon!" the parrot repeated.

"Good Napoleon." Max gave him another cracker as the phone rang.

Rita was on the other end, letting him know that Fitz had arrived, she'd sent him to his cabin, and she was off the clock.

Max liked Fitz. The kid was smart and had potential. If he didn't self-destruct before he realized it. But people made their own choices and a person could do only so much to help another. Still, a little fear of God often went a long way.

Max gave Napoleon one more cracker then headed for the front door. Hand on the knob—

"Max loves Daisy!"

—Max groaned, then left the loud-beaked parrot behind.

"I like your picture," Fitz said of the lone print.

In the Naugahyde chair opposite Fitz on the sofa, Daisy looked at Denali as if she hadn't been sure what print. "Thanks. I got it in An-chorage."

Ferris Fitzsimonds was a couple years younger than Daisy, originally from Montana, and had been kicking around Alaska for the last eight years, ever since he'd earned his commercial pilot's license. He was the youngest of five boys, three of whom were still back in Montana working the family ranch—"I had t' get outta there." His youngest brother, Martin—Marty, for short—had died years back in a hunting accident on July Fourth. Fitz didn't say it, but Daisy could tell that the loss lingered.

Ferris had been his grandfather's name on his mother's side and Fitz had given his share of black eyes because of it. Which explained his nickname *Fitz*. Apart from that, he had a shy smile and an infectious twinkle in dark eyes on a sweet face that seemed incongruous with a five-o'clock shadow. Tall and lanky, he wore his Levi's tight and his boots pointed and sported a well-cared-for silver buckle on his belt, won for bull riding ten years earlier.

"We called 'im *the old man*," Fitz said, accepting his third refill of wine from the bottle he had brought. "'Cause he was older than most bulls on the circuit and 'cause he made old men out of us young'uns."

There it was again, that shy smile. Daisy sipped from her first glass of salmonberry wine and smiled back.

It would've taken real effort not to like Fitz. The man was open and honest and self-effacing and, borrowing from Charity, puppy-like, although Daisy sensed something simmering beneath the twinkle and the smile. However, compared to Max Kendall and his suit of armor, Ferris Fitzsimonds was naked as a jaybird, his life an open book.

"Is that your turtle?" Fitz asked, oblivious to the obvious.

Without Daisy realizing it, Elizabeth had made a U-turn from the kitchen and returned to the living room.

"Her name's Elizabeth."

Fitz bent over and cocked his head at the turtle stretching her neck toward the cowboy. "Well, howdy, Elizabeth. Ain't you a fine-looking gal." He gently reached a finger toward her and touched her nose.

"Wow," Daisy said, impressed that Elizabeth didn't shrink into her shell. "She likes you."

"Me and critters get along pretty good. It's people I have problems with."

"I don't see that."

Fitz shrugged. "Well, I suppose I've roped enough of your evening." He downed the remaining wine in his glass. "Unless you need help unpacking." He nodded toward the stack of unopened boxes that had arrived not too long before Fitz. "Seeing as how I made you dig in there to find these glasses."

"That's really sweet, but it won't take long to unpack and I had to find these glasses eventually. Besides, you brought the wine."

"I hope it was okay. I mean, I know you're a fancy chef from Seattle and the Seldovia general store don't carry that Don Perryman guy—"

Daisy kept a straight face.

"—and I'm pretty much a Wild Turkey man, so . . ."

"It was an excellent wine," she embellished, picking up the bottle. "I had no idea there were wineries in Alaska." She studied the sketched label of a brown bear, a mountain, a kayaker and . . . a Russian Orthodox church? "Kodiak Island Winery . . . I'll have to remember that."

"They have blueberry and raspberry, too—"

A sudden flashback of Boone's Farm and her senior prom.

"—but I thought you'd like something really Alaskan. Otter Bite has salmonberries, y' know."

"I do." She cocked her head at Fitz. "You said you got this in Seldovia? Before you came here? But how did you know about me?"

Fitz grinned. "Shoot, Daisy, ever'one from Homer to Nanwalek knows about you."

That was a bit unsettling.

"You're big news. 'Course, anything that happens out the ordinary round here is big news. It's local entertainment." Fitz rose and maneuvered around the boxes to leave his glass in the sink. "But don't worry about it," he added, heading for the door. "Soon enough you'll be as local as the yokels."

That was a sobering thought. Daisy put down her wine on the coffee table and joined Fitz at the door. "Thanks for coming over. And for the wine. It was very thoughtful."

"Well, I have to give my mama credit. It's her advice I'm following—"

Wow, Daisy thought, a man who follows his mom's advice. And isn't embarrassed to say so.

"—If she told me once, she told me a hundred times. 'Ferris, wherever you hang your hat, make nice with the cook.'"

Daisy's smile was spontaneous—in spite of the *cook* reference—remaining even after Fitz had thanked her for her hospitality and made a beeline for his cabin. He waved to her at his front door and she waved back. After he disappeared into his cabin, she turned for her door but stopped short. Her boxes could wait. The evening called to her and since it was only—Daisy could scarcely believe her watch—nine o'clock, she answered.

Low in the sky, the sun had not yet dropped to the horizon, which meant she had time for a short walk before dusk. She grabbed a jacket, stepped off her porch, then made a one-eighty back inside to find her bear bells and king-sized pepper spray.

His knee throbbing, Max chastised himself for walking to Fitz's cabin instead of taking his truck. At the very least, he should've brought his crutches, although following a dirt path through the woods using crutches was no easy task either. It was just damn hard getting used to the idea of limitations, even temporary ones, but if he didn't start heeding his doctor's advice—which up 'til now he'd followed sparingly—he feared this splint might become a permanent fixture. Acknowledging that, Max found a stump in an island of crusted spring snow and he sat, stretching his injured leg and feeling relief as the throbbing subsided.

After a few more minutes of rest, and with dusk descending, Max decided it best to head home. The distance back was shorter than the distance forward, and sacrificing his knee for Fitz was just plain dumb. Wishing he'd come to that conclusion *before* he'd left his house, he hefted himself off the stump, took two steps forward and stopped in his tracks. He waited, unmoving, training his eyes a hundred yards down the trail. Soon enough, his suspicions were confirmed as the black blotch ambled a dozen steps toward him.

Far from being alarmed, Max merely looked around for an intimidating tree branch should he need a defense. But the scenario wasn't likely. Yogi was easygoing and, like most bears—even the dreaded grizzlies—avoided confrontations. With poor eyesight but a keen sense of smell, Yogi most likely hadn't realized Max's presence. Which explained why the bear continued in his direction.

"Yogi! Yogi!" Max shouted, waving his arms in an arc. "Go away, buddy!"

The bear stopped. He thrust his nose in the air and raised himself on his hind legs.

"It's me, Yogi! Off y' go!"

But the bear stayed in the air.

"Yogi!" Max shouted sternly. "Go!"

The bear's front feet landed on the ground, but, typical of a bear who'd grown accustomed to people, he showed no intention of surrendering the path.

Max could continue his current course, relying on the assumption that Yogi would give way. But bears, however predictable, could be very *un*predictable, especially in the spring when they were hungry after a long winter. Wild Man Lodge had been sharing these woods with Yogi for years and had never had a serious encounter, but that had been due as much to Max's diligence in educating his staff and guests as it was to Yogi's good nature.

Besides, thought Max as Yogi shredded a rotting log in search of grubs, even those with the kindest of dispositions had bad days, and that went for bears as well. Why risk being on the receiving end of those claws?

However, that meant going forward to the staff cabins. Rita could drive him home, bitching all the while that she was off the clock. And for the next week she'd peck and hover like a mother hen for not taking care of his knee. He'd rather tangle with Yogi, thank you very much.

That left him one option. The woods.

Still early in the season, the alders and willows had months before they matured and created an unfriendly thicket between the trunks of hundred-year-old spruce. The thorny devil's club was still low to the ground and tame, while patches of snow kept winter alive. Tonight, with a little effort and a few snags, he could still get through and cross over to the greenhouses and the adjacent driveway. From there he could get home. It was longer than the direct route through Yogi, but better than putting up with insufferable Rita, his only other choice. But just for the hell of it, he gave Yogi another go . . .

A shout stopped Daisy as she walked past the greenhouses. She looked back from where she'd come, then forward to where she was going, seeing nothing and no one. She started walking. With each step of her right leg, the bells that wrapped around her ankle happily sang.

The shout came again. And another. She stopped to quiet the interference of her bells. She frowned at the woods on either side of the road, first to her left and then to her right. She waited. For several minutes, it seemed, then she gingerly took a step. *Tinkle* . . .

She stopped. Had someone called *yogi*? She looked to the woods behind the greenhouses from where she was almost positive the shouts had come.

She quickly crossed between the greenhouses to the edge of the woods.

Tinkle-tinkle-tinkle-tinkle-tinkle. And stopped. She jerked back at what she heard. *Yogigo*? What did *yogigo* mean? A call for help, perhaps? Or a warning? In Japanese, maybe?

Had guests arrived today? Were they lost trying to find the hot tub? Or maybe it was a new employee like herself who didn't know the lay of the land—

There it was again! Only one voice. One *stern* voice. Maybe even a little angry. *Yogigo*!

Daisy knew some Japanese—mostly of the food variety—but also a few words of conversation that might be an advantage in this situation. But how many *bears* spoke Japanese?

Should she get help? Or first go to the source of the shouts? Was there time? What if this voice was attached to an injured body? What if, by the time Daisy had summoned Rita, the voice was still? She stared into the woods.

Somewhere in Daisy's past, she'd read something about not staring too deeply into the woods for fear of what you might see. She suspected that was a metaphor, but with dusk descending and the trees taking on that Sleepy Hollow spookiness, Daisy saw a lot of merit in the literal interpretation.

"No way am I going in there," she mumbled. She turned—*tinkle-tinkle*—intending to fetch Rita. The voice came again, sounding faint, tired, and hopeless.

"Hello? Anybody there?" she asked softly, not really wanting to know. She stepped into the woods. "*Konnichiwa?*" Another step and another as her bells softly tinkled.

* * *

Max found a branch to use as a staff, taking the weight off his knee. Mumbling a curse at Yogi, he slowly set off through the trees toward the greenhouses, wending his way around the more imposing thickets of brush.

Gathering courage, Daisy called out, "Hellooooo? *Konnichi-waaaaa*? Is anybody there?" Her eyes strained to see through the murky dusk that veiled all but a few feet in front of her. Her next step landed in a slush of snow, leaving a fuzzy impression of her sole. She took a few more steps, stumbled on exposed roots, but regained her balance with the help of a tree. That got her adrenaline surging. She took a calming breath.

"*Anata no namae wa nandesuka? Eigo o hanasemasu ka?*" Asking someone their name and if they spoke English probably wasn't the best of search and rescue questions, but it was that or rattling off menu items, which really seemed dumb.

The trees closed in around her. Young devil's club snatched her sweat pants. Her heart pounded as she tugged her leg free. *"Kon-nichiwaaaaaa!"*

Max stopped. Was that Japanese? Spoken by a *woman*? None of his Japanese regulars were due to arrive for weeks. They certainly wouldn't be bringing wives or mistresses. So who in the world would be out in these woods speaking Japanese?

Max was just about to answer when—

"Hello? Anybody there? *Eigo o hanasemasu ka?* Helloooo?" *Screw this*, thought Daisy, after her repeated entreaties were met with silence. If there was a body in the woods, there was no way she could find him. Better she should get Rita and let *her* organize the search. She turned—the alders rustled—and she froze. Peeking over her shoulder, Daisy vigorously shook her right leg. *Tinkle-tinkle-tinkle-tinkle-tinkle-tinkle-tinkle!*

It was all Max could do not to laugh aloud. Bear bells! Of course, Daisy would have bear bells. As if a little tinkling was going to scare anything, let alone a bear. He was about to call her name, when a devilish thought stopped him.

* * *

Daisy listened to the silence, then gingerly took a step forward. Her bells barely registered, their sweet sound muted by the woods. She stepped with her left foot, paused, then her right, paused, then her left, as if she could sneak away from whatever was behind her. She was just starting to feel safe when she heard something coming through the brush, snapping branches.

Max no longer had his makeshift staff, but he would retrieve it as soon as Daisy fled the woods—any second now. He felt guilty for the fear she must be experiencing, but a little terror might be the push needed to send her packing. Besides, a *cheechako* shouldn't be roaming these woods at night. What if she'd run into Yogi?

Bottom line, he was actually doing Daisy a favor. Next time she might think twice before waltzing around the woods unprepared. If, of course, there was a next time.

Daisy listened intently to her surroundings. Something didn't make sense. First, there was something behind her, then something crashed in front. She reined in her instinct to flee, fearing she might run smack dab into that from which she was fleeing.

She'd read about bears in her *Alaska Almanac* and nowhere did it describe this kind of stalking behavior. On the other hand—Daisy's heart quickened—Ted Bundy once used a fake leg cast to get a woman to help him to his car, where he then strangled her!

Were the calls for help a maniac's ploy to lure her into the woods where he'd then—

"Daisy, get a grip." She eyed the trees and took a tentative step forward. This was Otter Bite. What were the odds that a serial killer was in these woods? Then again, she'd heard how the isolation in these little villages could make a person go berserk. But cabin fever struck during the long, cold, dark, relentless winter, not during the spring. But maybe too much light could make a person go nutty just as easily. She thought about that pilot friend of Rita's who had leered at her the day of her arrival. Men in Otter Bite outnumbered women fifteen to one. Good odds if a woman wanted to find a mate. But what had Rita said? The odds are good, *but the goods are odd*. Was one of those *odd goods* stalking her now?

But whoever, or whatever, was out there, she was not alone in these woods and Daisy knew that for damn sure.

* * *

Ignoring the throbbing in his knee, Max crept closer to Daisy. Crouched behind a spruce, he reached for an alder to rustle the leaves, but his hand found a thorny stem of devil's club instead. "Dammit."

Daisy didn't need to be hit over the head with a fake leg cast! Hearing the curse, she bolted, but a few strides into her sprint a rotted log snared her foot and sent her sprawling into a young thicket of willows. Deaf to everything but the blood pumping in her ears, she scrambled to her feet just in time to confront a shadowy figure reaching for her. But Daisy would not be a victim. Not this time. Not ever again. Her hand shot toward her assailant and blasted cayenne-pepper bear repellant into his muzzy face!

To the sounds of tormented howls and snapping branches, Daisy scrambled to her feet and fled the woods, faltering when she heard the anguished call of her name.

Chapter Twenty-Seven

"Yes, ma'am." Ferris Fitzsimonds nodded into the phone, his eyes on Daisy.

A living, breathing contradiction, Daisy gently tended to Max while her brow knotted irritably and her lips pinched angrily and her eyes burned with malice. Taking a moment, she finagled a twig from her curls, and with a roll of her green eyes, tossed it on the coffee table.

Max did his part, being as surly as an old mule. The few times he had tried to fend for himself, Daisy had barked at him to lie back down on the couch. After he'd knocked his good shin on the coffee table in blind stubbornness, he'd grudgingly done as he was told. But it didn't stop him from complaining. Loudly and repeatedly. He moaned from the burning in his eyes, groaned at the ice pack on his throbbing knee, and swore at the cold, wet compress flooding his eyes and pillow.

Napoleon made the situation worse with his incessant squawks. "Tina is hot!"

"Can't you get that bird to be quiet?" Fitz asked, his palm over the mouthpiece.

"A parrot fricassee would probably do the trick," Daisy shot back.

"That's not funny," Max snapped, blindly addressing Daisy.

"Lie back down. I was only kidding."

"See how you like it when I kid about turtle soup."

Daisy puffed up. "Elizabeth is not annoying. Your *bird* is."

"That's because Elizabeth has no personality. She doesn't do anything."

"She does plenty . . ."

Fitz shook his head and moved away from the chaos. "I un'er-stand," he assured the medic issuing instructions from her home in Seldovia. She was the closest thing to a doctor the coastal villages had; the nearest doctor was across Kachemak Bay in Homer—an hour by boat or fifteen minutes by plane. But the cayenne pepper wasn't fatal and its blinding effects would be short-lived. Unless he had an allergic reaction, Max would be fine.

"Twenty-four hours. Yes, ma'am," Fitz repeated into the phone. "Cold compress, no rubbing, and flush the eyes." Fitz thanked the medic and hung up the phone. He looked at the squabbling pair, took a breath, and waded in.

"The doc said you've got to just wait until the effects wear off, which should be in a few hours, but you can't be doing anything like flying for twenty-four hours—"

"Twenty-four hours!" Max cast off the wet towel and leaned forward. The ice pack slid off his knee and crunched onto the carpet.

Daisy winced at his swollen eyelids and painful squint. But she would not, under any circumstances—no way, no how—feel guilty about a situation Max created himself. "You're not helping yourself by getting upset." She reached for the ice pack.

Max squinted in her direction, his jaw granite. "Under the circumstances, I don't think you're entitled to an opinion. You've been itching to use that pepper spray from our first date!"

Daisy remembered their banter about serial killers and pepper spray and recoiled at Max's accusation. "Yeah, that's what happened." She lobbed the ice pack into his abs, causing a flinch and a curse. "This was my grand plan." Then she rose from the overstuffed chair she had earlier wrestled toward the couch. "You wouldn't be in this mess if you hadn't been trying to scare me. So you can stew in your own rotten juices for all I care!"

Having the last word, she was jerking open the front door before Fitz could stop her. "You can't leave," he said in a low voice; he glanced at Max battling an uncooperative ice pack that kept sliding off his knee.

"Watch me," Daisy said, ignoring the smell of liquor on the young pilot's breath.

Fitz stepped outside into the cobalt haze with Daisy and softly pulled the front door to. Lights on either side of the door frosted the night with silver. "Someone has to take care of Max, and since we can't find Rita . . ."

Rita was probably on a date, Daisy figured, but that didn't mean *she* was backup. "*You* take care of Max since you're so concerned."

"Guys can't take care of guys. Not like this."

"Oh, please."

But Fitz didn't budge from that conviction.

"Max will be just fine without anyone hovering over him," she insisted.

"But what if he isn't? And under the circumstances . . ."

"This is not my fault!"

"Look, if I knew someone else to call, I would. But I just landed here. Do you know anyone else?"

She sighed. "We could both stay."

Fitz hesitated, then, without enthusiasm, said, "Okay."

"Never mind." She made an exaggerated sweep for the door. None of this was Fitz's fault. Why should he have a miserable night?

"You're a good person, Daisy," Fitz said with a shy but victorious smile.

"Yeah, yeah." She waved him off. "Get some sleep. I'll take care of Attila."

Fitz wasted no time in making his escape. "Watch for Yogi," she called after him, although she wasn't completely convinced such a bear existed. A backhanded wave and soon Fitz had blended into the heathered dusk. Mentally shoring herself up, Daisy stepped back into the house.

"Fitz?"

"Unfortunately not." Latching the door behind her, she dragged herself toward her patient. Max peeked out from under the compress.

"Will you keep that towel over your eyes? *Pleeeease?*"

"I thought you left."

"Someone has to stay with you."

"I don't see why—"

"Exactly. You don't *see.*"

"Thanks to you."

"You ought to be damn thankful you didn't get shot!"

Lifting the towel from his eyes, Max squinted at Daisy. "You . . . have a gun?"

Daisy clicked off the table lamp—wondering why she hadn't done that sooner—and sank into her voluptuous chair, relieved to be off her feet. The kitchen lights faded into the living room. "Sobering thought, isn't it?" she said, without actually confirming. "You might think about that before you pull another Ted Bundy."

In the subdued lighting with his blurred sight, Daisy looked all soft and fuzzy—in sharp contrast to the hard edge of her voice. Then her fear—and what he'd put her through—registered. "*Ted Bundy?*"

"I'm going to duct tape that towel across your eyes."

"I wasn't trying to scare you. Not . . . like that."

It was, Daisy figured, the closest thing to an apology Max could muster. Not that it was good enough—not for what she'd gone through. Not for the terror that had coursed through her veins. Not for the life that had flashed before her eyes. But it was something. And Max was suffering for his sins. Really suffering.

"I think you'll be more comfortable in bed."

"I mean it," he insisted. "I wasn't thinking. I was just . . ."

"Being a jerk?"

For a moment, Max had the look of a puppy who'd been scolded. Daisy felt like the jerk wielding the newspaper.

Max laid the towel across his eyes as if trying to hide. "So how'd Fitz escape bedpan duty?"

"He's got this thing about men taking care of men."

A smile lifted Max's lips. "Yeah."

"You too?"

"You don't know much about men, do you?"

Daisy grunted. "I know plenty; none of it good."

"You'd be miserable if you didn't have men to complain about."

"If that's the case, then let me be miserable."

Max rolled his head toward the kitchen. "Where's Napoleon?"

Daisy looked around, realizing, as had Max, that the parrot hadn't been heard from recently.

Max started to rise.

She pushed him back. "I'll find him." A few steps toward the kitchen and she smiled. Teal tail feathers jutted toward the ceiling; Napoleon was head deep in the cracker jar.

"Take these," Daisy said, holding two codeine capsules and a glass of orange juice.

With a few groans, Max maneuvered himself to a sitting position against his headboard. Light from the bedside lamp caressed his bare chest. She had convinced Max to go to bed and to take pain-numbing drugs for his knee. Convinced him that a good night's sleep would be the best thing for him. Convinced him *after* she'd put Napoleon to bed in his cage precisely as Max had dictated, draping a black sheet over the wire to quell his squawks.

"The last time you gave me drugs, you vanished."

She put the glass in his right hand and the drugs in his left. "You won't be so lucky this time."

Max handed back the empty glass. "*Bad* luck, maybe."

Daisy ignored what might've been a compliment. Max was not going to schmooze her, not after everything he'd put her through. "Do you want more ice for your knee?"

"I think it's sufficiently glacier-ized."

"Your eyes look better. How do they feel?"

"Not terrible."

"Then go to sleep."

"What're you going to do?"

"Sleep on the sofa."

"There's plenty of room here."

She flicked off the bedside lamp. "Good night, Max."

"Right. You've got that sheet phobia thing."

She headed for the door and the light beyond. "Holler if you need anything."

"They were put on clean this morning."

Daisy turned at the threshold. "Which gave you time for at least one blonde."

"I thought you were on a ferry back to Seattle!"

"Which makes it all okay." Daisy pulled the door to—"Sweet dreams, Max"—and latched it.

No longer kept at bay by interior lights, a cobalt glow swarmed the bedroom, entering through the undraped sliding deck doors

Max stretched under the sheets, trying to eke out a little comfort from a body that wasn't cooperating. Years of hard work and hard play had taken their toll. Physically *and* mentally . . .

Daisy made it impossible for a guy to apologize. Not that he was apologizing for the blonde. Or anything else, for that matter. But if he was inclined . . . well, she made it impossible.

Frustrated—by just about everything, including his ambivalence about Daisy—Max threw off the sheet and slipped his legs over the side of the bed. He labored to stand, hitched up his boxers, then he hopped around the bed toward the glass doors.

Daisy frowned at the thumping coming from the bedroom. Max Kendall was worse than a six-year-old! Daisy marched to his room. She swung open the door, intending to lay down the law, when the empty bed stopped her. Then she caught sight of Max, sitting on his deck in the gleam of the night that wasn't quite night, his gaze somewhere out beyond the shore.

Don't go there, don't go there, don't go there, Daisy told herself as she headed there.

"You should be in bed." She stood in the track of the open slider, not quite in, not quite out.

"Too much going on in my head."

"You should use your crutches."

"I *should* do a lot of things."

"Like going back to bed." Daisy pushed open the screen and the glass to its full width. "C'mon. I'll help."

"Do you ever watch the ocean, Daisy?"

Daisy paused against the jamb, crossed her arms, and listened to the surf. Across the bay, Homer twinkled. A beacon swept the twilight. A breeze brushed past her like a ghost, leaving goose bumps in its wake. Clouds with silver Mylar tops and ominous metal-gray bellies were moving in from the west.

That poor slice of moon doesn't have a chance, Daisy thought of the sky's lone defender.

"Daisy?"

"It's going to rain," she answered as her curls fluttered against her cheeks.

"I take that as a *no*."

"I don't have the time . . . or the view."

Max gave her a quarter-turn look, but otherwise ignored what he heard as a complaint about her accommodations.

"There's something sad about the waves," she finally said.

"Sad?"

"Never mind."

"Oh, c'mon. Finish."

"It's just . . . well . . . Jason and I used to vacation in Kona. And we always had a room with an ocean view. I would sit on the balcony when the sun was just coming up, sipping my vanilla latte, and I'd watch the waves crash on the shore, over and over, like they were trying to escape, but the ocean just dragged them back in . . ."

"*Trying to escape?*" He looked across his left shoulder at her. "From what? The ocean?"

"Sure. Why not?"

"The waves *are* the ocean. That's like my hand trying to escape my arm."

"No, it's not," Daisy said. "The ocean isn't one entity. It's made up of billions of little entities. And some of those entities want to see what life is like on land."

Max frowned. "The waves are not trying to escape; they're reaching."

"Reaching?"

"Reaching, exploring, checking things out. Seeing what they can find on the beach to claim as their own."

"Your waves might be reaching. *Mine* are trying to escape."

Like two interpretations of a Rorschach, Max thought. "Maybe it was *you* who wanted to escape. From Jason."

Refusing to go there, Daisy turned the tables. "Who's Molly-Anne?"

"How do you know about Molly-Anne?"

"Your boat told me."

He chuckled.

"Men don't name their boats after just anybody. Who is she?"

"The love of my life."

Her thoughts screeched to a halt. At his admission? At the idea that Max Kendall could *love*? Or at the unexpected inkling of jealousy she felt? But Max Kendall suddenly seemed, well, *less* Max Kendall.

"So what happened?"

"She died."

"Died?" It was so unexpected . . . *soooo* unexpected, Daisy hadn't the wherewithal to come up with a sympathetic response. Or even an unsympathetic response. But it explained a lot, she thought, feeling uncharacteristically ambivalent about further prying. However tough it was to compete with the living—Tina, for example—it was impossible to compete with the dead. Not that she was trying to compete for Max. No way, no sir, no how!

Max obviously didn't talk about Molly-Anne—had never told Rita about her—but here he sat, confiding his sorrow to Daisy. Was this the same man who, only a week before, hadn't wanted Daisy to know how many suits he had? But here he was, trusting her with one of the most painful moments of his life. How could she not feel—

"It was a long time ago," Max added.

Maybe Charity was right. Maybe the blonde *was* a misunderstanding. Maybe Max was just a puppy trying to find his way. Maybe Max Kendall deserved a second chance. Maybe Max Kendall . . .

"I'm sorry, Max."

"Yeah, what can y' do?"

Daisy tried to brighten the moment. "Move to Alaska?"

"It's not called the Great Escape for nothing." One heartbeat. "Right?"

He looked *into* her, at least that's what it felt like to Daisy. "It's cold out here," she said, rubbing her goose bumps and ignoring his insight. "Aren't you cold?"

"If you think this is cold, you're going to love winter."

Rain hit her cheek. "It's raining."

Turning from Daisy, Max lifted his face to the tumbling clouds as if inviting the assault.

"You're going to catch cold."

"I'm fine."

"Please, Max, come inside."

"In a minute."

"I'm going back inside. You're on your own."

"Naturally."

"What?" Daisy asked.

Max side-glanced her. "I said . . . thanks."

Caught off guard by yet another unexpected response, Daisy brushed it off. "I don't know what for. You're impossible to take care of." But she quickly retreated into the house. Stopping at the bedroom door, she glanced back at Max, sitting alone on his deck in the gloom of the impending storm, his gaze returned to the ocean vastness . . . and shook off the impulse to—

She shivered and wrapped herself in her arms, wishing she'd made Fitz stay.

* * *

Max never claimed to be the brightest bulb in the box, but he knew enough to come in out of the rain. Once the drops assembled into an army, Max pushed himself from his comfortable deck chair and hopped for cover inside. Closing the glass door, he left a few inches for the indoors and out to mingle. He lingered, watching and listening as the rain hit, realizing as he stood there that his knee wasn't throbbing. He finger-raked the rain from his hair and remembered his doctor's warning.

"Pain is not necessarily a bad thing," she had told Max. "It's your body telling you to take it easy. It keeps you from repeating your mistakes. Pay attention to your pain."

When it came to pain, Max was a wuss. He didn't like it, didn't need it, didn't want it. So why the hell was he reaching for that which would only cause more hurt? He was smarter than this; a long time ago smarter. And yet, here he was, being stupid. If only there was a pill he could pop to numb his feelings for Daisy.

He'd work on that tomorrow, when his mind was less jumbled and she was out of his reach. Right now, he needed a hot shower to ward off this midnight chill.

He turned from the glass and headed to his bathroom, slowing when the scene registered. Light peeked from under his unlatched bathroom door and leaked around the edges. Was that the shower he heard?

Cautiously he approached the door as a cat might approach an un-suspecting mouse. Inching the door open, he was met by a warm mist that felt good against his chilled skin. If he was smart, he'd leave his curiosity at that. But Max Kendall, admittedly, wasn't the brightest bulb in the box.

She felt his presence long before she felt his eyes.

"It took you long enough," Daisy said, standing beneath the hot spray of the dual shower heads, her back to Max, her racing heart quivering her breast. She glanced at him over her naked shoulder, trying to be coy and worldly, as if seducing a man was something she did every day. Trying to be unaffected by the magnificence of him, scars and all, standing in the V of the open shower door, looking con-fused, uncertain, but nonetheless melt-in-her-mouth hunky, his eyes questioning her presence in his territory, suspicious of a rebuff or ambush or worse . . .

Not that she blamed him.

"Are you in or out?" she asked, trying to keep the inexperience from her voice.

After a moment of visible indecision, Max slipped off his boxers and joined Daisy beneath the sprays, turning her to face him and pulling her close.

Close enough to feel his expectations.

She saw the question in his face. "It's complicated."

"Fair enough," he said in not much more than a whisper. He met her lips halfway as his hands, silky like the water, cascaded down her back, along the curve of her spine, and the swell of her hip. Her heart surged and her breath stopped when his hand gripped her thigh and lifted.

Daisy clung to his shoulders as their kiss turned feverish, her hands grasping his knotted muscles, his slick flesh. Her fingers plowed his hair as he tasted her skin, sucking the water from her neck, her throat purring vulnerability and acquiescence. She gasped at the cold tile pressing her back as Max drove into her and then everything jumbled together into a whirlpool of soft, hard, cold, hot, give, take, and, and, *and*—

Yes, yes, yes, yes . . .

—Damn the torpedoes, crazy-for-you, no turning back, now you've done it . . .

"Ohhhh, *Max!*"

Chapter Twenty-Eight

"Daisy ... I have to tell you ..." Max sighed, fighting to keep his eyelids from closing.

"You sure these sheets are clean?" Daisy asked, hoping to avoid the inevitable caveats men used to warn women about getting too serious.

Spent and sated, they lay in murky twilight, beneath the covers in his bed, Daisy in the comfortable crook of Max's arm, her cheek against his chest, her fingers meandering through the soft whorls, listening to the rain gently pelt the glass in a rhythmic lullaby.

She could fall asleep if only he'd let her; if only he'd shut up and not say something that would make her regret the second chance she'd given him—

—*to lie, cheat, break her heart.*

She tried to push the doubts from her mind, doubts that only a short while ago had swirled down the drain.

"Daisy," Max began again, in a sleepy whisper, "I ... shouldn't have scared you tonight ... in the woods. I was just ... you've been so ... bitchy—"

"You had the start of a really great apology going."

"Sometimes ... pride takes over. I just wanted to get even. But I shouldn't have done that," he finished with effort; from the drugs pulling him into a sleep or his own male ego, it was hard to tell which. "It was terrible what I did. You seem to bring out the worst in me ..."

"Hey!" Daisy lifted her head and poked him in the ribs.

He flinched, and with a brief awakening, popped his eyes at her indignation. "I mean that in a *good* way."

"Yeah, it sounds like it." And then, "People should bring out the best in each other, not the worst."

"From now on we'll bring out the best in each other."

"From now on?"

"From this day forward...," he added, nestling Daisy back against his chest.

"From this day forward...?" she squeaked.

"You've been quite the surprise, Daisy Moon," Max said in a fading voice. "I never... expected..."

"Never expected... what?" But no answer followed. "Max?" Only the steady rise and fall of his chest. "Max?"

Max Kendall had left the building.

Trying not to read too much into his disjointed choice of words, Daisy settled against him, but her mind was anything but settled. Unexpected scenarios swirled in her head.

It hadn't dawned on her that Max might actually take their relationship seriously. But isn't that what Daisy wanted? To be taken seriously?

As opposed to just being *taken*?

Wasn't that what her rage over the blonde had been about? That Max *hadn't* taken them seriously? That he had defiled their union by bringing another woman into her bed?

Daisy groaned at her dramatics. Bringing another woman into her bed had been tacky, but had the stink she made given Max the wrong idea about her feelings? Had it made Max think she seriously cared about him?

Of course, it might help the discussion if Daisy knew exactly what her feelings for him were. Her thoughts traveled along the rocky road of their relationship, from the first moment her eyes lit on the stubbled, rumpled hunk to now, lying beside him after the best shower sex she ever had. Hell, forget the shower—

But... sex wasn't love. Attraction wasn't love. And, although on some inexplicable, crazy level, she liked the challenge of him, that wasn't love either. True, he had experienced her at some of her worst and lowest moments—not to mention her most embarrassing—and he hadn't fled the scene...

Y' gotta love the guy for that!

But gratitude wasn't *that kind* of love. And, yes, snuggled next to Max, she did feel a warm glow of serenity, but that wasn't love either . . . was it? Even if she added all her feelings together, did they add up to love? Vow-making, to have and to hold, *from this day forward* kind of love? If you loved someone, wouldn't you know it? Wouldn't it scream at you? Or would it whisper, like the ripple of a new tide?

It didn't matter what her feelings were. Loving Max was not in her plan and she simply would not entertain the possibility. Somewhere in Seattle, there was a restaurant with her name on it and a career waiting to be resurrected. She couldn't waste her talents in Otter Bite. There were no gold spoons at the Wild Man Lodge! Not a silver one; not even copper. The best she could hope for was a Teflon spatula.

Daisy calmed her thoughts with a deep, slow breath. She was overreacting to a few words of indecipherable meaning from a man too groggy to know what he was saying. Max wasn't the kind of guy who took a relationship seriously. It was as obvious as the hairs on his fabulous chest that she now burrowed her fingers into. Every now and again, she and he would end up in bed. A little way down the road, the two of them would part. She'd go back to her life; he'd stay in his. No harm, no foul.

Yep, Daisy insisted, snuggling closer to Max. There was no other way for this to play out. In the cold light of morning, when she demanded monogamy and commitment, Max would make his dishonorable intentions known. And she would . . . what? Throw things? Storm from his house? Or maybe she should just quiver her lip and walk out. That, of course, would make Max feel guilty—surprisingly, an emotion Max was capable of after all. Then Daisy would have him right where she wanted.

Hello, cinnamon coffee—so long, campfire sludge!

Chapter Twenty-Nine

D aisy woke, gasping for breath.

Invited in by the glass doors, the pale, misty morning made itself at home in the comfortable bedroom. Max was gone, the space where he'd been now cold. She lay in bed and wondered what had caused such an abrupt awakening.

She had been dreaming. Of the ocean. Of spoons. Of swimming in spoons. Of *drowning* in spoons. Bright, shiny, gold spoons. Daisy shuddered. *Be careful what you wish for*, she heard her mother say.

Shaking off her nightmare, she checked the clock on the nightstand, relieved that it was only 5:11. She had menus to plan, staff to train, a kitchen to organize. Lying around in Max's bed would get none of that done. Especially if Max came back.

She stretched from her fingers to her toes, then eased out of bed in search of her clothes.

Max settled in his favorite chair with a cup of coffee and the morning newspaper. Unfortunately, the *Anchorage Daily News* never arrived in Otter Bite until afternoon, so his news was yesterday's. Not that he cared; it was the ritual he liked. And the satisfaction of doing exactly as he wanted. Of being in complete control. Surrounded by evidence of his success. The king of his castle. Who now had a queen.

An unexpected blip on his screen. Lifting the corners of his mouth, softening his eyes, melting his granite jaw. He almost felt *goofy*. Not something he particularly enjoyed.

But today, everyone was going to benefit. Today was *be nice to everyone* day—even Fitz, who was slated for Max's sermon on *pilots who booze, lose.*

Max liked the kid. He reminded him of him. But the whiskey on his breath last night told Max all he needed to know. He would give him one chance to clean up his act. If Fitz chose to kill himself, he wasn't going to take any of Max's clients with him.

But that was later. Right now he had a woman in his bed and he wasn't going to waste that. He put the newspaper aside and sipped his coffee, reflecting on the first time he saw Daisy Moon. Selling off her possessions. Looking tired and worn, her hair wild—the same hair he now loved to spiral around his fingers—but with a spark in her kryptonite eyes that had snagged him, if only momentarily.

Then their second meeting, at Mama Mia's . . .

Crashed and burned. Max lowered the flaps on further thoughts or he might get cold feet about keeping Daisy around, but he made a mental note to call his attorney. Also to check with his mom on the *Superman* comics. If he was particularly brave, he might mention Daisy. Then again, not. She would undoubtedly get the wrong idea and fast-forward Daisy into the mother of her grandchildren. From here to there was a long flight Max wasn't sure he wanted to make. First, he and Daisy would spend time together. With both of them working days, that meant nights. Yeah, he could spend nights with Daisy, no problem. But Daisy would expect an exclusive relationship. And she wouldn't be shy about demanding it. He'd make a great show of his sacrifice, however, so she wouldn't think him a pushover. After a while, he might even ask Daisy to move in with him . . .

How would that feel, sharing his life again? Good? *If* he could actually do it. It had been so long since he'd even considered such a move, and look who he was considering. The woman who'd blasted him with pepper spray. Then seduced him in his shower.

Yep, Max thought, rising from his chair. Tough combo to ignore.

Daisy splashed water on her face, rinsed the night from her mouth, and finger-fluffed her hair, trying not to be too critical of her reflection. After all, she'd had a tough night. Too little sleep, too much thought, and just the right amount of Max Kendall to make her doubt all the conclusions she'd come to last night. But you can't change the recipe once the cake is in the oven.

You can't switch horses midstream.

Can't make a U-turn on a one-way street.

Can't stop a shot arrow.

"Can't mend a broken heart," Daisy finished, shutting off the annoying flow of idioms, but not before recognizing that *idiom* was awfully close to the word *idiot*, which made her wonder if she was exactly that for thinking she could beat Max Kendall at a game he'd practically invented.

But she didn't have a lot of options. No matter what feelings she *might* have for Max, she was not about to end her career in Otter Bite. No, she was not going to rethink this. She'd figured this out last night and she had a plan. As long as Max Kendall acted like, well, *Max Kendall*, everything would come up roses. Which always struck her as an odd saying given the thorns . . .

"Good Morning."

Daisy jumped at the unexpected intrusion into her war room. Loosely robed, Max stood only a few feet away, stubbled and rumpled, but with a softness to his gaze and a lift to his lips that flip-flopped Daisy's stomach.

"Sorry," Max said at her surprise, offering a mug of coffee. "The door was open. I hoped you'd still be in bed."

The intent of his hope was obvious in his voice. Daisy smiled, not completely without that same hope. She tried to ignore her rampaging heart as she made her first move.

"I have a real terror of a boss who pays me to be in the kitchen, not in bed."

"He's just misunderstood."

"Yeah, I'm sure that's it." She took the offered mug and sipped. Not cinnamon, but not campfire sludge, either. Just good old-fashioned coffee with a splash of cream.

"This is good. And as usual"—Daisy pecked his lips—"so were you."

A tiny flinch struck Max's brows, but just that quickly it was gone and she wondered if she'd imagined it.

Max closed the gap between them, then added depth to her original kiss that almost had Daisy forsaking her mug for his shoulders. His kiss ended in the nick of time to save a collision between ceramic and tile.

"I'm making waffles."

Something about *waffles* niggled at her.

He nuzzled the soft underside of her jaw. "With strawberries and whipped cream. I whipped it fresh this morning." Then he nibbled her earlobe, flicking the small gold hoop with his tongue. "Take off your clothes and join me in the kitchen." But Max smiled and his blue eyes twinkled, dashing any hope that he was serious . . . or was that a serious gleam in those baby blues?

"Your eyes . . . ," Daisy said as she regained her focus. "They look good."

"I woke up this morning and everything was crystal clear."

She escaped his embrace—before she ended up naked. "That's a relief."

"It's a mixed bag."

"A mixed bag?"

"Let's have breakfast." He turned for the door, leaving Daisy wondering about his reply.

After a final mirror check, she followed him to the kitchen with her mug in hand, and slid onto a stool, the island between them.

"Shouldn't I be making breakfast?" Within her reach was a bowl of whipped cream; she swept a finger through the white peaks and into her mouth.

"You can supervise and tell me all the things I'm doing wrong."

"That's not nice."

Max tossed an eggshell into the garbage. "Old habits."

"Old habits?" At this rate, she'd be storming from his house faster than even she had planned.

With mixing spoon in hand, Max looked at Daisy. She was going to make this tough. He took a breath, shifted his approach. "The thing is . . . I'm in some weird territory here—"

Her brows peaked like the whipped cream. "Weird territory?"

"—And it would be really helpful if you'd just sit there, hear me out, and not repeat every damn thing I say."

Daisy clamped her jaw.

Leaving his spoon in the batter, he came around the counter and sat on the stool beside her. "I've been thinking—"

"*¡Buenos dias!*"

They jerked.

"That damn bird!" Max drew a bead on the perched parrot in the living room.

"*¿Dónde está el dinero? ¿Dónde está la cocaína?*"

Daisy looked at the bobbing parrot. "Why does Napoleon speak Spanish?"

"Because he's Mexican."

"And the cocaine request?"

"He's an addict."

"Uh-huh. I have to get to work."

Max grabbed her arm as she left her stool.

"*¡Policia! ¡Policia!*"

"I got him from a drug dealer."

"Friend of yours?"

Max released his grip. "No, but *you* would think that."

"Okay." Daisy raised a palm in truce. "How did you get Napoleon?"

"This really isn't what I want to talk about."

"You kinda started it with the drug dealer comment."

Max parted his lips, then shook his head. "You'd never believe me."

"Thanks for giving me the benefit of the doubt."

"Okay, fine." Retrieving a bag of sunflower seeds from a cabinet, he headed toward Napoleon as Daisy patiently waited. He filled Napoleon's bowl and the parrot immediately snatched a seed.

Max turned toward Daisy. "I *took* Napoleon from a drug dealer."

Daisy narrowed her eyes on him. "Really?"

"It's kind of a long story."

"Hit the highlights."

"When I got out of the navy—"

"You were in the navy?"

"Yes. And when I got out, I ran a fishing charter in Acapulco. Had some clients from Alaska. They raved about it. I came up for a visit. Sold the charter. Got a job as a bush pilot. Made some connections, made some money, et cetera, et cetera—"

"Et cetera, et cetera?"

"One day a navy buddy called. His daughter had gone down to Acapulco on spring break and got mixed up with a guy who turned out to be something of a drug dealer, and since I knew my way around, maybe I could help. I did, and Napoleon came back, too. End of story."

Daisy stared at Max for what seemed like forever. *End of story?*

Hardly. Her head cocked slightly. Then a tiny knot formed between her brows. "This *daughter* person. Tell me her name isn't Ellen."

"As a matter of fact—"

"Oh, please, Max. You just *parroted* back the story *I* made up for you!"

"Coincidentally, it does bear some resemblance."

"*Some* resemblance? The only thing missing are the Rottweilers!"

"No Rottweilers. Only a couple of very unfriendly bodyguards."

"Of course."

Max put the bag of seeds on the counter and took the stool beside her. "You don't believe me."

Her chin dipped, a single brow arced. "Would you?"

"Yes."

"So if I told you I came by Elizabeth as I was foiling a poaching ring down in the Florida Everglades, you'd believe me."

"Of course not. Elizabeth is a western box turtle. What would she be doing in Florida?"

Daisy sighed. "Fine. It was a poaching ring in . . . Arizona."

"What were they poaching?"

She threw up her hands as if beseeching the heavens. "Cactus!"

"Were they giant saguaros? Because saguaros are a protected species and they are poached—"

Daisy stared Max into silence, then shook her head. "I don't know why I keep doing this to myself."

"Doing what?"

"This, *this*," Her hand flip-flopped between them.

"Daisy—"

She squirmed from his grasp. "I've got a kitchen to organize."

Two steps, three steps, four steps, five steps . . . heading for the front door, nabbing her jacket from the chair where she'd left it last night. Not the storm she'd planned, but . . .

"Daisy, wait . . . I think we've got something here—"

Slowing, slowing . . .

"—I think we ought to give this a go."

Stopped in her tracks. Then she spun around. "What?"

"I . . . think we ought to give this a go."

"No. Give *what* a go?"

"*This*," he said, mimicking her prior hand action. "*Us*," he added, when Daisy only stared.

"There is no *us*," she told him, standing her ground and keeping her distance. "There's a *that*—" She shot a pointed finger in the direction of the bedroom. "But *that's* not an *us*."

"*That* could be an *us*."

Daisy took a single step toward him. "Are you kidding me?"

"No, actually." Max mirrored her forward step. "Although . . . well, it kind of took me by surprise, too. But then, last night—"

"Last night was just—"

"Last night was not *just*. That was *my* shower you were in. I was there, remember?"

Vividly, Daisy thought, trying not to remember . . . all her feelings before, during, and after. Trying not to make it more than she could afford. Trying, trying . . .

"The thing is, it got me thinking—*you* got me thinking—and well—" Max shrugged. "'*Ducunt volentem fata, nolentum trahunt.*'"

"What the hell is that?"

He cocked his head at her. "You know French, you know Japanese. You don't know Latin?"

"When someone orders from the menu in *Latin,* then I'll learn Latin."

"*Fate leads the willing; drags the unwilling.* So why fight—"

"*Seriously?*" She interrupted him with a hard look. "And which one are you? Willing or unwilling? As if I don't know."

"I'm neither. I mean, I'm willing, but that's not the point."

"You sound *resigned*, Max, not willing. Not exactly the kind of romantic gesture that sweeps a girl off her feet."

"Daisy—"

"Max loves Tina!"

Eyes wide. Breathing stopped. Faces shot to Napoleon. Then Daisy did a one-eighty for the door. Only this time, she meant it.

"For God's sake, Daisy, Napoleon doesn't know what he's saying. He just puts words together. It doesn't mean *anything*!"

"Max loves Daisy!"

"Oh, jeez." Then, to his surprise, Daisy turned from the door.

"I just realized . . . *waffles*. These are your morning-after waffles.

The same waffles you make for every woman who shares your sheets. I'm just another batch of waffles to you!"

"You're way more than waffles and you know it."

"How do I know that, Max? How exactly do I know that?"

"Well, for one thing, I don't have this conversation with every waffle."

"*What* conversation?"

"The conversation I've been trying to have for the last twenty minutes. I've been trying to tell you—"

"Look, Max, in spite of Napoleon" Glancing at the offending parrot—"maybe you've got good intentions here—"

"Here it comes. Another excuse to run away."

"Hey! I've got good reason to run."

"Which is the kind of thinking that makes *you* a risk for *me*."

Daisy frowned. How had Max managed to turn the tables?

"If you walk out that door, I'm not chasing after you."

An *ultimatum*? Was Max actually giving her an ultimatum? She puffed up. "Who asked you to?"

"Damn it, Daisy! Why are you so—"

"Cautious? Unyielding? Demanding?"

"Blind!" Clenching his fists, Max exploded with the first words that came to mind. "I want more than waffles and I thought you did, too! I want to wake up beside you. I want to have morning coffee together. I want to share my newspaper. I want—"

Daisy's mind spun like a Tilt-A-Whirl. Nothing was happening like she planned. Max wasn't Max. He was supposed to be unavailable and unattainable; he was supposed to be weaseling out of their affair, but this man in front of her, this man who *looked* like Max Kendall—all rumpled and rugged and still very hunky—this man was actually suggesting . . .

"—you and me to be *us*. And not just in there," he added, shooting his thumb toward the bedroom. "But everywhere."

Her future flashed before her. But it wasn't *her* future; there wasn't *her* gold spoon or *her* fabulous restaurant in downtown Seattle. It was the future of Daisy somebody else, Max Kendall's lover, hired *cook* for Wild Man Lodge in Otter Bite, Alaska. And yet . . . would that really be so bad?

"What do you say, Daisy? Fish or cut bait?"

Fish or cut bait? Daisy looked at Max. Really, really looked at Max. She'd never experienced anyone so uncommitted to commitment; so horribly, terribly bad at making a proposal.

Then it hit her, like a brilliant flash of light. Something so bold, so daring, so outrageous . . . she could scarcely believe she contemplated it, let alone—

"Yes!" she gushed, reaching him in record time and nearly bowling him over as she jumped into his arms. "Yes, Max, yes! Of course I'll marry you!"

Chapter Thirty

"Oh, Max . . . this is so unexpected," Daisy cooed between kisses to his lips, his jaw, his neck. Her hands slipped inside his robe. "Let's celebrate," she murmured as he swelled from her touch.

Before Max could catch up, Daisy had a spatula of whipped cream. "*Je vais te sucer lentement . . . un pouce à la fois.*"

Her provocative French fogged his brain, then her provocative mouth shut it down completely. He didn't even notice the front door opening . . .

"Good morn—" Rita froze midstep, then did a one-eighty, her long, loose braid whipping behind her. "Sorry!"

Max jerked back, calling to Rita. He helped Daisy up and wrapped his robe as Rita peeked around the door.

"I didn't mean to interrupt." Coming inside, Rita ignored Max's crotch. But she couldn't ignore the whipped cream. "Um, Daisy . . ." She pointed to her own nose, then motioned to Daisy's.

Daisy swiped her nose, then giggled at the whipped cream on her fingers before licking it off.

"Fitz told me about the pepper spray," Rita said. "Obviously you two have worked things out."

"I was just about to make waffles," Max said awkwardly. Stupidly.

"Is that what you call it."

"Oh, Rita," Daisy gushed. "Max proposed! We're getting married!"

Rita's chin all but landed on the floor. She looked at the animated expression on Daisy's face, at the pain on Max's.

"You two have waffles without me," Daisy suggested. "I've already eaten." She winked at Max. "And I want to call my mom and

Charity and, well, there are a million things to do . . ." She kissed Max on the way out. "We'll finish this later." She beamed at Rita, and shut the door behind her.

Rita stared at the closed door, then turned to Max. "You *proposed*? I suppose that's one way to keep a cock—uh, cook."

"Chef," Max corrected, looking stunned. "And I did not propose."

"Then this is quite a misunderstanding." She reached inside a cabinet for a mug.

"Exactly!" Max followed Rita back into the bright kitchen. "It's a misunderstanding. A horrible misunderstanding."

Rita helped herself to coffee. "The same kind of misunderstanding you two had in the woods last night?"

"That was just plain stupid."

Rita stopped the mug at her lips—*Is Max admitting he was wrong?*—then she sipped the hot coffee. Taking a stool at the counter, she watched his thoughts through his changing expressions.

"From pepper spray to whipped cream in less than twelve hours. You should write a book."

With a groan and a grimace, Max dragged fingers through his hair.

Rita softened. "Do you need to, uh, clean up?"

"I'm fine."

So how do you suppose this misunderstanding happened?"

"No idea. One minute I was quoting Seneca—"

"Who?"

"Your grandmother."

Her generous brows lifted.

"Fate leads the willing . . . ?"

"Daisy got a proposal out of *that*?"

"Actually, it pissed her off. And then I got pissed off that she got pissed off and then that damn parrot—"

"What name came up?"

"Tina."

"Tina?"

"Max loves Tina!"

A twin glance at Napoleon. Max silenced him with additional sunflower seeds. "A year ago. The Alaska Air pilot? Had a tattoo of a winged horse on her shoulder?"

"Oh, right. I like Tina."

"Daisy doesn't."

"Daisy knows Tina?"

"In a roundabout way."

"And she knows that *you* know Tina?"

"It came up."

"Small world. So then what happened?"

"It all came out in a rush. Sharing the newspaper. Her, me, us. Fish or cut bait—"

"Fish or cut bait? That's some pretty heavy poetry. No wonder she said yes."

"I'm glad you're enjoying this." He swallowed coffee. "Obviously Daisy is in love and she's hearing what she wants to hear."

Rita stared at Max. "Poor, delusional Daisy."

Max slowly shook his head. "I know."

Rita pulled in her smile. "Did you say the L-word?"

Holding his mug near his mouth, Max frowned. "Does Napoleon count?"

"I wouldn't think so. Especially after the mention of Tina."

"Then no."

"Hmm."

"That's it? *Hmm?*"

Rita shrugged and sipped her coffee.

"I guess you know this is all your fault," Max said.

Her face pinched. "Me?"

"If you had been home last night—"

"You're not the only one who has needs, Max. Although I prefer my whipped cream on actual waffles."

"It was unexpected."

"Like marriage?"

"You're not helping."

"I guess I just don't believe in accidents or coincidence."

"How 'bout mistakes?"

"Everything happens for a reason."

Sometimes he wished he had that same unquestioning faith that had kept Rita hopeful in spite of a personal tragedy that would have drowned most mothers along with their sons. But Seneca notwithstanding, he always figured that even in the worst storm, people had rudders.

"Maybe subconsciously you really do want to marry Daisy."

"Uh-huh . . . no," Max said. "So how the hell do you tell a woman who thinks she's getting married that she's not?"

Rita held out her mug for a warm-up. "You don't."

"Are you nuts?"

Daisy held the phone away from her ear. Three thousand miles didn't dampen Charity's outrage one decibel. She waited for silence, then tried again.

"I'm *not* getting married. Max *didn't* propose. But he thinks I think he did, so now he'll have to break up with me, which makes me the injured party and gives me all the power. I've explained this once. Weren't you listening?"

"Believe me, Daisy, I heard every word. From the pepper spray to the whipped cream. Nice, by the way. But you're in very dangerous territory."

Daisy scowled at the phone, then eased down to the kitchen floor and sat against the wall. "But you said—"

"I said you should try a little flirting, a little flattery, a little *nice* to soften Max up. I never said to marry him—"

"I'm *not* marrying him! I'm just giving him the taste of his own medicine. He scared the hell out of me last night. And now he knows what that feels like."

"Are you *sure* that's what's happening? Are you sure you haven't fallen for the man? Are you *sure* you don't actually *want* to marry Max?"

"Are you kidding? I was engaged for ten years! I'm thinking I never wanted to be married at all."

"I'm thinking you never wanted to marry *Jason*."

"Good heavens, Charity, the *last* thing I need is to be married! What I really want is my restaurant and my spoon and this is just part of my plan to get my life back."

"Interesting plan. But I'm not so sure Max will cooperate. He might really love you. And you said *yes*, Daisy. What if Max takes you up on that? What if he really did propose?"

"Please. *Max* and *marriage* are two words that will never again be in the same sentence. And Max loves himself more than he'll ever love me. I'll bet my Cuisinart that right now he's conniving a way to break our engagement."

* * *

Max's blue eyes hardened on Rita. "So I should just order my tux now . . . ?"

Rita ignored the hard stare and sarcasm. "As much as I'd love to see you in a tux, you'd make Daisy miserable."

"I would?"

"Wouldn't you?"

"Uhhhh—"

"You're not husband material."

"I'm not?"

"Are you?"

"Women seem to think so."

"That's because they experience only a *snippet* of your life. And I just used today's word," Rita proudly added.

"Snippet?"

"They experience you at your best. You give them romance and attention and incredible sex—"

His eyes flinched.

"—It's no wonder they think a lifetime of that would be great. But if they experienced the real you—"

"The real me?"

"You know. Selfish, self-centered, rigid, uncompromising . . . forgetful."

"Forgetful?"

"My birthday was two days ago."

"Okay, okay, I get the picture. Let me know what you want."

"You need to paint that picture for Daisy," Rita explained. "And she'll be the one who breaks your engagement. But you can't be obvious."

"Obvious?"

"No blondes-in-the-bed kind of thing."

Max remained conspicuously silent.

"In fact, I'd ask her to move in."

"*Move in?*"

"A few weeks of day-in, day-out living, and Daisy will be over you before you can say *I do.*

Is that what he wanted? For Daisy to be over him? "Sounds risky."

"As risky as . . . Acapulco?"

Max narrowed his eyes on her, wondering what she knew, how she knew, and who else knew.

Rita waved away his concern. "Your secrets are safe with me."

Max relaxed . . . a little . . . and answered, "Different kind of risk."

"And you'd rather have a gun to your head?"

"I'm not sure I don't have one now."

"Fine. Do it your way. March over to Daisy's place and hit her with the truth. But put on some clothes first and don't forget your knee thingy. You'll need all the sympathy you can get not to come off as a jerk. And one more thing . . . I assume you'll never want to make *waffles* with her again."

"Why?"

"Because after you tell her she's an idiot for thinking you want to marry her, she'll feel too humiliated to even *think* about waffles with you . . . ever again."

Max visibly mulled that over.

"It's certainly a good thing I put those ads in for a chef. We're going to need one," she reminded him. "But if you must know, I'm kinda relieved to be rid of her."

"Yeah?"

"Ever since Daisy came into the picture, you've been a little moody."

"*Moody?*"

"I'm not the only one who's noticed it. Fitz said you were as surly as an old mule last night."

"He did, did he?"

"He really felt sorry for Daisy. But then it all works to his advantage—you and Daisy being on the outs, I mean."

Max drew back. "How so?"

"Duh. It leaves a clear path for him."

"Fitz isn't Daisy's type."

"That would explain the bottle of wine they shared at her place. *Before* she blasted you with pepper spray."

"Daisy and Fitz? I don't believe you."

"Ask her. After you tell her you don't want to marry her. Should be an interesting conversation."

"Wait a minute . . ."

Rita looked at Max with big, brown, innocent eyes.

A gleam electrified his blue eyes. "I can't believe I almost fell for this."

Wider and more innocent. "What?"

"You can cut the act, RJ. I'm on to you and I'm on to Daisy."

"I don't know what you're talking about."

"And while I might be able to—on some level—*admire* Daisy's gamesmanship, *you*, Rita, are supposed to be on *my* side."

"I am on your side, Max."

"Then cut the crap and tell me what you *really* think."

Rita dropped her eyes to her mug as if it might offer advice, then she looked up. "I like Daisy. More importantly, I think *you* like Daisy. A lot. And I think Daisy likes you. A lot. But I also think you and Daisy are about the stupidest people I've ever met. Each of you trying to want something different than you both want because it will ruin what you *think* you want and you're both too damn obstinate to accept that what you *really* want is a lot better than what you think you want."

"Don't sugarcoat it, RJ."

Rita pressed the counter. "I mean it, Max. Happiness doesn't show up on your doorstep every day. Not like this. Not in Otter Bite. You're lucky if it finds you once. And you keep slamming the door in its face. What're you afraid of?"

Max twitched back at the unexpected question . . . at the unexpected answer. He ditched the sarcasm. "It's not that simple."

"It's as simple as you make it."

"Daisy has plans—"

"We *all* have plans . . . until something—or someone—changes them."

Admiration softened his eyes as he thought about the heartbreaking changes Rita had endured. "You're the one I should be with."

"Oh, please. I wouldn't have an old fool like you."

A grin pierced his dark stubble. "Wise woman."

"Yes, I am, but flattering me won't win Daisy."

His grin faded. "I'm not sure I want to win Daisy."

"But you're not sure you don't."

"She's a lot of work."

"Anything worth having usually is."

"I wouldn't know where to start."

"Geez, Max . . . you start with a conversation."

"That's how I got here in the first place. And look what happened. I lost money and golf clubs, and wrecked my knee."

"Max—"

His palm shot up. "Some things are not meant to be. It's best I throw in the towel now, before lightning strikes twice." Shaking off his mixed metaphor, Max left Rita at the counter and headed for his bedroom.

"You're making a mistake," Rita called after him. "Difficulties are just a test of your resolve. Max? Are you listening?"

The discussion was over. Fifteen minutes later, groomed and determined, he was out the door.

Forty-five minutes later, tousled and vexed, he was back in.

Rita forked a mound of whipped cream onto a bite of waffle. "How'd it go?"

"Great."

Rita put down her fork and watched Max drain the coffee pot into his mug. "Daisy wasn't upset?"

"Noooo." His spoon clinked the ceramic as he noisily stirred cream into his coffee. Then he took his mug and headed for his deck.

"Max?" She slid off her stool and followed him. Standing in the threshold, she spoke to his back as he stood at the rail in the mist and stared beyond the shore. "What happened?"

Max sipped his coffee and slowly shook his head as if he couldn't quite believe . . ."I'm an idiot."

Chapter Thirty-One

Alone and unnoticed beneath a canopy of towering spruce, the last frozen patch of winter pooled into crystal drops of summer. Carpets of dogwood sprouted tiny white blossoms, scenting the shaded hills and valleys surrounding Otter Bite with their sweet fragrance. Crops of lupine, their spears of petals unfurling into a profusion of purple, basked in the long days of the short summer.

Like a spell lifted, Otter Bite shook off its winter hibernation, refreshed and renewed.

Dall lambs, under the watchful eyes of their moms, tested their coordination on the granite outcroppings as they plucked tender shoots from among the rocks. Leaving the ocean, schools of salmon fought against the current to fulfill their destiny in the shallow streams and creeks where life ended, then began anew. Riding the waves, *awww*-dorable otters, some with babies, floated belly-up among seaweed beds as eagles circled high above, their chittering banter carried on pristine wind, eyes keen for the king gasping its last breath.

Shrieking seagulls boldly hovered over the docks demanding halibut scraps from the fishing charters. Perched above a colorful FOURTH OF JULY banner, sassy ravens, sleek and shiny like black patent leather, greeted visitors to the festivities with clucks and caws.

The population of Otter Bite swelled to a thousand-plus as tourists milled about Main Street, visiting the docks, patronizing the mercantile and the general store, before savoring clam chowder at the Kachemak Kaffé or relaxing with a bottle of Alaskan Amber on the deck of the Lighthouse Inn, aflutter with tiny American flags. Hearty visitors hiked the hill to the historic Russian Orthodox church, its open doors an invitation to light a candle, say a prayer, and stuff a dollar into the vintage monk cookie jar.

Summer had settled in Otter Bite, bringing with it a nest egg for the long, cold winter ahead.

"Busier than a one-armed crabber," Jen Owens happily answered Rita from behind the candy counter at the Otter Bite Mercantile. Rita barely had time to introduce Chef Daisy before Jen excused herself to help a tourist with a purchase.

"This is so cute," Daisy said of the old-fashioned decor. It was her first visit to the store since she'd arrived in April. The lodge had kept her so occupied that her infrequent trips into town had been limited to quick stops at the general store or post office. Today, however, Rita had insisted that Daisy get out of her stainless steel cave and experience the lighter side of Otter Bite before they met the ferry.

Daisy turned from the candy counter that tempted her with fudge and truffles, and mingled with the shoppers. One young girl—maybe eight or nine—followed Daisy as she drifted from ceramic bowls and cups painted with forget-me-nots and fireweed, to displays of gold and silver charms of moose and bear and dogsleds. The little brunette stopped when Daisy stopped, and walked when Daisy walked, to tables of carved wood toys and a wall with Alaskan art prints. She watched Daisy slide hangers of T-shirts and night shirts, each silkscreened with Otter Bite's namesake and slogan, *Where you otter be . . .* , then stood behind her as she perused books, books, and more books on anything imaginable about the Last Frontier.

Finally Daisy turned. "Can I help you?"

"Are you *the* Chef Daisy?" the girl asked.

Apparently the moniker Rita had chosen for Daisy was starting to stick. "I guess I am. And who are you?"

"Emily. Me and my dad live in Anchorage. We ate dinner at your restaurant last night. He's been real sick and doesn't eat much, but he ate all your chowder. I thought maybe I could get some to take home."

Daisy glanced around the shop for a possible dad, then smiled at Emily. "I wish I could, sweetie, but . . ." Health regulations swam in her head. She knew them too well from researching how to bottle and sell her sauces. "Tell you what, Emily. Come to the restaurant to-night for dinner. The maître d'—"

Emily sucked her lower lip.

"—the person who greets you at the door and seats you," Daisy explained. "He'll be expecting you. Tell him your name, and you and your dad will be my guests. Then order anything you want and as much as you want and whatever you don't eat, I'll make sure it's wrapped to take home."

Emily beamed.

Daisy scanned the store again. "Where's your dad?"

"He had to get batteries."

At the general store, Daisy presumed.

"After here, we're going to the church."

"Emily."

Emily turned toward the voice . . . and lit up. A man came toward them wearing a baseball cap. Attractive but thin, he bore a second-look resemblance to Daniel Craig's brooding 007. His long-sleeved, blue T-shirt stated I SURVIVED CHEMO AND ALL I GOT WAS THIS LOUSY T-SHIRT.

Was that shirt his idea or, more likely, a gift from someone special? Judging by the pride in Emily's gaze, Daisy had a pretty good idea who that special someone was.

When Emily's dad introduced himself as Ian MacIntyre, Daisy faintly heard a rolling *r*. Then words tumbled out of Emily as she parroted Daisy's dinner invitation. But Daisy couldn't tell whether Ian was embarrassed or grateful.

"That's very kind, but really we couldn't."

Emily, however, was clearly disappointed.

"It's no big deal, Ian. We do this all the time."

He looked skeptical.

"But in return, could you do me a favor? Emily says you two are going to the church." The young girl nodded enthusiastically, so Daisy addressed her. "If I give you a dollar, will you put it in the cookie jar and light a candle for me?"

"I think we can spring for the dollar," Ian said.

Daisy smiled at his lyrical *r*'s; Ian's Scottish roots were close to the surface. He carried himself confidently, although he seemed re-served, cautious even. Probably a transplant, Ian might be connected to Alaska's multibillion-dollar oil industry. Or an agent with MI6.

"What should I pray for?" Emily's eyes radiated faith.

Daisy didn't believe her problems merited divine intervention—not like Ian's—but she wasn't about to rain on Emily's parade. "Well, Emily, when I was little, my grandmother told me to pray however the Spirit moved me."

Emily sucked her lower lip.

"It means, you'll know what to pray for when you get there."

"What was that all about?" Rita asked, joining Daisy after father and daughter had left the mercantile.

"Just two adoring fans of my halibut chowder."

"Don't let it go to your cranium."

Daisy stared at Rita—was *cranium* today's word?—then laughed. "Not with you around." But come to think about it, she had been receiving more than the usual number of accolades on her chowder lately. Could it be the new ingredient?

"Are you about done?"

"I want to look at cards."

"No one sends cards anymore."

Ignoring Rita, Daisy perused the turnstile display. With all the e-cards available, was Rita right? Would traditional cards become extinct? She lifted a belated birthday greeting—*I missed your birthday and I feel so empty*—then read the message inside—*Any cake left?* Giggling, she slipped it back in its slot. Her eyes cascaded down the turnstile when another card caught her attention.

I love you more today than yesterday . . . She opened the card. *Yesterday, you really pissed me off.*

Chuckling, she chose another. *I have one simple rule when it comes to loving someone . . . it has to be you.* Daisy sighed, held the card a little longer, then put it back.

Rita came up from behind. "Are you getting anything?" She stuck her hand into a plump paper bag of gourmet jelly beans.

Daisy put on a smile. "I suppose I *otter* get something." *To support the locals.*

"Want some?"

Daisy filled her mouth with the sugary flavor of watermelon. She bought a quarter pound of marble fudge and offered Rita a piece. Taking a chunk for herself, Daisy put the bag containing the rest in her jacket pocket.

"The ferry is probably here by now," Rita said, before biting into the rich confection. Pulling open the door, she waited for a group of chatting tourists to make their way inside.

Daisy jerked to a stop on the covered porch. "Is that a—"

"Buster," Rita answered.

Big and brown, with his ears laid back and nose in the air as he nibbled on the red geraniums cascading off the mercantile's hanging baskets, the horse almost looked like a moose.

Rita clapped her hands to scare Buster away from the flowers. "He's going to be glue if Jen catches him eating her geraniums."

Buster stopped snacking but looked beseechingly at the two women. Rita stepped off the porch onto the ground and dipped a hand into her bag of jelly beans, then offered her palm to him.

"Is it okay for a horse to eat candy?" Daisy asked.

"It's only sugar."

"Can I try?"

Rita poured a few jelly beans into Daisy's palm; Daisy reached her hand toward Buster. His lips were as soft and nimble as fingers. Daisy beamed; she'd never been this close to a horse. Stroking Buster's face, she looked into his big, luminous eyes.

"We've gotta go," Rita said, patting Buster's neck and warning him to eat someplace else.

Daisy looked across the street at FLuke Eleven-Nine; customers were jammed up at the door trying to enter. "Can we stop at FLuke's?"

"No time."

As they left the mercantile, Daisy glanced back. Buster was reaching for a geranium.

"It's just like *Brigadoon*," Daisy said as the two women walked toward the docks.

"Like what?" Rita weaved around a slow-moving couple.

Daisy scampered to keep up, leaping a puddle from last night's rain. "*Brigadoon*."

"Is that a town in Washington?" Rita hailed a group of locals outside of the Lighthouse. Fitz was among them, his hand wrapped around a beer, his cowboy hat tipped back in friendly fashion, his boyish face one big smile. He called after the pair, but Rita shot back with, "Why are you drinking?"

"Not flying today."

Rita stopped. "Is Scully with you?"

"Inside. Hittin' on Mavis."

"Tell 'im Buster is at the mercantile eating Jen's geraniums."

"Come sit a spell. I'm buyin'."

Rita started walking. "No time. Just tell Scully."

In the adjacent parking lot, volunteers assembled booths for to-morrow's Fourth of July carnival. Games, native crafts, and jewelry, as well as food, would all be represented, including two hundred rhubarb tarts from Daisy's kitchen. The Bay City Trollers, a band from Homer, would provide the music.

"So where'd you say Lornadoon was?"

"*Brig*-adoon. In Scotland actually, or at least in the movie."

"I'm not following." Rita had her eyes on their destination, her Mudruckers splashing a puddle.

"Brigadoon is a place unaffected by time, y' know, pristine and idyllic—"

Rita glanced at Daisy. "And that's how you see Otter Bite?"

"Well, in the movie—"

Another glance. "There's a movie about Otter Bite?"

"No. There's a nineteen fifties movie called *Brigadoon* starring Gene Kelly and Van Johnson—"

"Van who?"

"*Johnson*. Really nice-looking. My mom had a crush on him. I bought the DVD for her a few years ago. Of course, he's dead now."

Rita led the way down the long ramp toward the docks. "I don't get the connection."

The tide was out, the ramp was steep, and Daisy grabbed the rail. "In the movie, Brigadoon only wakes up every hundred years, but to the locals, it's like the next day. And Van Johnson and Gene Kelly stumble into the village the day it awakens and Gene falls in love with Cyd Charisse."

"This is a movie about gays?"

It took her a moment. "Cyd Charisse is a *woman*. One of the lo-cals. But if she leaves Brigadoon, the magic is broken and the village disappears forever. And if Gene Kelly stays, he can't ever go back to his big city life."

Off the ramp and onto the dock. "This sounds like one weird movie, Daisy."

Daisy followed Rita along the narrow boardwalk. "Yeah."

Engines idling, the small ferry was gliding toward the dock. Rita hailed a deck hand, who tossed her a bowline. She pulled the line taut and the *Kachemak Princess* gently bumped the landing.

Minutes later, passengers spilled from the boat onto the boardwalk. Hanging back and out of foot traffic, Daisy scanned the crowd for the Wild Man wannabes. Not the family of five, nor the gray-haired foursome. And for sure it wasn't the young couple whose eyes kept darting back to each other as if magnetized. A trio of middle-aged men with duffel bags and fishing poles looked promising, but Rita let them pass. More families, more couples, a congenial group of thirty-something women who made Daisy really miss Charity, and then a pair of flannel-shirted, all-American men—father and son?—veered toward Rita as the remaining passengers headed toward solid ground.

A hug for Rita from the older, distinguished man, a handshake from the younger, and Daisy knew they'd found their wild men.

Rita waved Daisy over. Going against the current of passengers, Daisy joined them.

"This is Commander Knife Newton. Chef Daisy is our four-star chef."

"Call me Pete," the former commander corrected. "No one calls me Knife except at reunions. This is my son-in-law, Dylan James."

Handshakes all around and the four trekked down the dock, up the ramp, and across the dirt lot to the parked Land Rover, splattered with mud. When all the bags were loaded, Rita excused herself for a quick jog to the post office, leaving Daisy with the pair in the parking lot.

"Would that be navy?" Daisy asked about his title, shielding her eyes from the sun.

"Thirty years," Pete answered. "Annapolis into flight school. Great life except for the separations from family. My wife gets all the credit for keeping it together."

With an answer like that, Pete was instantly likeable.

"But you're making it up to her now," Dylan remarked. He looked at Daisy. "My father-in-law owns a very successful construction company."

"We do okay," Pete said. "Personally I think Clutch is the real success. How can you beat this life?" His gaze swept the sheltered waters of Sedna Bay, then lingered on Kachemak Bay and the distant mountains.

"Clutch?"

Looking at Daisy, his pale blue eyes sparked with mischief. "*Max* to you."

"Interesting nickname."

"Actually it was his call sign in the navy. He always came through . . ."

In the clutch, Daisy silently finished. "So you've known Max a while."

Before Pete could get past a grin, Dylan warned, "Don't get Dad started. He's got more Clutch Kendall stories than Alaska has salmon. And he's not shy about telling them. It was worth the trip just to meet the man."

"So you haven't met Max?"

"This is my first visit. But I've certainly heard about him. Sometimes I think Pete got the wrong son-in-law."

Pete laughed and roughed the blond hair on Dylan's head. "Ellen married wisely and we both know it."

It was just friendly ribbing, Daisy knew, and Dylan obviously thought the world of his father-in-law. Gears ground to a halt. "Is Ellen your daughter?"

"Our youngest," Pete answered. "And only girl. Our little rebel. There were times—"

"Dad."

Daisy recognized the warning. Some topics were off-limits to strangers. But she'd gotten all the information she needed—for now. Pete was an old navy buddy with a daughter named Ellen. Coincidence? Or the opening line of a true story?

"So, Daisy, a four-star chef, huh?" Dylan asked, obviously eager to shine the spotlight elsewhere. "How did Max find you?"

"Actually . . ." She paused. "At a garage sale."

Pete and Dylan shared a glance.

"But the official version is, I had a restaurant in Seattle. Was engaged to the owner. Was un-engaged to the owner. Otter Bite seemed like a good place to regroup."

"Out here, a good-looking gal like you must beat 'em off with a stick."

"Dad." Dylan shook his head, looking embarrassed.

"You know what they say," she said, preferring not to disclose that no one, save for Max, had paid her much attention. And even that had gone to seed. "The odds are good, but the goods are odd."

By the time the laughter faded, Rita had returned, a stack of mail in the crook of her arm. Saying nothing, Rita handed Daisy a certified letter. "Anyone need anything from town?" she asked, herding her charges into the SUV. "Then let's roll."

The drive seemed long with an unopened letter from her attorney in her lap, but Daisy assumed it expressed the tying of loose ends. She'd known for weeks—after she'd pried into his duffel bag and found the correspondence from his lawyer—that Max had dropped his lawsuit. Her letter was probably official notification of that discovery. Probably a final bill. Probably a mention of his unreturned phone calls. Three, to be exact, in the last two weeks. But her days had been hectic and by the time she could get to a phone for a private conversation, Seattle business hours were long over. She'd have more time to put this to bed after the July Fourth celebration. After the barbecue. After the fireworks. After the two hundred rhubarb tarts. And then, this outrageous ordeal would be behind her.

Except, of course, for one little thing.

Somehow she'd have to muster up her courage and swallow her pride and thank Max for finally being reasonable. She'd have to manage a smattering of gratitude for something that wasn't her fault to begin with! She'd have to praise his generosity in ending something *he* had started. And she'd have to do it with sincerity . . . and less anger than was churning her stomach right now.

For such a little thing, it would take huge effort. Especially in light of their last encounter. Eight weeks gone and she was still at the lodge and in her cabin, like a CD on continuous play. Truth is, she hadn't expected him to be so concerned, hadn't expected kindness in his crystal-blue eyes or warmth in his touch or gentleness in his words.

Of course, he didn't want to marry her; that was a given from the start of her charade. But she never expected the truth from him, never expected an honest reaction. Never expected her own startling emotions . . .

She had been only seconds away from playing the abandoned lover to Max's unfeeling cad—as she'd planned. But what she hadn't planned was the ambivalence gnawing at her gut. When Max sat with her on the sofa, his blue eyes intent, his jaw granite, his hands hugging hers . . . the tears threatening her eyes were not manufactured from thoughts of her departed mutt, Sophie. In fact, she had no idea where they came from.

Suddenly benevolent, she had decided to make it easy on him, to let him off the hook, to break their engagement that never really was. *Before* Max beat her to the punch . . .

"Daisy—"

"I don't want to marry you," she blurted.

A second of silence, then Max had answered, "You don't?"

"God, no." She turned away from eyes that read her like a polygraph.

"Not even a little bit?"

"I just wanted to watch you squirm." She slipped from his grasp and stood. "Last night, you scared the bejeezus out of me. I wanted you to know how it feels."

He relaxed into the sofa cushions. Relieved? Disappointed? Daisy couldn't tell.

"And to think I came over to set the date."

A second of silence, then Daisy had said, "You did?"

"God, no." He grinned, although his eyes didn't go along.

"Well, then . . . no harm, no foul," she said with more air than a spindle of cotton candy. "I better get to work."

"Right. I hear your boss is a real ass."

"I think he's just misunderstood."

"Yeah," Max said, rising from the sofa. "I'm sure that's it."

Daisy watched his departure, wishing he would get there faster. Then, to her anguish, Max had turned at the door. "Move in with me."

"Sounds like an afterthought," Daisy had said.

"Actually . . . a *fore*thought."

"Let's just call it a bad idea."

He shrugged. "I thought you might say that."

"So why ask?"

"So you know I did."

His last words had left Daisy speechless. He left her cabin and left *her*, or so it seemed. She'd barely seen him, and spoke to him even less, and always about the lodge. Was he avoiding her or just occupied with work? The days he spent fishing were long, she knew that.

Sometimes late at night, she'd be finishing up in the kitchen and hear him in his office. More than once, she had headed to his door only to turn away at the imposing slab of wood.

It's better this way, she reasoned. She and Max had no future, so why go there? Why give her heart to a man who only wanted to shack up? She'd been there, done that . . . for ten years. Besides, she wasn't even sure Max meant it. Had he asked her to move in *because* she'd say no—and thus be off the hook—or did he ask *in spite* of the expected rejection? Had he really laid his pride on the line or was it just strategy?

Trying to decipher Max Kendall was like reading Latin, and Daisy had other things to concentrate on—like the review from the *Anchorage Daily News* restaurant critic. He had been in her restaurant last weekend and his review would be in the paper any day now. Not exactly *Bon Appétit,* but it was a start, and better than working her buns off in obscurity with no hope of discovery.

Max Kendall was part of her past, she vowed . . . *again.* This time she meant it. This time—

"Here we are," Rita announced, turning past the sign and into the drive.

"Wow, this is something," Dylan exclaimed.

"It is something." Daisy remembered the first time she'd seen the impressive structure with its herculean timbers and soothing waterfalls.

"But it's not exactly the rustic pit you've been telling Mom about," Dylan teased Pete.

"Sure it is," Pete insisted. "That's our story and we're sticking to it."

"Sounds like a conspiracy," Daisy said, before the wheels in her head started turning. The brochures, the website. Even the Wild Man Lodge postcards. None of it conveying the truth. And not a single woman on the guest register. Ever. But women—and one man—going into and coming out of the guest rooms late at night; Daisy saw them when she occasionally walked through the guest wing to her cabin after the kitchen was tucked in. *Massages*, Rita had told her.

Daisy knew Jasmine, of course, early forties and gorgeous; she lived in the cabin next door. The other five masseuses, including Scottie, seemed to be on a rotating schedule, leaving and returning to the lodge every couple of weeks. Although late-night massages made sense—guests were gone during the day, returning with sore muscles—something about those women, and Scottie, niggled at her. Maybe *conspiracy* had merit.

"Ignorance is bliss," Pete retorted. "My darling wife is enjoying a fabulous week at a spa with her girlfriends, feeling no guilt or envy at my two weeks *roughing it* with the guys."

"Marie isn't as gullible as you think," Dylan said as the Rover eased to a stop in front of the carved double doors.

"*Pretense*," Pete began, "is the foundation of a happy marriage."

Rita cut the engine. "Everybody out." She tapped the horn and a teenage boy slipped between the heavy doors to collect the luggage.

"So where's our venerable host?" Pete asked Rita as they headed toward the entrance.

"I'm sure he'll be here any second. I phoned him from the post office that we were on our way."

"Pete, Dylan," Daisy said. "It was a pleasure meeting you. Sorry I have to rush off." She backed away from the front doors where Max was certain to exit.

Rita wrinkled her brow. "Where're you going?"

"I need to check on something."

"On what?"

"*Something*," Daisy repeated emphatically, before turning on her heels and stopping dead in her tracks. For a breathless heartbeat, her eyes locked with the wild man himself; Max stopped, too. Then, as if Daisy didn't exist, he strode past her.

Daisy breathed, and without looking back, continued on as the old friends exchanged greetings. As fast as she could, without actually *fleeing*, she rounded the corner of the lodge and willed her heart to slow and her breath to regulate. Then she released her chokehold on the crumpled letter.

Chapter Thirty-Two

"So what the hell was that all about?" Pete asked.

Max poured two fingers of Glenfiddich into a crystal rocks glass. He slid it across the polished wood to Pete. "What the hell was *what* about?" He poured a glass for himself.

"Old friends, new adventure," Pete said, toasting Max, the rims of their glasses chiming before the obligatory taste. "You and Daisy," he said after a second swallow. "As if you don't know."

"We don't get along."

"Before or after you screwed her?"

Max came around the bar and claimed a stool in the quiet lounge. In the middle of the afternoon, all his guests were elsewhere enjoying the activities they paid well to enjoy.

"Before, during, after—does it really matter?"

"Something tells me it does."

"That ship has sailed."

Pete sipped his scotch. "Interesting thing about ships . . . they return to port."

"Yeah, well, this ship sank. It ain't returning nowhere."

"Sure it ain't."

"How's Marie?" Max asked.

"As bodacious as the day I married her."

"And Will, Matt, Steve?"

"All great."

"And Ellen?"

"Sends her love."

"The grandkids?"

"Awesome."

"Business?"

"Booming."

"You?"

"Like a clam in sand."

"Then all is right with the world." Max took another swallow.

"*My* world. *Yours* is a little fucked, I think."

"Look, Knife—"

"You saved my daughter's life," Pete interrupted. "That gives me not only the right, but the *obligation* to meddle in yours."

"Meddle all you want. It won't change squat."

"How's the knee?"

"Had surgery some weeks back. Had to hire a pilot to help out. Could be worse."

"How 'bout a loan until you're back on both feet?"

"If I want debt, I'll go to a bank."

"You wouldn't have to pay me back. I owe you."

"I don't see it that way."

"Pride is a double-edged sword, Clutch."

Max softened. "If I need your help, I'll ask. This isn't about pride. It's simple economics."

"Insurance is paying?"

"Sure."

"I like what you're doing here, Max. Let me help."

"I'm good. The lodge is good. There's just no need."

"And your building plans?"

Max shrugged. "Bigger isn't always better. I may hold off."

"I've been looking for a good investment."

Max looked him square in the eyes. "Then you should look somewhere else."

Pete wasn't convinced, but he let it go—for now. "About Daisy . . ."

Max huffed. "Surely there are other things two old friends can talk about."

"She's really gotten under your skin, hasn't she?"

"Like the Ebola virus. Want me to book Jasmine? She asks about you."

Pete smiled. "I could use a few sessions to blow out the pipes."

"I'll have Rita schedule it."

"Do you ever use the ladies, Max?"

"I sign their paychecks; it would be awkward. Besides, I have Rita."

"I'm sure Rita's great, but she's not a professional."

"Hey, guys," Rita called, coming into the lounge from the kitchen. "Sorry to interrupt, Max, but Clyde Standish is on the phone. Says it's urgent."

"Keep Knife company."

Rita took the stool Max had vacated. "I'd love to be a fly on the wall for that conversation."

"Why's that?"

"Well," she began in a confidential tone, "I'm not supposed to know this, but Clyde Standish is an attorney from Seattle. I've seen his name on some envelopes in Max's office."

"Why does Max need a Seattle lawyer?"

"I don't know all the details," she said in a hush. "But it has something to do with Daisy. Today I picked up a letter at the post office addressed to Daisy from a different Seattle attorney."

"And you think the two are related?"

"A couple weeks back I saw some papers on Max's desk."

"*Saw?*"

"Saw, read . . ." She shrugged.

Pete checked a grin. For someone who wasn't supposed to know anything, Rita knew a lot.

She glanced over her shoulder at the door, then leaned into Pete. "Max is suing Daisy."

Pete jerked back. "Suing Daisy? Okay, Rita, start at the beginning."

"Well . . . Daisy was having a garage sale . . ."

Max shot forward in his chair as he barked into the phone. "I told you weeks ago to drop this! How the hell did this happen?"

"Calm down, Max," Clyde said. "I've been in court the last three weeks. My PA mailed out the wrong letter, that's all. Nothing we can't retract, if you really want to. But you should know that Ms. Moon's attorney called me after he got the letter and I got the impression he might support a settlement. So this little mix-up could be to your benefit."

"Believe me, this little mix-up is gonna cause me nothing but—" He stopped short; a lit stick of dynamite stared at him from the doorway. "I'll get back to you," he said, hanging up the phone.

"You bastard!" Daisy shook her lawyer's letter at him. "You scheming, conniving, vindictive, lying sonofabitch. I can't believe I let my-self . . . that I actually thought—"

Max leaned forward. "Thought what?"

"That you might have some redeeming qualities—"

He settled back.

"—but you keep proving me wrong."

"Look, Daisy, if that letter is what I think it is, it's a mistake."

"You better believe it's a mistake. And if you think I'm giving you one penny . . . well, you're just stupider than I thought."

"If you shut up, I'll explain."

"I don't need your explanations. It's all very clear what's going on. This is payback for my *rejecting* you."

Max stared at her. "Talk about stupid—"

Daisy stomped toward his desk. "I happen to know that you dropped this lawsuit—"

"I did?"

"Weeks ago. I found the letter from Clyde Standish in your duffel bag—"

"What letter?"

"The letter that said he was withdrawing the complaint. And don't try to deny it," she added when his face pinched.

Max swiveled from their conversation and opened a side drawer. He thrust papers toward her. "Is this the letter?"

Hesitantly, Daisy took the sheet and started reading.

Dear Mr. Kendall:
Based upon our recent discussion, I am withdrawing the com-plaints filed with the court on 3 May against Ms. Daisy Moon.

"Yes!"

"Read *all* of it."

She returned to the page. *Yadda, yadda, yadda . . .*

I will submit an amended complaint deleting the assault and fraud charges, but retaining all other charges . . .

Daisy looked up. "That's awfully big of you."

"The point is," Max began, snatching the letter back from Daisy, "I never—" His mouth clamped, his brow furrowed. "Wait a minute—" Max rose from his chair. "What do you mean, you *found* the letter in my duffel bag?"

Realizing her accidental confession, Daisy punted. "You brought another woman into my bed!"

"Nice try." Max leaned across the desk. "You were snooping in my things. I *knew* you were up to something!"

"You brought another woman into my bed!"

He circled the desk. "You little hypocrite."

Daisy backed toward the door. "The two are not even remotely the same."

"You invaded my privacy, went through my stuff, and you're not even the tiniest bit sorry."

"I was just trying to find out who I was sharing my cabin with."

"You always have an excuse. Nothing is *ever* your fault. You manage to justify everything you do, no matter how crazy, vindictive, or selfish."

Daisy's jaw all but dropped to the floor. "That's . . . not true."

Max pressed into her space. "Let's recap, shall we? You sold off Jason's things at a garage sale because he cheated on you. You broke thousands of dollars' worth of innocent china because you lost the restaurant which, by the way, was never actually yours to lose—"

"Fireflies was mine in every way but legal!"

"Yeah, right. And the mess at Mama Mia's was somehow my fault because I dared question the waste of a perfectly good drink. I bet you have all kinds of excuses for not getting a job in Seattle, but not one is about your impossible personality. You have used me, left me, and treated me like a leper even though I give you a place to live and work. And I have yet to hear one little squeak of thanks."

Outrage lunged her forward. "I work my fingers to the bone around here!" she thumped one index finger on the Wild Man logo on his T-shirt. "From sunup to sundown, making the most exquisite dishes this pathetic excuse for a town has ever tasted. I get compliments from all your guests. We have a full house practically every night from locals and tourists. I've put Wild Man Lodge on the map and all I've heard from you is *real men don't eat mango chutney, real men don't put nutmeg in coffee, real men don't like bananas Foster* and apparently *real men don't say thanks* either. So ex-cuuuse me," she said, with two more final thumps of her finger, "if I'm not genuflecting at the mere sight of you, but I'm just too damn busy adding stars and making you money!"

Max wouldn't have been surprised to hear a clap of thunder, so thick was the electricity between them. Now would be a good time to capitalize on that energy—a good time to screw both pride and caution . . . and screw Daisy instead. Atop his desk, on his sofa, against the wall . . . until they were just too tired to fight any more.

Kiss me, Daisy thought, feeling his pull. *Kiss me until I stop thinking about all the ways this can't possibly work. Kiss me now and I'll forget everything, forgive everything . . .*

A shrill jangle cut the moment like a razor. Like prizefighters, Max and Daisy separated to imaginary corners.

Max snatched the phone before its third ring. He held his hand over the receiver and looked at Daisy. "Anything else?"

Daisy wanted to say *everything else*, but how could she compete with the urgency of the telephone? She shook her head and awkwardly turned toward the door. Feeling very *un. Un*satisfied. *Un*certain. *Un*wanted. *Un*happy.

She would escape into her kitchen and all of those *uns* would disappear. Outside his door, she heard Max snap, "Hello." Seconds later, expletives exploded from him. Then he shot past her like a bullet . . . clutching a rifle.

Chapter Thirty-Three

The Jeep careened around the corner, its tires skidding on mud from two weeks of rain.

"Max is gonna be pissed," Rita warned for the third time.

"Fitz is my friend," Daisy said yet again as they chased flashes of Max's red truck. "If he's in trouble, I want to help."

Rita grabbed the armrest as the Jeep fishtailed on a curve. "The kind of trouble Fitz is in I doubt you can help, and Max is gonna be pissed that you're butting in and that I gave you the keys to do it."

"The keys were in the Jeep."

"I'm still an accomplice."

"You could've stayed at the lodge."

"And miss the excitement?"

Daisy brushed away the frizz dancing around her face, then raised the window. Muddy water splattered the windshield when the Jeep hit a puddle. Daisy flicked on the wipers as her adrenaline spiked. "You don't know for sure this will be exciting."

"The way Max is driving, I do know."

The road ahead was a landmine of flooded potholes. Daisy backed off the accelerator to give the wipers a break. "I wish people would just get over Max Kendall." *Myself included*, she thought. "He's not God, for Chrissakes."

"More like the marshal of Dodge City," Rita said. "And Fitz, for all his charm and talent, is still an outsider."

"Like me."

"Like you," Rita agreed. "And to be blunt about it, for all your brilliance in the kitchen, you can be pretty dim-witted everywhere else."

Daisy slammed on the brakes to avoid a squirrel dashing across the road. Their seat belts locked. Stones and mud pelted the Jeep's belly. "Don't sugarcoat it, Rita."

"See your glass as half full instead of half empty and cut Max a little slack."

Daisy pressed the gas. "Me? My blade is dull from all the slack I've been cutting!"

"Oh, please!" But before Rita could elaborate, the drone of an engine caught her ear. Seconds later, the roar of that same engine had Daisy hitting the brakes. They ducked in their seats as a blue and white Cessna buzzed the Jeep.

"What the hell—" Daisy watched the plane sail off, wings bobbing.

"More like, *who* the hell," Rita corrected.

They shared a look.

"You don't think—"

"Wheels up!" Rita ordered.

The Jeep came to a screeching halt at the landing strip, where a small crowd of locals and tourists had gathered to watch the Cessna 185—WILD MAN LODGE emblazoned across its fuselage—terrorize Otter Bite.

Leaving the Jeep, Daisy and Rita joined the group and confirmed that Fitz was the pilot. Spectators oohed and aahed as the plane swooped into treeless clearings, then rocketed toward the blue, barely missing towering spruce on the hill. The plane circled, pointing one wing at the ground while aiming the other skyward, making Daisy queasy just thinking about what it would be like inside the cockpit during that maneuver.

Aimed at Sedna Bay, the plane buzzed low over the dock, scattering seagulls and fishermen, then repeated the attack over Main Street, causing tourists to run for cover.

The plane disappeared behind the hills, the drone of its engine resonating across Kachemak Bay. Daisy took advantage of the interlude to search for Max, spotting him by the trio of hangars with a small group of locals, his red truck parked nearby. Leaving Rita behind, she hurriedly wended her way through the crowd, passing an unshaven, flannel-clad, beer-swigging quintet of locals making bets on the outcome of the impromptu air show.

"Fifty bucks says he hits Dall Mountain," one of the grizzled men offered.

"One hundred bucks says Max takes him out with his Remington next time he passes."

Daisy stopped. *Max wouldn't actually shoot Fitz . . . would he?*

"Max ain't that good a shot," the first man countered, before wrapping his lips around a bottle of beer.

"Fifty bucks says he *is* that good," the third interjected.

"Fifty says Fitz'll ditch in the bay," the fourth offered, upending his own beer.

"Not enough spectators," the fifth disagreed. "I say he lands her."

"Max'll kill him the minute he falls outta the plane."

"Maybe he'll land in Nanwalek," the fourth suggested. "Let things cool down."

"Nah. Man's got a death wish. Scully's got it right," the third said. "Kaboom into Dall Mountain. Too bad about the turtle, though."

Daisy spun around. "What turtle?"

The five stared at her.

"What turtle!"

The man with the Dall Mountain theory shrugged as if it *weren't no big deal*. "Fitz has got a turtle with him."

"What *kind* of turtle?" Daisy demanded. "What's it look like? How big is it?"

"About so-so." Dall Mountain spread his hands about six inches. "A *turtle* turtle. Green."

"Kinda brown, too."

"Had her at the Lighthouse," another offered. "Bought her a beer." The group chuckled.

Daisy sputtered her disbelief. "He gave Elizabeth *beer*?"

"Fitz drank most of it hisself," Dall Mountain said. "Turtles ain't known for holding their liquor."

The group laughed, elbowing each other.

Daisy fumed. "You people are all idiots!" She stormed off as the Cessna reappeared on the horizon. "I'm gonna shoot Fitz myself!" She made a beeline for the hangars *and Max*.

The plane was nearing the landing strip, dropping toward earth. Maybe Fitz was going to land this time; Daisy stopped to watch his approach. *Dear God, please, please, please . . .*

Down, down, down, the Cessna floated, its engine calming to a purr. The crowd behind her held its collective breath.

The tires touched gravel and bounced. Caught by a crosswind, the Cessna fishtailed. The crowd let out a grateful holler. Daisy trembled with relief.

"Just get here as soon as you can!" she heard Max shout into his cell.

The engine revved. The wings caught air.

Daisy froze. The crowd moaned as the plane was once again airborne.

Max looked through the sights on his rifle.

"No, no, no!" Daisy screamed.

Max swung around.

"He's got Elizabeth," Daisy screeched. "He's got Elizabeth!"

"Who the hell's Elizabeth?" someone asked.

Max waved off the question as Daisy reached him. "What're you doing here?" It was a mix of anger, concern, and dread.

"We followed you," she answered, breathless with fear.

Looking for Rita, his eyes darted to the crowd behind.

"Fitz has Elizabeth," Daisy repeated. "Up there." Motioning to the sky. "He's got Elizabeth."

"That doesn't make sense. How? Why?"

"I don't know, I don't know! His drinking buddies told me. That's all I know. He's got her."

Max raked fingers through his hair. "Christ."

"He's coming back around," one of the men said. "Now's your chance."

Max turned away from Daisy and raised his Remington, sights on the Cessna.

"You can't shoot Fitz. He's just a kid!" She grabbed his arm.

Max roughly shook her off and regained his sights.

"What about Elizabeth?"

Someone repeated the question. "Who the hell's Elizabeth?"

But Max wasn't about to make the situation worse by explaining. Daisy, unfortunately, didn't know better. "She's my turtle!"

"Christ," Max mumbled.

Faces went blank, then laughter rolled.

"Shoot the sonofabitch," a stocky woman said. "Before he takes out Main Street."

But Fitz stayed over Sedna Bay, circling the blue skies. Max lowered the rifle. "Let's try the radio again."

Relief settled Daisy's stomach as the group moved into the hangar en masse.

Max spoke calmly into the microphone. "Wild Man six-eight-zero, this is Otter Bite radio. Come in." One collective heartbeat, two collective heartbeats, three collective heartbeats . . . "Wild Man six-eight-zero, this is Otter Bite radio. Come in."

The group focused on the empty skies. "Do you see 'im?" the stocky woman asked.

"Come in, Fitz," Max said with authority.

"Uh-oh," someone warned, as the drone of the engine got louder. They ran outside as the 185 raked the hangars, splitting the crowd on the field like Moses parting the Red Sea.

"Cut it out, Fitz!" Max demanded into the mike. "You're going to hurt a lot of innocent people. Land the plane!"

Max was holding it together better than most, but Daisy saw granite invade his shoulders and jaw. "Maybe I could try," she said.

Max dipped his chin at her, waited a thought, then handed her the mike.

"Wild Man six-eight-zero, this is Otter Bite radio. Fitz, it's Daisy. Do you copy? Fitz? Please, Fitz, come in."

Max lifted a brow at Daisy's easy use of flight lingo.

"Fitz, it's Daisy. You're really scaring me. Please, talk to me." At the silence, her expression sagged, along with her spirits.

"So much for plan B," Max said. "Don't take it so hard, Daisy. He probably doesn't have the radio switched on."

"He's just a kid, Max." Eyeing the rifle. "You can't kill him."

"He's not a kid, Daisy. He's a grown man *acting* like a kid. And it's not my intention to kill him, but I have to stop him before *he* kills someone. Or a whole lot of someones."

"Why you? You're his friend. Why *you*?"

Max shook his head; Daisy couldn't possibly understand. "It comes with the territory."

"There's got to be another way."

"If you think of it, let me know." He turned for daylight.

"Max—"

The radio crackled. "'Daisy, Daisy, gimme your answer do . . .'"

If they'd been dogs, their ears would've pricked up. Daisy grabbed the mike and pressed the button to send. "Fitz. This is Daisy. Come in, *please*."

"—I'm half-crazy all for the love of booze . . ."

"Fitz! Please land. You're scaring everyone! You're scaring *me*!"

Max was again beside her, followed by the rest of the group. Together, they hung on Fitz's every slurred word.

"Daisy, baby, I'll be true-ooo-ooo,"

"Buddy Holly," someone in the group muttered.

"Didn't he die in a plane crash?" Another asked.

"This is ridiculous," the husky woman spat. "Just shoot the s-o-b."

Max spun around and shoved the rifle toward her. "Here, Marge, you do it."

She eased back. "Hey, I'm not the trooper."

"That's right, you're not. So why don't you shut the hell up?"

"Give a man a badge . . . ," Marge grumbled.

Max turned to Daisy. For a moment he was taken aback by what he saw in her eyes. *Respect? Gratitude? Admiration?* Her lips lifted slightly and then, as if remembering what was going on, she turned her attention back to the microphone.

"Fitz, this is Daisy. You know your mom wouldn't be happy with you flying around like this."

"Mama?" came the response.

"Keep talking," Max whispered.

"That's right, Fitz. Mama."

"I love Mama."

"I know you do, Fitz. And she wants you to land and come home."

The drone of the plane became louder. As if one entity, the small group moved outside and looked toward the sound. "He's awfully low," a voice warned.

"I'm gettin' sleepy, Mama."

"He's awfully low!" someone repeated.

"Wake up, Fitz!" Daisy shouted. "Pull up!"

The Cessna arced toward the ozone. A sigh escaped the group.

"You're doing great, Daisy," Max said.

But Daisy didn't feel great. Her stomach clenched, her mike hand trembled, and sweat covered her palms. "Fitz? Mama wants you to stay awake and land the plane. Mama's waiting for you. Land the plane, okay?"

" 'Here we go loop t' loop . . .' " Fitz began singing.

"No loops!" Daisy shouted as the crowd oohed and aahed. Daisy dropped the mike and joined the spectators, who watched the Cessna shoot skyward then belly over and slip back down. "Oh my God. Elizabeth," she whimpered, rushing back to the mike. "Fitz? Come in, Fitz!"

"I don't feel so good, Mama. That loop the loop has thrown me for a loop! Uh-oh. I'm gonna be—"

Sick, Daisy silently finished for him.

"We're losing him," Max told her. "Give it your best shot. It may be the last one you get." *Before my best shot.*

Daisy sucked in a breath and tried to steady her nerves. "Fitz . . ." Her brows knitted as if something tangled her thoughts. "Fitz," she began again with more certainty. It was risky, what she was about to do, but it might be the only chance Fitz had. "Martin's waiting for you at the hangar, Fitz. Come on home."

Max looked at her as if to ask, *Who's Martin?*

"Did you hear me, Fitz? Marty's here. Marty's here with your mama and they want you to land the plane. And we'll all have a nice barbecue."

Several heartbeats of silence. "Marty's home?"

"Marty's home. And he wants you to land the plane. Will you do that for Marty? Will you land the plane for Marty?"

"I'm so sssorry," Fitz breathed as if he'd lost all hope.

"Marty knows you're sorry. It wasn't your fault." Then she held the mike toward Max and quietly said, "Tell him you're Marty. Tell him it wasn't his fault."

"What wasn't—"

"Just tell him."

"Fitz? This is Marty. It wasn't your fault. Now come on home. We're all waiting for you."

"Marty?" And then a few sobs and a sniffle before the radio went dead.

"Fitz?" Daisy asked. "Fitz?"

Nothing.

"Fitz!"

"He's coming back around," someone announced.

Daisy hung up the mike and quickly made it to daylight; the Cessna buzzed the field and headed straight for Dall Mountain.

"Pull up, pull up, pull up," Daisy prayed, shutting her eyes and waiting for the explosion.

Max looked down at her, at her eyes scrunched shut and her balled fists. He corralled her in his arm. "You did everything you could."

She felt tears starting to well and then someone yelled, "He's turning!"

Her eyes popped open. The Cessna banked past the mountain and returned to Sedna Bay, circling wide around the docks, straightening until it almost disappeared, then banking once again toward Otter Bite.

"What's that sonabitch doing now?" Marge asked.

"Shut your damn pie hole!" Daisy snapped.

It was an unexpected moment of levity and Max allowed a bitter-sweet smile. He squeezed her shoulders.

"I guess she told you," one of her companions said.

"Bitch," Marge grumbled.

"I think he's landing," someone voiced with surprise.

"I think you're right," another said.

Her heart racing, Daisy left Max for a better view. She watched as the Cessna floated toward earth, wings bobbing from the cross-breeze, but very much on final approach. Then the tires hit the ground and bounced, once, twice, before steadily rolling along the strip, past the crowd that ran toward the Cessna like a wave on the shore. The brakes screeched as the plane greedily used the whole length of gravel and kept going, going, going . . .

The Cessna rolled off the runway, down the embankment, and slipped into the slough, tail in the air.

Daisy gasped and raced toward the plane. She didn't know how she managed it—Rita would later tell Daisy that she muscled her way through the crowd while screaming *Elizabeth!*—but she made it to the plane ahead of the others, jumped over the embankment and slid down the muddy slope, coating her jeans in the process, as most of the crowd peered over the edge from higher, dryer ground.

The propeller was dipped in muddy water, as if taking a drink. The engine died and the plane was unmoving, creaking and sizzling. Daisy saw Fitz through the windows, slumped forward over the wheel, his seat belt cinching his waist. She pounded on the door, yelling his name, her eyes searching the interior for her turtle. She grabbed the recessed latch and pulled, but the door remained resolutely shut.

Looking dazed, Fitz lifted his head from the steering column and started to move; that's when she saw the revolver. A few brave souls approached the plane, then someone yelled, "He's got a gun!" and the onlookers scrambled as the warning bounced around like a pinball.

Even the booze couldn't mask the pain radiating from Fitz's boyish face as he lifted the 9mm toward his head. Daisy screamed and pounded on the window.

It all happened so fast, it barely registered. Like a flash of lightning. You don't see it coming and in an instant it's gone.

The butt of the Remington exploded the passenger-side window and it was only later that Daisy realized the power behind it. In practically the same moment, Max reached through the fractured Plexiglas, sprung the lever on the door, and yanked it open.

On reflex, Fitz flashed the gun toward Max. Stunned at the sight, Daisy banged on the window with all her might, screaming Fitz's name.

His face flashed at her and then back at Max. Fitz looked dazed, confused, cornered, as if he wasn't sure who posed the greater threat. The gun pointed in her direction, then at Max, before Fitz pressed the barrel to his own temple.

Her heart stopped. Visions of splattered blood and brains filled her head. She wasn't prepared . . .

Her eyes moved off Fitz and caught Max on the other side of the cockpit.

"Daisy! Get down!"

Her knees miraculously folded. She dropped to the mud as the fuselage rocked and thumped. A blast deafened her, its power thundering through her as it fractured the windshield and echoed into the wilderness.

The Cessna started to slip down the embankment, farther into the slough. Her eyes popped as the tail threatened to roll over her.

She scrambled to get out of harm's way, but the muddy slope held no leverage. Her only other choice was to go with the plane as it inched farther into the creek. As water lapped her mud-caked feet, the Cessna stopped.

For an eternity she crouched there, unmoving, staring at the water, her senses muted by the blast still echoing in her ears.

She jumped at the pressure on her shoulder and shot her eyes to the blood-streaked hand resting there. She followed its natural course and found Max's face. Blood smeared his right cheek like paint. She winced, wide-eyed.

"Daisy?"

She just stared at him.

"Daisy?"

Somehow her name made it through the blast. She blinked, softened.

"Are you hurt?"

She managed to shake her head *no*.

He offered his hand. "Come on. Let's get outta here."

How Max pulled her up the slippery slope, she didn't know. She was equally surprised by the human chain of townsfolk and tourists latched onto the tail of the Cessna, keeping it from sliding farther into the water. Max and Daisy cleared the plane as volunteers secured the rear fuselage with ropes.

Strange arms grabbed her and pulled her onto firm ground. Voices came at her with words that didn't quite register. The crowd parted as Max led Daisy toward the hangars. Behind her she heard shouts as the rescue began. She looked up at Max, then started to turn. "Where's Fitz. Is he . . . ?"

"No. But tomorrow he's gonna wish he was."

Daisy didn't know what Max meant by that, but it didn't sound good. She could only imagine the frontier justice Otter Bite would mete out.

Another fifty feet; another dozen friendly faces.

She stopped. Started to turn for a second time. "Elizabeth."

Max kept her moving. "She wasn't in the plane."

"Are you sure?"

"I looked everywhere. She's not in the plane."

Her knees weakened. Max held her up. "We'll find her. People are looking. I'm sure Fitz left her somewhere safe."

Daisy stopped, stared at Max. "Why . . . are you sure Fitz left her someplace safe? He kidnapped Elizabeth. People who kidnap turtles don't leave them someplace safe. The man is flying on fumes. This whole crazy-ass town is flying on fumes. Not one of you has full tanks! People were actually making bets on how Fitz was going to die. What kind of people do that?"

"You're upset—"

"Someone has to be! You sure as hell aren't. What's wrong with you? What do you have in there"—she poked his chest—"a big ol' glacier?" She cocked her head at him as reality hit. "You were gonna shoot Fitz. Shoot to kill, weren't you? You don't care about Elizabeth. You don't care about anything except your stupid lodge. People are just expendable, you ice-hearted bastard."

"We'll find Elizabeth," Max assured her.

"Don't put yourself out!" She stomped away.

Max released his clenched fist, but the quiver in his hands remained. He took a breath and started after Daisy.

"Miss! Hey, miss! You! *Turtle Lady!*"

Daisy stopped. One of the bet-makers came toward her with something in his grasp. Something round and not too big, but big enough. Something that looked very much like—

"Elizabeth!"

She ran back toward him, converging with Max.

"Is this your turtle, miss?"

Daisy reached muddy hands toward her turtle, tucked safely inside her shell. "Thank you. Thank you!"

"Fitz had her in his truck."

"Thank you," she repeated.

"She's a fine turtle," the bet-maker said.

Tearing up, Daisy only nodded and clutched Elizabeth to her.

"Y' did good with the boy," the bet-maker said, looking at Max. "Too bad about your plane. Coulda been worse all the way around, I guess."

Max looked back at the scene, the tail of his Cessna cresting the embankment. A few more pulls and it would be back on solid ground.

"Yep," Max blandly agreed. "Could've been worse."

"Whaddaya gonna do with Fitz?" the bet-maker asked.

"Don't have a lot of choice."

The bet-maker looked down at the ground then up at Max. "He won't do good locked up like that."

"Nope," Max agreed.

"He done it to himself, I guess," the man solemnly offered. "Sure gave folks a helluva show. Better'n fireworks." He gave that a moment to settle then he walked back toward his buddies.

Daisy glared at Max.

"What?" Max asked.

"Nothing," Daisy grumbled, turning away.

Chapter Thirty-Four

"*What?*" Max snapped for the third time.

"Nothing," Daisy grumbled for the third time, diverting her eyes from Max to Elizabeth, safe in her lap. Max's red truck thumped, bumped, and splashed its way down the road, and before Daisy expected it, they arrived at the lodge. Max steered the truck past the impressive entrance toward the employee cabins. He braked, shifted into park, and looked at Daisy.

"Are you going to be all right? Do you want me to get someone to handle dinner?"

Daisy stared incredulously. "Is that all you can think about? *Dinner?*"

"Hardly. Dinner is just one of a dozen things I have to think about. I have a busted-up pilot, a busted-up plane, and a lodge full of guests who don't give a rat's ass about either, but they'll care if they don't get fed tonight. So, are you going to do dinner or do I get someone else?"

"Are you really going to send Fitz to jail?"

Max eased back. "That's none of your business."

Daisy tensed. "You really are cold. Cold and unfeeling."

"I don't have the luxury of breaking dishes every time things don't go my way."

From tense to venomous. "And when do things ever *not* go your way? When are you ever *not* in control?"

He puffed up as if he might explode. "Be damn thankful I am in control because right now—"

"Right now *what?*" Daisy leaned into him.

"Right now—"

"*What?*"

He stared at her, his eyes stormy, his voice low, deep, and thunderous. "*Right now* . . . I might forget that you saved Fitz's life. I might forget what kind of day you've had. I might forget that you're emotionally distraught."

"Emotionally *distraught*?"

Max managed to find a little sympathy. "When was the last time you faced a gun?"

It took a moment. "Fitz wasn't going to shoot me."

"Of course not."

Her brows edged together. She looked hard at Max, at the blood smear still on his right cheek, at the unfathomable ocean in his eyes. A stew of emotions boiled inside her. "Tim can handle dinner," she said, referring to her assistant. Hugging Elizabeth and unlatching the door, she scrambled from the truck, mud flaking off her clothes as she went.

"Hey," Max said as Daisy turned to slam the door. "Why are you so angry?" *At me*, he wanted to add. Instead, he let the question unwrap itself.

Daisy looked at him as if she sensed his real question, but she wasn't prepared to answer either variation. The truth was, she didn't know exactly *why* she was angry except that . . .

"It's the best choice I have." Then she shut the door between them.

The steamy water pelted Daisy, pooling at her feet in chocolate drops that disappeared down the drain. Her jeans lay in a wet, indigo heap at the other end of the small bathtub where she had shed them after hosing off the mud outside.

If only she could separate herself from Otter Bite as easily.

Without Daisy even realizing it, the tears came, silently at first and then in sobbing waves and breathless heaves. Her hands shook, trying to shampoo her hair as if everything were normal. Just another day of breakfast, lunch, and dinner. Just another day of almost getting shot, maybe even killed. Just another day in a life that had become a spinning top—going round and round and round in every direction while getting absolutely nowhere.

Light-headed, Daisy managed to finish her shower; managed to stop the tears with deep, quivering breaths. She spread the shower curtain and stepped into steam that prevented reflection.

By the time she had dried her hair to damp, the fog was disappearing. She knew her eyes would be puffy, her face blotchy. She didn't need the mirror to confirm it so she quickly left the bathroom in her robe.

She checked on Elizabeth, who was happily munching her last leaf of lettuce—*need more lettuce*—completely oblivious to her own mortality . . . or maybe just accepting it.

Acceptance wasn't one of Daisy's strong points. *Kicking and screaming* was more her style . . . although she couldn't say that approach made much of a difference in the outcome.

She curled up on her sofa beside Elizabeth's terrarium, remembering when Elizabeth had come to live with her. Daisy was only twelve, and Elizabeth was barely three inches long. Not exactly the kitten she'd begged her parents for, but, as her father had explained, a turtle has many merits. For one thing, turtles live a long time—a real plus for her dad, who seemed to suffer more from Daisy's grief over the passing of their dog, Sophie, than the death itself. For another, they didn't take much space. And you could travel with them—an important consideration for a duty-free corporate family who had lived in Honolulu, Paris, London, and New York by the time Daisy was eighteen.

For twenty-three years, she and Elizabeth had weathered life's storms. For twenty-three years, Elizabeth had been one of the few constants in Daisy's life. She had clipped her nails, given vitamin drops, oiled her shell, taken her for "walks" in the park, let her swim in the bathtub. Whatever else happened in her life, she would take care of Elizabeth. There was comfort in having responsibility for another. And her dad had been right about the advantage of a long life. No niggling dread—until today—of an impending funeral. If the Universe allowed, Elizabeth would be with her for another twenty-three years. Yes, Elizabeth had many merits. Certainly more than—

No. She absolutely would not go there. She snuggled into her robe and lay against the cushions. The day weighted her like lead. Would it be so bad if she just gave up? Threw in the towel and got out of the ring? How wonderful it would be to stop taking punches . . .

That was the last thought Daisy had before the day knocked her out.

* * *

Max popped a pill to dull the throbbing in his knee. The scotch chaser was for the quiver in his hands—a reminder of how bad he was at that at which he was very good.

He put his glass on the bathroom sink and leaned into the mirror to check the cut on his cheek. Like so many events in his life lately, he wasn't even sure how it had happened. Just one uncontrollable fiasco after another. And like a family tree, each could trace its roots back to Daisy Moon.

During the last few weeks, he'd managed to block Daisy from his thoughts. Well, most of the time. Going to her cabin on the morning after had been a mistake, he realized too late. Not his first one—that had been meeting Daisy at Mama Mia's. Or his worst one—he wasn't going to think about that. But how could he have predicted his feelings when he didn't know he was capable of them?

But when she told him she didn't want to marry him...he blanked.

He'd had a plan and suddenly he was improvising. Words came out that he didn't know were there. He wasn't Max Kendall, he was some other guy...who, maybe, just a little, didn't think marrying Daisy Moon was such a bad idea.

But Daisy was playing him just to watch him squirm. Payback for scaring her in the woods. Not that he didn't deserve it. Still, he couldn't quite believe there wasn't something *else* . . .

So he asked her. *Move in with me.* But Daisy dismissed that without taking a breath. Dismissed him, too, or so it felt.

They'd barely seen each other, and spoken even less, and when they had it was always about work. Sometimes late at night, he'd hear her in the kitchen as he worked in his office. Too often, he had headed to his door, only to stop before turning the knob. There was just no purpose, not when what Daisy really wanted was to escape from Otter Bite.

Max turned from his reflection and cinched his robe. Taking his scotch, he re-entered his bedroom. Glass on the nightstand, pillows stacked against the headboard, he eased his way onto the bed and stretched his legs, then reached for his scotch, the quiver finally gone.

Escaping from Otter Bite, from Wild Man Lodge, from me *is probably all Daisy thinks about*, Max conjectured, taking up from where his last thought left off. *Especially after today . . .*

Maybe it was time to help things along.

Rita had told him about the restaurant critic from Anchorage. He could have spit nails! It was hard enough trying to keep Wild Man under the radar—Daisy had no right putting *his* lodge on the map! Last weekend, the guy showed. Friday, Saturday *and* Sunday for dinner. He and his wife. They had stayed at the Mad Fish B & B and taken a halibut charter. She shopped at the mercantile and they rented bicycles. They had drinks at the Lighthouse—he an Alaskan Amber, she a rum and Coke. There were few secrets in Otter Bite.

Daisy, however, didn't even try to keep secrets. Her contempt for pretty much everything about Max was right out there in the open. And she had no problem thinking the worst of him.

"I don't need this." Max shot back the remainder of his scotch. He rolled the cut crystal between his palms and watched the light play. The sooner Daisy left, the sooner he'd get his life back. The sooner he'd be Max Kendall again and not that other guy. He just wished it wasn't going to cost him so damn much.

He pulled himself from his comfort like so much lead and headed into the den. He might as well be heading to the gallows for all his enthusiasm. He sat in his desk chair and pulled out his address book from his side drawer, found the listing, and punched in the ten numbers on his cordless.

The ringing of her phone roused Daisy from her nap. It took a groggy moment to figure it out, and then she left the couch and reached the phone, expecting no surprises. "Hello?"

She could count on one hand the people who called her with regularity, Charity being at the top of the list. Daisy hadn't yet phoned her with the news of all that had happened today.

"Is this Daisy Moon?" asked the husky male voice on the other end of the line.

"Yes . . ."

"My name is Geoffrey Blanchard, Miss Moon. I don't expect you'd remember me, but I was a guest at the lodge a few weeks back. I visited you in the kitchen one evening. Gray hair, short beard and moustache. I had your fabulous cioppino . . . ?"

Vaguely, Daisy thought. "Yes, of course, I remember."

"Just to be clear, Miss Moon, Max gave me your number and said it was fine to call. I wouldn't be doing this otherwise."

"Sure, I understand. Do you want the recipe for the cioppino, Mr. Blanchard?"

"In a way, yes . . ."

Ten minutes later, Daisy hung up the phone, completely baffled by her own ambivalence. But the knocking on her door gave her no time to think about it.

"Grand central station," she mumbled, reaching the door and turning the knob.

"Just checking to see if you're okay," Rita said, inviting herself in.

"I'd be lying if I said I was."

Rita took a side chair. "Stuff like that happens out here. Y' just gotta shake it off and go on. After all, no one died."

Daisy shut the door and sat on the couch.. "No, but poor Fitz is going to jail. That's hardly a happy ending."

"Jail? Says who?"

"Max."

"Max told you Fitz was going to *jail*?"

"Well . . ." Daisy mentally backtracked. "He said Fitz would be locked up. If that doesn't mean jail, then what?"

"Rehab. He's booked a flight into Anchorage tomorrow. Putting him in the hospital to dry him out. Gonna force him to face his demons." Rita smirked. "Fitz'll probably wish he *was* in jail. Or dead."

Daisy dropped her eyes to the floor, looking at nothing in particular. Remembering similar words from Max.

"Of course, there are a few locals who think Fitz ought to be in jail. He could've killed people, himself included. We could be having a whole different conversation right now." She paused. "Rumor has it, you got Fitz to land. Kinda makes you a hero."

Daisy looked up. "Hardly a hero. Not by a long shot. All I did was talk. That's all, just talk."

"That's worth more than you think—"

"Max is the real hero," Daisy blurted, vacating the couch and missing the beginnings of Rita's smile. "Max . . . got the gun from Fitz. And if he had to, he would've . . ." Standing at the kitchen counter, Daisy breathed deeply. "All I did was talk."

"Sometimes, when you say the right words, talking is all it takes."

Daisy looked at Rita, at the wisdom shining in her dark eyes.

"Guess I'd better check on my patient," she said, pulling herself from the chair.

"Your patient?"

"Someone's gotta take care of the flyboy," Rita answered. "And I've got a weakness."

"But you don't like Fitz."

"I like Fitz just fine. It's the booze I don't like."

"But—"

"You gotta separate the yolk from the white before you can make crème brûlée. Think about it," she added when Daisy just stared. "Come see him, if you want. On your way to dinner."

"Actually"—Daisy stopped, changed direction—"I'll do that. On my way to dinner."

Chapter Thirty-Five

"Welcome," Rita said, stepping aside.

Daisy glanced around the familiar surroundings, having visited a half dozen times before. The layout was identical to her cabin, but the environment was cozy. Daisy lived in her cabin; Rita had made hers a home.

"Fitz is in the bedroom with Jasmine. I just fed him."

"Smells good." Daisy recognized the aroma of chicken soup.

"There's more."

"Thanks. I'll grab something at the lodge."

Rita gestured toward the bedroom. "Go on in."

Daisy softly called Fitz's name, then pushed the slightly ajar door further open.

"Come in, Daisy." Jasmine rose from her seat on the bed. "I'm just leaving."

The bedside lamp glowed golden through an amber shade. Propped up with pillows, Fitz sat in bed with a bowl of soup in one hand, spoon in the other. Rita's cat, Samantha, curled near the lumps under the covers that were Fitz's feet.

"Please, don't leave on my account," Daisy said.

"Fitz and I are done." Reaching Daisy, Jasmine hugged her; Daisy awkwardly hugged her back. "I'm sorry I couldn't get there in time to help, but I heard you saved the day. Thank you."

Get there in time to help? What had Jasmine intended to do? Telekinetically massage Fitz into landing the plane?

"I'm here if you want to talk," Jasmine added with one of the warmest, sincerest smiles Daisy had ever seen.

Alone with Fitz, Daisy asked how he was feeling.

"Like I've been stomped by a bull." Fitz set his soup bowl on the nightstand. "And he's still inside my head."

That was probably an understatement. Fitz sported a purple eye and a swollen nose, where Max's fist had most likely landed. She suspected a few bruises and bumps were out of sight beneath his T-shirt.

"I guess I owe you an apology . . . and a thank-you."

Daisy shrugged as she eased into a vacant spot the other side of the lumps from Samantha. "I'm just glad you're okay."

"I'm sorry I took your turtle. I just wanted to show her to the guys." Fitz looked down at his lap where one shaky hand brushed the scraped knuckles of the other.

"It's all right, Fitz, really. We've all done stupid things."

Fitz looked up as if he doubted Daisy's confession.

"Not too long ago, I broke the china in my fiancé's restaurant. Smashed it to smithereens. Thousands of dollars. And I was stone-cold sober."

"He musta deserved it."

"Maybe." Another shrug. "But probably not." She diverted her eyes to the intimate bedroom, stopping at the framed photographs atop the dresser. Her eyes locked on an 8 x 10 photo of Rita with a toddler in her arms, standing beside a man, everyone smiling.

"The point is," she continued, dragging her eyes off the photo and ignoring the questions it inspired, "we all do stupid things. If we're lucky, we live to confess them."

Eyes back on his hands, he tugged on fingers. "Thing is . . . me and July Fourth . . . we don't get along very good."

When Fitz looked up, tears flooded his eyes.

"You were in there a while," Rita said when Daisy finally emerged from the bedroom.

"Fitz feels really bad about today."

"He should. He coulda killed people."

"You don't take prisoners, do you?"

Standing in the kitchen, Rita tilted her head at Daisy, at the curtness in her voice. "He could have *killed* people, Daisy. What would you say to the families and friends?" Her voice went dumb. "Duh. Fitz feels really bad?"

"I'm just saying . . . sometimes people do things for reasons that . . . aren't always their fault."

Rita looked incredulous. "*Really?*"

"Stuff happens."

"Yeah, stuff happens. And if you wanna take yourself out of the picture, that's one thing. But you don't have the right to take someone else with you. You just don't."

Interesting choice of words, Daisy thought, remembering the dresser photograph. "Well, it all turned out okay."

"It turned out dandy for everyone but Max. His plane is busted; his pilot is busted. *He's* busted. And he's got the rest of the season to get through. But, like you say, it all turned out okay."

"What do you mean, Max is busted?"

Rita brushed by Daisy for the sofa. "Nothing."

"No way." Daisy followed the few steps after her. "I know you want to tell me so I can feel really, really bad."

"Are you capable of feeling bad for Max?"

"For your information, Rita, the man is *suing* me. It's hard to feel bad for someone who's extorting money."

"He's only suing you because he has to."

"Yeah, right." Daisy headed for the door.

"It's true."

She stopped.

"Do you have any idea how much money his injured knee is costing him?"

"He has medical insurance, Rita. Everyone has insurance now."

"Yeah, Daisy, Max has insurance. And he also has a deductible and a co-pay. Add those together and Max paid almost $6,000 out-of-pocket toward his surgery."

Daisy, who rarely had an insurance claim other than for her annual checkup and birth control—*oh yeah,* and her emergency room visit after Mama Mia's—never gave her deductible or co-pay much thought. But $6,000? Wow. "Okay, but that's $19,000 less than the $25,000 he's suing me for."

"Six thousand is only the beginning. It's like dominoes. Max may be the boss, but he's a *working* boss. When he's out of commission, someone has to replace him. And what he does is expensive."

Rita wasn't whistling Dixie, her explanation proved. A good, experienced pilot—and why would anyone hire a bad, inexperienced pilot?—commanded $50,000 to $100,000 a season, depending on the type of aircraft and flying required. Fitz was making $65,000 for a short season; Max had another month of recuperation before he would be certified to fly again.

And now, with Fitz going into rehab, Max needed another good, experienced pilot. But one would be hard to come by mid-season. Ironically, even if he found a pilot, he was also down one plane. Aviation repair shops weren't as plentiful as automotive shops; getting the Cessna fixed could take months.

"But he has insurance, right?" Daisy asked.

"Sure. And a $5,000 deductible. With one less pilot and one less plane, he's gonna have to contract with charters *if* they aren't already booked solid with their own clients. I don't even know what that will cost, but it ain't gonna be cheap."

Plus, until Max's knee was fully functioning, *Molly-Anne* needed a captain.

Daisy dropped like a rock onto Rita's sofa. Roughly adding everything, she figured Max's knee had toppled $85,000 in dominoes. By comparison, the $25,000 Max wanted from her was chump change. Maybe . . .

Wait. What had Max inadvertently told her?

I banged it up pretty good a few years back and it's been an accident waiting to happen.

Chump was right.

"You almost had me," Daisy said. "But Max's knee was already banged up. He told me it was an accident waiting to happen."

"Can you honestly say you don't feel even the tiniest bit responsible for what happened to Max? That you had absolutely *nothing* to do with it?"

"I'm not responsible for Max's problems. I don't blame *him* for the china I broke."

"Max wasn't there when you did that."

Her brow pinched. "If he'd left the restaurant when I wanted . . ."

"So this is Max's fault?"

"Not completely. I mean, it's no one's fault . . . except for maybe Jason. And Tina."

"Sounds like it's everyone's fault but yours. Of you four, Max was the innocent bystander."

"Not completely innocent. He knows Tina."

"Is that why you're punishing him?"

From a pinch to a scowl. "I'm not punishing Max! And you've heard only one side of the story."

"I haven't heard *any* side. Max isn't much of a talker."

"Then how do you know about the lawsuit?"

"I get the mail. I answer phones. And I snoop in his desk. I've seen the letters from his lawyer. And I took a call from Tina once."

If the mention of Tina hadn't knotted her stomach, Daisy might've taken a moment to admire Rita's sleuthing.

"Max wouldn't sue if he had any other choice. He's a stand-up guy."

"Unless the situation calls for him to be lying down."

"Not that I think Max needs defending," Rita began. "But he hasn't been with anyone else since you've been here. And he's had opportunity. Including Tina."

"And I should applaud his restraint?"

"No. You should open your eyes and see what's in front of you. But if you can't do that . . . you should leave."

Rita's suggestion stopped Daisy's heart—or so it felt. Which was crazy, since leaving is exactly what Daisy had wanted to do—what she now *could* do—thanks to Geoffrey Blanchard.

"Max has an awful lot of stuff going wrong," Rita added. "He might have to cancel reservations for this season. If he loses income, on top of the extra expenses, he'll have to put his plans on hold."

"What plans?" That fast, she cursed herself for asking.

"Max was going to add on this winter. Guest cabins for next season. But that takes money."

Why her rum and Midori cocktail popped into her mind, Daisy wasn't sure, but a niggling sense of guilt followed. Still, this lodge *reeked* of money. "Max doesn't seem to be hurting."

"You don't know what goes on behind the curtain."

"He sure as hell isn't running a charity, I know that."

"Then you know diddly," Rita said. "You're not the only one who has dreams. Some people are just quieter about theirs."

Daisy didn't want to appear to be fleeing, but she couldn't get out of Rita's cabin fast enough. Stammering something about being late for dinner prep, she dashed out the door and kept right on walking.

All the way to the lodge, she tried to shake Rita's words. Rita was

Max's friend; of course she was on his side. But there wasn't malice in what she had said. Bluntness, yes, but Rita was going only for a wake-up call, not the jugular.

Which didn't mean Daisy had to buy any of it. Everything was more complicated than Rita had made it seem. Upside-down and backwards.

Open your eyes...

As if her eyes weren't open. They saw everything, real or imagined. What Daisy needed to do was *close* her eyes.

Because love, Daisy thought, reaching the lodge, *is blind.*

Chapter Thirty-Six

Dinner had been busy. There were lodge guests, of course, but also locals and summer residents with visiting friends and family. Ian and Emily had come; true to her word, Daisy had given them three jars of "leftover" chowder to take home. Every seating was full; Daisy had even extended the kitchen hours to accommodate a group of eight who arrived at nine thirty.

Finally, it was over. The dishes washed. The pots and pans hung. The tables set for breakfast. The last of the weary staff headed home, pockets flush with tips. At one thirty in the morning the lights dimmed, wild men slumbered beneath Egyptian cotton sheets, and today vanished into yesterday and tomorrow had arrived.

Daisy made it through, although Fitz had certainly been a topic of conversation. But work had overpowered gossip, and the day's excitement gave way to routine. Drink requests. Dinner orders. Food out. Dishes in. The kitchen danced in a well-timed choreography.

If only my life ran like my kitchen, Daisy thought, surveying her stainless domain. Then her sights drifted to the office door.

Max had been in the kitchen when Daisy arrived for the dinner shift, pitching in beside Tim just like one of the tip-reliant staff. After Daisy's assurance that she was okay, he retreated into his office. Not for the duration, of course. He had been in and out as duties demanded, but never interfered in her job.

Not that he ever had. Oh, sure, he rolled his eyes at the mango chutney and the cinnamon coffee and made an occasional sarcastic comment about the *bistro-dized* menu. But he let her run the kitchen and create the menus and never complained about the expenses—a rarity in the cost-conscious restaurant business. And every now and then, he'd leave a handwritten compliment magnetized to the refrigerator door for all her staff to share.

Rita had it right—Max wasn't much of a talker. But Daisy talked enough for two. She'd said some horrible things to Max. *Ice-hearted bastard* came to mind. And, as usual, she'd presumed the worst. Not that Max didn't deserve—

"Get over it," Daisy grumbled to her self-righteous other half. How long was she going to keep Max nailed to that cross?

She walked to the office door, curled her fingers into a fist, but stopped before knuckles met wood.

What exactly was her plan?

Her right hand dropped.

Apologize . . .

And then what? Her brain churned.

Maybe it was enough just to apologize. Maybe, right at this moment, she didn't need a *then what*. Maybe all she needed was a *now*.

Asleep on the couch, Max couldn't quite figure out the source of the banging that threatened to wake him. His brow wrinkled. Was it hammering? Sure. That's it. They were building his guest cabins.

When silence returned, his brow relaxed and he rolled away from the bright light of his desk lamp. He'd check on the builders later. Right now he just wanted to sleep.

That damn hammering, Max thought, slowly gaining awareness. He opened his eyes to dark leather and took a moment to get his bearings. Rolling over on his back, he eased himself up, stretching away the stiffness he felt. Papers littered the floor by his feet where they'd spilled from his hands.

He checked his watch, surprised at the time, trying to remember when he'd moved from his desk to the couch. He reached down to collect the construction contract he'd been reviewing before exhaustion won out.

Looking at the top page, he paused. All of his expansion plans—everything he'd been working and saving for during the last three years—had in one day slipped through his fingers like sand. The guest cabins would have to wait, that's all. He tried not to think about the people he was disappointing—the locals who were counting on winter construction work, his staff who were expecting year-round employment. And the men who came here for support, away from wives and girlfriends who tried—*Lord, how they tried*—but couldn't possibly understand. He tossed the contract on his desk and pulled open the top drawer. The check from Sotheby's stared back at him. Who would've thought a few old Superman comics could bring such a windfall? He took the check—already endorsed—folded and tucked it inside the pocket of his flannel shirt.

Exiting the lodge, Daisy snuggled into her fleece jacket against the early morning chill. Penetrating the dusky veil, voices and laughter reached her before she met the source of the happiness on the deck steps.

"Daisy?"

Through the grainy ambience, it took a moment to recognize the two men in their fluffy white lodge robes, each with a generous towel slung over their shoulders and each with a bottle of Alaskan Amber.

"Hi, guys," Daisy responded to Pete Newton and his son-in-law, Dylan. "Out for a swim?"

"Yeah, in the hot tub," Dylan answered. "Don't tell me you're just getting off work?"

"Holidays are always busy."

"Speaking of that, I had your salmon for dinner, with the mango on top. Absolutely fantastic."

"Thanks."

"I'd love to get that sauce recipe . . . for Ellen," he quickly added.

"I'll go one better. Stop by the kitchen before you leave for home and I'll give you a jar of it."

"Y' know, Daisy, you ought to sell your sauces. They'd make good gifts."

"You're not the first person who's suggested that. Maybe next year."

"We heard about the excitement in town today," Pete said. "Sort of wish we'd been there."

"If only we'd arrived a little later, we would've seen it all," Dylan said.

"Not that exciting. Just another day in Otter Bite."

"Everything turned out okay then." Sort of a question.

"Sure." She thought about Fitz in rehab, Max's busted plane, her big mouth, and now, her failed apology. Her knocks hadn't been answered. Sometime during the evening Max must have left his office without her noticing. Now she wondered if Fate was telling her to forget the whole thing.

"You probably want to hit the sack," Pete said, moving toward the lodge. "And I have a massage scheduled."

"Good night, Daisy," Dylan said. "Can't wait for breakfast."

"Pete, do you have a minute?"

Pete motioned for Dylan to go on.

"I . . . have a question. Kind of personal—"

He cocked his head.

"—about Max—"

"Yeah?"

"—and your daughter. I sort of heard something and I just kind of wondered if it was true. It has to do with Acapulco and a parrot."

Pete chuckled. "I'll cut to the chase. Max saved Ellen's life and all he got for it was a parrot, a busted knee, my eternal gratitude, and a couple of namesakes. Ellen has a son and a daughter, Max and Avery."

She sort of smiled. "Thanks."

"Y' know, Daisy, pilots have a saying . . . well, pilots have lots of sayings. As a whole, we're a philosophizing bunch. But one, in particular, might apply here—"

What pearls of wisdom were about to be cast?

"You can always make a one-eighty—up until you crash."

One brow lifted. "I'll think about it."

"You do that. Good night, Daisy."

Daisy was no sooner down the deck steps when she remembered and made a one-eighty back to the lodge. Going through the guest wing, she passed Scottie leaving a room, carrying a portable massage table. Three doors down, she saw Jasmine enter Pete's room, without one.

Max scooped up the last bite of salmon and mango from his plate and put his dish and fork into the stainless steel sink where they joined the small frying pan. No food since breakfast, but it still surprised him how hungry he'd been.

He screwed the lid on the jar of mango chutney, ignoring the dollop that had landed on the counter, and returned it to the refrigerator shelf next to the jar of blueberry sauce used as a garnish for rib eyes. It was a toss-up which he liked better—not that he'd ever admit liking either. But his guests certainly did. Without fail, feedback forms mentioned the great food; some suggested a cookbook; some wanted jars of Daisy's sauces.

Max shut the refrigerator, shaking his head. Maybe, as Daisy had said, he was in a *culinary time warp*. Turning, he stepped back, his heart thumping.

Daisy quizzically stared at him from the doorway.

Regaining composure, he asked, "What're you doing here?"

"I could ask you the same question."

"I own the joint."

Her heart pounding, Daisy approached Max, who stood between her and the refrigerator. "I was heading for my cabin when I remembered I needed lettuce for Elizabeth. In the fridge." She gave Max a pointed look until he stepped aside. "I didn't know anyone was here. I thought you'd gone." Retrieving a single lettuce leaf from a bag, she closed the refrigerator. "I knocked on your office door before I left."

"That was you?" He ran fingers through his uncombed hair. "I was zonked out on the couch. Thought I was dreaming."

A dollop of something on her previously spotless counter caught her attention. Her eyes wandered to the sink and the dirty plate and pan. She sniffed the air and caught the lingering aroma. "You were eating salmon with my mango chutney, weren't you?"

Max eased back at the accusation. "What are you, the salmon police?"

"*Real* men don't eat mango chutney."

"They do if it's the only thing they can find."

Daisy faced him. "Are you telling me, out of this whole kitchen, salmon with *my* mango chutney is the only thing you could find?"

"It was the easiest."

"The easiest?"

Max huffed. "Okay, fine. I ate your mango chutney."

"Be careful, Max, or you might be tempted to try the blueberry sauce."

Max remained conspicuously silent.

Daisy tilted her head. "You've had the blueberry sauce ... and you *like* it." She wagged her finger at him. "Admit it!"

"We were out of A-1."

"Liar."

"So, I tried your blueberry sauce. Big deal."

"It **is** a big deal, considering all the crap you give me over my *bistro-dized* food. Why can't you admit that you like my cooking?" She stepped toward him. "Would that be so hard?" Another step. "Would that be so tough? Would it totally and completely emasculate you to say, *Daisy, I like your mango*—"

His lips caught her next word. He snatched her at the curves of her shoulders and pulled her to him in one fluid move. When he released her, they both looked a little dazed.

"Sorry," Max said. "I just wanted to shut you up."

Not exactly the heartfelt sentiment she might've hoped for. But probably what she deserved.

"Want a ride home?" he asked, with something akin to resignation in his voice. "I'm going your way." Max was almost out the door. "It's not a hard question," he said when her silence seemed forever.

"I can walk."

"It's just a ride in a truck. Not a marriage proposal."

"I can definitely walk."

"It was a joke. Why do you always make a big deal about everything?"

"You're the one making it a big deal. I'm perfectly happy walking."

"God, are you stubborn."

"*Me* stubborn? What are *you*?"

"*Nice.* At least I'm trying. But you make it pretty damn hard."

She started to disagree, had the words right on the tip of her tongue . . . then sighed them away. "Fine."

Lettuce in hand, Daisy quickly passed him by. He flicked off the kitchen lights and followed her down the dimly lit hallway toward the back door.

"Just out of curiosity," Max began, holding the door for Daisy. "How'd you know about Fitz's brother? Marty. The one who died."

"I'm a snoop, remember?"

"Yeah." Down the steps. "But Fitz didn't tell you that he was the one who shot him."

"He told me his brother died in a hunting accident. I guess it was the way he looked. I made a short leap."

"Good leap. You probably saved his life. And maybe a lot of others."

It was weird thinking she might've saved Fitz's life, especially since it had happened without risk to her own. Weird and uncomfortable.

"How did *you* know?" she asked as he unlatched the truck's passenger door and pulled it open. "It doesn't seem like something a guy would confess to his boss."

"I recognized the symptoms and did a little digging. Do you want to talk about today?"

"No."

"No?"

Daisy climbed into Max's truck, understanding his surprise. She was an open book, after all, willing to talk about anything, and expecting the same from those around her, Max included. But this book she wanted closed. For the first time, she understood, just a little, why Max didn't like her snooping in his library.

"No," she repeated.

It was a short ride with some long thoughts, and Daisy was still waffling on an apology when the truck stopped at her cabin. "Thanks for the ride."

"It was on my way."

She looked at him, the dashboard lights warmly sprinkling his face, the scratchy stubble along his chin and cheeks, his eyes tired but nonetheless penetrating. Turning away, she started to pull the door latch, then, heart in her throat, she faced him. As if ripping off a Band-Aid, she blurted, "I'm sorry."

Max had the expression of someone who'd just seen a pig fly. The words tumbled from her lips. "I said some horrible things to you this afternoon. I was upset and angry and none of it was your fault. I assumed the worst and I was wrong about that, too, although you let me assume the worst. And I think it's awfully kind of you to put Fitz in rehab instead of jail, and I know you didn't want to shoot Fitz, but you had to protect the rest of us and I'm really sorry about your plane getting banged up, even though I had nothing to do with that, but it's still unfair considering how much you do for everyone around here and in spite of things that might be *questionable*, you really are, deep down, a decent guy."

Max blinked and Daisy was out of the truck. She shut the door on his astonishment and disappeared into her cabin.

Max wasn't sure how long he stayed in front of Daisy's cabin with the engine idling. But finally he pulled himself out of the shock of Daisy's ... *apology?* ... long enough to shift into gear and drive away.

Chapter Thirty-Seven

Daisy was climbing into bed when the knocking on her front door stopped her. She threw her pink terry cloth robe over her extra-large T-shirt, and shoved her feet into her slippers. Louder this time, the knocking repeated.

She flicked on the kitchen light. "Who is it?"

"Fitz."

Her heart sank; she realized how much she had wanted it to be Max. She flipped the deadbolt and opened the door, spilling light into the dusk.

Frozen at the sight of her visitor, she drew a blank before the obvious sputtered from her lips. "You're not Fitz."

"I wasn't sure you'd open the door if you knew it was me."

Her heart was back where it *otter* be, thumping madly. "That's just plain silly."

"I'm still standing on your porch."

"It's two thirty in the morning."

"I have a question."

"At two thirty in the morning?"

"Back in my truck . . . was that an apology?"

"You couldn't tell?"

"Well, you kind of blamed me for letting you assume some things and you included something about my questionable behavior, which sort of muddies the water."

"You could've told me that Fitz wasn't going to jail."

"It wasn't your business."

"You *wanted* me to think the worst."

"No, I just figured, given the choice, you would."

"You set me up."

"You set yourself up. You look for the bad and you find it."

Daisy snuggled into her robe. "I find it because it's usually there."

"You want it to be there so you can have moral superiority."

"Before you can speak intelligently about morals, you should at least have some. Or have you forgotten about the blonde?"

"Dwelling on past mistakes *that I can't change* doesn't do me any good. Obviously, you feel differently. And just out of curiosity, do you suppose there'll ever be a time when you won't hold that—and everything else—against me?"

Daisy parted her lips to say . . . what? That, without the blonde, she had no defense against him? That, without the blonde, she might let herself love him? That, without *everything else*, she might have to rethink her life and all that she thought she wanted . . . ?

"That's that, then." Max reached into his shirt pocket and pulled out the folded check. "Here."

Daisy unfolded it. "Jiminy Christmas! What's this for?"

"Your comics. From the garage sale. Remember that?"

"Yeah, but—"

"I said you might have some valuable issues."

"Y' think? But I can't take this." Handing it back. "You bought the comics. The money's yours."

"Why don't you let me have moral superiority just this once. Use the money for your restaurant. It's the only thing you really care about."

"It's not the *only* thing—"

"Geoff Blanchard made you a good offer. You should take it."

Daisy didn't have to ask how Max knew about the offer. "I wouldn't feel right leaving you in the lurch."

"I've been in the lurch before and it's heaven to where I am right now. Besides," he added, taking the edge off, "I've already hired someone."

Her heart dropped. "You've hired someone?"

"Yes."

She swallowed her protest, mustered her pride. "Then . . . this is my two-week notice."

"Two weeks or two hours. We'll manage."

"The least I can do is stay until your chef arrives."

"Not necessary."

"But—"

"Look—the sooner you're gone, the sooner you can stop blaming me for your unhappiness. And the sooner we can all get on with our lives."

Daisy had no words. No snappy comeback. No stinging retort.

He started to turn, then turned back. "What things are *questionable*?"

"What?"

"In the truck, you said there are things that are questionable. *What* things?"

"C'mon, Max. I'm not a complete idiot. The fake photos on your website, no wives. *Massages* in the guest rooms at two in the morning, *without* a table. It's as obvious as a red neon vacancy sign on a midnight highway."

"You think I'm a pimp."

"I think you run a legitimate business with a few *extras* thrown in. Which is why you want to fly under the radar."

Max wanted to say something else, Daisy could tell, but he let it go with his breath, as if he'd run out of steam. Seconds later, he was gone, the gray-blue dusk rushing to fill the emptiness as if he'd never been there.

Chapter Thirty-Eight

"Well, Daisy, you've had the grand tour, what do you think?" Geoff Blanchard offered a padded leather chair.

Daisy smoothed her suit skirt and took the seat as Geoff sat in the adjacent one. "Your kitchen is state-of-the-art, as you know. And the dining room . . ." She practically shivered at the elegance. At eight in the morning, Blanchard's was a sleeping beauty. Celadon china, cut crystal goblets, celery-colored linens, satin wallpaper atop bamboo wainscoting, and glittering chandeliers. The black baby-grand in the center, surrounded by snowy pillars and lush bamboo plants, inspired a forties retro ambience. All to magically awaken with the gentle kiss of the setting sun. She could hear the ivory keys and the clinking of goblets, smell the melting butter and the exotic spices, and imagined her reflection in the mirrored silver of the serving dishes. In short, Blanchard's was everything Daisy had ever wanted . . . "I can't think of a single thing I would change."

"Quite a difference from Wild Man."

Daisy smiled. "Worlds apart."

"A chef with your talent shouldn't be cloistered in Otter Bite, no offense to Max, of course. I love the lodge. But Seattle is the adrenaline in my veins, and I think you feel the same."

"I wouldn't be here if I didn't."

"I can imagine how Max reacted to mango chutney," Geoff continued, amused. "*Real men don't eat mangoes*," he added in a deep, mimicking voice before chuckling. "I bet you had your hands full dragging Max from his cave."

Daisy smiled, but shifted uneasily in her chair. "Actually, Max loved my mango chutney. And my blueberry sauce. I left two dozen jars."

"The wild man himself eating steak with blueberry sauce? Now that's something I have to see!"

"It's not that big a deal."

His smile eased. "It's funny how people surprise you sometimes."

"Speaking of surprises . . ." Daisy shifted from one cheek to the other. "There's something you should know . . . before you hear it from someone else."

"I'm intrigued."

"Well . . . there was this *little* incident at Fireflies—"

"If this is about the china, I already know."

Her shoulders sagged. "I assumed Max might've mentioned it—"

"Actually, Daisy, I talked with Jason." A wry smile. "No love lost there." Geoff leaned forward in his chair. "Admittedly, it gave me second thoughts. I mean, fifty thousand in damages—"

"It was only *thirty* thousand, and I paid for it," she countered, before realizing that didn't sound much better. "There were extenuating circumstances."

Geoff chuckled. "So Max told me."

"*Max?*"

"He didn't volunteer it, if that's what you're worried about. No, I spoke with Jason first, when I was thinking about making you this offer. And then I asked Max what he thought, knowing he wouldn't mince words." Geoff relaxed into the chair. "Quite honestly, if someone screwed me out of my restaurant, I might act the same. Besides, you spent ten years at Fireflies. C'mon."

So Max had pleaded her case. Probably gave her a glowing review just to get rid of her all the faster.

"You should know that Max wasn't in a hurry to let you go. I mean, it took a few weeks for the obvious to become apparent."

"The obvious?"

"What's in Otter Bite? A chef with your talent and ambition needs an audience who appreciates a brilliant performance. It's like Meryl Streep playing Walla Walla. Max flies under the radar, almost like he doesn't want people to know about the lodge. And you should be in the spotlight, Daisy, not working in obscurity."

Not too long ago, she had thought the same.

"But I admire his pragmatism. It was only a matter of time before someone came along and stole you away. Why prolong the inevitable? Face it, Daisy, you and Wild Man were just a fling. But you

and Blanchard's"—he leaned forward—"we're talking marriage."
After a moment to let things settle, Geoff once again relaxed. "So,
Daisy, what do you think?"

"Well, you sure put things into perspective."

"I knew you and I would think alike." Geoff lifted the forest-
green, leather-bound menu off his desk. He handed it to Daisy as if it
were the Bible.

Daisy checked out the cover—*Blanchard's* in gold script diago-
nally across the front. then opened it. A quick perusal and she looked
at Geoff. "It's in French."

"*Très élégant, oui?*"

"Yes, I mean, *oui*, but not everyone speaks French."

"They should, don't you think?"

"*Bien sûr,*" she agreed. "But for those who don't?"

Geoff waved away her concern. "We have a menu with subtitles.
Although most of our patrons either ask for translation or just give it
a go. Like opening a package on Christmas."

Daisy dropped her gaze to the crisp linen paper and the black
script. She started at the top with the hors d'oeuvres and then followed with the *salades* as Geoff continued talking.

"In time, you'll have an opportunity to add your own selections
and, of course, you'll be responsible for the *du jour* menu, within the
Blanchard parameters, of course. It's where we try out the exotics."

Daisy glanced up. "Exotics?"

"Pheasant, wild boar . . . *médaillons de cheval*. Et cetera, et
cetera."

Her brow lifted. "*Cheval?*"

"Is there a problem?"

"This isn't Tokyo." She remembered Buster's kind eyes and soft
muzzle. "I'm surprised Seattleites would eat *cheval*."

"People want the nouveau and the avant-garde—"

Daisy dropped her eyes to the *soupes*.

"That's what we give them—"

She blinked at the elegant words on the elegant parchment—*la
chaudrée de tortue Blanchard*. She read the words again—*la chaudrée de tortue*—as Geoff continued gushing.

"—with a few traditional selections which are the cornerstone of
Blanchard's."

"Chaudrée de tortue . . . ?"

"Chaudrée de tortue Blanchard. Very popular. Not another Seattle restaurant serves it."

Of all the restaurants in all the cities in all the world, I had to walk into this one. She closed the menu and forced a smile.

Ten minutes later, Daisy was on the curb by the VALET PARKING sign, waiting for her ride. Overcast but pleasant, the day held the promise of a sunny afternoon. People in suits passed her on the sidewalk as they exited the corner Starbucks. Cars, taxis, buses, delivery trucks crisscrossed the street. She scanned the buildings around her, the high-rise offices and the luxury condos; she could smell, albeit faintly on the same breeze that ruffled her red spirals, the fish coming off the docks near Pike Place Market.

Everything had worked out perfectly. Looking back, Daisy marveled at the circuitous route she'd taken to get here, standing on the curb outside of Blanchard's.

Like dominoes—Charity, Jason, Tina, Rita, Max—they'd pushed her back to the beginning, which is where she wanted to be. Blanchard's wasn't quite her own restaurant—but neither, as it turned out, was Fireflies. Still, the salary was great and the exposure, even better. Charity had been right. People forget.

Or, in Daisy's case, whatever you can't forget you stuff into a memory drawer and pretend.

Two taps from a car horn jolted Daisy from her thoughts. She quickly passed between the front and tail of two parked cars and slid into the passenger seat of Charity's silver Jaguar.

"Well . . . ?" Charity asked, checking the side mirror before pulling into traffic.

"I finally know someone more pretentious than me."

"How is that possible?" Charity maneuvered into the left turn lane behind a BMW.

"Believe me, it was a shock."

"Oh, Daisy," Charity said as they waited for the arrow, "there's not a pretentious bone in your body. So how was it really?"

"Three words. *Chaudrée de tortue.*"

"Oooh."

"*Oooh* is right."

"No way around it?"

"A cornerstone and very popular," Daisy said, paraphrasing Geoff's words. "I don't see how I can get around *that*."

A horn blasted from behind. Both women shot eyes forward. The BMW was gone and the arrow had changed to yellow. Charity gunned the Jag and whipped around the corner as the opposing traffic converged into the intersection. A screech of tires, a second, heavy-handed horn blast—then a shiny red truck bore down upon their back bumper. His engine revved and he roared past, the driver's middle finger shooting at them.

"Neanderthal jerk," Charity grumbled.

"Ditto."

They headed for the I-5 on-ramp and the Tacoma Narrows Bridge beyond, along with a herd of other vehicles.

"Y'know," Charity finally said as they cruised into the center lane. "It's not like you have to kill the turtles yourself." She paused. "Do you?"

"God, I hope not."

Charity waved away her own concern. "Don't know why I asked that. Of course, you don't. By the time the turtles arrive at your kitchen, there's probably nothing distinguishable about the meat at all. Kind of like looking at a rib eye and trying to visualize a cow."

"True. But it's better not to have a personal relationship with your food."

"I'd feel the same way if someone served up a dog . . . or a horse." Daisy glanced at Charity.

"Some things are not meant to be eaten," Charity concluded.

"I'm not sure anything with a heart is *meant* to be eaten," Daisy said, knowing that philosophy didn't mesh well with her profession. "But in spite of the turtle chowder, it's a great offer."

A red truck sped by them in the carpool lane.

"It's not him," Charity said; she steered into the carpool lane behind the red truck, which was rapidly escaping reach.

"What's not him?"

"The red truck. It's not Max."

"*Max?* Of course, it's not him. Why would you even say such a thing? Geez, Char."

"Because every time there's a red truck you stop breathing."

"That's ridi—"

"Don't bother. I'm a psychologist and even if I weren't, I know you too well. You've been here two days and not a single word about Max. You haven't trashed him; you haven't praised him. You didn't even volunteer that he dropped his lawsuit; I had to *ask* about it. You're acting like he doesn't exist."

"He doesn't exist."

Charity softened. "What in the world happened between you and Max?"

"Nothing." Daisy turned her gaze to the passing landscape. "Because I wouldn't let it. And now for my punishment, I have to make chowder out of Elizabeth's family." She shuddered.

Charity kept her equally repulsed reaction to herself. "You could always go back to Otter Bite."

"No, I can't."

"Why not? I don't want you to leave Seattle again, but hang out in Alaska until another offer comes along. You know it will."

Daisy turned toward Charity. "Promise me you won't meddle."

"I never—"

"Promise!"

Charity surreptitiously crossed her fingers. "Fine."

"Max asked me to leave. He sort of arranged my job at Blanchard's and told me to take it. Then he gave me a check for $42,000—"

Charity gasped and shot her eyes to Daisy. "Forty-two thou—"

"Charity!" Daisy screamed at the glowing red lights on the stopped Jeep in front of them.

Charity slammed the brake pedal and the Jaguar skidded to a stop inches from the Jeep's bumper. "Forty-two thousand?" Charity repeated, as the traffic started to creep along. "That's quite a severance package."

"It's for my *Superman* comics. You probably don't remember, but Max bought them at my garage sale. He sold them at auction."

"And gave *you* the proceeds? That's . . . *impressive*."

"What's impressive is how much he wanted me gone."

Charity contained her smile. "That's impressive, too."

"So now can we stop talking about Max Kendall?"

"You love him, don't you?"

They started across the bridge. Daisy gazed out onto the water at the single sailboat battling the whitecaps. "I'll get over it. Pretty soon I'll be too busy to even think about him."

"So you're taking the job at Blanchard's?"

"I'd be crazy not to." She looked at Charity with beseeching eyes. "Just don't tell Elizabeth about . . . you know."

Charity glimpsed Daisy long enough to catch the *I'm kidding, but not really* glimmer in her eyes. It was ridiculous, of course, worrying about Elizabeth's feelings, but it was equally endearing and *sooo* Daisy. Was it any wonder Max loved her?

"Not a word to Elizabeth," Charity promised.

Chapter Thirty-Nine

Max Kendall braked his mother's black vintage Mercedes in front of the diner. He considered the odd-looking establishment that was tucked between a print shop and a dressmaker along a narrow side street dotted with parked cars. THE LOBSTER SHACK glowed in red neon above the mustard-colored double doors. Small windows on either side gave no clue as to what existed behind the brick front.

"Are you sure *this* is where you want to have lunch?" Max asked his mother in the passenger seat beside him.

"Yes, dear, absolutely," Maeve Kendall insisted.

"Blanchard's is only a few blocks away. Why don't we eat there instead?"

For the third time, Maeve said, "I don't want to eat at Blanchard's. The Lobster Shack has the best cioppino I've ever tasted and the seafood chowder brings back memories of Ireland."

Max scrutinized the diner again. "Really?"

"Y' can't judge a book by its cover."

"Let's hope not."

A foursome of suits came up the sidewalk and one by one entered the diner through the mustard doors.

"It gets quite busy at lunchtime," Maeve said. "I should go in and nab a booth while you park the car."

"If you're sure." Max shifted into Park.

Maeve stopped his exit; she grabbed her black patent leather purse and swung open the door herself. "Try to park next to a nice car," she said before gently closing the door.

Max waited until his mother was safely inside the diner, then he checked over his shoulder for traffic. A taxi passed and then a Mazda before the way was clear.

A parking space was available a few cars down, in front of an In-
dian boutique named Nirvana, but Max would be putting his mother's
beloved Mercedes between a work truck with a dented front fender
and a rusted van with a hand-painted peace symbol on its rear.

The next space in front of an architect's office looked promising.
Behind was a silver Jaguar and in front was a shiny red Pathfinder
with a Greenpeace bumper sticker on the left and a SAVE THE TURTLES
proclamation on the right. He parked the Mercedes and an unexpected image of Elizabeth appeared in his mind before he banished
that and every related thought.

Seven weeks had passed since he loaded up Daisy's remaining
boxes into the Homer Air 206 for the first leg of a long trip back to
Seattle. Seven weeks and two days, to be precise, as if precision
changed anything.

It had all blended together, one day into the next as he tried to
keep it together with a lodge full of guests and one less plane, one
less pilot, and one less chef. But the Tilt-A-Whirl was finally winding down. Fitz had returned two days ago, Max's plane was due back
next week, and Rita had a line on a chef after weeks of trying to du-
plicate Daisy's recipes with mixed results. Now, after repeated calls
from his doctor, he'd finally found the time for a post-surgical
checkup and a visit with his parents—a quick two-day trip to Seattle.

Max locked the Mercedes and stepped onto the sidewalk. For the
first time in years, he had no pain, no hitch, no limp. He walked
briskly toward the diner, past the businesses lining the sidewalk
while thinking that, one of these days, he'd have to thank Daisy for
forcing the cure. *If* he ever saw her again. But what would he say if
he did? *Remember me? I'm the guy who sent you packing . . .*

What had he been thinking, suggesting Blanchard's for lunch?
Was he hoping for a glimpse of Daisy? Intending to spy on her? Or
did he think seeing her happy would make him forget her?

Whatever he'd been thinking, he hadn't been *thinking*, or he
never would've entertained such a sentimental urge. Relief washed
over him that he wasn't at Blanchard's now, making a fool of himself.

He arrived at the mustard doors in front of a trio of casually
dressed women, but entered behind them after holding the door open.
Their penetrating gazes and inviting smiles spoke volumes, but Max

dismissed them with a smile, like background noise. A quick scan around the diner, rapidly filling to its small capacity, and Max found his mother hailing him from a corner booth. He passed the counter with its many occupied stools, doing a double take at a familiar blonde whom he couldn't quite place, before shrugging it off and joining his mother.

The waitress had already delivered water and menus.

"How in the world did you find this joint?" he asked, perusing the laminated selections.

"A friend."

"A friend?" Max looked up from the soup choices. "Which one of *your* friends would come to a place like this?" He checked out the rustic decor, reminiscent of a surfer's shack If you stretched your imagination. Otherwise, it looked like a run-down café with fake palms crowding every corner. An untalented attempt at a mural of blue skies, ocean waves, and sandy beaches spread across one wall. But the real scene-stealer was a bubbling glass tank behind the counter filled with—no kidding—*plastic* lobsters.

"The food is excellent," Maeve said. "And when did you become a snob?"

Max looked at his unmatched flatware, one tine on his fork slightly askew. "I have no idea." He returned to the menu. Too bad the prices weren't as cheap as the decor.

"Are you ready to order?" the waitress asked, appearing from the crowd. She wore a white T-shirt with the words THE LOBSTER SHACK emblazoned in red across her modest bosom.

"Yes," Maeve answered brightly. "I'll have the half plate of co-conut shrimp to start, along with the salmon nuggets and a cup of chowder."

"And I'll have—" Max began before being silenced by a glare from Maeve. "Sorry. Thought you were done."

"And I'd like a bowl of cioppino—"

"No cioppino today. Cook didn't like the mussels." The waitress sighed as if disapproval was a common, albeit annoying, occurrence in the kitchen.

"Then I'll try the curried halibut with a side of chipotle salmon penne pasta and . . . let me see . . .

Max stared at his mother. "Are you kidding?"

"...the garden salad with blueberry vinaigrette," Maeve contin-ued. "For dessert, save me a bananas Napoleon. And I'll have a Kil-lian's."

The waitress finished writing on her pad, then turned to Max. "And for you?"

"Just bring me a Killian's and a plate."

The waitress nodded, took back the menus, and went to the next booth.

"You're not eating?" Maeve asked.

"I'll be eating plenty. Everything you don't." He trained his eyes on Maeve. "What's going on?"

"I don't know what y' mean."

"You drag me down to some obscure diner that I *know* you would never go to, and then you order for a group of dockworkers." The seconds ticked. "I'm waiting, Mother."

"Fine. You're so stubborn, y' never would've come otherwise."

"What are you talking about?"

"I've found you a cook—"

Max jerked back. "What?"

"—for the lodge."

"Mother—"

"Don't *mother* me, Maxim Avery Kendall. Y've got poor Rita running ragged without a spare second for a personal life. Just be-cause you aspire to be Uncle Arvis—"

"Enough with the pigeons."

"—doesn't mean y' have to force that on your employees."

Max sighed. "This summer has been tough on *everyone*."

"So I'm helping out. I've found y' a cook. And for your informa-tion, Jeanne brought me here and I've come back three times since, once with your da. And each and every time the food was the best."

Max glanced around. "Uh-huh."

"You'll see."

"Even so, Mom, you're presuming a lot to think this cook would want to move to Otter Bite. The guy's probably married...with a dozen kids...and has his own double-wide. He's undoubtedly happy right where he is."

"Well, now, depends on your offer, don't y' think?"

"Why don't we try the food before we even go there."

As if on cue, the waitress arrived with two beers, the coconut shrimp, the salmon nuggets, a cup of chowder, and the salad with blueberry vinaigrette. She placed an empty plate in front of Max.

"Y' forgot the dipping sauce, dear, for the salmon nuggets."

She surveyed the table. "Be right back."

"Y've got to try this," Maeve told Max as the waitress delivered a small bowl of pale orange sauce with bits of something vaguely familiar.

Max eyed the concoction, forked a salmon nugget, and dipped.

Maeve followed suit, blowing delicate puffs of air onto the hot salmon before popping it into her mouth. "Have y' ever tasted anything so delicious?"

Stabbing salmon, Max repeated the process. "As a matter of fact, I have."

"Order!" the waitress called, ripping a sheet off her pad and stuffing it in the turnstile.

"What is it?" Daisy whisked curry sauce in a small saucepan as halibut chunks cooked on the grill.

"Two salmon burgers and a spinach salad. And a woman at the counter wants *consommé tort*-something. Do we have that?"

Daisy softly laughed as she turned off the flame beneath the curry. "I'll take care of it." She flipped halibut chunks with a spatula. Then she grabbed a plate, scooped rice onto it, nested the halibut, and poured the curry over the mound. She set the steaming dish in the garnish line for her assistant to finish.

From the fridge, she grabbed two fresh salmon patties and placed them on the grill. Before they started sizzling, she was dishing out baby spinach from a large bowl onto a small oval platter. She set it in the garnish line for almonds and sweet mustard dressing. Then she ladled out a hearty helping of chowder and cut a slab of sourdough bread. "I'm taking a quick break," she told her kitchen staff. "Watch the grill."

"Daisy doesn't know I'm here, does she?" Max asked his mother.

"Mmmm. Not exactly."

"Then we can leave without her ever knowing."

"But you haven't tried the curry or the pasta."

"I'm sure they're delicious. Daisy's an excellent chef."

"I'll tell her you said so," the waitress said, delivering the two entrées.

"Don't bother. I mean, I'll tell her myself—" *Not.* His escape from the booth blocked, Max drummed his fingers on the table.

"Anything else?" the waitress asked.

"The check."

The waitress looked perplexed. "Should I bring the bananas Napoleon at the same time?"

"Yes."

"No."

Maeve scowled at her son. "Yes!"

"Be right back," the waitress said.

"Max, you're acting foolish. A half hour ago, you were practically begging to go to Blanchard's, as if I don't know why. Now here's your opportunity to do what y' wanted to do all along and you're like Haemish Hamlish."

"*Who?*"

"Your cousin, twice removed. Youngest boy of your Aunt Eileen's oldest daughter, Anna."

Clueless, Max craned his neck for the waitress with his check. "I give. How am I like Haemish?"

"You're being foolish."

"Yeah, Mom, I got that. Look, I don't know how you know about Blanchard's or what you *think* you know about Daisy and me—"

"Rita told me everything. How grumpy you've been ever since Daisy left, your twenty-hour work days, you refusin' to hire another cook."

"I'm grumpy *because* I'm working twenty-hour days and I'm working twenty-hour days because I'm understaffed and I haven't hired another *chef* because there haven't been any good applicants and putting Daisy and me on a collision course will not change any of that. Can we go?"

"I differ with that opinion. And so does Dr. Wagstaff."

"Who's Dr. Wagstaff?"

"Don't y' remember? We met her at Daisy's garage sale. She introduced herself as Charity."

The honey-blonde at the counter. He spun around to find Charity and was stunned by the sight of Daisy in these cheap surroundings, wrapped in a stained Lobster Shack apron, a ridiculous fifties hair net unnaturally helmeting her cherry-colored spirals.

Max always seemed to be there at her worst moments.

Then, unexpectedly, Daisy's gaze left Charity; she casually scanned the crowd and stopped—along with his heart. Her eyes lost their smile and widened into horror—or so it seemed to Max. She gawked at him, then exploded into motion, dashing from the counter like a sprinter at the gun, crashing through the kitchen doors and disappearing from sight.

Max turned to Maeve. "You still think this was a good idea?"

Sadness tugged at her mouth. "I don't understand. Charity said—"

"Apparently you and Charity don't know everything." He tossed a pair of hundred-dollar bills onto the table. "Let's go."

Reluctantly, Maeve obeyed, leaving plates of untouched food behind. They passed a speechless Charity, who looked as chagrined as Maeve. Max herded his mother out the door and into the drizzle of a typical Seattle afternoon.

Beneath the dim light of a bare bulb, Daisy stared at her reflection in the small cracked mirror of the employees' bathroom. She looked absolutely hideous in her hair net and tacky apron, and imagined how much worse she appeared surrounded by fake palms and plastic lobsters.

In her fantasies, when she and Max met again, she was gorgeous and successful, in a starched white chef's jacket, surrounded by expensive linen and gleaming china, and commanding a kitchen army. Not in a cheap diner like a whore on a street corner.

Why was Max always seeing her at her worst?

Three knocks on the bathroom door, and then Charity called her name. Daisy opened the door and Charity crowded inside.

"Are you okay?"

"No. I look like crap. Why did he have to see me like this, *here*, a complete and utter failure."

"That's why you ran? You're ashamed?"

Tears welled. "Max is probably gloating up a storm right now. A short-order cook surrounded by fake palms and plastic lobsters, paper napkins and bent forks. And not even the head cook. The *lunch* cook."

Charity cupped Daisy's cheeks. "Listen to me. You're not a failure. You're the bravest person I know. You have principles and you're willing to stand up for them. I'm proud of you for leaving Blanchard's. Every night you made that stupid turtle soup, you died just a little. And you'd hate it if this diner had real lobsters. And I don't believe Max thinks any less of you for working here. But if he does, then he's a bigger moron than Haemish Hamlish—"

"Who?"

Charity waved away the question. "Some nut case. Tried to marry a goat. But that's a different story."

Daisy sat on the lidded commode. "Why did he have to come *here*? Of all the diners in all the cities in all the world, why'd he have to walk into this one?"

Charity innocently shrugged. "Who knows? But maybe this is a good thing. Maybe, now that he knows where you are . . ."

"He'll what? Beg me to come back? Yeah, that's going to happen. And I couldn't, even if he did. It would seem like I was returning to get out of this dump instead of—"

"Going back because you want to?"

Sadness flooded her eyes. "It's my *Brigadoon*."

"Funny story." Charity digressed. "I gave the DVD to my mom for Christmas. One of her favorite old movies. But she just stared at the case and then I realized she didn't have a DVD player." Charity chuckled but stopped when Daisy looked wretched. "Right. Gene Kelly and Cyd Charisse. He gave up his world to live in hers." Charity sighed. "You love Max that much?"

"I don't know. But I think I'd like to find out."

A pounding on the door startled them both. "Need some help out here, Daisy," her assistant said.

Daisy wiped away an escaping tear. "I've got to get back to work." She checked herself in the mirror, then turned away in resignation.

"Hey, I've got an idea. Let's go out tonight. We'll have a few drinks at Mama's and forget all your problems."

"I wish it were that easy."

The pounding repeated. "Daisy!"

"Coming!" Daisy looked at Charity. "I'll call you tonight."

"Chin up, Daisy Mae. I promise, it'll all work out."

Daisy nodded without believing and then said, "I only caught a glimpse, but the woman with Max looked like his mother. Was that Maeve?"

"I think so." As if Charity didn't *know* so.

Daisy moaned. "I can imagine what *she* thinks."

Chapter Forty

Daisy whipped off her hair net, shook out her curls, and grabbed her purse, jacket, and the evening newspaper. She dashed out the front doors, passing a couple collapsing an umbrella before entering the diner. Hugging the buildings, she hiked up the sidewalk past the closed print shop toward her parked car, hurriedly stuffing her arms into her jacket as she went, then snuggled into the fleece against the cold drizzle.

She passed Nirvana as a woman in a sari locked the front door while her two daughters in blue jeans waited under the awning. Slowly the street emptied of its parked cars, headlights shining, wipers sweeping windshields, as businesses closed and people left for brighter, warmer locales. A jovial group of four men in similar tan trench coats spilled from the architect's office into the fading daylight, then dispersed as the sky rumbled. Daisy stepped beneath the overhang and searched her purse for her car keys as the drizzle became a shower that turned into a downpour.

As she waited beneath the overhang, Daisy glanced at the front page of her damp newspaper. "Downtown Park Renovated and Re-opened." "Carjacking Leaves Driver Wounded." "Cat Returns Home After Cross-Country Adventure."

Drops of rain from her wet hair splattered the newsprint. Daisy folded the paper as a woman raced by, her heels splashing the rivulets. Across the street, a man and woman waited as she did, beneath the awning of a contractor's office, their features obscured by the sheets of gray rain and encroaching dusk.

This is ridiculous, Daisy thought, as if a little—or a lot—of rain could make her look or feel worse than she already did. It had been a miserable, dismal day and all she wanted was to go home to her tiny apartment and curl up on the couch with her laptop and Restaurant.com, searching for an available, *affordable* eatery she could make her own. Adding the money from the sale of the comics with her previous savings, she had $221,000 to spend on her dream.

A car stopped in the street and the woman from the contractor's office dashed for the passenger side. Daisy decided to make the same dash for her car. She pressed the door unlock button hanging from her key chain; her car beeped and its lights blinked. She made her move as the man across the street made his.

She leapt over the gutter and threw open her door, tossing her purse into the passenger seat, then dove in after, slamming the door behind as the rain drummed her roof. She settled inside the fogged interior, then wiped the water from her face with the sleeve of her wet jacket. Someone pounded on her window. By the time she shot her finger to the lock button, her door was opening. But she wouldn't give up her car without a fight. She grabbed for her purse and the small canister of pepper spray in the outside pocket, then spritzed the face leaning into her car.

"Daisy—" Max jerked back.

"Max?" Daisy froze, realizing what she'd done . . . *again.* Then she bolted from her car, intending to save the blinded man from the dangers of the street. Max stood by the red Pathfinder, blinking away the rain and sniffing the air, but otherwise unaffected.

"I'm so sorry, Max. Are you okay?"

"What the hell did you spray me with?"

Daisy looked at the Marc Jacobs purse-size perfume spray in her palm and laughed. *"Daisy."*

"Nice," he said.

"Jesus, Max, I thought you were a carjacker. What're you doing here?"

Max looked at Daisy. Mascara smudged her eyes and her wet hair was plastered to her head, making her look like one of the Kewpie dolls his mom collected. He cleared the auburn strands from her face. Daisy closed her eyes for a long moment. "I don't know," he finally answered. "I mean, *I know,* but I'm thinking maybe I'm just another Haemish Hamlish."

"The guy with the goat?"

"My cousin . . ." His expression pinched. "What goat?"

Daisy stared at Max; he stared back.

"Can we get out of this rain?" he asked.

She hesitated at what she wanted. Her tiny apartment? *The bed* in her tiny—

"Is there a decent bar nearby?"

"Up the street," she said.

Daisy grabbed her keys and her purse. Max grabbed her hand.

"Bailey's and coffee," Daisy ordered from the waitress. "With extra whipped cream."

Max ordered the same, but without the topping. He scanned the subdued bar, ran fingers through his damp hair, and looked at Daisy as if he wanted to say something.

Daisy abruptly scooted her chair back. "I'm going to dry off." Max stood as she rose, although Daisy didn't feel enough like a lady to deserve it.

She escaped into the bathroom, almost falling to her knees in gratitude at the electric hand dryer on the wall, then balked at her reflection in the mirror—she still wore her ridiculous apron. When she left the bathroom, spirals had returned to her hair, her eyes were more doe-like than raccoon, and her apron was in the trash.

Max said nothing, but his expression spoke surprise at the transformation. Daisy sat down and reached for her coffee, the mountain of whipped cream reminiscent of Mount St. Helens. Licking away the creamy top peak, she sipped from her cup.

He laid a postcard on the table. "This came for you a few days ago."

Daisy contemplated the photograph. Nighttime fireworks exploded over the Magic Kingdom. The flipside held a child's writing.

Dear Chef Daisy,
The doctor says Dad is doing good so
we're celebrating in Disneyland. Dad
says it was your chowder that cured him!
We lit a candle at the church and prayed
for a second chance for Dad, and you
too, since you didn't say what to ask for.
Dad says everyone needs a second
chance sometime so now you have one if
you want it.
Sincerely yours,
Emily MacIntyre

Fighting unexpected tears, she took a deep breath. And another, her eyes still on Emily's message. When she felt in control, she looked at Max, who was watching her.

"I guess I was right," he said.

"About?"

"The postcard being important."

"You read it?" Then Daisy shook her head and shot her eyes to the heavens, knowing her question was stupid.

"It's hard not to read a postcard." Smiling. "So . . . what happened to Blanchard's?"

She sighed. "*La chaudrée de tortue.*"

He tried to keep a straight face. "Elizabeth wouldn't like that."

"Me neither." Sipping her coffee, she licked whipped cream from her lip. "I guess I'm not the chef I thought I was."

"The *person* is more important than the chef."

"Yeah, well, Blanchard's wanted a chef."

"Daisy . . ."

"How's Fitz doing?" As if she didn't know. She'd talked to him two days ago as he was leaving rehab.

"One day at a time."

"And Rita?" As if she didn't know. She'd talked to her last week.

"She's fine, too." He took a breath. "Daisy . . ."

"And Napoleon?"

"He's fine. Buster is fine. Everyone is fine. As if you don't know."

She settled her eyes on her coffee, wrapping both hands around the warm cup.

"Look, Daisy, the reason I came . . ."

She swiped a forefinger through the whipped cream, sucking it off her skin.

"I'm not a pimp—"

Her brow pinched as if to ask, *That's why you're here?*

"—But you're right, there's more going on than massages."

Her hope for a second chance vanished. Like she wanted to. How stupid was she to think . . . "Look, Max, I'm not ratting you out, if that's what you're worried about."

"Good to know." He definitely smiled. "But the women you've seen, *without* massage tables, are therapists, not hookers."

"*Sex* therapists?"

One spontaneous burst of laughter. "No. The regular garden variety. There's Jasmine, of course, who has a PhD, by the way. And I employ five therapists for the summer who rotate out of Anchorage, where they have their own practices."

"I'm not following."

"It was Jasmine's idea . . ." Researching her thesis, Jasmine had worked as an escort; she discovered that many of her clients wanted someone *safe* to talk to, but feared the stigma of being "in therapy." The secrets they shared with her—she could write a book! Max had found a similar mentality among his military buddies, who couldn't confide in their families but desperately needed to unload. Unlike most women, who were willing to confront their demons, men often avoided therapy, feeling it meant they were weak and not in control. And there was an unspoken rule in the military—*if you want to advance, you don't see a shrink.*

"The five stars? They're for friends I served with in Afghanistan. Each one a suicide."

Daisy felt like the breath had been knocked from her. Suicide was as much a casualty as an enemy bullet, but no one liked to talk about it. She couldn't fathom the horrors of war—to kill or be killed. She couldn't imagine the burden soldiers carried; the guilt of living when others had not.

"I'm sorry, Max." It was lame, but Daisy didn't know what else to say. She wasn't alone; she suspected most nonmilitary women simply couldn't relate to their military men—husbands, boyfriends, fathers and brothers—let alone help.

"The stars remind me, but they no longer haunt me." Max blamed his unhappy marriage on that same combat stress, which sometimes made him moody, explosive, and critical. He finished his explanation—"I had to lose my wife before I finally faced my demons."

"Oh, Max, that's awful. How did Molly-Anne die?"

He looked perplexed. "She died in her sleep. Why?"

Her face pinched. "Had she been sick?"

"Just the usual aches and pains that come with old age."

"Old age?" She envisioned a May-December romance. "How old was she?"

"Fifteen, I think. Why?"

"Your wife was fifteen?"

"What're you talking about?"

"Molly-Anne. The love of your life. The one who died? You named your boat after her."

Laughing, he shook his head, looked at Daisy's confused expression, and laughed more. "My *ex*-wife is Kimberly. As far as I know, she's very much alive. Molly-Anne was my Irish setter when I was a kid."

Daisy couldn't believe how silly she felt—and how relieved. A beloved Irish setter she could compete with; a beloved dead wife, not so much. "You've always liked redheads, then."

He grinned. "I guess so."

She drank her coffee—licking the whipped cream from her lip—and considered everything Max had told her. "So, the website, the brochures, even the postcards. The reason you fly under the radar. One big ruse to keep women out?"

"Not to keep women out, to keep them from *wanting* to come," Max said. "Women are welcome. But over the years, we've only had a handful. Some were military; others came to support their husbands. Wild Man gives men a safe environment to try therapy without anyone knowing."

Of course, many of the guests knew exactly what was going on, but they were in it together. After they returned home, some found the courage to talk to their families, others continued therapy, and a few, like Pete, only needed to "blow out the pipes" for two weeks to be perfectly happy the other fifty.

But Wild Man wasn't cheap. Depending on the circumstances, Max discounted the all-inclusive $8,000-a-week price for those who couldn't pay, which is why he pinched pennies, and why he had sued Daisy.

"The domino effect," Daisy said. "Rita told me. I just wish you had."

"Rita didn't tell you everything." Max hesitated; his confession was going to be as painful as his knee once was. "The truth is, I saw your house and the neighborhood and then you told me you were a chef at Fireflies. Considering all that, I didn't think the money would be that big a deal. And . . ." He paused. "I liked you."

"You liked me?"

"From pretty much the moment we met."

"So you sued me?"

"It was the best way to make sure nothing happened between us."

"Seriously?"

"I know I've changed since my divorce. I just wasn't sure I'd changed enough to make a relationship work."

Daisy could scarcely believe her ears.

"That leap surprised me, too," Max said, reading Daisy's face. "But at the same time, I was afraid my past would repeat. And then, dammit, you showed up on the ferry. And at my lodge. And then in my shower. It seems I was doomed to have you in my life."

She swiped the last of the whipped cream.

This time, Max did something about it.

"Took you long enough." She smiled from his kiss. "I'm down to my last lick."

He leaned back in his chair. "When you left Otter Bite, I thought you hated me. And then today at lunch, when you ran, I was sure of it."

"There's not a single recipe with only one ingredient . . . which isn't to say I haven't hated some things in a loving sort of way."

Max slowly shook his head. "You, Daisy Moon, are beyond my comprehension. Which is why I must rely on my mother's uncanny ability to know what's best for me. Not to mention a few choice words from Rita . . . although . . . her story about Lorna and Sid didn't make a lot of sense. But the upshot is, they came from two different worlds and made a go of it." He paused, his thoughts in a debate. "Then this afternoon, Dr. Wagstaff called me."

"Oh, God." Had Charity divulged her Lobster Shack shame?

"She told me to grow a pair."

Daisy breathed. Then made a mental note to thank her meddling friend.

Max pulled an envelope from the inside pocket of his jacket that he'd draped over the chair back when he sat down. He slid it toward Daisy. "My mother suggested I make you an offer."

She stared at the envelope as if she'd never seen one before.

He stood, tossed a twenty on the table, and grabbed his jacket. When Daisy finally looked up, Max held a very small purple velvet box that had seen better days. He set it on top of the envelope. "But this is my idea."

Max started to walk away, then turned back. "One more thing—" One heartbeat, two heartbeats. "I love you."

Her pulse racing, she flipped open the box. It wasn't just a ring; it was a *spoon* ring—antique gold with scrolls and millefleur and just a shadow of tarnish, but nothing a good cleaning couldn't remove. A little polish and Daisy would have that ring blinding like the sun!

She slipped it on her ring finger where it twirled, so she traded fingers to her middle where it hugged her skin. She looked for Max, but he'd vanished. She reached for the envelope. Her expression changed a dozen times by the end of the three pages.

She barely found her breath. Words were cheap. But this—in black and white and *notarized*—was *love*. Clutching the papers, she bolted from her chair, grabbed her belongings, and flew out the door into the mist.

Streetlights punctuated the dusk, cars came and went, people passed. She searched one direction and then the other. "Max?" Two heartbeats. "Max!"

His voice came from the shadows. "Took you long enough." He stepped into the light.

"It's a lot to digest." Daisy held up her hand. "The ring?"

"It doesn't fit." He sounded disappointed.

"It's a *perfect* fit. But I'm not sure I understand."

"It's a promise ring. If we don't kill each other, I *promise* I'll get you a better one."

"I . . . kind of like this one."

"Then I promise I'll get it sized." Max stepped closer. "What about the rest of the offer?"

"Do you mean it?"

Max corralled her in his arms. "I love you, Daisy Moon. Most ardently."

She took a fortifying breath. "I . . . love you, too. Dammit."

"Was that so hard?"

She shrugged, kind of whimpered. "Just out of curiosity . . . why?"

"Truthfully?"

"If possible."

"I'm down to my last jar of mango chutney."

Daisy unconvincingly smacked him.

"And you're beautiful with the most amazing green eyes, but mostly, it's your humongous vocabulary. And you know Roman emperors. Now you."

"You call Elizabeth by her name."

"You're kidding."

"And you chose this ring."

"*And?*"

"You're the biggest stud in the world."

He puffed up. "That's what I'm talking about. So, my offer . . ."

"It's very generous."

"You think so?"

"You're making me a partner."

"A *junior* partner."

"I get my own restaurant."

"In Otter Bite," he reminded her. "No stars, no reviews."

"Somehow, *those* stars don't shine like they used to. And the best review of my life is written on a postcard. The truth is, I would've come back without any of this."

"*Now* you tell me."

"But I have a confession."

"The past is the past," Max said.

"Actually, it's kind of the present, since it was one of your reasons for this offer. The thing is, I *don't* know Roman emperors, other than Caligula. Well, I sort of know Tiberius, since Caligula probably poisoned him. And Julius Caesar, but then, who doesn't? And Claudius from the PBS series. And Nero, since he 'fiddled' while Rome burned, which he couldn't have because the fiddle didn't exist until the eleventh century, so if he played anything, it was most likely a cithara, but the expression is just a clever way of saying that Nero was uncaring and ineffectual—"

"Oh my God, shut up!"

"I was just—"

"I'm sorry, Daisy, I can't do this." He snatched the contract from her hand and tore it into large confetti. The scraps littered the sidewalk; some drifted into the gutter and were carried away by the rain streaming into the sewer.

Eyes shimmering with tears, Daisy looked as if she'd lost her puppy.

"I deserve better," Max said.

Daisy wanted to run, to escape this humiliation, but her feet were lead while her legs were rubber. She feared she might collapse. So much for candles and prayers . . .

"And so do you," he added. "I don't want a business partner. I don't want clauses and conditions and everything in black and white." He bent down on his rehabilitated knee to the wet sidewalk and took her right hand in his. "Marry me, Daisy. Marry me and be my *life* partner."

Daisy brushed tears and rain from her cheeks and looked hard at Max. She opened her mouth to answer but the only word that squeaked out was, "Really?"

"You had me at cithara." *Whatever the hell that is.*

She took a shaky breath. "To be completely accurate, Nero might have been strumming the lyre and not the cithara."

"Daisy, I'm not staying down here forever."

As the situation registered, she pulled him up and wrapped her arms around his neck. "Are you sure about this?"

His expression twisted. "So-so."

"Good enough. Can we get out of this drizzle now?"

"I think it's sexy and romantic."

"There's nothing sexy or romantic about cold and wet."

"I was thinking about the hot shower after we strip off our clothes."

"Well, yeah, when you put it *that* way." Daisy looked at Max as if seeing him for the first time. The glow from the streetlights illuminated his face; love illuminated his eyes. She felt warm all over.

"Babe, I can put it however you like."

Daisy laughed, but inside she tingled. "You promised me a hot shower."

As down payment on the *hot* part of that promise, he seriously kissed her; then lacing her fingers with his, he hurried them down the street.

Turns out Charity was right. The stars, the reviews, her golden spoon—Daisy had everything back. None of it the same. All of it *better.*

Daisy glanced at her future husband—a sinfully delicious man who was familiar with a cithara.

How lucky can one chef get?

Please turn the page for an exciting sneak peek at
Maggie McConnell's next Otter Bite romance
EMBRACING FELICITY
coming in November 2016 wherever ebooks are sold!

Chapter One

"C'mon, Dad, you're sooo slow!"

"Wait 'til *you're* forty," Ian MacIntyre mumbled, hiking with ten-year-old Emily to the end of Bobrovie Spit. Twenty minutes earlier they'd been dropped off at the trailhead by Victor Dudnik, Otter Bite's postmaster, plumber, and occasional cabbie.

Ian and Em had flown over this spit, but until today had never walked it. Flanked on each side by a beach, the mile stretch resembled a soup spoon: broad at the attached end, then long and narrow before it spread into an eight-acre oval patch that supported thigh-high grasses and a grove of venerable Sitka Spruce. From the clouds, this trek looked easy. On the ground, the trail was plagued with ruts, roots, and rocks that only a Dall sheep—or *we'an*—could navigate.

"Wait up, Pup."

One hundred feet in front, Emily turned to Ian, but instead of stopping she walked backward. "We have to be there by eight!"

Pushing up his sleeves, Ian checked his platinum Omega. "Em, it's barely seven thirty."

She spun forward and kept going and going and going . . .

They had plenty of time. Despite their late takeoff from Merrill Field in Anchorage. Despite the headwind between Kenai and Otter Bite. Despite scrambling for alternate transportation when the Jeep he'd been promised wasn't at the landing strip.

Passing a second *No Trespassing* sign, Ian spread the zipper on his fleece jacket and stepped up the pace. Breathing in the chilly May morning air, he exhaled wisps.

The sun had been shining for two hours, but with formidable mountains to conquer, it was only now showing its face to Otter Bite. In Alaska, however, the summer sun was rarely below the horizon.

Mist rose off the calm bays and vanished into crystal air seasoned with salt and flavored with fish. Waves softly lapped the beach, retreating into a low tide that, in another hour, would expose clams and mussels on the muddy sea bottom. Bald eagles reigned from the tops of spruce that pierced the sky like castle spires. Below, like peasants, squawking seagulls scavenged in the wet sand, their footprints disappearing behind them.

Everything in this moment reminded Ian of the seaside village on Scotland's west coast where his maternal grandparents had a summer estate.

"Dad!"

Well, *almost* everything.

Looking back, Emily stamped her foot. "Hurry! Up!"

"I should've given y' to Granny when I had the chance," Ian mumbled, passing a third, hand-painted warning. He'd underestimated the toll of this trek when he rented the house. Hiking one mile through nature was a lot tougher than jogging three miles on a treadmill.

Pausing to enjoy the view, he spotted the Kachemak Princess. Sailing from Homer—where access by road ended—the 150-passenger ferry coursed through open water toward the rocky promontory known as Mermaid Point. Behind that landmark, tucked into Sedna Bay, was Otter Bite and the catamaran's first port; from there it would dock at Halibut Cove, Seldovia, Nanwalek, and, finally, Port Graham before reversing the route and returning to Homer in the evening. Last winter he and Em had taken that ferry and visited those coastal villages, all originally Alutiiq settlements. On every sailing, she had pressed the rail.

Emily loved the ocean, but any water would do. As a toddler, she'd kicked and screamed when he lifted her from the bath. *Though she be but little, she is fierce,* his mum liked to say of Emily. She'd be swimming in the bay right now if it weren't a heart-stopping forty degrees. And she was fast, *really* fast. One day his little mermaid would be sporting Olympic gold.

"Dad! Orcas!"

The black and white bodies with the tall dorsal fins were unmistakable. As they cruised past, Ian counted five. A little too close for *his* comfort, but surrounded by postcard-perfect scenery, he sometimes forgot that Alaska was wild down to her knickers.

"Good eye, Pup!" Ian called back. Emily glowed. When the pod turned for open water, he sensed her yearning to be swimming with the whales.

Emily's aquatic gene hadn't come from him. Sure, he lounged poolside in Monte Carlo and enjoyed the knee-high surf at Waikoloa; he'd even barreled down Disney World's Summit Plummet water slide. Nonetheless, when it came to the deep, he was chicken of the sea.

But he'd found a way to give Emily the ocean without setting foot in it. Suddenly he was as impatient as she to reach their beach house. However rocky their morning had been—and this trail in particular—no more obstacles lay in their path. This was the first day of a summer they would remember for the rest of their lives.

"There it is!" Emily pointed to a stone cottage topped with blue shakes that peeked between towering spruce trees. "Look!"

Ian *was* looking, but that was not it. The cottage was quaint, as far as he could see, and cozy, but it was definitely not the home he'd paid $2,800 to rent for the summer. Where was the modern, two-story cedar house with expansive decks and eight-person hot tub he'd seen on the internet? All these two properties shared were the views.

Had he gotten the directions wrong? How many Bobrovie spits could there be?

"Emily, wait!" Ian shouted as she abandoned the path and waded into spears of tall grass. Three *No Trespassing* signs weren't exactly an invitation to visit. Who knew who lived here or how welcoming they'd be? Alaska wasn't called The Last Frontier for nothing.

But Emily ran toward that cottage as if the Seven Dwarfs were inside to greet her.

Ian chased her, cursing his Gucci loafers when sand and pebbles got inside and assaulted his feet.

It's not the mountain in front of you; it's the pebble in your shoe.
Not now, Mum.

"Emily!" Losing sight of her, Ian hopped with one shoe while emptying the other. A pair of ravens swooped low, flapping and screeching. "Bloody hell!" Shooing them away, he cast his loafer at them; an eagle snatched it mid-air and flew off. "What the—" But he didn't have time to dwell; the ravens were back, diving and soaring like Spitfires. He dropped to his knees and ducked, arms up, to protect his face and head.

"Oy! Leave those ravens alone!"

It took a moment, then Ian looked up and peered around. The birds were gone, as if he'd imagined them. Cautiously relaxing his arms, he stood and tried to regain his dignity. He felt like a real poindexter.

It didn't help that the woman chastising him looked like an airbrushed centerfold.

In a gauzy, mid-calf nightgown, with her waist-length blond braid draped over one shoulder, Felicity Arhnaq considered the expensively attired urbanite who had defied her three *No Trespassing* signs. If not for the dark-haired, light-eyed sweetie with him, he'd be facing the double barrels of her 20-gauge shotgun—the first defense in The Last Frontier.

"You should be ashamed, harassing helpless birds."

"Helpless? Those bloody corbies attacked *me*!"

Buckshot unnecessary. She could chase this Scot off with a flyswatter.

"Then an eagle stole my shoe!"

Felicity lodged hands on her hips. "How? At gunpoint?"

Ian started to say he had thrown it at the ravens, but considering her sarcasm . . . His eye caught the splatters on his shoulder and arm. With growling disgust, he tugged off his soiled fleece jacket.

Reaching out, she huffed. "Give it here."

Instead, Ian gingerly rolled his jacket inside out and draped it over his elbow. "It's a *Patagonia*."

A two-second stare. "Suit yourself."

With as much dignity as his shoeless foot allowed, Ian marched to the thirty-something stunner who stood on the deck. Glancing at her bare feet, he momentarily drew a blank, then he looked up at the woman who was looking down on him—in more ways than one, he suspected. "What've you done with my daughter?"

Felicity jerked back. "What have I *done* with her? I lured her into my gingerbread cottage and stuffed her in my oven, what else?"

"How is that funny?"

"Don't get your knickers in a twist, she's using the bathroom. And by the way, you're *trespassing*, so lose the attitude."

"I'm *not* trespassing. I rented this place for the summer."

She snorted. "I don't think so."

"Is this Bobrovie Spit?"

"Anyone who *rented this place for the summer* would know that it is."

"I have a lease."

Her brows jumped. "Show me."

"Actually . . ." The document was in his briefcase safe in his Cessna along with their luggage. "It's in my plane."

"Sure it is."

"I didn't think I'd need it."

"Because I'm too stupid to know who I rent my cabin to?"

"Look, I don't know what you're trying to pull—"

"What *I'm* trying to pull?"

The melancholy blast of a ship's horn drifted across Kachemak Bay; the ferry was arriving in Otter Bite. Pulling her eyes from Ian, Felicity gazed past him toward Mermaid Point. After a disappointed sigh, she looked expectantly at him. "You were about to say?"

Usually Ian could wield words like a Samurai wielded swords, but he'd been rendered dumb . . . and felt even dumber. First, the ravens and eagle, now this cheeky chick. Thankfully Emily hadn't witnessed his fowl encounters.

"Dad!" Emily raced around the corner, footsteps pattering the weathered planks. Her sneakers squealed when she slammed on the brakes. "Come see the otters! They're *cramazing*!"

"We're leaving." He targeted Felicity. *"For now."*

"We just got here!"

"And now we're going." Face-to-face with four-foot-three Emily, who stood on the two-foot-high deck. "Don't argue."

Pleading eyes shot to Felicity.

"It's okay," Felicity said. "You can visit another day, after your dad has found his shoe"—she focused on Ian—"and lost his attitude."

"My attitude is appropriate to this situation." Grabbing Emily from the deck, he set her on the ground. "And don't be tellin' my daughter what she can do."

"Where's your shoe?" Emily asked, staring at his feet.

"Never you mind. Let's go."

"But we live here—"

"That's right—" He whipped his finger at Felicity, who flinched. "I want my money back."

"*What* money?"

"The twenty-eight hundred I paid for summer rent."

Felicity's luscious lips parted and her jaw dropped.

"Not only is this place like a chapter out of *Zoo,* it's completely different than the house you advertised! Where's the second story and the hot tub? I'm of a mind to sue you for false advertising!" Ian spun around and steered his daughter into the tall grass toward the path.

"Hold on," Felicity said.

Feeling smug, Ian stopped. Turning, he aimed his fully-loaded .45-caliber expression at Felicity. She appeared unimpressed; if anything, she seemed . . . *sympathetic*?

"I don't know who you gave money to—"

"Don't play dumb with me. I handed a check to your father, Dr. Bricker."

"I don't know any Dr. Bricker; *my* father is an attorney. Either this is all a terrible mistake—"

"And you, miss, are the one making it. You have no clue with whom you're dealing. Are you returning my money?" He carefully unrolled his soiled jacket and pulled his cellphone from an inside pocket. "Or am I calling the authorities?"

"Doubtful. No local *authorities* or cell service."

Ian inflated at yet another lie. "Your ad promised phone and internet."

"The same ad for the two-story house with the hot tub?" She took a deep, calming breath. "You can use my satellite phone to call the state troopers. Fourteen dollars a minute. Cash up front. While you're at it, feel free to report the eagle. Maybe provide a description? Height, weight, feather color?" She bobbed her head. "Tattoos?"

Ian felt like a firecracker with a faulty fuse. "Oh, for the love of—" He stuffed his phone back into its pocket and gruffly re-rolled his jacket.

Felicity glanced at Emily, whose eyes were wide and frightened. With her forefinger, she beckoned Ian to come closer.

Ian warily looked around. "What?"

"We're scaring your daughter. Holster your bravado and come here . . . *please*." That took effort. But his shoulders sagged just enough to inspire Felicity's compassion.

Ian stepped tentatively toward the deck. When he was near enough to whiff Felicity's fresh, breezy scent, she bent over. Suddenly he was facing unfettered breasts as formidable as the Alaska Range.

You're wrong, Mum; it's the peaks not the pebbles.

Pulling his eyes away from Felicity's distracting cleavage, he stepped back for perspective.

"I'm sorry, little girl's dad, but—"

"I don't want your apology. I want my money or the house you advertised." He stared into irises the color of his mother's favorite aquamarine broach. "I'm not some *cheechako,* fresh off the ferry for you to scam."

"Hate to tell you," she said softly. "But I think you sorta are."

Photo credit: Portrait Park by J

Golden Heart nominee Maggie McConnell spent her childhood overseas as the daughter of US diplomats. Attending college in Illinois, she earned a BA in art and an MBA while working at the local animal shelter. At twenty-six, she packed her dog and cat into a Ford truck and drove the Alcan Highway to Alaska, where she spent twenty-three years exploring the Last Frontier in single-engine Cessnas. An animal-rights advocate and vegan, Maggie provides a sanctuary on her Arizona ranch for all creatures great and small. Every year, like the gray whale, she returns to Alaska. Readers can visit her website at www.MaggieMcConnellRomance.com